LUCILLE'S LIE

LUCILLE'S LIE

❀

Camille Howland

Writers Club Press
San Jose New York Lincoln Shanghai

Lucille's Lie

All Rights Reserved © 2002 by Carmelia M. Howland

No part of this book may be reproduced or transmitted in any form or by any means, graphic, electronic, or mechanical, including photocopying, recording, taping, or by any information storage retrieval system, without the permission in writing from the publisher.

Writers Club Press
an imprint of iUniverse, Inc.

For information address:
iUniverse, Inc.
5220 S. 16th St., Suite 200
Lincoln, NE 68512
www.iuniverse.com

This is a work of fiction. All characters and events are fictitious.

ISBN: 0-595-23216-7

Printed in the United States of America

To my brother Timothy Fogg, whose infectious enthusiasm for writing inspired me to return to this long-neglected novel. Many thanks, Tim.

Fear is the tax that conscience pays to guilt.

—George Sewell

Introduction

❀

Lucille turned to her side, adjusted the oxygen tube, and buried her face in the soft pillow, damp and sour-smelling after a long, restless night. She closed her eyes, mentally taking inventory of her life and her wealth…the fine house in which she was dying, her valuable possessions, the lumber mill she had operated so successfully, the town that her family had founded and still, in essence, owned. All this finery. The good life.

Her cough ended in a sighed whisper. "My good life. All a lie."
Who would care when she was gone? No one. Not one…except…
"David." She owed her younger brother so much. "Oh, dear."
She had hurt him terribly. She must make amends for that. She could do it. There was still time. It was just a matter of finding someone who could help her, someone who could help her die at peace with the most painful corner of her conscience. Then she would be free of that one terrible lie.

CHAPTER 1

❀

Sheldon stared in disbelief. This couldn't really be the home of David P. Bradford. Could it? She felt the slow crawl of apprehension. She sat with the engine running, not anxious to get wet in the downpour, wondering what she had taken on when she said she would be happy to interview the hospital's most generous benefactor for a newspaper profile. The weathered two-story farmhouse, with broken shutters and upper windows boarded up, was right out of a Gothic novel, a behemoth enlarged by a long ell. It seemed to loom out of fog, like an eerie house on the moors. All it lacked was a vicious dog barking and straining against its tether.

She had heard him referred to as eccentric. "David Bradford? Now there's a real character for you. You never know what he'll do next," Ashton's general store owner had said. But when she pressed him for details, he said no more. "You'll find out, if you're going to interview him." With a sweet smile, the librarian had said, "He's our dear eccentric. What would we do without him?"

The longer she looked at the place, the more hesitant she became. At left, a drafty barn, precariously tilted, harked back to the days when the village of Ashton was a farming community. A pole propped the sagging double doors shut. One end was suspended in air where foundation rocks had fallen away, and on each side of the barn doors was a small window, one broken and stuffed with a dark rag.

She turned the ignition key off and listened to the rain splattering against her venerable Dodge Dart. She had driven up the long driveway as far as the saw-horse barrier, and now she hoped the car wasn't stuck in the muddy ruts. Hard to believe it had been so dry, but the county needed a month of rain, not this flash shower which seemed to have been designed expressly to dampen her spirits and sully her mood for this important interview.

"Oh well," she muttered. She tied her plastic rain bonnet under her chin, scooped up camera bag and purse, opened the door, swung her hips around...and stepped into a mud hole.

"Oh no! My new shoes." She looked down at her white canvas ballerinas, now grungy brown, and curled her toes to hold them on, attempting an exit that wouldn't mire her completely.

"You'd think a man worth his weight in gold could have a paved driveway instead of a quagmire." Sheldon envisioned Mr. Bradford as a miserly old man, at this very moment watching her slosh through water and mud, rubbing his hands together, and laughing.

The heavy, soaking air smothered her in a miasma of moldering barnyard residue. How many years had it been since this place was farmed? Probably long before Ashton was bypassed by the super highway. Yet, in the rain, its cattle aura carried a haunting memory, as vivid as the old farmstead.

Avoiding the muddy driveway, she picked her way beside it, through scratchy grass that snagged her hose. Head lowered, she squinted through the rain to focus on the ancient farmhouse ahead and tried to imagine the type of man who had built beautiful public buildings for Ashton, given many thousands of dollars to medical research at laboratories and universities, funded scholarships for local young people, provided for the poor, and yet lived in a decaying house surrounded by overgrown bushes. Fields of juniper, the weathered barn, a rusting truck, all confirmed what locals asserted about David P. Bradford. He *was* eccentric to live like this. She wondered if he would be crotchety. Funny no one described the man himself. Mostly they talked about his money and what he did with it. One man went so far as to say, "He's a crackpot." Obviously he was a man who marched to his own drummer.

Sheldon hesitated at the front door, her hand raised to knock, her eyes following a long crack that split the upper right panel. She tried to think of her prepared questions, but she had the sinking dread that she would blurt out, "Is it true that you go to the junk yard for parts to repair your truck?" or "Do you really get food scraps from the local restaurant to feed your dogs?" or…

The door swung open and, her knuckles just short of banging the man's nose, Sheldon found herself looking into a pair of cool blue eyes and hearing a voice boom, "Miss Merrill?"

"Ahhh…yes…yes, I'm Shellie Merrill." This must be the butler, she thought.

"I was watching for you. Come in out of the rain. I'm David Bradford."

He took her raised hand and tugged her inside. Of all the mental pictures she had formed of David Bradford, this definitely was not one of them. This was no old man with a long beard and patched coat. This was a young, virile, six-foot Paul Newman image. Certainly not yet forty, he had dark auburn hair with just a fringe of curl along the collar line, high cheekbones, and square jaw.

Now she wished she hadn't cancelled her hair trim yesterday, and she definitely should have dressed in something classier than a plain white blouse and ancient gaucho skirt. She glanced down at her filthy shoes. Lord. Who knew? Eccentric? What age group did that apply to? Wait until she got back to the office. She'd tell Harry just what she thought of him for leading her to believe she was interviewing a curmudgeon. "Write a good profile on the guy. You'll find him…*interesting*," Harry had said. His emphasis on the word interesting left Sheldon with the distinct impression that Bradford was old and wily, not young and virile and…so-o-o handsome.

"Sorry about the smoke," he said. Now she glanced down the dank hallway, saw faded yellow wallpaper and two closed doors, a long table and mirror, and realized that it was all hazy. The fog swirling around the house must have been smoke.

"It will clear up in a few minutes. I thought a fire would help cheer up this dismal day. Besides, it was rather damp and cool in here. Haven't opened the front parlor for some time. I guess the flue needs cleaning."

He opened a door and stepped back for her to go in. She hesitated by the stairs leading up to the second floor, pushed her bags back on her shoulder, and balanced herself against the dark banister to tug off her shoes. Her stockings were a mess, too. Just brave it out, she thought.

"Think I'll just leave these muddy shoes here, if you don't mind." When she walked into the living room she got another surprise, a bit like entering the land of Oz, going from black and white to color, all light and cheerful, almost blinding after the dark hallway.

In front of the blazing fire, a linen-draped table, set with gleaming silver service and a plate of delicate desserts, stood on an oriental rug woven in rich, dark hues. Antique chairs with colorful petit point on black background flanked the table. It could have been a scene set for a photo shoot of a nineteenth century drawing room. Mahogany furniture, marble-top tables, deep green velvet sofa, velvet flocked wallpaper. The grandeur drew an "Oh my!" from Sheldon.

"I take it you like the room?" His eyes lit up as if he savored her approval of the decor. His guileless manner went contrary to what she had heard of Bradford. Some had gone so far as to call him a ruthless man. She knew he was a shrewd Wall Street broker. The librarian had told her that he had inherited a financial house and turned it into one of the most prosperous brokerages in New York City.

"It's beautiful, Mr. Bradford. Just beautiful. I would never have expected…that is…uh," she fumbled for a way to praise without at the same time insulting the exterior appearance. "It's gorgeous, so elegant."

Surely this man, most likely a billionaire, didn't need praise for having a pleasant room in his house. Yet, he grinned like a new father being told he had a beautiful baby.

"This room is kept closed and the furniture covered most of the time. Only on special occasions does it get used. Entertaining is not something I do on a regular basis, but when the occasion arises, I can put my best foot forward, so to speak."

So, Sheldon thought, being interviewed for a newspaper profile is a special occasion. Perhaps she should relax. It would appear that it was as special for him as for her. She'd interviewed plenty of notables, from visiting dignitaries to local bigwigs, but never had she encountered anyone who piqued her interest more.

"Let me take your coat," he said. She set her bags on the floor, and handed him her rain apparel. In an instant he was out the door again, carrying her wet coat and rain bonnet. She took the opportunity to look around, and wondered who had put the room together. It had a woman's touch, with Royal Doulton figurines, silk lampshades, velvet pillows. It all looked much too feminine for Bradford, unless he had hired an interior decorator. At that thought, Sheldon smiled. Not likely. Or maybe he was married. No one had told her. Of course, he would be married. She should have realized that sooner.

From another room she heard a telephone ring twice.

Sheldon went to the polished brick fireplace, relishing the warmth of the fire, and ran her hand along the satiny hardwood mantelpiece. Over it was the only piece of art work in the room, a large portrait of a young woman with a tender expression and almost regal bearing. This would be his wife. Her light blond hair curled softly about her face, her sensual brown eyes focused just beyond the viewer, as if welcoming her lover. Maybe David Bradford, standing beside the artist? If in flesh and blood she looked like the painting, then this was a beautiful woman, indeed, just what one would expect a man of charming good looks and enormous wealth to have on his arm at an elegant *soiree,* presuming he attended such affairs. But, of course, he would have to. There must be many occasions when he was the guest of honor for his philanthropies. Sheldon sighed. How come some women got it all?

But she never let herself wallow in self-pity. Maybe her mother wasn't the most insightful person in the world, but from her Sheldon had learned at least one important lesson about life. You don't sit around feeling sorry for yourself and wait for good fortune to smile on you. You get to work and take pride in your own accomplishments, however meager they may be. Hadn't Mum done just that? She started work at the hardware store thirty years ago and was still there, walking the mile each way every day, five and a half days a week

"Sorry to keep you waiting. I had a phone call."

At the sound of Bradford's voice, Sheldon whirled around and found herself looking not just at her host, but at an unexpected sight in the corner alcove. She squealed in disbelief, "Oh, my goodness! That's a bear!"

His resonant laugh was hearty, like his voice, as if echoing in a cave.

"Don't let old Ernie scare you. He's thoroughly dead and stuffed, I assure you. Sit here by the fire. You'll be dry in no time. Sorry you got wet, but it's good to see the rain."

"If only it would go on for several days. The weather report is that it's only a passing shower. I never thought I'd get tired of seeing sunshine."

"Too bad. So little rain won't do a thing to help the farmers." Then he grinned again. "You see I do read your page, Miss Merrill. You do the farmers a good service."

With some surprise and a blush that he read her work, Sheldon thanked him. She had been creating the Agriculture Highlights page for the *Westburgh Press* for over a year, in addition to her regular reporting duties at the daily. For months now she had been focusing on the Great Drought of nineteen seventy-seven. Farm auctions were held almost weekly as dairymen gave up in the wake of withered crops and dried up water sources. To make matters worse, army worms had pitched a battle against surviving crops. Sheldon had stood beside farmers, their crops hit by invading army worms, and listened as the hairless green grasshoppers crunched their way through corn fields. Corn stalks folded over and clattered like bamboo sticks in the dry wind, then the marauders marched on to the next field for their next overnight raid.

She sat in the chair that Bradford held for her.

"You shouldn't have gone to so much trouble."

"It's no trouble, I assure you. I have a lady come in for this sort of thing. She even does the baking. She makes my life much easier. When you live alone you need all the help you can get. Especially someone like me. I'm good with high finance, but no good at keeping house."

Alone? Then who's the woman in the picture? How Sheldon wanted to ask the question, but, on the other hand, why should it matter to her? It was as if she'd mentally laid claim to the man. But wasn't it every woman's fantasy to find a rich, handsome man with no strings attached? Sheldon turned her head to look at the bear again. To her it was an appalling sight. Why would he have a stuffed animal, a big one at that, in his otherwise elegantly appointed living room?

"Did you shoot it?"

"Yes." He poured coffee for both and passed the pastries. Sheldon noted the outmoded style of his blue suit and narrow blue necktie. She wasn't fashion conscious, but doubted that these were designer clothes.

He looked up and smiled. Oh lord, he was good-looking. She shifted in her chair and ducked her head. When she peeked up again he had turned his attention to the bear. She swallowed hard and took a deep breath.

"Ernie the man, Ernest Pelletier, was my guide in the Maine woods when I hunted there a few years back. I'm sorry to say, he died three winters ago. I used to go to the Mooseneck Lake area each fall, mainly for bird hunting, but once in a while I'd shoot a deer for camp meat. One year this bear had caused all kinds of trouble, breaking into the camp and smashing things up. So Ernie offered a free two weeks at the camp if someone could shoot the animal. I got the free two weeks."

His eyes shone with deviltry over the absurdity of his needing to get free lodging, and Sheldon began to understand something about him. Here was a man who enjoyed making people believe he was eccentric. She'd bet he put it all on just for the fun of having the reputation, leaving people to guess about him.

But she took a dim view of hunting.

"So you shot the bear. Such a drastic measure." She had always thought there was something barbaric about hunters' displaying animal trophies. It was impossible for her to hide her disgust.

"You sound as if you don't approve."

"I don't believe in killing."

"Killing." He studied her for a long moment, his eyes moving from her head to her hands which circled the coffee cup, then back. "Not even shooting animals for table meat?"

"No. Not even that. It's taking life, and I feel that life is precious."

"You're a vegetarian, then?"

"Well, no. I'm not."

He laughed heartily. "And where do you think the meat you eat comes from?"

She felt her face heating with embarrassment, as it always did under attack of an aggressive man like this.

"I do make a distinction between animals that are raised for meat and animals that are in the wild. I just feel they should be left there to live free like nature intended."

"A Bambi lover. Well, you see nature isn't exactly kind and understanding like you are. Animals in the wild, like deer, unless culled in an annual hunting season, will over populate. Then, according to nature's design, they become diseased and die, starve to death, or maybe maimed or killed fighting over food. Venison is one of the tastiest meats you can eat. For that matter, Ernie there provided several fine meals in camp, too. I respect your tender feelings, but they are misplaced."

Sheldon wanted to crawl under the table. Why had this topic arisen? Now she was on the defensive. Not that she wanted to argue with her handsome host. She'd just like vindication for her own belief.

"You may think that, Mr. Bradford, but I don't. Isn't life precious to you?"

"Life? What life? Animals? Humans?"

"Both."

"That's a question that's not as simple as it sounds. It's like most things in life, without a single blanket answer. If you want to know whether I would shoot an animal, yes I would and obviously do. If you want to know whether I would shoot a person, again the answer is yes. But if you ask whether I would deliberately kill an animal or a human being out of perversity, then the answer is no. I respect life. Very much so. I do not hold it sacred."

"You could shoot a person?" Sheldon was horror struck at that thought.

"Yes, under certain circumstances."

"You think there are circumstances that justify shooting someone?"

"You think there aren't?"

"I can't envision ever being in such a circumstance, no."

"What if someone threatens to kill you?"

"Then you negotiate, you talk them out of it."

Again Bradford tipped back his head and laughed. "Oh, my dear Miss Merrill. I won't insult you by calling you *naive*, but obviously you've never had a knife held at your throat by a drug addict. You've never had someone burst into your home with a gun. You've never faced a crazed rapist. I assure you if you had experienced any one of those circumstances, you would try to find some way to stop the assault, even it meant to shoot the attacker."

Sheldon studied the table top. Since she couldn't relate to those offenses in any way, it was difficult to judge what she would do.

"I'd try to escape somehow. At the very least, I'd try to talk my way out of the situation." Her voice sounded tentative to her own ears.

"If you could get away. There are few...and I daresay that includes you...who would wait to be killed without doing something about it. I would kill under unusual circumstances. And while we're on the subject, not all killings are with guns. The bare hands can be just as lethal as a gun."

Sheldon knew that it would be pointless to go on with an argument she was ill prepared to make. She only knew that deep in her heart she could not kill. She had seen hunters drive through town, honking their horns to attract attention to the fact that they had a deer carcass tied to the fender. It turned her stomach. And killing a human being was just unthinkable.

She reached into her bag to get her mini recorder, placed it on the table between them. She had to concede, for now. But she wished he didn't look like he had just taken a refreshing dip in the pool while she felt like she had nearly drowned in it.

"I doubt that you and I will see eye-to-eye on that issue, but now I know why you named the bear Ernie."

He nodded. "In honor of my dear friend. And that's why I have him in the best room in the house. He's my special guest. He reminds me of very special times at Mooseneck."

It was Sheldon's opinion that the camp life for hunters was what most hunters really cherished. It had to be a male thing, she decided, this macho business of carrying a gun and shooting prey and then gathering around the fire with a drink in one hand, a cigar in the other, telling a raft of stories about their exploits against defenseless animals. Bambi lover, indeed! It was simply inhumane to kill.

Peripherally, Sheldon saw Bradford's focus rise from the fire to the portrait, and he seemed transported to another place. She waited for him to break the silence though she would like nothing better than to ask who the woman was. Something in his expression just now told her not to ask, at least not yet.

Then Bradford stiffened. He leaned forward, his arms on the table, and looked Sheldon square in the eyes, thrilling her with the intensity of his own.

"Miss Merrill," he said in a firm voice. "What is the single most important quality a person can possess?"

Did he intend to carry on this reverse interview, tricking her into saying something that would make her feel even more childlike in her convictions? Did this have to do with killing? She had never thought about a single most important quality, and she was bereft of thought and words.

"Well…I don't know. I suppose I'd have to say love."

"Ah. A typical woman's answer." He leaned back in his chair as if he were a judge about to exact a stiff sentence. "Love. A passion. Not all business and not all life is conducted on a level of passion. You can hardly take love into the boardroom, not in my boardroom anyway."

He snorted a sound that could pass for derision.

Sheldon moved her chair slightly away from the table, as she tried to understand what he was getting at.

"No," he said, his brow furrowing. "Love doesn't do it. So what is it? It's loyalty." He slapped his hand on the table rattling the cups in their saucers. "Pure and simple. Loyalty. That's the most important quality a person can possess. Without loyalty you have nothing. Love be damned…a brief interlude in someone's arms or a tumble in bed, call it love if you like, lasts how long? Just until a test of loyalty arises."

He leaned back, turned his head in the direction of the portrait, then quickly back. Again Sheldon wondered what the outbreak was about. The woman in the painting? Or just the rambling of an eccentric?

She fidgeted and ran her finger around the rim of the fine china cup, so thin it could cut a person's lip. Was there more? Should she get on with her interview? Her unease must have shown.

He threw back his head and laughed again, as if he had told a joke.

"My philosophies bore you, do they? Consider this. Loyalty, or lack of it, is what makes or breaks a family, a business, a system. Yes, even a government. Betrayal topples governments. And what lies behind this great dearth of loyalty in the world today?"

He pointed his finger at her. "You know as well as I do. It's self-interest. Self-interest overrides everything else. Love is easy to give, but loyalty takes introspection and self-denial."

He heaved a great sigh, then looked at Sheldon again. "Do get on with the interview. Just don't get too personal."

Her surprise at this speech left her breathless. Now, so quickly, he was asking that she not become personal in the interview. Personal. Like asking how loyalty or disloyalty had affected his life? Why he lived alone? Was the beautiful woman someone he'd loved? Had she been disloyal to him?

The librarian had told her that Bradford was not long on patience if he thought someone was trying to outwit him. One thing was certain. He had very definite opinions and wasn't shy about expressing them.

"Let's start with the new wing that you've built at Westburgh Hospital. What prompted you to do this?"

"More than one thing, but only one that I care to mention. My mother. Theresa Trent Bradford. Everyone called her Aunt Tess. She was the kindest, most generous, most loving woman you would ever meet. Held an open house for townspeople after church every Sunday. Went to homes of the sick. Knit clothing for the poor. Just a real good woman."

His head lobbed to the side and he shifted his weight. With a little sniff, he went on.

"When she was seventy-one she had a heart attack one day, and I found her on the kitchen floor at the Trent House. That's across the road, where my sister Lucille lives. She'd gone over there to see my sister, but Lucille wasn't home. I got my mother to the Westburgh Hospital, but they couldn't perform the surgery that she needed. Their facilities were limited. So she had to be transported to Mid-State General. She died in the ambulance on the way. That was six years ago."

Sheldon said nothing, but frowned in sympathy. She reached for the urn and poured more coffee for both.

"I don't fault anyone for her death. It was simply that the hospital was ill equipped. They had to send all such cases to a larger facility for critical care. After we buried Mama, I knew that I needed to do something about it. The people of Dedham County deserved to receive the same kind of health care that they could get in any other county in New York State. So, I told the hospital board members I wanted to build an intensive care unit with all the latest equipment. Of course the offer was accepted. And now it's finished and we'll dedicate it next week in memory of my mother. As you know, it's the Trent Intensive Care Unit."

He shrugged his shoulders as if it were an everyday occurrence.

She checked her notepad for another question and looked up only to find that he was studying the portrait. He quickly looked away when she asked, "Didn't you also give the town of Ashton an ambulance?"

He nodded, and remained quiet.

"When did you do that?"

"Three years ago."

"And the school?"

"Mmm…" he rolled his eyes in thought. "In nineteen seventy-one. Six years ago."

She had already gotten the story on the fire station and the school from the fire chief and the principal. She had hoped he would elaborate, but he was still in that far-away state.

"Do you have other family?" she asked.

"No. Just my sister and myself now." Distant. So distant. What was he thinking?

"You're not married?"

"No."

"You grew up here in Ashton?" Sheldon took a sip of lukewarm coffee. His brevity left her disappointed. Why? He had started out seemingly eager. Such a changeable man. Once again his eyes sought out the painting.

"Yes. I was born here, went through all the grades here. That's why I had the school built. I wanted the kids to have better than that four-room building with outhouses."

Now he took a deep breath and focused on her with more interest, but still Sheldon had the impression that he would rather conclude the interview.

"I had planned to become a doctor and was admitted to Bretton College in Maine. The reason I chose to go there was that my uncle, my father's brother, used to take me fishing summers in Maine. I liked the state very much and decided I'd try to get into that college so that I could enjoy the hunting and fishing the state offers. The fact that my uncle was an alumnus probably did more to get me in than my scholastic ability."

Then he grinned with boyish deviltry, and Sheldon felt a touch of intimacy. David Bradford would never be mistaken for a common man. His voice rolled with the ease of a practiced orator, mellow and rich, and now his gaze bored into her, commanding her full attention. Sheldon was compelled to concentrate on his words, partly mesmerized by his expressive eyes, partly lost in her own fantasy world of over-the-rainbow male perfection, a world that she knew never did and never would exist.

She looked at her notepad, preparing for her next question, when her host continued.

"I didn't go on to study for the medical field, however. My uncle suffered a mild stroke during my senior year and insisted that I come into the firm with him, which I did. When he died I inherited the enterprise, Bradford Investment Associates. And I continue to operate it."

"And you don't live here all the time."

"No. I come here when I can get away, often on weekends and holidays, and several weeks during the summer, too. I have an army of associates now and feel quite comfortable leaving things in their hands."

"Someone told me you have hunting dogs."

"Yes. Four. I house them on a farm which a friend operates on the other side of town. In fact, it's not far from my cottage on the lake. I still like to fish and hunt."

"Your sister, Lucille. Is she married?"

"No. Her name is still Bradford. Lucille and I both inherited businesses that we hadn't really sought to enter. Mine was the brokerage firm, and hers, from our mother's brother Saul Ashton Trent, the Ashton Sawmill. She has done an outstanding job of running the mill, an unusual occupation for a woman. But she has a good business head. Or at least she did before she became ill."

"Oh, I'm sorry. Is it serious?"

"I'm afraid so. Emphysema. She lost one lung last year to cancer. She has always been a heavy smoker." After a second's pause, he added, "But I hope you won't find it necessary to impart that information to the public. We try to remain as private as possible. We don't discuss our problems with outsiders."

His sister's ill health must be another reason for the intensive care unit. Sheldon nodded assent to his request.

"Our father, Nicholas Bradford, was the Baptist minister here. He died ten years ago. While my sister was a faithful Baptist for many years, I'm afraid I felt no calling to religion."

His eyes twinkled. "Maybe I missed my calling. I probably was trying to peek through the hole in the women's dressing room at the lake the day it came."

Sheldon laughed. "You said Saul Ashton Trent was your mother's brother. The same middle name as the town. Did the family found the community?"

"Yes, we're descended, not just from the Mayflower Bradfords, but also from Henry Ashton who came here in seventeen eighty, when the living wasn't easy. Westburgh was then a trading post. Of the estimated ten thousand Indian members in the Five Nations, some were friendly, some weren't, depending partly on their perception of how honestly white men treated them. Guess they weren't skeptical enough, huh?"

Sheldon watched as Bradford got up and pulled a poker from the fireplace tools and with it pushed a checkered black log back into the fire bed. She instinctively jumped as sparks exploded. Replacing the poker, he watched the fire for a moment before turning his attention to her again.

"I don't mean to bore you with a history lesson, Miss Merrill." Obviously an impatient man, he started to pace a few steps toward the bear, then came back and stood with his back to the fire, slightly hunched forward, like a racer waiting for the gun to fire.

"Not at all. It's fascinating. I know nothing about the area's history. Please go on."

"Henry Ashton was a peaceful man." His hand went to his chest, and with a touch of insincerity he said, "Like me. He established a grist mill on the river, the present-day sawmill, and he did something that gave him security in trading with the English, French, and Indians."

"What did he do?"

"He married an Indian chief's daughter and traded furs with the French. So it all worked out to his advantage. There's no written history of our family back before nineteen hundred. That's when my great-grandmother started to keep a journal and wrote all that she had heard about the family, passed down orally through the generations. I don't know why no one had written it all down before that."

Scratching his head, he said, "Maybe they were illiterate."

"Oh, I doubt that," Shelly blurted. Then they both laughed. Now she could see the Indian features, the high cheekbones, the slightly aquiline nose, the taut skin. But English and other genes had mixed with the Indian to create a distinguished blend, right down to the lighter hair and blue eyes.

He paced again while he spent the next fifteen minutes telling Sheldon more about the regional history and his family ancestry. When he appeared to have exhausted the subject, she looked at her watch and said that, unless he wished to add more, she should take his photo and return to her office. He doubted that there was much more to say which would enhance the profile a great deal.

"I can't think of a better place to take your photo than there by the fireplace. The portrait is lovely and would make a good backdrop. Is she a relative, Mr. Bradford?"

"No. She isn't a relative."

"Do you mind if I take the picture there?'

"Yes, I do mind."

Although Sheldon could see the flexing jaw muscle and lowered eyelids, she plunged ahead in her quest to learn something about the subject in the portrait.

"Oh. Is she…is she your fiancee?" She kept her voice light, uplifted with interest.

He drew in a deep breath and let it out slowly. Irritation was apparent in his stiffened body, the tight lips. His eyes looked almost menacing.

"That's really no concern of yours. We'll take the picture in my library."

Without another word he marched out the door to the hallway. Sheldon scrambled to gather her bags and hurry after him. What on earth…? Why was he angry because she asked about the woman? Whatever the problem, Sheldon wished that she hadn't said anything about it.

When they were finished and she had squeezed her feet into her shrinking shoes, she turned at the front door to thank him for the interview.

"I'm sorry if I upset you," she said quietly.

To her surprise, he smiled and clasped her hand, as if nothing untoward had happened.

"Miss Merrill, I don't get upset. I don't get frightened. I don't get bored. And I don't get taken. A man in my position can afford to remedy all of those conditions. To date, I've found only one condition that I can't reverse. That's death."

CHAPTER 2

❊

Thoughts of David Bradford haunted Sheldon on the drive back to the office, thoughts that ranged from fascination to disapproval. On the one hand, he possessed superior intelligence to have garnered a fortune at his young age. He cared for family and the disadvantaged, that was obvious from his many philanthropies and the circumstances that prompted him to have the hospital wing constructed, then naming that wing for his mother. He provided for his town. Yes, he seemed to be a caring, smart, generous man. And he was handsome. Oh yeah. He was that all right.

Yet, his eccentricity bordered on obnoxious and rude, his moods were a roller-coaster of unfathomable emotion. He both thrilled and frightened her. Instinct told her that she could fantasize about him, if she must, but never get close to him.

The rain had stopped before she arrived at the newsroom in the afternoon. Wire services fidgeted on and off while reporters were typing late stories and answering telephones. This small newsroom was home to Sheldon. No other career could have given her the satisfaction she felt by interacting with humanity, writing about the world around her, and reading her own stories, which instilled in her a sense of pride for having contributed to the pages of regional history.

"So how did it go with Mr. Moneybags?" George was at her elbow as soon as she sat down at her desk. Disheveled as usual, he looked as if he had just gotten out of bed, with five o'clock shadow, his dark brown hair curling wildly in all directions, his wide-legged jeans wrinkled, shirt hanging loose. He carried his five-ten, medium build with a swagger, a bit like John Wayne, but he was unpretentious, had a pleasant face with a quick smile and laughing light brown eyes, as well as a mustache that most usually needed a major trim. A reporter for many years, George talked little about his past life, lived alone, loved the outdoors, was a steady worker and an excellent writer.

"It had some…how can I put it…surprising turns."

"Like what?" Dee had joined the pair. Sheldon's best friend, confidante, exact opposite, petite Dee dressed to complement her black hair and unblemished pale complexion. Sheldon often wondered why every eligible bachelor in the county wasn't pounding down her door. But Dee had an aloof quality which warned the opposite sex that she would be friends at arm's length only.

"Like just about everything." Sheldon laughed and looked out the window at the few shoppers returning to their cars in the parking lot across from the *Press* office. How could she characterize a man who had mood swings, but not lasting ones? A man who apparently loved humanity, yet seemed not to be loved for anything but his wealth? A man who enjoyed the great outdoors, but made his fortune in the heart of New York City? A man who was generous and tightfisted all at the same time. He was, indeed, a man of contrasts. But how could you fault him for his individuality?

She laughed. "He's one of the most interesting people I've ever interviewed."

She hesitated. Page one editor Manfred Gray and sportswriter Jon Phelps were both reading AP wire copy as a start toward tomorrow's publication. The others seemed to be absorbed in their work, too. Yet she knew they were all listening to her. It couldn't really be otherwise in their cramped quarters.

"He's certainly different from what I expected. I thought he'd be old. Everyone just sidestepped the fact that he's young, in his mid or late thirties, I'd say. Imagine, being that young and having millions." She sighed.

"Must be a terrible burden," George said with an exaggerated frown.

George was, like Dee, a good friend. When she came to the *Westburgh Press*, Sheldon had needed a friend, not just to show her the ropes of the daily, but also to encourage her and to help her adjust to the barbs of the Two Wicked Sisters, as the society and obituary writers were referred to privately among the reporters. George had been patient and non-judgmental. She could forgive him almost anything for making her early days here so much easier.

"Yeah, terrible. But what's really funny is that he lives like a poor farmer. Oh, he does have a beautiful parlor, where I interviewed him. Otherwise the place is a dump. And yet across the road his sister Lucille lives alone in a big white house with two-story columns and a black Cadillac parked out front. His home is an enormous old farmhouse with everything a shambles. I mean, the fields haven't been mowed, the driveway is gravel…mud, when it rains." She swivelled her chair and held up her feet for them to see her muddy, ruined shoes. "There are holes in the roof shingles, the barn is so open you can see right through it. But he just doesn't look like the type of man to live poorly. He's handsome, Dee. He's got these beautiful blue eyes…"

The rapture of the moment was interrupted by the banging of the composing room door. Harry, in his usual breathless manner at deadline, called out, "Is everything out? Any more copy to come? Dee? George? How about you Sheldon? Got anything else?"

Dee gave Sheldon a quick wink. Obviously Harry singled them out because they were idling at deadline. As a boss, he was fair and honest, and he protected his reporters by taking flak for their mistakes, but he was also serious about his product and demanded that his staff be the same. At this time of day when the newspaper had to be put to bed, he became irritable. At other times, the short, affable, overweight Irishman with a generous heart might be telling a joke or joining in office trivia.

In chorus, the three reporters answered, "It's all out."

Candy Hart, one of the Two Wicked Sisters, held up her hand. "I'm not quite finished, Harry. Just another paragraph."

If ever Candy were finished by deadline, George had once said, they would have to mark it on the calendar as a memorable event. She moved with amazing slowness. Her working pace was painful to watch, each word seemingly sucked from some deep, dark tunnel that she peered into from time to time, with glazed, blank eyes.

"Hurry it up. We don't have a lot of space left. Get it out here fast." Harry pushed back through the door to the composing room. Candy scowled and re-read what she had just written, then pulled the page from her typewriter. She leaned across her desk and whispered something to her compatriot, Janet Kelleher, and the two laughed. Janet was a fiftyish woman with a desperate desire to remain young, her red hair a little too flaming for her fading complexion. Never married, she wrote obituaries at the *Press* and occasionally had an assignment to cover a speech or social event. One of her claims to independence was that she had just two dresses to her name. She wore the gray print daily. For the special occasions, she wore a navy dress, made from the same pattern as the gray one, long-sleeved and straight cut.

"So he's young and handsome. And?" Dee's dark eyes sparkled with enthusiasm.

"And he has this portrait of a beautiful blond woman in his living room and seems to want to keep her identity a mystery. Oh, yes, and a stuffed bear, too, but he told me about that."

"A bear!" Dee's eyes widened. "He has a bear in his living room?"

"Yes. A bear that he calls Ernie, of all things. I think it's repulsive. He named it for a hunting guide he knew in northern Maine. He said the man died three years ago."

"Well, there's your headline for the story: The 'Bear' Facts About David P. Bradford."

Dee groaned and Sheldon rolled her eyes heavenward. "I'm far more interested in the portrait than I am the bear. When I asked to take his photo standing by the fireplace, in front of the painting, he turned angry and said we'd take it in his library, which was a very small room lined with bookshelves with hundreds of old books. Very hard to get a good photo there. I tell you, I didn't know what to think. I felt that somehow I had touched a very sensitive nerve, and it just makes me wonder why. Then when I was leaving, I apologized for upsetting him. He laughed, and said I hadn't upset him. So there you are. What do you make of it?"

"You think he really was upset?" George asked.

"Oh yes. No question about it. He had been smiling and going on about his family history and was generally pleasant. Then when I mentioned the portrait, he scowled…no, he glared at me, almost menacingly. He spoke in very terse sentences, and barely gave me time to take the pictures. No, he was upset all right. So strange. Maybe that's what everyone was hinting at, sudden mood swings. You just wouldn't believe he was the same man. And then at the door, he had changed again, acting as if we were the best of friends. Weird."

Dee tried to rationalize Bradford's behavior, "Maybe she was his ex-wife. Maybe she had left him and he might not want the embarrassment of having that mentioned in your story."

Sheldon studied her for a moment. Dee was probably the most down-to-earth woman she had ever known, and it was always worthwhile to listen to her. Sometimes Sheldon wanted to shake her friend when her self-assuredness turned to pig-headedness. But she had a good mind and a good heart. They had become like sisters, not just working together, but also partying, shopping, visiting, swapping books and records. They were at each other's apartment so often that they had talked about leasing a large one and sharing it, but the idea fizzled when Dee became involved with Conrad Drew, a college administrator at Tandy State.

"Yes, that could be it," Sheldon said. "He isn't married now. If she left him, though, I should think people in town might have told me. I only talked with a few people, but none of them said anything about his ever having been married. It could be just a sweetheart who backed out of the relationship."

"I'd say townspeople know which side their bread is buttered on when it comes to the biggest philanthropist in the area," George offered. "Hell, I wouldn't say a whole lot about a man's private life if he were giving me food baskets, or sending my sister to college for free. Would you?"

"Maybe not. He did carry on a bit about the importance of being loyal. Maybe everyone in Ashton knows how much importance he places on loyalty." She shook her head and looked down at the blank piece of paper in her typewriter. "I don't know. I only know it has me wondering. Just one of those things. Something about the way he would look at the painting, and then quickly look away as if he didn't want me to see his interest. Well, you'd think he'd put it someplace else if he doesn't want anyone to see it."

She thought about the man's odd behavior and his emphasis on loyalty, his lapses into deep thought. "You ever get a niggling curiosity about something that you've just got to get the answer to, George?"

His deep chuckle was a familiar precursor to one of his irreverent remarks. "If I do, I fight it real hard. Sleuthing is hard work, in case you didn't know it. If the man wants privacy, it's for damned sure he has good reason. I wouldn't upset his applecart, if I were you. Men like that can get real mean." He yawned and stretched. "I've still got work to do, ladies. If you need me, you know where you can reach me."

That drew smiles. It was a narrow editorial room, desks bumped together two-by-two against each concrete wall with an aisle down the middle, and at each pair of desks two reporters faced each other. At the very back of the room where there was one door to Harry's office and another door leading outdoors behind them, George sat across the center aisle from Sheldon. Dee was her desk mate. She could talk to either of them in a normal voice and they would hear her. Unfortunately, so could most of the others in the room.

"Well I'm curious." Dee slipped back into her typing chair and stacked some papers.

"Are you going to try to find out about who she is? Yes, of course you are. I can see it in your face. Where do you think you'll start?"

Sheldon thought for a few minutes. Maybe someone would answer a very straightforward question. Bradford didn't, but surely someone else in the town of Ashton would know the background on that portrait.

"Oh, I know. I'll start with his sister Lucille. She would probably be flattered if I went to her and asked for some information about her brother as a child, growing up. And somewhere along the line, I can slip in a question about the painting in his living room. I'll just bet she'll tell me about it."

Sheldon felt a prickle of anticipation. There had to be a story here, maybe not one she would print, but one that would help her to see David Bradford a little clearer. At the same time, maybe she would get a clue from his sister as to his odd ways. After all, it wasn't really normal to live poorly with that much money.

"Good idea. When will you do it?"

"I'll call her tonight. Maybe she can see me sometime this weekend."

"But this is your free weekend. Why don't you wait until Monday?" For Dee, the three-day weekend in their rotational schedule was almost sacred. Sheldon knew Dee would never give it up even to do a little interview.

"I don't have a lot planned. It won't interfere with anything."

Dee pursed her lips, but said nothing.

Sheldon began to type, but soon found herself staring out the window at the quiet side street where a white-haired shopper trudged by, crossed to the parking lot, and loaded herself and packages into her car. What must it be like to be able to shop during the day, any day, and take your time about it? Sheldon wondered if it would be fun or if it might not seem as if she had no great purpose in life except to indulge her own impulses.

The earlier rain had washed away some of the dusty haze that had hung over Westburgh. Every time she thought about the day two years ago when she first came to the city trying to find the *Press* office, she had to smile. Buildings were so drab and the main street so narrow that she thought she was on a back street. To the right across the intersection she could see the sleek black front of Shandler's, the one upscale dress shop on Main Street, a place she had avoided for too long. But she couldn't think about new clothes now.

David Bradford intrigued her, he and his mystery woman. And his talk about loyalty. Why had he inserted that topic so suddenly, and apparently so unrelated to the discussion? He was, himself, a man of mystery, though there was no mystery where he stood on killing animals, or people for that matter. Well, she disagreed with him. There was no valid excuse for killing.

It was because of her interest in people's lives that she had become a journalist. Good old Ben Bentley had taken her under his wing and taught her the ropes of good journalism. She'd never be a muckraker like he was, but she had learned to dig for a story and how to write it.

What would Mr. Bentley think of this story? Would he say she was being melodramatic even to think there was something unusual about Bradford's refusal to reveal the identity of the woman in the portrait? He'd probably say, just like George did, that an eccentric multi-millionaire could hide whatever he wanted to hide, and the rest of the world could go hang. And they were probably right. She was being silly.

She snapped her attention back to the last few paragraphs of the agricultural story she was writing for her weekend page, a page she had to finish today before leaving for the long weekend off. These three days off together were always a treat in the rotating schedule the reporters followed, and for Sheldon this one would be a real respite, unlike the normal procedure of going to New Hampshire to stay with her mother for at least two of the days and then returning to do mundane chores. Going to Mum's created a certain amount of tension, though. She always spent the six-hour drive steeling herself for the guilt trip her mother laid on her. Why did she have to work so far from home? Why couldn't she come back and save expenses by living at home? Why had she left in the first place? Why wouldn't she make up with Joe? So many whys, and so many lies.

But this weekend would be different. She was staying in Westburgh, regardless.

She would be out of the office on schedule at five and start her weekend by joining the others at Pat's Pub. She'd have a beer with a light supper at the pub, go home, call her mother, shower, and relax with the used book she had just bought, *War and Peace*. She should have read it long ago, but never felt she had the time for it. Her spirits rose in anticipation. To the monotonous clack, clack of the wire services and the banging of Royals around the room, she typed on.

After finishing the story and going over the page layout and headlines with the composing room staff, she returned to her desk and looked at the clock. Just ten minutes to go. She began tidying her desk, putting away notes, sliding pens and pencils into the top drawer, stacking her reference books at the side. She was about to speak to Dee when her phone buzzed.

"A call for you on line two," Della, the front office secretary, said.

She pressed the button and said hello.

"Miss Merrill? This is David Bradford."

"Oh, how nice to hear from you, Mr. Bradford," Sheldon said in her most pleasant voice, as her heart began beating in triplets. She looked at Dee and mouthed, 'It's him,' pointing to the phone.

Dee stopped her work and stared, all attention to Sheldon's words.

"I'm calling to ask you whether you have started writing the profile on me yet."

Sheldon felt the dread of a different kind of anticipation now. She instinctively knew what he was going to ask. She hated to have to turn him down.

"No, as a matter of fact, I haven't. It's not due until next Thursday, for the weekend issue next week. I'll be writing it Tuesday."

"Oh, I see." He didn't try to hide the disappointment in his voice. Neither said anything for a moment.

Finally, just for something to say and hoping to divert his request, Sheldon said, "I'm just about to start my long weekend, Mr. Bradford. I'll have three whole days off." She gave a nervous little laugh. "It doesn't come often, so it will be a big treat. I may be out your way, however. Thought I'd like to look around the village a little more and go around the lake, which I didn't see."

She squeezed her eyes tight. Why was she rambling like this? Did she subconsciously think he might offer to escort her around? No, no. Of course not. That was ridiculous.

Then it became a moot point as he said, "I should like to read that story after you write it. Just to be sure you get the important facts correct, you understand."

Her shoulders slumped. This was always the difficult thing to explain. Would he get angry? She crossed her fingers and jumped in.

"I'm so sorry, Mr. Bradford. It's newspaper policy that no stories may be read before publication. It's a long-standing policy. Nothing I have any control over."

"What kind of policy is that? No wonder the paper has so many mistakes. Surely in my case, you can make an exception."

Oh no, he's getting angry, Sheldon thought. Now what do I do? He obviously won't take no for an answer. She looked at Dee, who wrinkled her nose in sympathy.

"Well, I can't rule on an exception, but I'll tell you what. If you care to talk with the editor, I'll have him pick up and talk with you."

"Harry O'Brien? Yes. I will talk with him. You put him on."

"I'm going to put you on hold. Don't hang up. He's in the composing room. Stay on the line. Okay?"

"Yes. Fine. I'll wait."

She pressed the hold button and set the phone on its cradle. "Oh lord, Dee. I hate this. I might have known he'd want to read the story. There was no way I could deal with him. He was beginning to get angry."

"Harry will know how to deal with him. Don't worry."

Sheldon used the intercom to get Harry on the phone, then told him who was calling and why.

"Okay," he said. "I'll get it."

The editorial room was soon being vacated, some leaving by way of the front through the composing room, and some past Sheldon. Candy was beside her, but before opening the door, she said, "So you have a mystery with David Bradford?"

Sheldon smiled and nodded, inwardly wishing she had waited to tell George and Dee about Bradford when they were alone. Candy wasn't a sinister person like her "sister" Janet, but she didn't strain to keep confidences.

"If there's anything I can do to help you find out what you want to know, just let me know," Candy said. She talked as if she were about to yawn, and her eyes were constantly moving. "I've never heard that Dave was married. You did know that we are acquainted, didn't you? Frank's on the hospital board along with Dave."

"Oh, of course." Sheldon recalled that Candy's fiancé Frank Youngman was on the board. This buttonhole relationship, however, fell short of impressing Sheldon. Candy brushed at her well coiffed and sprayed hair, as if an auburn lock could possibly be out of place. With a buttery complexion and full figure, she was an attractive forty-year-old with a quick laugh, the kind of woman who could and did wedge into society's upper echelon with ease while clinging to Frank's coattails.

"We meet socially from time-to-time. He's a very nice man." Candy said.

"But he never brings a woman to the social functions that the hospital sponsors? Or maybe some other gatherings?"

"No. I've never seen a woman with him. And I've never heard that he even had a woman friend. There has been speculation that he might be…oh, ah, you know. That he might prefer men to women." She said the last in a barely audible whisper.

Candy gave a high-pitched titter as she flung her hand in the air. "But, of course, I wouldn't repeat that to anyone. And I hope you won't ever say that I told you that."

"No. Of course not. And thank you for your input."

"Any time. Just ask me."

It occurred to Sheldon as Candy left that the woman meant to be sincere. If only she weren't so affected

Dee mimicked, "'Just ask me.' Why didn't you think of that in the first place, Shellie?"

"Yeah. Right. Oh well. She tries."

"Yes. As Harry would say, be charitable."

Dee finished tidying her desk and got up. "Are you coming to the pub?"

"Not just yet. I'll wait and see Harry. I want to know what he decided."

By the time Harry came to the editorial room, everyone but Sheldon had left. She looked up from the notes she was studying to ask, "Harry? What am I to do about the Bradford story? Shall I show it to him?"

"No. Of course not. We stick to policy."

"He seemed quite angry."

As they talked, Sheldon followed Harry into his office, where he gave short shrift to tidying his desk and stuffing papers into a well-worn briefcase. He was a good journalist, with a real nose for news. But tidy he wasn't. Out of the chaos of papers and clippings, he could find just about anything on his desk or in his briefcase, but Sheldon never knew how. The papers he was taking home were probably notes for his editorial, which he wrote late at night when his wife and two children were asleep.

"He was angry. But I don't bend on that rule. Ever. We let one person edit a story that we write, and the first thing you know we no longer operate an independent newspaper. He may not like it, but that's the way it is, and that's the way it remains."

Sheldon backed away from his doorway as he came toward her.

"I'm fifteen minutes late," he said. "Supposed to pick up Kate at the hospital. Oh, by-the-way, that last cutline you wrote has something wrong with it. Looks like the typesetter may have missed a line. You want to take a look at it and correct it before you go?"

He was already out the door. "See you Monday. Have a good weekend."

"Thanks. And say hi to Kate for me. Tell her I appreciated the private tour of the new wing."

He nodded as he pushed through the outer door. Sheldon smiled. Kate certainly deserved the promotion to supervising nurse of the new ICU unit, and she had been so excited about it the day she showed Sheldon through. How the woman handled such a responsible job as well as two active children and Harry was more than Sheldon could imagine.

It was five-fifteen already and she was hungry. Well, this wouldn't take long.

Reading the lines under the photo she'd taken of an angelic three-year-old boy with his arms wrapped around a lamb, Sheldon quickly saw the mistake, pulled the strip off, stuck it sideways, and wrote the correction in blue pencil. With no one around, the composing room seemed dead, ancient boards occasionally snapping somewhere. Even though she could hear the faint sound of voices in the distribution department out back, this area felt creepy. It was an old wood building with three stories, converted to house the newspaper operation. The concrete editorial room was an add-on. When she came to work here, the changeover was being made from hot lead to paste-up. It had been a traumatic change, old-time compositors unwilling to give up their art for this paper doll paste-up, as they called it. But now the days of reading lead type backward were gone and just about anyone could do the job of composing a page. Sheldon herself often pasted up her agricultural page.

About to leave, she swung around, startled by the creak of floorboards behind her.

Then she relaxed. "You startled me, Hugh."

Hugh Webster not only did normal janitorial duties each night, but he had the unenviable job of scraping up discarded strips and pieces of paste-covered photo-copy paper stuck to the floor.

"How are you, Miss Merrill?" Though he had tiny teeth, set in thick gums, Hugh always smiled. He came to her side and stood grinning, his eyes bright behind horn-rimmed glasses. He wasn't an old man, maybe in his early forties, but he had the stooped bearing of someone either ashamed of his considerable height or simply too weary to stand straight.

"Oh I'm fine. All finished up for this week." She smiled warmly, but felt a certain repugnance, a feeling she always tried to hide. The man was ignored by everyone here. Someone had to befriend him.

Realizing that he wasn't going to say anything, Sheldon said, "Well, they didn't leave too bad a mess today, Hugh. You'd think they could learn to use the waste can instead of the floor, though. It would make your job a lot easier. And maybe we wouldn't have to scrape the stuff off our shoes when we get home."

His mouth stretched even wider. Obviously he felt flattered that someone was concerned over his hard work. He seemed starved for attention. He reminded her of a poor farm boy who had been in her high school class, always so left out of things. She felt sorry for people with low self-esteem.

"It sure would. But I don't mind. I get paid to clean it up. Is there anything I can do special for you, Miss Merrill? You want your desk washed?"

He had seen her cleaning her metal desktop at the end of a day about a month ago and had expressed the wish that she let him know whenever she wanted it done. She didn't tell him that all of the desks could use a good cleaning at least once a week, to remove the newsprint ink. Long-sleeved white blouses had to be bleached after each wearing.

"I'm off for the long weekend and don't intend to think about my desk for three days." she said. "But if you have time to clean it while I'm gone, that would be fine. And thanks, Hugh."

With that she hurried out through the editorial room to join her friends, but as she got to the outside door, she heard him call behind her, "My pleasure, Miss Merrill. I'll do anything for you."

Revulsion rippled through her. Poor Hugh. Must be a terribly lonely man.

CHAPTER 3

The pub was buzzing as patrons tried to make themselves heard over the juke box music.

Thursday was the one day the pub offered happy hour, two-for-the-price-of-one drinks from five to six o'clock, and it invariably packed the place. On other days, only a handful of regulars came in at this hour. It certainly confirmed the long-known American fact of life, everyone wants something for nothing.

In the dim light Sheldon could see a hand waving at a back booth. As she headed toward it, she thought how she had changed over the past two years. Before coming to Westburgh, she would never have entered a barroom, let alone drink a beer. The first time she had come to the pub with George she'd nearly choked on her first intake of cigarette and alcohol fumes, and then she had to force down the bitter-tasting beer. But she had wanted to make changes in her life. It was time to live in the real world, to satisfy the restless curiosity she'd always had in her insulated haven with her mother. Even with Joe, she wouldn't cross certain boundaries...no booze, no overnights, nothing but straight sex. Somehow, living with her mother, she felt that just having a sexual encounter with Joe was *risque* in itself. But the desire for new experiences was always just beneath the surface, and when she landed the new job, she determined that she'd join in, no longer under the restrictive censure of her mother. She had asked

George if he would object to her tagging along for the after-work pub gathering. To her surprise she was soon relaxed and enjoying herself as others joined them from the office. She relished the camaraderie and had even developed a tolerable taste for beer.

Dee, with Coke in hand, shoved over to make room for her, while George said, "I just ordered your hamburger and fries along with mine." She nodded thanks.

"What kept you so long?" Dee asked.

"I had to correct a cutline on my ag page after I saw Harry. He said he told David Bradford he couldn't read my story." She cocked an eyebrow. "I'll bet that went over like a lead balloon. Lord knows, I hope I don't make a mistake. Both of you promise me you'll proof it for me?"

"Sure." They said in unison.

Beers and hamburgers arrived and were set in front of George and Sheldon.

"Let me guess. You're having dinner with Conrad tonight," Sheldon said to Dee.

"Right. Not as exciting as hamburger and beer, of course, but…" They all laughed.

"No. Filet mignon never is," George said. "When am I going to meet this paragon of integrity, Dee? You keep telling us what a gentleman he is. I should meet him, you know, if for no other reason than to gain some pointers on which fork to use, just in case I ever get to one of those fancy restaurants he's always taking you to."

Dee's midnight eyes sparkled. "You could use instruction on a little more than just the right fork to use, George. How about some grooming tips, maybe where to find a good tailor, and a barber and…"

"Okay, okay. I got ya." He leaned over the table and pointed a finger at Dee. "But you better be forewarned, miss bandbox lady. You'll be very surprised when you see me all dressed up some day. I clean up real well."

"When is that going to happen?" Sheldon asked, feigning surprised interest.

George held up both hands, palms out, as if defending himself from attack. "I give up. I'm outnumbered."

Sheldon reached across the table and patted his arm. "That's okay, George. We love you just the same, slob or not."

"You're just saying that to make me feel better," he pouted.

Laughing, Sheldon said, "As if you care! But speaking of slobs, Hugh sneaked up on me while I was in the composing room and jumped me out of my skin. That poor man. He's so…so…" What could she say? He was a human being with redeeming qualities, even if no one recognized that fact. "He's so pathetic, really. He just stood there grinning at me. He never seems to know what to say to anyone."

"He gives me the creeps," Dee said. "If he'd just not shuffle so when he walks. And that dirty hair, all pasted down on his head like a wet mat. Brrr." She shuddered.

"He is a mess, all right. But I still feel sorry for him. He tries to be friendly. I wonder if he's married. That's a daunting thought, huh, Dee? Being married to Hugh?"

"Please. I don't want to get sick. I wonder where he lives. I never see him around town."

"He lives in Ashton," George said. "I saw him one day when I went out to go fishing at the lake. He was outside a small house, not much more than a shack, not too far from your David Bradford's cottage, Shel. Kitty-corner across from it. Did you know that?"

"I don't even know where 'my' David Bradford's cottage is. How do you get there?"

Already the pub was growing quieter. The loud music had stopped and patrons began leaving shortly after six. From behind the bar came the thud and clink of glasses being washed at the stainless steel sink.

Sliding his paper plate aside, George pulled a white napkin from the box at the end of the table, took a pen from his shirt pocket, and drew a map as he explained the route through Ashton to the Lake Road.

"It's about a mile out the Lake Road on the water side, like so," he swept a line from an X marking Ashton. "Sort of hidden by a lot of pine trees and firs. You should see his Keep Out sign. It's hand lettered in black paint on a shingle and nailed to a tree by his driveway."

"I believe it," Sheldon said. "Now you talk about a strange one, that's David Bradford. *He's* not married. Probably women take one look at that house he lives in and run the other way. On the other hand, seems to me a person could get used to it, given the advantages that come with the eccentricities."

"Meaning money, looks, and sex appeal, no doubt," George said, his expression a mix of question and disappointment.

"Well...yes...that would be about right." The women laughed, but Sheldon observed a sudden change in George, from carelessness to contemplative. He turned cloudy eyes on her, not angry, but definitely pensive. She had never seen him disturbed by her frivolity before. It was time to change the subject.

"Dee, I plan to go shopping Saturday in Wintertown. It's time I bought a couple of new outfits. Are you shocked?"

With an appropriate open-mouth stare, Dee said, "I guess so! What prompted this outbreak? I hope it's not catching. Well, maybe I do. I'd like to get a new suit."

"Good. Why don't you go with me then?"

"All right. What time are you leaving?"

"How about eleven? We can have lunch at The Maple Grove."

Dee agreed. Sheldon knew that her friend could afford a whole new wardrobe, if she wanted it. Her mother was a rich woman, although they didn't seem to be close. It was Dee's grandparents who had left her money, income from a trust fund. Though Dee didn't need to work, she wouldn't know what to do with herself without a job to go to each day.

"Doesn't Conrad usually take you someplace on Saturday?"

"Not this week. They're having a science fair at the college. Connie invited me to come, but I'm really not into scientific stuff. I am into shopping, however."

Sheldon hoped Conrad Drew knew what a gem of a woman he was courting. She'd make him a good wife. He certainly seemed to care for her, and it wasn't for her money since she hadn't told him yet about her wealthy family. It had to be love.

Dee looked over at George. "What about you, George? What are you doing Saturday?"

"Oh, no thanks. I really don't need a new suit."

"Cute."

George gave a "What do you mean by that?" look. Despite his attempts to appear unconcerned about everything and everyone, Sheldon knew better. She had walked in on him in the archives room one day after he had covered an accident. She was in the room before she realized that he was there, sitting in a corner next to a tall bookcase, his head in his arms. She walked to the central table where various bound volumes of newspapers were scattered about, sat on a stool, turned and faced him, then realized he was crying.

"It must have been a bad one," Sheldon said in a half whisper.

His husky voice was muffled in his arms. "Yeah. Real bad. I've seen people die in Vietnam, but this little boy wasn't any more than two." George looked up, his eyes not quite meeting Sheldon's, his face tear-streaked. He sniffed and heaved a big sigh, his body shuddering. "He was alive when I got there. He was in shock, just staring, not crying. I watched as the paramedics worked on him. A chubby little blond boy, so terribly hurt, like a broken doll, blood all over. Then he was just gone. And his mother…saw him, tried to touch him, but her arm couldn't reach and she was too hurt herself to move. It was awful, Shellie. Just awful."

He got to his feet, took out his handkerchief and wiped his face, strode to Sheldon and put his arms around her. He held tight for a long few moments, as if she might absorb some of his pain. Then he slowly released her, turned and walked out. Neither one mentioned it again.

But Sheldon remembered. She'd seen into the man's heart that day.

Now Dee had to leave, and Sheldon, digging in her purse for money, said, "I have to go, too. A ton of things to do. I'll call Lucille Bradford and see if she'll talk with me tomorrow. Maybe I can take a drive around the lake, too." She pasted on a false smile. "Too bad you two have to work."

"Low blow," George said. "You want to borrow my fishing rod?"

"No thanks. I'm fishing for information only." She stood to let Dee slide out.

"Don't leave just yet, Shel," George said.

"Oh?"

"I need to speak with you."

Dee had already gone to the bar to pay her tab. Sheldon called to her, "Go ahead Dee. I'll call you later."

She sat back down facing George once more. "What's up, doc?"

"You've had a tough week, Shellie. You look tired."

"I guess I am. Three farm interviews in two days, then that agricultural conference that went on and on into the night. And, of course, David Bradford. But I got it all written up, except for Bradford's story. Yeah. It's been a busy week. I'll be glad to have the weekend off."

"Then why go on working tomorrow? You can wait to talk with Lucille Bradford next week without any problem, you know."

"I know. It's just that..."

"You just have to push it, don't you. I never saw such a snoop as you are."

"I'm no more of a snoop than you are, George Durant. You never rest until you get all the answers you want for a story. Now don't go pointing a finger at me."

The bartender came to clear the table, then asked, "Anything else here, folks?"

"Sure, why not?" George looked at Sheldon with a question mark, and she shrugged an okay. "Bring two more beers."

"You pay for both this time around. It's past six," the bartender said.

"Good enough."

"Oh, I owe you for that first one," Sheldon said, reaching for her bag once more.

"Put it away. You had the freebie."

"Next week, you'll get the freebie."

"Fine."

They sat quietly for the few minutes it took for the fresh beer to arrive, George intent on tracing with a spoon the outline of the map he'd made, and Sheldon brushing crumbs off her skirt. Her thoughts returned to David Bradford, the inconsistency of the run-down exterior of his home and the magnificent parlor in which he had talked with her so charmingly at a tea table complete with silver tea service. What would it be like to have such a handsome man at her side, walking into a reception hall, and being envied by every woman there? Or just relaxing together on a sand beach after a swim, maybe rolling into a kiss on a blanket? She felt her face heating, and knew she shouldn't let her thoughts go there. She cleared her throat as the two beers arrived. That tiny voice of conscience, which always sounded like her mother's, told her to stop day-dreaming. Bradford lived in a different world from hers, one that would never include her. She had as much chance of becoming part of such a life as she would have of becoming Miss America.

She took a sip of beer and focused on George, meeting his warm, smiling eyes with a smile of her own. He was a good man, a good friend. She could talk as openly with him as she could with Dee. He was like an older brother, full of sympathy and understanding.

"I had something I wanted to ask you, Shellie." He smoothed each side of his mustache with a finger, that nervous habit of his. "We've known each other now for what, about two years? And we, ah, we've become friendly. Maybe just a little more than friendly. At least that's what I'd like to think."

He smiled at her with eyebrows raised, and she nodded, wondering where he was heading with this and why he was so nervous.

"It seems to me that we might be able to do a little better than sharing a beer here at the pub. I was wondering if you might like to join me for an evening in Ottawa…dinner, then a show at the Arts Theatre. I had in mind to pick you up about five on Sunday after I get off work. Since it's only a half hour drive, we'd have plenty of time. I'd say Saturday, but I promised Harry I'd cover the Founders' Day Festival that afternoon and evening."

A date. He was asking her for a date, and actually the glamorous Ottawa dinner and show date that Dee so often did with Conrad. Somehow she had never considered George as a suitor, and wasn't that what a date usually implied? What should she say? He was always good company. She had no problem with that. The only problem she had with the whole idea of going out on a formal date with George was that they worked together.

He placed his hand over hers on the table. "I'm no David Bradford, I know. But maybe you'd consider a ride in a Ford instead of a Cadillac right now?"

"Oh George," she said, feeling guilty for her thoughts about Bradford. "Don't be ridiculous. I was just thinking that we work together. Sometimes it's not such a good idea to mix work and play. You know?"

"I know. I can't blame you if you say no."

"I'm not saying no. I'm very tired right now. How about letting me sleep on it? Will you call me at about ten tomorrow morning? I'll be thinking more sensibly then."

"Sensibly? A question of a dinner date has to be weighed sensibly?" He laughed, but without bitterness. He stroked the sides of his mustache thoughtfully, fixing a wicked smile on her. "I promise not to shave it off, Shelly."

She lowered her head, smiling, remembering their exchange and the uproar in the office six months ago. They had been bantering all morning, first one landing a verbal punch, and then the other. When she couldn't come up with anything more clever to say, Sheldon said, "When are you going to shave that bird's nest off your lip, George?" He didn't miss a beat. "Just after you go to bed with me, Shellie." Ever since then, all he had to do to win an argument was to smooth lip hair and level a sexy look at her.

"I wasn't thinking of that," she said.

"It's okay, Shel. I'll call you tomorrow at ten."

"It's not that I don't like you, you know. I like you a lot. I mean, I just need to think about this. I'd hate to mess up a perfectly good working relationship."

"I understand." His voice was disappointed, as if he guessed that she would refuse his offer. "But I hope you'll say yes anyway. You think about it and give me your sensible answer in the morning. I just want you to know that I won't regard you any differently at work, whichever way it goes. We're adults, and we respect each other. At least I think we do."

"Yes, of course. Exactly. We do respect each other."

"And it will remain that way. So. Let's get out of here. What are you doing this evening?"

❦ ❦ ❦

As she drove home, Sheldon could see George's face, so sincere, so full of disappointment when she hadn't instantly said yes to the date.

Why hadn't she said yes? He was a good friend, a lot of fun, a fine person. She shouldn't have been thinking about David Bradford. She realized that now. And how stupid of her. As soon as George said Bradford's name, she knew he'd almost read her mind, and it embarrassed her to think that she would let her fantasy hurt a good friend. And George was a good and true friend, she knew that for certain. Besides, an evening in Ottawa with him would be great fun. She didn't have to think it over any longer. She would go with him. In fact, she'd buy a new outfit just for this date. She'd…

Her thoughts were suddenly interrupted when she looked in her rear-view mirror and saw a black pickup truck with tinted windows. It had been following her ever since she left the city, she realized. And she was almost certain it was the same truck she'd seen trailing her twice before. "What the…?" She felt a nervous surge in the pit of her stomach. Why would someone be following her? She speeded up, and the truck speeded up. Then she slowed down. The truck slowed, always keeping that same measured distance between them. Oh God, what's this about, she thought uneasily, recalling that just two weeks ago a woman in the neighboring town of Ember had been accosted just outside her home, dragged into the woods, and raped. The woman had been so traumatized that she couldn't remember the man's face, though it was uncovered. Whoever it was, he was still at large. Sheldon looked again, just as the truck turned to the right onto a gravel road. "Oh," she sighed. Her hands felt slippery on the wheel. "Now just calm down. You're just imagining things. No one's out to get you."

CHAPTER 4

❀

Sheldon came awake with a start. In the distance she could hear sirens, but that wasn't what woke her. It was the telephone. In an instant she was out of bed and down the hall to her desk under the skylight. Fumbling for the lamp switch and picking up the receiver at the same time, she whispered, "Hello?"

"Shellie." Harry's voice didn't really surprise her. Who else would call at this hour?

"There's a fire at the Mollison Farm."

Harry O'Brien spoke in that rush of urgency that a breaking news story always excited. At his words Sheldon felt a shot of adrenaline that wrenched her wide awake and took her breath away.

"Oh no. That's what the sirens are about. How bad is it?"

"Sounds bad. The barn is pretty well gone from what I heard on the scanner. You're the closest. Get right over there. You got your camera with you?"

"Yeah. I'm all set."

"I'll send George out, too. We need plenty of photos and a couple of sidebars. Any human interest stuff. You both know what to do."

"Okay. I'm on my way."

"Oh, and Shellie?"

"Yes?"

"You can take some time off later for losing time today."

"Yeah. Sure."

She hung up and raced back to the bedroom. Looking at her Little Ben, she saw that it was six o'clock. Friday. Her long weekend would be shot, but so what? She had never covered a big fire before, but this was one she wished she didn't have to witness. She had been a friend of the Mollisons since publishing a full agricultural page spread on their farm. This was a real disaster. Theirs was the most productive dairy farm in the county, a genuine showplace. They were leaders in the agricultural community and a fine couple, to boot. Sheldon's heart pounded. This was so too bad

It briefly crossed her mind that she would wake up the Spencers downstairs in her haste to dress. Well, she'd just have to apologize later. She tugged on a pair of jeans and while zipping them up, pulled the window shade, let go of it too soon and cringed at the clatter it made flipping around the roller. More noise. Oh well. The Spencers would understand.

She blinked in disbelief at the western sky, glowing like a Canadian sunset, and wished she could drive straight across the old woods road to the farm. It couldn't be more than a half mile that way, but by the main roads it was at least three miles. The sight of sparks, like fireworks, shooting skyward jumped her to faster action, and she pulled on a pink cotton blouse without tucking it in. Old sneakers came next. She barely tied them. Running to the bathroom, she gave short shrift to necessities, rushed to the kitchen and snatched up bag and camera, then all but slid down the outside stairs to her car.

Her mind jumped from one thought to another as her car barreled down the road toward the intersection, leaving a wake of dust from the gravel road. Country living had its advantages, but the dirt road was definitely not one of them. Dust in dry weather and mud in rainy spells, to say nothing of frozen ruts in winter. After yesterday's morning rainstorm ended, it had taken only a couple hours for everything to return to its desert dryness again. Her car was more spotted than usual, but it always looked like it had been driven on safari. Come to think of it, so did she. She smiled at that thought, then wondered if George thought she looked too plain. And why should she think of him when she was on her way to a serious fire? George was just a friend, like Dee. The fact that he asked her out on a date didn't mean a thing. Did it? Did she want it to? She sighed, and shook her head. Now's not the time to think about it, she told herself.

Dense woodlands on each side made the road dark enough for headlights, though the morning sun was beginning to peek over the eastern horizon. When she had gone apartment hunting two years ago, the day was hot and clear, and Meadow Run Road had seemed idyllic, cool, inviting. Then the old house, practically overrun with climbing roses, added to the illusion of coming onto a Miss Marple hamlet. Before she had even entered the garret apartment, Sheldon had made up her mind to take it. She wasn't disappointed. The three rooms and bath, with it hallway and alcove for a desk stirred her imagination. Warren and Julia Spencer showed her through the entire house, so proud of their hard work in restoring vintage aspects of the antique cape. When Sheldon leaned back on her bed pillows that first night in the apartment and listened to her radio, she felt truly at peace. She had been so lucky, first in getting the reporting job, then in finding this home.

Now she took a deep breath, feeling a certain self-satisfaction at having become independent, having left her mother's home, her home town, her journalist mentor. She stopped the car at the corner to make a U-turn onto Mollison Lane. These were not busy roads as a rule, but already there was a stream of traffic heading toward the fire. When she could make her turn, she found herself once more under a dark canopy of knotted branches. Then as the car canted around a sharp bend and into the openness of cleared fields and early morning light, she gasped at the sight of the Mollison Farm on the left. She had expected bad, but not this bad. Everything was ablaze…barn, house, sheds.

"Oh God, oh God," she said over and over. She felt sick, incredulous, dumbfounded. How could it have happened? The Mollisons were meticulous in their care of everything. They put equipment under cover, protected their huge investments. They wouldn't be careless with wiring or combustibles.

The three Harvestor silos, apparently untouched by the flames, stood like royal blue sentinels behind the barn and milkhouse, both of which were burning and steaming. Sheldon had greatly admired this set of buildings. The farm had been her inspiration to suggest that the newspaper devote a special weekend page to agriculture and related topics. It was the first big farm she saw after her arrival in the area, and it awed her. She had sat in her car and studied the sprawling farmstead, the long white barn, the black and white Holstein herd that might have been painted onto the lush green pasture at the south side, and a shimmering farm pond between the road and the barn. Graceful maple trees, overhanging the long drive, added a touch of southern plantation grandeur to the spread. She had always been fascinated by prosperous farms and suddenly the whole agricultural industry, a major economic factor in this northern New York county, intrigued her. She felt drawn to it.

The Mollison interview was a fitting catalyst for the new ag page and from that point forward, Sheldon's respect for farmers continued to grow. She admired their tenacity, their independence, and yes, their sense of humor. They could laugh at their mistakes and at the vagaries of Mother Nature. They saw serious injuries, horrible accidental deaths that she couldn't bear to think about, and strange diseases associated with their work. Yet, in face of it all, they remained uncannily optimistic, even when they had to vacate, as so many did this summer. She recalled the woman who said to her, "We have to go now and earn money enough to come back and start over. We still own some land. We'll be back."

Hot emotion burned in her lungs as she watched firefighters pitching a futile battle against flames playing an impossible game of hide and seek. It's true, she thought, flames *are* angry. Idling the motor at the driveway entrance, she saw that the rear end of the barn, parallel to the road, had caved in. For some reason, water was being played over flames at the front, but it looked like wasted effort. They might better fight the fire at the house, where flames were glowing in shattered windows and cutting like lasers through the roof.

The wind. Where had it come from so strong? A flag in one of the several decorative flower beds flapped wildly, as if choreographed in a dance with the furious flames. She looked back at the barn and moaned.

"The brand new tractor," she said in a whisper. Now it was a rusted iron frame without tires or glass. A year ago Don Mollison had pointed to that shiny new John Deere and said, "It's my Caddy. It even has stereo and air conditioning." Then he'd added that farmers like himself were never out of debt. They simply passed on their mortgages to their children when they decided to retire.

"Hey! You! Lady!" The shout jumped her. "Get out of there. We gotta get trucks in and out of here."

The man bearing down on her wore the tan uniform of a sheriff's deputy. Someone new in the department, she reflected, since she was sure she knew all the deputies. He carried a walkie-talkie in his left hand. His scowl and tone of voice told her she had no time to argue.

Through her partly open window she shouted, "I'm the press. The *Westburgh Press*." She pointed to the sign on her dashboard. "I need to get pictures and a story."

His expression softened. "Well, you can't stay here. Pull her over into the field there. It's dry enough. You won't get stuck. Follow me."

He walked backward, beckoning her his way until there was ample clearance to the driveway, then held up his free hand and called, "Okay. You're okay here."

He was right. Yesterday's hard but short-lived rain had done nothing to soften the ground. The pond that had dried up a month ago was still an ugly cavity of cracked dirt, a dark muddy bottom the only sign that rain had fallen. She gathered up her camera and bag and quickly jumped out of the car. She could hear popping and crackling as black smoke and huge sparks shot skyward. The stench of burning hay, manure, wood, and animal flesh assaulted her lungs, and she fought against coughing.

Four uniformed men stood farther up the field to keep back a gallery of spectators, obviously rapt by the awful show.

"Anyone injured?" she asked the deputy, while she slung her bag over her shoulder and started to snap pictures.

Someone yelled, "Just let 'er burn. No sense wasting water now."

The deputy heard it, too, and shook his head at Sheldon as if to say they could do without the fire chasers. She wondered if all these people had monitors next to their beds.

"One fireman," he said. "Smoke inhalation. He's okay, though."

"What's his name?" She reached inside her bag for note pad and pen.

"Joe Winehart. Rookie fireman. This is his first real fire. He tried to get a cow out of the barn. Took a good gulp of smoke. He's okay, though. Wait a minute."

The deputy ran back to the driveway, where another car was turning in. After some discussion with the driver, he returned, and Sheldon watched the car back out and edge into a space in the field across the road.

"See what happens? You let one in and the others all have to try it."

"I'm sorry. I can leave and park somewhere else if you want."

"No, no. It's okay."

She smiled her thanks and looked up into his eyes. She realized that his were the first really green eyes she'd ever seen. And playful, too. From his reddish coloring and golden red hair, she guessed he might be Irish. Not that it mattered, she reminded herself. Probably married, anyway. Aren't all the good-looking ones married?

"Water's a big problem," he was saying. "Real low. None left in the farm pond. This damned drought. If only yesterday's rain had continued, there might have been enough to save the house, but now with the wind getting stronger, there's not a hope in Hades. They lost almost all the stock in the barn."

Sheldon felt a wave of nausea and shook her head.

"Ninety-five head. This is awful. I wrote a feature story about the Mollisons a while back. We've been friends ever since. They're such good people. Do you know how it started?"

"No. Chief Rosen said there was an explosion. Probably had dynamite stored in there. Who knows how it got ignited. Farms burn all the time, especially in bad times."

Sheldon would have taken exception to that statement that implied the Mollisons might have set the fire, but decided to let it pass.

"And when did it start?"

"We got the call about five-twenty. Apparently they tried to put it out themselves, at first. But it got way out of control in a hurry. When I got here the barn was all ablaze and the house had already caught. Pretty hopeless, I'd say."

"Dreadful." Sheldon looked at her watch. It was almost six-thirty.

He left to direct a water truck to the right of the house. This time Sheldon stayed close behind him, and when he turned back, she stopped taking pictures and started writing again.

"I wonder how many spectators we have," she said.

"I'd say between fifty and sixty. And they're still coming. Must be parking way up around the bend." Sure enough, several men, women and children were walking and running down the road.

The two of them were now at the drive entrance and Sheldon needed to get closer to the action.

"I'm expecting another reporter to show up soon," she said. "His name is George Durant. Will you tell him to take some close-up shots of the barn? I'm going to the other side, near the house."

Sheldon hated the lurid aspects of reporting, like fatal accidents. She knew there would be dead animals all over the barn area and George was welcome to witness that carnage.

"Sure," the deputy said. "Glad to."

"Where's the fire chief?"

"He's the one with the walkie-talkie, telling me and everyone else what to do. See him up by the porch there?'

He took her arm and turned her slightly to see where he was pointing. Sheldon nodded without enthusiasm. She flipped a note page and looked up to find the deputy's smiling green eyes studying her with interest.

"What's your name?" She asked, and hoped he didn't notice the sudden flush in her cheeks. It was there, for certain. She always blushed when someone stared at her closely.

"Eugene Luce. Just call me Gene."

"You look very Irish. Luce doesn't sound Irish, though."

"My coloring comes from me Irish mither, Colleen Shannon. My father is a mongrel American."

She grinned and said, "You've been very helpful, Gene. Thanks."

"Any time. What's your name?"

"I'm Sheldon. Shellie Merrill."

"Good to meet you Shellie."

She nodded and reddened. He was looking at her too intently, and she was very conscious of her overbite and the much too-long straight hair and the worn-thin clothing. This wouldn't do. She had work to do.

"Gotta go," she said, pulling her arm from his firm grip.

"Before you do, let me give you a hard hat to wear. It's not safe without one. This way, over at my car." The walkie-talkie crackled and she heard the fire chief bellow orders to a patrolman to get the crowd back farther.

She ran to keep up with the deputy, but stopped short of the car to snap a picture of a hog at the edge of the driveway, then moved on and took the hat from him. As she turned to leave, a little cry escaped her when she realized what she had just photographed.

"Oh dear God. Look at that pig. It's burned. Just look at it," she said.

The hog stood, unmoving, chunks of flesh hanging like loose scales from its hairless red body. Sheldon could hear its labored grunts, exhaled in quick breaths. Fluid oozed from its eyes.

She moaned. "It's burned to a crisp. Someone ought to put it out of its misery. Can't you do that?" She nodded toward Luce's holstered gun.

"Afraid not. We aren't allowed to shoot an animal without the owner's permission."

"What a stupid rule," she murmured, and strode off feeling as much repulsion for the system as for the animal's condition. Law and mercy, she decided, were definitely not synonymous. But, then, when were they ever?

To add to her queasiness, she was now close enough to the barn to see three steaming dead cows, lying on their backs with legs all stiffly cocked upward. A shudder rocked through her, and she envisioned how terrible it must be when, instead of cows, human corpses were found in a fire where there was a large congregation. She recalled reading about the Coconut Grove fire in Boston during World War II, when so many partygoers were trapped and burned. What a sickening business firefighters are in, she thought.

She shouldered her way through the crowd, tiptoed around a patchwork of smoking cinders in the dry grass, and was given the okay by another deputy to continue on toward the house. Snapping pictures as she walked, she nearly stepped on a ratty-looking dead cat.

"Shit," she intoned and moved far to the right, toward the driveway where fire engines, water trucks, and firefighters charged against the tricky flames, in what looked like mass confusion. Just when it appeared that the fire was quelled on one side of the house, it burst out on the other side. Never having been this close to a raging fire, Sheldon found the noise level almost unbearable…firemen yelling, water pumps grinding, engines roaring. She would definitely commend the firefighters in her story. To withstand the intense heat and the imminent dangers of falling debris and moving trucks took greater courage than she had imagined.

For now she had to summon up her own courage to talk with the fire chief. He had badly intimidated her in two telephone interviews. She braced herself. "Obnoxious jerk. I won't be intimidated this time."

Near the front veranda now, she noted that it was barely dangling and decided to move away in case it should collapse. She held her notepad beside her head as a shield against the wind-driven heat and walked around the front flower garden to where the six-foot fire chief, in black rubber coat and hard hat, stood. His husky voice boomed over the din, "Get some men around here fast. This wind's against us. If we don't get more water flowing, we'll lose it all for damned sure."

Sheldon stepped beside him and cleared her throat. "Excuse me, Chief Rosen. I'm Sheldon Merrill of the *Westburgh Press*." She coughed in an attempt to clear the tremble from her voice. "I won't bother you. Just wonder if you know how the fire started and how many departments are here?"

He had bent his head to hear over the roar of a pumping truck just as a fireman ran by and whipped the hose, hitting her ankle. She staggered forward, and Chief Rosen grabbed her arm in a vice-like grip. His leathery face reflected no amusement or friendliness in response to her quip, "Big enough feet. You'd think I could stand on them."

"What the hell are you doing here?" If he'd been a dog, he couldn't have barked it more fiercely. "We've got four departments here. Not sure how it started. Don't have time to talk. If you want to call me after it's over I'll try to fill you in."

He waved his arm and pointed for a water truck to go to the far side of the house, then turned to her again. "Just get the hell out of the way. We can't be looking out for you reporters."

Again he pointed, this time to the field beyond the back of the house.

"Get out there with the others. And don't bother me now."

His bilious attitude not only bore out the chief's reputation for hating the media, it brought out an old grade school stammer which Sheldon had successfully worked to control through the years.

"Thank you. I will...call...is...will you...ah, before press time."

Perfect, she thought. How cowed can a person sound? Been reporting for seven years and still you let a boor like that fluster you. Get a grip. He's only a man. A big, ugly, mean, rotten, arrogant man. You'd think he ruled the world or something.

The words were half thought, half spoken as she circled the house and spied Pat Mollison across the wide field near the woods, surrounded by eight or ten people, all absorbed in watching the fire. A sudden shower of sparks flew over the rooftop, sending a spurt of flame streaking along the dry grass in front of Sheldon. She instinctively stomped it out with her feet, then rushed forward to Pat.

"I'm so sorry," she said, folding her free arm around her friend. "Are you all right? Is the family okay?"

Wearing work jeans and plaid camp shirt, Pat wiped a tear from her eye. She held a pink lace-edged pillow hard to her chest as if it were her most precious possession. A tan over-the-shoulder bag dragged from the crook of her arm.

"Thank the good lord, we're okay. Don got some of the cattle out, but we lost most of them. We could hear them screaming in the fire, in terrible agony." She caught her breath. "Then after a while all we could hear was the fire, and walls and things crashing, after the animals died. It's so horrible. We couldn't do a thing. We tried. But we just couldn't. It was too hot and went too fast."

"I know. I know." Sheldon gave her lean body a squeeze and wondered what she could say that would sound even remotely helpful or even sensible at this time.

Pat sighed. "Thank God thirty heifers were out to pasture."

The woman's quivering chin contrasted sharply to her perpetually calm eyes. Sheldon had admired Pat's cool manner the first time she met her and had never seen her lose that air of self-assurance. In public forums Pat easily spoke at length about her travels with Don to foreign countries as they exchanged agricultural information. She never became flustered, and she fielded questions as easily as a politician.

A man who had been talking with Pat stepped back to give Sheldon more room. Like the other men and women surrounding her, he continued to gape, openly fascinated by the conflagration and the organized confusion among firefighters.

Sheldon raised her camera and began snapping. Nearby at her right, two women were talking and laughing loudly. The men near them moved away, scowling.

"How many cows do you think are lost?" Sheldon asked.

"About eighty-five."

Pat hugged the pillow closer and lowered her head, the very picture of despondency. How Sheldon wished she could do something, but there was absolutely nothing that could be done. Only time would help to heal this great loss.

"I know this is very hard for you," Sheldon said. "But, unfortunately, it has to be reported. That's my job. This is one time I wish it weren't my job."

Pat lifted listless eyes and attempted a smile. "I know. Ask what you have to. It's all right."

"Do you have any idea how it started?"

Before Pat could open her mouth, they both turned in the direction of the shout, "Shellie!"

George Durant was hurrying toward them. He looked just a little more disheveled than usual, as if he hadn't bothered to put comb to hair, and he badly needed a shave.

Coming up to Sheldon, he said, "I took a few shots of the barn, like you wanted. Can't imagine why you didn't want to do that. Probably Harry won't print any of them anyway. You know how he is about running pictures of dead bodies on his pages."

"Yeah, I know. Just thought we should have them in case they're needed for some reason." Often officials would call on the newspaper for photos of a catastrophe.

"Who've you talked with so far?"

"The deputy that spoke to you, Chief Rosen, and now Pat. Do you know Pat Mollison, George?" She made the introduction, then quickly suggested that George scout around for a good sidebar. In the meantime, she told him, she would do the same.

"Have you seen Channel Nine here yet?" she asked.

"Just saw them coming in. They won't get very good film of the barn burning. It's just smoldering now. Even the house is nearly under control."

Sheldon eased him away from Pat, realizing that the banter between reporters could seem callous to the one suffering the loss. A little like doctors treating the sick, reporters tended to treat the problem in front of them in a clinical manner.

"I hope they try to talk with Chief Rosen," she said.

"Vicious. You're vicious. Say, can we get together after we're through and go for a quick coffee and donut? I didn't get breakfast, did you?"

"No, of course not. That sounds good to me."

"I'm parked right next to you. We'll meet there," he said and hurried away.

It was important that they both hurry in order to get their films to the lab and write their stories for today's issue. She returned to her friend.

"I'm sorry, Pat. I guess I was asking you if you know how the fire started."

"No idea. Don got up a bit late this morning. Must have been nearly five o'clock. He looked out the kitchen window and saw flames coming from the back end of the barn. He called to me, and when I saw what he was yelling about, I threw on some clothes and ran after him. Neither of us thought to call for help at first. There were a couple of fire extinguishers in the barn and we both took one and tried to get it out, but the flames just spread so fast. We couldn't stop them." Pat closed her eyes, as if trying to rid herself of the stark memory.

"We were running back and forth, trying to put it out, then we'd see it somewhere else. And the next thing you knew, we were surrounded by fire. Then Don yelled for me to get to the house and call the fire department, and he started leading cows outside. Then that explosion, followed by another one in a few seconds, just set the whole thing going. Don would have gone back in if our next door neighbor hadn't arrived just then and held him back."

She clapped her hand over her mouth and Sheldon noticed how blunt her fingers were, like they'd been sanded off, with the short, stained nails typical of farm women. When she could talk again, Pat said, "I thought he was dead when it exploded. What would I have done if he had been killed? I guess it's the one thing we can be thankful for. We're all alive and not hurt."

Sheldon gripped her arm and squeezed in sympathy. "Thank God for that. Somehow everything will work out all right, Pat. Just hold up. Where's your son?"

"I had a neighbor take him to my parents. I felt he didn't need to witness this loss, like I did when their farm burned."

"Oh? I didn't know that."

"Yes, when I was twelve. They lost everything, too."

She pinched her lips together, but her eyes glistened and tears began trickling down her cheeks. She made no effort to wipe them away, even when they ran into the corners of her mouth. Life definitely is not fair, Sheldon thought. Good people like this family don't deserve to be so devastated.

"You don't think this was arson?" Sheldon asked. "Anyone ever get real angry with you or Don for some reason?" She knew it was a stupid question, but wanted to cover all bases.

"We don't have enemies," Pat said quietly. "I can't think of anyone who'd..." She hesitated, then shook her head. "No. I don't think he'd do such a thing, but I was thinking of the man who came in while Don was building the milk house. He wanted the job of wiring it for him, but Don told him he did his own wiring and then had it inspected. The man was quite upset with that, and he said, 'Wiring should be left to those who know what they're doing. I hope you don't have a fire. You'd lose a lot.' He's the only one I've seen get upset with Don, ever."

Sheldon had the feeling she knew the answer when she asked, "Who was that?"

"Warren Spencer. But I'm sure he wouldn't do this."

Warren Spencer. Her landlord, the electrician. "No, I agree with you. He's my landlord, you know."

"No. I didn't know that."

"Yes. And you're right. I'm sure he wouldn't do such a thing, either. He's a real sweet man." She had never seen him get angry and was surprised to hear what Pat said. The thought was dismissed quickly as Sheldon asked more questions. Finally she had to move on.

"I need to talk with Don," she said. "Do you know where he is?"

"I'm not sure, but I think he's in the metal storage building. They were taking some of our things over there."

"Where will you go tonight?"

"I don't know. Maybe we can make do right here somehow. Don will know what to do. I just don't know."

Pat turned completely around, her back to the house, and seemed to talk to the woods. "I can't think what we'll do. Don will have to decide. I just don't know."

The man who had moved back for Sheldon now came closer and eyed her with interest while she and Pat talked. He watched as she wrote notes and took more pictures of the crowd, the metal shed in the distance, the back of the house where firemen could be seen on the roof under the giant poufs of smoke.

"Some fire, huh?" he said.

Sheldon looked the man square in the eye to see if he were truly serious by such an understatement. His grin told her only that he might be insensitive.

"You could say that." Her tone was deliberately flat.

"I helped get furniture out." His boast begged for her approval.

"Gee. You must have been here early."

"Yup. I live the next farm up. Saw the flames shootin' up and came right over. You a reporter?"

Before she could reply, he lunged into his discourse.

"Well you never saw nothin' like it. Fire goin' every which way. My name's Stan Shopman, in case you want to use it. I looked out the winder and saw flames shootin' straight up in the air. Still dark then. Looked like the Fourth. Just as I got outta my truck I heard a big boom. Then I saw Don with a wet towel over his head goin' back in the barn. I grabbed him and just then there was another boom. He wanted to get more cows out. Well, you can't blame him. It's a big investment, a dairy herd is. Still they ain't worth your life for."

He kicked a rock with his boot and Sheldon watched it bounce over the rough terrain and roll to a stop in straw-grass. So dry. Everything was so dry.

"Cows don't know as much as once. They'll eat barbed wire as soon as hay. Just plain dumb. No way you can manage 'em when they get rattled like that. Just gotta let it all go."

Sheldon nodded. "I guess it started at the back of the barn."

"Yup. Shame. That new tractor gone. More'n likely it was…"

He looked at Pat, who stared vacantly at a burning maple tree near the porch.

Shopman put his hand around Sheldon's elbow and walked her toward the stone fence. Without pretense of civility, Sheldon jerked her arm free. He didn't seem to notice but said, "It was faulty wiring. Mark my words. Just between you and me and the mailbox, Don always does his own work. Not to put him down, mind you, but I don't think he ever really knew what he was doin' when he wired that new milk house and the tractor shed."

"You don't think it could have been spontaneous combustion?"

"Naw. Bad wiring. Fire marshal will come up with that. I'd bet my eye teeth on it."

"Hmm." She thought about it for a minute while watching two cows beyond the stone wall chewing their cuds, looking curious about the people and the activity. Sheldon felt another wash of sadness. The whole existence of this family was practically all gone. The only difference in this demise and that of a loved one was that these buildings and even the animals could be replaced, a difference that afforded little comfort at the moment.

She excused herself, went to Pat and told her she'd be there for her if she could do anything, then left with the promise that she'd be back tomorrow. Sheldon watched as a lone fireman atop the house hacked a big hole in the roof. There won't be a thing left, she thought.

Along the route to the metal shed, she took more photos, talked with more bystanders, even got to ask a couple of firemen a few questions. Just as she approached the shed Don was coming out. She yelled, "Don, I need to talk with you."

He took off his cap and wiped his forehead with the back of his hand. He had a leathery face and bushy white hair, despite his young age, which Sheldon guessed at about forty-two. He and Pat were a handsome couple, both tall and wiry, and both moved and talked in the same crisp manner.

"What do you need, Shellie?" he asked with a sigh that signaled fatigue and hopelessness. "Have you seen Pat anywhere?"

As he spoke his eyes wearily took in the fallen, smoking barn, the mounds of indefinable smoldering refuse, and the tangle of equipment that were so recently his livelihood and pride.

Sheldon swallowed hard, trying to loosen her tight throat. "She's over there by the stone fence, in that group of spectators."

"Enough here to see the sights, I'd judge. Wonder where the dog went. Did she have him with her?"

"No and I haven't seen him, either."

She reached in her bag for the tape recorder to save time.

"You couldn't get many cows out, I'm told."

"Only six. It went too fast after the explosion. Had thirty heifers out to pasture, though. That's a help."

"And you got some things out of the house?"

"Some, but not everything. I was just getting some things arranged in here so we can stay the night. We'll probably stay with Pat's parents tomorrow, but for tonight we'd better be around here for the animals and to watch that fire doesn't break out in the woods. We've caught a few patches here and there already, but no telling how many sparks have landed hot enough to start a fire under these dry conditions."

With a sweep of his hand, he said, "I have to tell you that some of these people are here to help. Several have come up to me and offered this or that, places to stay, food, help with the cattle. I expect a bunch of them will be here tonight to help keep watch, too. Oh God." Another sigh that was more of a moan. "It's our paycheck, you know. All gone. Everything. The milk cows. The antiques. My boy's bike."

With that, his voice broke and he covered his eyes with one big hand.

Sheldon caught the irony of what he said. Of all the losses, his son's bike made him break down. She pictured him giving the boy that bike as a surprise, probably at Christmas, and then helping him learn to ride it. Just as her father had done.

He took a blue handkerchief from his back pocket and wiped the inside of his cap. Where the tan of his face stopped under the cap, a white streak circled his forehead. He blew his nose.

"I don't know just how much of the house is lost. Maybe we can repair it, bring it back. But from what I saw the last time I was up there, I'd say it's pretty far gone."

"That's about the way it looks to me, too. Any idea what the total loss will amount to?"

"Oh, I don't know." He stuffed the handkerchief in his back pocket, and his bloodshot eyes met hers. The lines in his face seemed to be etched deeper than ever.

"I'd say probably in the neighborhood of a million or so."

"Really? That much?"

"Farming on the scale we do it is not inexpensive. I had a brand new milking parlor. You saw that. And the house. That's irreplaceable. I was born there."

He took a few steps as if to walk away from her.

"We'd done so much to it. Added a family room with fireplace and redid the kitchen two years ago. I made Pat a sewing room."

His voice trailed off and he stopped walking.

From a nearby pasture a plaintive moo-oo pierced the air in a bawling crescendo that strained for an elusive high note. Sheldon took off the hard hat and waved it at a wasp persistently targeting her chin. She felt hot and tired and could only imagine how much more so the Mollisons must feel. If only it had rained. If only she could go back to bed. She was hungry, almost to the point of feeling faint.

"Anything else?" he asked. "I want to get back to the house. Fire is just about out. Not much I can do there, but I want to see how bad it is."

"No. Thanks. Oh wait. Yes. Just one thing. Do you know for sure how it started?"

"Haven't a clue. It got a good start before I noticed it. Then the dynamite stored in the shed started exploding. But I don't know what touched it off."

"Could it have been set?"

"Oh God, who'd want to do that? No, I don't think so."

"Are you insured?"

He sounded sardonic. "Yeah. Insured for about a quarter of the replacement value."

"Do you think you'll start up again?"

He shrugged. "Of course. What else can I do? All I know is farming. It's my life."

Without another word, he walked away. Sheldon watched him, arms hanging loose at his sides, shoulders sagging, and she knew he had just given her the lead to her story, a good quote.

All I know is farming. How typical of the breed, she thought, as she picked a route around the house and down the front field toward her car. They're never down long, no matter what the tragedy.

Elbowing her way through the spectators and down the gravel lane, she looked ahead and saw a very tall man with a stoop, wearing a long raincoat, walking fast toward the road.

Hugh? Could it be Hugh Webster? She wouldn't expect the night janitor to be out this early to watch a fire here in Westburgh or even that he would have heard about it in Ashton.

CHAPTER 5

As Sheldon approached George, where he waited behind his car, she called, "Was that Hugh Webster I just saw? Did you see him, George?"

"I didn't notice him. Where?"

"Well, he's disappeared now. Funny. I wouldn't expect him to be here this early in the morning, so far from his home."

"Just another fire chaser I guess. Lots of them here today."

"Still, it's odd." She looked at her watch. "Almost nine. We really don't have time to stop and eat. Why don't you take my film in and I'll stop and get us coffee and donuts and bring them to the office."

"Sounds good to me."

"Did you get any sidebars?"

"Yeah. One that's pretty good. Did you know a rookie fireman had suffered from smoke inhalation?" She nodded. "Well, he quit. Just up and told Chief Rosen that he was through and he walked away from the fire. Said he had a family and was damned if he was going to risk his life in this kind of work."

"Really! Did TV get it?"

"No. I happened to be right there and heard it all and followed him out to a friend's car for the interview. Then they drove off, so I know Jill didn't get to him. Just between the two of us, he opened a can of beer the minute he got into the car. Drinking buddies, I'd say. Still it'll make a good story."

Sheldon got into her car, happy that Jill Minot didn't have that story for Channel Nine. She liked Jill, but there was natural rivalry between the media when it came to breaking a story first, and friendship had nothing to do with it.

By the time she arrived at the office, Harry had his sleeves rolled up and was already hurrying everyone to get the job done. She dropped everything onto her desk and took coffee to George. He told her he'd just come back downstairs from the photo lab. Just as she announced that there were donuts for everyone, Harry said, "George, Shellie. Come in."

Their notes in hand, the two faced Harry at his cluttered desk. As always when she came into his office, Sheldon had the urge to swipe everything into the wastebasket. She was naturally neat and clean, systematic enough to draw jabs from the Two Wicked Sisters.

"What'd you two do, roll in the ashes?" Harry asked, his face dead-pan despite the twinkle in his eyes.

Sheldon looked at George and laughed. He had streaks on each side of his nose, running into his mustache. She took a tissue from her jeans pocket and wiped her cheeks and forehead randomly.

"How bad was it?" Harry asked.

"Real bad," George said. "Barn and outbuildings are totally gone. Just part of the house left standing when we left. Lack of water was the major problem. That and the wind."

"They did get some household items out," Sheldon said. "But almost all of the dairy herd is lost. Thankfully, no one was hurt."

Harry nodded, his round face slightly flushed, and ran his hand over his crew cut that was a blend of dark and gray hair. Breaking news was his meat and potatoes. He loved every exciting minute of it. Whenever he could, he still went out on police runs, drug busts, accidents. But today he had needed to get someone there in a hurry, and Sheldon was nearby. So Harry had concentrated on getting lab and typesetters ready to work on this one project. Just as soon as Sheldon and George turned out their copy, it would be processed. The fire would be the focus of news this day, and Sheldon would bet that he would be at the farm later in the day. He wouldn't be able to stay away for long.

"Sidebars?"

George said he had one good one and proceeded to tell Harry about the young rooky fireman who quit on the job.

"Did you get a picture of him?"

George nodded, "I had just shot him with the chief. I didn't know until after I took it that he was quitting, but as I walked up to them, I heard the last of what he was saying. Then I went after him and did an interview. He gave his okay to use the photo."

"How did Chief Rosen take it?"

"Not too well." George grinned. "He had a few colorful words to say, and then he looked like he wanted to kick his ass all the way down the driveway."

"It's a wonder he hadn't done just that," Harry said.

"He wasn't too pleasant to me, either," Sheldon said. "Wouldn't give me more than a couple of words. Said he'd try to fill me in after the fire was over. So good luck to me to try to catch up with him before deadline."

"You can bet he'll be on Channel Nine tonight, though," George said.

"Oh, yes. He'll have time to be interviewed for TV. He and the sheriff make a good pair. Funny I didn't see the sheriff there, did you George?" George shook his head. "Well I don't need the fire chief, actually. I can get everything I need from someone else. What do you think, Harry? Should I just go ahead and get everything and then ignore him as far as a quote is concerned?"

"We might like to do that, but it wouldn't be a good political move to leave him out of a big fire story. We'll need him again, and he could be even more difficult. We'll follow the usual procedure. Give him at least a graph, even if he's uncooperative."

Sheldon nodded, though she still resented the chief's put-down. "I got a sidebar, too," she said. "A farmer next door saved Don Mollison's life. He had to physically keep Don from going back into the barn for more animals. Grabbed him just before the second explosion. The stock are a terrible loss, though. Eighty-five head."

"That's rough. It sounds like you've got a lot to write up. Better hop to it. I'm devoting most of page one and a double-truck to it. We'll have an early deadline today and get those papers on the street before Channel Nine comes on."

By the time everything was finished and both Sheldon and George had checked page one and the inside sections for possible errors, she was weary and anxious to go home. And she knew everyone around both her and George must be anxious for them to leave, too, just to get their obnoxious odor out of the office.

"Did you plan to see Mr. Bradford's sister today, Shellie?" Dee asked the question as Sheldon checked through her notes one last time to be sure she hadn't missed anything.

A feeling of horror rushed over her. Lucille Bradford would be waiting for her.

"You forgot, didn't you? I was afraid you might have."

"Yeah. I forgot. What time is it?" She looked at her watch. "Two. I can still make it, but she'll have to take me as I am, stink and all. I don't have time to go home and clean up."

"She should understand. When did you tell her you'd be there?"

"Well, she told me, really. The doctor was coming in this afternoon, so she couldn't see me before two-thirty, and I told her that was fine with me. I guess I'd better get going right now."

"Oh, and Shellie? You really do, you know."

"I do what?"

"You stink to high heaven." Dee laughed, and Sheldon wadded a sheet of paper and threw it at her just as her phone rang. She made a face, but picked it up.

"So have you done some sensible thinking?" It was George.

"Where are you?" Sheldon cupped her hand over her mouth to keep others from hearing, and Dee turned back to her work pretending not to notice.

"Right around the corner at the pay phone."

"You idiot," she said, unable to keep the laugh from her voice. "We've been working side-by-side all day."

"Didn't want the whole office to hear. So what's it going to be? You going with me to Ottawa Sunday?"

"Oh…" She said this with a long sigh. Might as well give him a few anxious moments.

"It will be okay if you don't, you know. I can always explain that I simply felt like shaving off my mustache. Nothing to do with you whatsoever."

"That's blackmail," she growled.

"Naw. That's just the worst scenario."

"Okay, okay. I don't have time to argue. You win. I'll go. But you'd better keep your promise. You don't shave your mustache after this date. Understood?"

On the road to Ashton, Sheldon tried to think as she pushed the speed limit to make up for lost time. Lucille Bradford had sounded friendly on the phone last evening, but she had hesitated to let Sheldon come see her. It was only when Sheldon said she wouldn't use her name if she preferred, that Lucille agreed to talk about her brother's childhood. Now Sheldon had to forget the fire…and George…and turn to the questions she would ask Lucille.

It was easier now to forget the fire than it was George. He'd floored her by calling from the phone booth, although she shouldn't have been surprised. Doing the unexpected was one of his trademarks. She wanted to go to Ottawa with him now more than ever, if for nothing more than to forget the sadness at the Mollisons. It would be a really enjoyable evening. They always had a good time together. Then why did she still feel this knot of doubt? Was it fear of what George might expect from her? For goodness sake, she was a grown woman. She didn't have to worry about a come-on from George. He wasn't at all like Joe. He wouldn't pressure and then not take no for an answer. He was a gentleman, as rough as he looked, and had always acted with integrity since she had known him. Besides, was it such a repulsive thought that he might want a little more than a goodnight kiss at the door? It had been two years since Joe. Well, now…

Sheldon shook her head. This would never do. She had to be ready to interview Lucille Bradford, and right at the moment she only wanted to go home, shower, and go to bed. She yawned. Okay. Now. First ask what David did as a boy, what were his hobbies, his interests? Then go on to…

George once said he learned how to fish from his aunt. Strange. Why his aunt? She hadn't asked him if his father had died or had left or what. Come to think of it, she didn't even know where he grew up. He was so secretive about his past. She knew from office gossip that he was a Vietnam veteran and that he had been married but that his wife left him for another man before he returned from service. But George never spoke of those things, nor did Sheldon ever ask. How different men are from women, she thought. She knew so much about Dee and vice versa. She knew that Dee had spent more time with her grandparents than with her mother on the coast of Maine. She knew what Dee liked to eat, where she went to college, the dates she'd had since they knew each other, the books she liked to read.

Whenever they were together they spilled everything about what they had done the evening before, or what they hoped to do, or what they had heard from home. Men seemed to stay with the issue at hand, no chit chat about their past or about their families. Certainly no suggestion of emotional involvement and no trying to find a deeper meaning to something other than just what was on the surface. Or so it appeared.

Darn it. Stay on the subject. Focus. Lucille Bradford, not George or Dee. Ask her if David was artistic. After all, that painting may have been something he had done. Now where did that thought come from? Sheldon hadn't thought about that possibility until this minute. Perhaps it wasn't anybody special, just someone who posed for a nice portrait for him to have in his parlor. And maybe he was just too shy to have his art work appear in a newspaper. That was certainly a reasonable possibility, though she couldn't imagine David Bradford having a shy bone in his body.

She had made the turn onto the Ashton road and was now approaching the gradual hill that ran past the Bradford homes. She glanced to her right at David's dark house, surrounded by withered brown grass, and noted that it didn't look any better in sunshine than it did in rain. Then she chuckled at sight of a red retriever leashed in front of the barn. Well, now it's complete, she decided. A combination of the *Hound of the Baskervilles* and the *House of Usher.* What a contrast to his sister's home. At the top of the grade she turned left onto the driveway and stopped the car in front of the tall columns. She glanced at the view, a wide vista of faded fields and a stream with only a trickle of water, bordered by gentle hills.

Leaving the car, she felt tiny approaching the double front door, half of which was open and screened. Everything was massive. This had to be the most impressive house in Ashton. It seemed odd that David didn't live here, too, since she was sure it was large enough for two people to live and stay out of each other's way, if they wished.

A huge black cat, startled from sleep by the front door, jackknifed in a second and spit at her with fire in its eyes, then hightailed it to the flower garden at the end of the house. Sheldon pressed the doorbell button and the sound of musical chimes made her smile.

"Come right in. The door isn't locked." The voice was faint, but Sheldon heard it through the screen door and did as commanded.

She found herself in a spacious vestibule with a mirrored coat tree on the left. A long, high stairway curved graciously from the wide hallway with its light hardwood floor. A glance at her reflection stopped her short. Good grief. Miss Bradford would think she was a beggar or a thief, for sure. She thought she had cleaned soot off her face at the office, but now she saw streaks of it on her chin. Her tangled hair drooped lifelessly over her shoulders, her shirt was dirty. She gave an open-mouthed smile to be sure nothing was stuck in her teeth, but the teeth were clean…and, of course, obvious. Dark shadows under her hazel eyes announced loudly how tired she was.

"Oh well," she whispered, just as she heard the woman's voice again call to her. "Come in here. Straight ahead of you, to the left."

The house had the feel of rich comfort to her as she walked on thick emerald green carpet atop gleaming hardwood floors to the open door on the left. Sheldon's mother kept a clean house, but it was small and sparsely furnished. Everything about her mother was sparse, come to think of it. Especially the house. It had none of the plush and polish that this house had. No interesting alcoves, no built-in bookshelves and glass curio cabinets filled with hundreds of Hummel figurines, no room like this one she entered, probably called a sewing room. In the middle of the room, a basket of knitting stood beside a green plush recliner containing a heap of a woman with white-streaked permed hair and wearing a gray dress with a white lace collar. Her thin hands rested on top of a colorful granny afghan in her lap, and a tube extended from prongs in her nose to an oxygen tank half hidden behind her recliner. A cherry wood magazine table on one side of her chair held a variety of items that included tissues, pill bottles, and a bedside bell.

"Miss Bradford?" Sheldon asked.

"Yes. And you must be Miss Merrill. Come over and sit in front of me in that straight chair where I can see you. I don't get around much now, or I'd take you into the living room. But you won't mind this."

She spoke in a halting, soft voice, giving the impression of utter exhaustion.

"This is lovely." Sheldon sat down on a white chair with green velvet seat and back, almost directly in front of her hostess. "First of all, please excuse my appearance and my odor. I had to get up early this morning to cover a very large fire at a farm just outside Westburgh. I've been working all day on it, so I didn't have time to go home and change."

"I don't smell much with this contraption in my nose. And as far as your appearance, I guess you look as good as most young people do today. No one seems to care about their appearance any more. Personal pride is a thing of the past."

Sheldon wanted to reply that she did care how she looked. She always dressed neatly in clean and pressed clothes. Today was an exception, as she'd just explained. But she remained silent. Of course she'd be swept under the same rug as hippies by someone over fifty. She tossed back strands of hair and silently vowed to get something done to it first thing in the morning.

"You have a huge collection of Hummels," she commented to break the ice.

"Yes. I've been collecting them ever since my uncle sent some back to me from Germany when he was in the war. He was killed just after he had sent the Umbrella Boy to me in nineteen-forty-four. That's my most cherished figurine. Are you a collector?"

"No. But I think they're most interesting. Very cute." She thought of adding 'and very expensive' to that, but instead craned her neck to study one of the three overflowing cabinets in the room.

"So many. It's hard to see the individual pieces. Like not seeing the woods for the trees, I guess." She laughed as she tried to distinguish them. When she saw the boy sitting beneath an umbrella in front, she got up and looked closer through the glass. "This must be the Umbrella Boy."

"Yes. And the one next to it is Umbrella Girl. They're very valuable today, because of their age, condition, and size, with the original crown mark. They're rare pieces."

Which is just a bit of Greek to me, Sheldon thought as she studied the boy in clunky shoes, wrinkled stockings, short pants and orange shirt under the dark umbrella. Like all of the figurines, the boy had a cherubic face with wide eyes, the perfect image of innocence.

She returned to her chair and said, "I didn't know that you had an uncle in the war."

"Yes. Thomas Bradford. My father's brother. All of them are dead now. David and I are the only survivors in the family."

"None of your uncles had children?"

Miss Bradford simply shook her head slowly, then asked, "Well, how may I help you? You did say you wouldn't use my name."

"No, not if you don't want me to."

"And I don't. For my part, I don't think David should have consented to being interviewed. He seldom does. This family has never been fond of publicity. Our father taught us to do good works quietly. He was the town's minister for nearly fifty years, you know."

The hand that reached out for a cigarette lighter on the stand was thin and white. She tipped the lighter end-over-end as they talked. What if she lit that lighter? Surely she didn't still smoke, especially when she was connected to an oxygen tank.

"Yes. I heard that. Your brother talked with me yesterday, and the profile will be non-controversial. I thought it would be nice to get a little background on his boyhood. What he was like. What he did. Whether he had particular talents. Things like that. Maybe an anecdote or two."

Lucille Bradford leaned forward slightly. Unlike David, Lucille had dark eyes. Eyes that seemed not to smile but to maintain an impenetrable stare. Was she terribly unhappy? Or did she just have the bug-eyed look of someone on drugs?

"He was the sweetest little boy. I was twenty when he was born. And I took care of him every chance I got. He seemed almost like my own child. And, of course, I never married and never had any children, so I've always had that maternal feeling for him."

Which may account for the interest in figurines of active children, Sheldon thought.

Lucille flopped back with a sigh. "Seems like yesterday he was so tiny and delicate, interested in everything. I remember when he was just learning what things were called that he pointed at a butterfly and said, 'Birdie.' Now look at him. Six feet tall and a Wall Street giant at the age of thirty-five. I'm proud of him. I wish he could be as proud of me as I am of him. But sometimes, Miss Merrill, fortune shines on the male of the family. Oh, I took over Uncle Saul's sawmill when he died, but it could hardly compare with David's accomplishments."

She studied her hand holding the lighter, then looked up again, blinking fast.

"Life is so very unpredictable. Can you believe it? I wanted to become a concert pianist when I was a young girl, and I practiced and practiced so that I could win a scholarship to a music conservatory. Then look what happened. Oh my."

Sheldon gave her a moment to rest, then asked, "Was your brother musical? Or maybe artistic?"

"No. He had no talents along those lines. Just liked to go into the woods or out on the lake. Hunting and fishing, those were his interests. I almost got to attend Julliard. I was ready to audition for a scholarship when my uncle called me into his office one day. He said he badly needed a secretary and wanted me to take the position."

She began to cough, took a sip of water from the glass on the stand next to her, then continued. Sheldon caught the faint odor of lavender when she pulled a white lace handkerchief from her pocket, shook it out and dabbed at her lips.

"Of course, I didn't want to, but my parents both urged me to forget music as a career and take Uncle up on his offer. So many times I've wondered what my life would have been like if I had refused to do as they wanted. If I had only been more independent. But I was young, only nineteen at the time, so I didn't dare go against their wishes. A girl didn't defy her parents back then, you know. If only I had…"

Her voice faded and she drew back into herself, apparently unmindful of Sheldon's presence. She had been a good-looking woman, no doubt, when she was young, with high cheekbones and narrow, upturned nose. But now she was thin, her sallow face weathered and wrinkled. The dress hung loosely about her arms and small bosom. She looked to be in her seventies, not mid-fifties.

Again her hand started to tip the lighter end-over-end. Despite their wateriness, her eyes maintained that bulgy stare, and now Sheldon was sure it was caused by pain killers. She remembered the same look in her father's eyes when he became so ill with cancer and took great doses of pain killers…before he left her forever.

"I asked if he might be artistic because of the portrait hanging in his living room. I saw it when I interviewed him and thought how lovely it is, how beautiful the woman is. Then I thought maybe he was the artist?"

As soon as Sheldon spoke of the portrait, Lucille's hand flew to her mouth, which she rubbed as if her lips were sore and chapped. If possible, her eyes widened even more, and she looked in the direction of the front door.

"He has it hanging in plain sight?" The question was almost a whisper. She turned her head to the side and seemed to be studying her pill bottles. "I can't talk about that. He didn't paint it. That's all you need to know."

"Oh, of course. Well." Sheldon was caught off guard. She wanted so much to know who the woman was, but obviously neither brother nor sister would talk about her. Why the mystery? The picture *was* in plain sight, and it would seem that anyone might ask the same question: Who is she?

Sensing that Lucille had slammed that door shut, Sheldon asked, "David went to school here in Ashton."

"Yes," Lucille's voice quavered, but she answered as if the portrait subject hadn't come up. "He attended the same school I did. Back then it was also the high school. He was able to go on to college. But I couldn't. Girls just didn't get the same privileges that boys did, you know. We weren't really poor. I could have gone on if my betters hadn't reversed my fate by consigning me to the lumber mill for life. Oh, I didn't hate the work after a while. Not the work. But it was a far cry from concert halls."

Her speech was refined, as if she had studied at a finishing school, Sheldon noticed.

"While I was going to high school, Mama did alterations and mending for women in town. And I learned to do that, too."

Miss Bradford seemed to be more interested in her own story than filling in some details about her brother for the profile. But she was probably lonely. After all, being sick and shut in made for long and dreary days.

"You have lovely, precise diction, if you don't mind my saying so, Miss Bradford."

The smile was fleeting. "Yes. I had a tutor for a couple of years. My uncle thought that I should learn more math and English. She was a strict teacher, with a fondness for proper diction."

"Was David a good student? Did he get high grades?"

"Oh, yes. Studies were a breeze for him. He studied all the time. Used to read those financial magazines that Uncle Charles sent from New York. I guess that's why Uncle Charles took such an interest in him. For me, studies came hard. Like I said, all I wanted to do was play the piano. Then when there was no out and I had to learn all about the lumber business, life seemed to just pass me by. I spent long days and sometimes evenings at the mill. With Uncle Saul. No one noticed, I guess. I don't think even Mama did." In a fading voice she murmured, "She should have known…oh, well, it's all in the past and forgotten."

Sheldon wondered what the woman was driving at. Whatever it was, she certainly was not forgetting it. Obviously she was unhappy about her life, her years in the mill work, even though David had said she had a good head for business and had done well with the mill. Was it possible that everyone ignored the fact that Lucille was miserable?

"What kind of games did David play as a boy? Was he athletic?"

"What? Oh. Yes, I guess he was to some extent. He liked to play baseball and basketball, and he rode his bike all the time. I never had one. Daddy said I'd get hurt and that it wasn't ladylike to ride one, anyway. I didn't care too much. Uncle Saul gave me a rubber doll once. One that you could feed from a little bottle filled with water, then it would wet the diaper and you'd have to change it. It was my favorite doll back then, when I was young. Then when David was born I had the real thing to play with, only it wasn't quite as pleasant at times, changing the diaper."

She laughed for the first time, a weak, gurgling laugh, and Sheldon laughed with her. She wished she could visit Lucille from time-to-time and just let her get it all off her chest, but as it was, the woman wasn't being very helpful with the story at hand. The next words startled her.

"It's been a hard life. Much harder than anyone knows. David certainly doesn't know."

Lucille turned her hand over and reached out, and Sheldon placed hers in it. Such a cold and frail hand.

"Thank you for listening to me ramble. You're a very nice girl."

Sheldon felt her face redden.

"And you're a very nice lady. I do appreciate your talking with me. I have another question, if you don't mind?"

Lucille nodded.

"Did your brother ever marry? I know he's not married now, but maybe he's divorced?"

The hand went slack. Lucille pulled it away, her body stiffening.

"Oh where is Ruth? She's such a useless nurse. When I need her she's never around. She's not like Karen…" A look of horror crossed Lucille's face. "I mean…"

Quickly, as if to cover up what she had just said, Lucille reached for a pill bottle. When she opened it, the pills spewed onto the floor, and Sheldon jumped to her feet.

"I'll get those for you," she said. In picking them up, she noticed that they were merely aspirin, though she could see that there were three other bottles on the stand, all prescription drugs. She sat again in the straight chair and wondered what to do next. Perhaps she should just leave. From another room she heard a clock strike three.

"No," came the unexpected answer. "David never married. I doubt that he'll ever marry. Unless…"

Her voice trailed off.

"I'm sorry if it was a question I shouldn't have asked. I wonder why you think he never will marry, though. He is so charming, and certainly must have many women acquaintances in New York."

"I don't know. But sometimes it's better not to be harpooned by love."

With that, Lucille made three sharp raps on the call bell, bringing a ruddy, full-bodied woman in pink uniform to the doorway.

"Ruth, I'm tired and need to lie down for a while. Will you show Miss Merrill out?"

When goodbyes were said and Sheldon was out of earshot in the vestibule with Ruth, she said, "Miss Bradford seems like a very nice lady, but very sad."

"Yes, well, she doesn't have long to live. Maybe a couple of months. Maybe less."

"Her recollections seemed to cause her to be sadder."

"They would. I guess she had a life of hell with that uncle of hers. But we don't talk about it."

"Oh?" Since Ruth didn't offer to comment further, Sheldon said, "She mentioned a former nurse. Karen?"

"She did?" Her husky voice became defensive. "I was told never to say her name either in this house or outside. And I don't. But for her to say it. Well, I'm surprised, that's all."

"Can you give me her last name?"

"It was…no, I can't say any more about her. I was told not to, and I just won't. I'm sorry."

Sheldon nodded. "I understand."

It would take a long time to understand that family, Sheldon decided as she drove away. They seemed to have so many little hang-ups, secrets, and taboos. She wondered what the parents and uncles had been like. They must have been social people, considering their stations in life. So strange that the two uncles had never married. And now David. Was there a reason that the males didn't marry? But, of course, their father had married. And who knew about the uncle who had died in the war? Funny David hadn't said anything about him, since he was quite thorough in telling her the family history.

Just how far did she want to go with this? She had enough for a good profile, and that was all that had been assigned to her. But there was something about David Bradford, aside from his sexual magnetism. His odd behavior concerning the portrait bothered her. And there was some reason why the nurse Karen was blackballed by Lucille Bradford. Was there a connection between the painting and Karen, or were they just two separate problems?

The more she thought about it, the more Sheldon wanted to know the answers. And she knew just who could tell her about Karen.

CHAPTER 6

❀

The Westburgh General Hospital seemed to have miles of corridors, especially in this new wing, its floors so shiny they looked wet and slippery. Kate was already working in the new unit, even though the dedication was a week away, and it appeared that they were particularly busy, judging from the number of cars in the parking lot.

Pretty outdoor pictures on pastel walls invited a slow walk in order to study them, a change from old-time institutional tan walls. Sheldon used to think that all hospitals smelled of disinfectant. That was one of the outstanding memories she had of visiting her father the day he died. The day he told her, "Take care of your mother, Shellie. You're all she has now. You be a good girl. Make your old Dad proud. I'll be there, you know. Right in your heart. You'll know I'm there."

With a start, Sheldon realized that she hadn't thought of his words for years. She used to pray at night, "Please, God, tell Daddy that I was a good girl today. And let him come back home."

She knew he had no way of coming home even though she wanted him to and after a while there didn't seem to be reason to continue praying. It was only when she became a teenager that she experienced a wrenching conversion and thought she had been called to save the world. She could almost laugh now at the memory.

But still, good things had happened, admittedly because she had taken the initiative to make them happen. When she was close to failing in plane geometry, she had decided to do something about it, and went to the math teacher for help. Until then she had been too proud to ask for help. But once she did, she passed the subject with a B and felt good, both for overcoming her own pride and for digging in and studying. And when she needed a job, she looked everywhere. She wanted to stay home to help her mother, but jobs were scarce in Middleton. So she gathered her courage, took a high school report that she had written, and asked Mr. Bentley for an apprenticeship in reporting. He was taken aback at the request, but after talking with her for several minutes and reading her essay, he smiled that toothy smile of his and said, "Sure. Why not. But you'll have to learn it all, from the ground up."

When she reflected on her accomplishments, even getting the job at the *Westburgh Press*, she had to believe that there was something extra working in her life, some unseen guidance that steered her to make right moves. She felt all prickly when she thought about it, though she had long since given up the notion that God was at her beck and call. Were there supernatural powers working in our lives? How could one ant-size individual believe that his or her voice carried to the ear of God? Did God even have ears? And why did humans believe that God had the same emotions and weaknesses that they had? Yet, she could recall her father saying, "It makes God sad when you lie, Shellie."

So she stopped lying when she was eight. She told the truth even when she climbed up on the boxcar at the railroad track and jumped from the top of it to impress her friends, scraping her knee badly. And for that truth-telling, she got a spanking.

As she approached the nurses' station in ICU, she shook off her thoughts. Lessons she had learned as a child seemed contradictory now and, so often, questionable. But of late she had been thinking about some of those lessons, and the possibility that not everything was as she had been taught.

The nurse looked up from the records she was studying, a little scowl creasing her forehead at the sight and smell of Sheldon. "Can I help you?"

Sheldon smiled sweetly and involuntarily swept her hand over her hair, acutely aware of her dishevelment beside this young, glowing, springtime clean young woman.

"I hope so. Is Kate O'Brien on duty? And is it possible for me to see her?"

"She is on duty, but she's in the OR right now and I don't know when she'll be out."

"Oh, I see. Well, I guess I can't see her then. Perhaps you could help me. I need to locate a nurse who used to work here, I believe. Her first name was Karen, but I don't have a last name. Did you happen to know a Karen?"

It was almost a sure thing that she would answer, "No, I'm sorry, I don't know a nurse by the name of Karen." After all, this was a young girl just out of nurse's training, Sheldon guessed.

She probably was as new to the hospital as the wing in which she worked.

"Okay. When Kate is free, would you give her this note?" She hastily wrote a message on a sheet from her notepad, folded it over and put Kate's name on the outside. Like Harry, Kate knew just about everyone in Westburgh and certainly all the nurses that had ever been with the hospital over the past ten years. If there had been a Karen working in the area, she would know.

The nurse took the note and smiled. "I'll see that she gets this," she said.

Disappointed that she hadn't immediately found out about Karen, Sheldon wound her way back through the corridors and out to her car, then drove the nine miles to her apartment. Why did this Karen nag at her so? If ever intuition had driven her, this was it. The mystery was like a giant Christmas box under the tree. She just had to unwrap it.

As soon as she opened her car door at home, she could smell roses even though a pall of smoke drifted from the Mollison farm. The air was always filled with the comforting fragrance of the prize roses that Spence and Julia grew, "instead of children," as Julia once put it. Climbing all around the house were various shades of pink roses, and in the garden out back, where Sheldon could see them from her apartment, other shades of the delicate flower grew in a kaleidoscope of color along even rows of trellises. Although he worked in his converted three-bay garage on electrical projects, Spence more often was in the rose garden.

"Hi there, Shellie." She turned at the sound of Spence's voice. He was just coming from his kitchen, walking toward her as she started up her stairs.

"Hi Spence. How's it going?"

"Well enough, I guess." She stopped short and stared at him. The dejected tone of voice didn't sound like Spence, who ordinarily was bubbling over, anxious to tell her some trivial thing about a new rose bush he had just planted or a restaurant where he and Julia had eaten the night before. He was one of the most energetic men she had ever met, a good match for Julia who had to be on the go every minute.

"Is something wrong?" Sheldon walked back down the steps and stood with her hand on the rail while he came toward her. "You sound unhappy."

"I'm okay. A little lonely. Julia left yesterday to be with her sister for a few weeks, until she has the baby. The house seems quiet."

"I know what you mean." Sheldon laughed aloud, hoping to see a smile on Spence's face over the obvious reference to Julia's constant chatter. But he looked down without a smile and twirled a big yellow rose in his fingers.

A man in his late fifties, Spence had married a woman eighteen years his junior. But they were happy together, sharing the two hobbies of rose-growing and restorative work, both on the house and on antique furniture. Their age difference was hardly discernable, he being a stately, slender man with only slightly gray sideburns against sandy hair and she, nearly as tall as he, with a full figure and prematurely graying black hair. A complementary couple, they were always the center of attraction wherever they went.

"Cheer up, Spence. She won't be gone very long. Anyway, you can go be with her, if you want. Where is it? Syracuse?"

"I don't want to go down there. Her sister talks twice as much as she does. Between the two of them, I go crazy. Julia's okay. At least she listens, as well as talks, but her sister doesn't stop to hear an answer if she asks a question. No. I'll wait here."

Sheldon half turned to go up, feeling that she couldn't do anything to cheer him up.

"This is for you, Shellie. Thought you might like to have one in a vase for a day or two."

He handed the rose to her, his expression blank and sad.

"It's beautiful. So big. Is this one of the prize-winning yellow roses?"

"Uh huh."

He looked as if he wanted to say more, so Sheldon stood, waiting with her foot on the first step, smelling the sweet fragrance of the velvety petals in her hands.

Finally, he said, "I hear there was a big fire over at Mollisons. You cover it, did you?"

"Yes. Got an early morning call from my editor. I hope I didn't wake you up with all my racket getting out of here."

"I did wake up. But it was no problem. The mailman told me they lost everything."

"Well, almost everything. It was the worst spectacle you ever saw. Eighty-five cows lost. And that beautiful set of buildings almost completely destroyed. It went so fast, there was no way they could save much more than some furnishings out of the house. It's just fortunate that no life was lost."

"Well that is a good thing." Spence scowled and looked down at the ground, then wet his lips and said, "Do they know how it started?"

"No. Maybe spontaneous combustion, or maybe bad wiring…" Sheldon stopped abruptly, remembering about Spence and his anger toward Don Mollison for not hiring him to wire the new milk house. Her voice fading, she said, "Anyway, the dynamite that he stored at the back exploded and sent fire everywhere."

Spence's gaze moved away from her to the direction of the Mollison farm. "I could see the flames and smoke from my window."

Only half a mile straight across, Sheldon thought. Only half a mile, and Julia wasn't home. Would a nice man like Spence do such a thing? Surely he wouldn't stoop to setting fire to someone's barn. Could he have such a vindictive nature? She had never seen any sign of it in him. Never a time when he lost his temper, even for a few seconds, when Julia got irritated at him for not tying a rose bush right or for walking into the house with muddy shoes. Julia had enough foibles to drive any man to a fit of temper once in a while, but Sheldon had never seen Spence lose it. Could it be that he was one of those who dwell for a long time on having been wronged and finally let all the fury out in one rash and destructive act?

No, not Spence. Sheldon shrugged the thoughts off and headed up the stairs.

"Thanks, Spence. I'll put this in water now. I need to get this soot and grime off me. Had to live with it all day. I never knew you'd get so dirty just being around a fire like that."

At the top, she stopped and called, "If you need anything, Spence, let me know. If you want some cleaning done, or get too lonely and want company for supper, I can't replace Julia, but at least I can cook spaghetti."

He nodded and waved absently at the air as he walked toward the kitchen door. For heaven's sake, Sheldon thought, whatever was I thinking? Offering to do his housework, indeed. I hope he doesn't take me up on it.

But she knew why she had offered help. She had needed to make amends for her unkind thoughts about the man. "I was good today. You hear that, Daddy?"

🍁   🍁   🍁

Sheldon couldn't remember when a shower felt so good. She could smell smoke washing out of her hair, and she let the soft warm water flow over her body long after she was clean. Finally ready to step out of the shower, she wrapped a towel around her head, and then remembered. She had forgotten to call for an appointment to have her hair done.

She picked up her watch from the sink counter and saw that it was five-ten. Sometimes Adrian worked late. She ran to the telephone, found the number and dialed. She closed her eyes in relief when Adrian answered.

"Thank goodness you're still there. This is Shellie. Can you possibly work me in for a perm tomorrow morning? It's a real emergency. I have a date, believe it or not."

"Well, I guess this is an emergency. Let me see. Can you come early? Like seven-thirty?"

"You bet I can"

"All right, I'll work you in. Hey, I just got the paper. That was quite a story you wrote on the fire."

"Oh thanks, Adrian. I haven't seen it yet. Guess I'll have to go get a paper."

"Terrible tragedy. Pat's one of my customers. I feel just awful for her."

"Yeah, so do I."

Half an hour later she walked into the newsroom. As was customary, a newspaper had been left on her desk and she picked it up, anxious to see the results of all their hard work. No one was in the office, and she sat down to quickly review the layout, a sense of hype growing as the impact hit her hard. The pictures told the tale all too graphically: the raging flames, the blackened barn and the unidentifiable mounds. She noticed with a little smile that Harry cropped her picture of the hog and left only the background of spectators viewing the blazing scene. She wanted to share the triumph of their reporting skills with George, and she thought she might still find the gang at the pub.

The composing room door opened and Hugh Webster walked in, grinning from ear to ear, like a kid ready to play outside. His blue flannel shirt looked much too warm for this weather.

"Hi Miss Merrill. You had to work today, didn't you?"

"Yes, I did. We had a big fire to cover."

"I know. I'm sorry. That you had to work, I mean."

"That's the nature of this business. We can't always choose when we work."

"You work too hard. I read all your stories. You write real good, but you do too much."

"No. No more than anyone else here. We learn to write fast and to be on the run. It's exciting work, really. Of course, I love it or I wouldn't do it." She checked herself from adding that she certainly didn't do it for the money. "Excuse me. I'm going to try to find George and Dee."

"Okay. I'm glad I saw you."

Sheldon didn't share the feeling, but she smiled and then she asked, "Were you at the fire this morning, Hugh? I thought I saw you just as I was about to leave."

"Me? No, not me. Must've been someone else."

Somehow she felt that he was lying, though he never changed expression, still wearing that silly grin. She ran across to the pub and found that it was much quieter than last evening. However, at their usual booth sat Dee and George, and with them were Manny and Jon. She stopped at the bar to order a sandwich, then went to the booth.

"Well, this looks like a table of friendly Indians," she said as she pulled a chair from a corner table and put it at the end of the table to face everyone. She slapped the newspaper onto the table. To George, she said, "Quite a spread."

"We make a good team," he said. Something in his eyes told her there was a double meaning to those words.

Dee raised her Coke and said in ceremonial style, "To George and Sheldon. Fire reporters *extraordinaire*. You deserve a Pulitzer for this day's work, my friends."

Manfred and Jon raised their glasses and said, "Hear, hear."

Red-faced, Sheldon sucked in her lips and studied the paper in front of her.

"Now you did it, Dee," Jon said. "You've embarrassed Shellie."

A knowing round of laughter followed.

When her vision kicked in, Sheldon picked up the paper, for the first time taking note of the box insert in her page-one story. "What's this?" She read aloud, "'Fire Marshal Suspects Arson.' He does? When did you get this, George?"

"After you left. It was just before we were going to press. He's an old friend of Harry's, and he came into the office and said they'd found signs that indicate arson."

"Wow. My goodness. Arson. I remember Don said to me, 'Who'd want to do that?' when I asked if he thought someone might have set the fire. Well it appears someone did. How terrible. But he's not sure?"

"He is, but he can't make an official ruling, as the story indicates, until after the lab tests are completed. Seems you can't put kerosene-soaked rags around dynamite, even, and not leave traces, although this arsonist was careless to the point of stupidity. He spread the kerosene all over the place, and then threw the can in. Apparently he thought all the evidence would be blown away."

Sheldon's sandwich and beer were set before her, and she eagerly began to eat while they continued to discuss the fire, before moving on to less formidable subjects.

"I'm surprised to see you here, Manny," Sheldon said. "You don't usually come over here."

"Manny couldn't go home," Dee said. "His wife called and said they didn't have the cake ready and he couldn't see it until everything was ready for his birthday party."

"Birthday? This is your birthday, Manny?"

"It is. And before you ask, I might as well tell you since the others wormed it out of me. I'm thirty-four."

"Gee, I wouldn't have guessed that. I thought you were forty-one."

For her smart remark, Sheldon caught a flying pretzel in mid-air.

"I can't be too mad at you today, Shellie," Manfred said. "You made my work easy with that page one story and photo. Didn't leave much for me to do."

"Boy, I'll tell you, it's been some day, hasn't it George? Up before six and running ever since. Whew! Now I can smell you. I just had time to get home and shower. Been out at Lucille Bradford's. Just as well she couldn't smell much. I didn't realize how bad it was."

George looked as if he'd been on an all-day construction project, still wearing the smudges on his face. He brushed at the front of his short-sleeved shirt and ran his fingers through his hair.

"I thought I looked pretty good, myself. You know how to hurt a guy."

Jon, who seldom engaged in lively conversation unless it centered around a sporting event, asked, "Does Miss Bradford have a lion in her living room?"

Everyone laughed, recalling the story about David Bradford's bear.

"No, but she does have a collection you wouldn't believe. Hundreds of Hummel figurines. If you're familiar with Hummels, you know that they represent many thousands of dollars. Considering her feeble condition, it's a wonder someone doesn't break in and steal them. They're all over the place."

That launched a conversation about various things that their mothers and friends collected, until finally Manfred said it was time for him to go home.

"I've got to go, too," Jon said. "Got a date for evening fishing on the river." He slid off the end of the banquette where he'd sat beside George. "Why don't you sit here, Shellie? I'll put that chair back."

"I'm going to be late," Dee said. "Better get going, too. Are we still on for tomorrow, to go shopping, Shellie?"

"Yes. But you don't have to leave, Dee."

"Oh yes, I do. Connie is picking me up at seven-thirty."

"Where are you going?"

"Alex Bay for dinner and dancing."

"Have a good time. I'll pick you up at eleven tomorrow. I have some things to do first."

"Fine with me. I'll need the extra sleep." She gave a bold wink, her dark eyes playful. However, they both knew it was all show. Dee intended to hold all men at bay until she was ready to marry, and that included Conrad.

Sheldon watched Dee leave. "She could go just as she is, without changing, and outshine all the other women there. How can she be so well groomed at the end of the day? She's one pretty woman."

"Not a bit prettier than you are, Shellie, well-groomed or all covered with soot."

George's words surprised her. She knew all her faults as far as looks went and, had it come from anyone else, would have taken exception to an obvious false flirtation. From George it didn't sound false. Or was she just imagining sincerity because she wanted to hear it?

"Yeah, sure," was all she could come up with.

George frowned. He had been very quiet when the others were here, she thought. Probably tired just like she was, but she had the terribly annoying problem of getting very hyper the more tired she got.

"I wanted to tell you that you wrote a super story today. The reference to the pig was genius. The whole thing was so well put together anyone would think you had worked on it for a week. I don't know how you do that."

"You do the same thing. I thought your sidebars were very good, too. And your photography is a hundred percent better than mine."

They looked at each other, then burst out laughing.

"So much for the mutual admiration society," George said. "But I told you that, not just because it's true, but because there was a bit of a problem. And I don't want you to think you did something wrong."

"Oh? What kind of a problem?" Sheldon felt a shot of disappointment.

"Sheriff Beaulieu was on deck for the first issue off the press. As soon as he saw your reference to the burned pig and what the deputy said, he stormed into Harry's office and yelled at him. Wanted to know what the hell he was trying to do, making the law enforcement officers appear to be heartless. He said it was bad enough that Harry was out to get him in his column, but a news story should be objective, and on and on."

"Oh God." Sheldon put her shaking hands over her face to hide the mounting tears. This was the worst of being a reporter, the part that she didn't handle well, being criticized whether the complaint was justified or not. It was a reflection on the imperfection that she saw in herself, and it always shook her up when her work was brought into question. It was the legacy of her father's view of bringing up children…if they don't do just as you think they should, or if they seem slow to absorb what you're trying to teach them, resort to verbal and physical abuse. She had loved her father, but she had also feared him. The fear of failure had never left her.

"No, no. Don't feel bad, Shel. I told you. You didn't write anything wrong. Believe me. Harry didn't let Beaulieu get away with his bullying tactics. First of all, you reported it like it was, just what the deputy said. You didn't fabricate that. Harry asked him if you had given out the wrong facts. Were the deputies allowed to shoot a suffering animal without asking the owner's permission? And Beaulieu said no, of course not. So what was he bellyaching about? Harry said that all his reporter did was report the facts."

"Well, I did embellish on it a bit," Sheldon said in a weak voice. "I said that three hours later, when I left, the pig was still standing there hurting. That was editorializing. I implied that no one would take the time to get permission to put the animal out of its misery."

"You know as well as I do what was griping the sheriff. It wasn't your story. For one thing, we were the first with the arson angle. But, of course, the real problem is Harry. That little incident was all it took for him to have his chance to jump all over Harry with the accusation of harassment. It was nothing. And Harry told him that. He said if he wanted to make a case of it, do it. The newspaper's lawyer would handle it."

A few weeks ago, Harry had been furious with the sheriff's handling of a youth, arrested for possession of marijuana. The boy's father happened to be a neighbor and close friend of Harry's, and when they went to pick up the youth at the station, it was obvious that he had a black eye. The boy said the sheriff had hit him when he refused to say where he'd gotten the hash. For some time rumors had been circulating that the sheriff mistreated his prisoners, so Harry lashed out at the sheriff and called for his resignation in his previous weekend column.

"Forget it, Shellie. Nothing's going to come of this. It's just the ranting of that pea-brained sheriff, and everyone knows what a jackass he is."

George took both of her hands in his and looked deep into her eyes. Even in her state of self-flagellation, it didn't escape her attention that he cared. Over his intense brown eyes, his brows were drawn together in a single line.

"If he gives you any trouble you call either Harry or me. But he won't, I'm sure of it. Now listen. I mean it. Don't you worry. Okay? You got that?" He shook her arms for emphasis.

She sighed. "Yeah. I got it. Thanks George. I worry too much about those things. You know that."

"Yes, I do know that. But you need to know that you're okay. No one's going to harm you. Even making a mistake isn't the end of the world. We all make mistakes. But this was no mistake. This was straight, good reporting."

She attempted a smile.

"Let's talk about something else," he said. "How did your interview go with Miss Bradford? Learn anything new? Get anything on the portrait?"

She wet her lips and gathered her thoughts. If she could just let the criticism go. But she knew it would eat at her until she could get it out of her system and go onto something else.

"She's a very nice lady, very sickly, on a respirator. Her nurse says she doesn't have a lot longer to live, poor woman. And she's too pathetic. Seems to regret her life."

Sheldon sighed again, feeling empathy for Lucille Bradford.

"She wouldn't tell me anything about the portrait. Very strange. But she gave me something else to wonder about, too. She said a name, apparently of a former nurse she had, and then she got all flustered and quickly changed the subject. And the nurse she has now, who saw me out, wouldn't tell me a thing about the other woman. I asked for her last name since Miss Bradford said only the first name, Karen. But she said she was told never to mention that name, and she just wouldn't do it."

George called to the bartender to bring two cups of coffee, then said, "Now that's curious. Is there a connection with the portrait, do you think? Maybe the woman in the portrait is Karen. Maybe there was something between Mr. Moneybags and this nurse. Maybe it caused trouble in the family."

"It would be quite a coincidence. But...well. You never know." Sheldon thought for a few seconds. The idea of a nurse working for Miss Bradford and having an affair with David didn't seem to be cause enough for dismissal with such acrimony. In fact, why should there be any problem at all?

She shook her head. "No, I don't think so. But maybe the nurse stole from Miss Bradford. I would sooner think that, since she is *persona non grata* in that house. Anyway, I'm trying to track her down. Harry's wife will know if there used to be a nurse working in the area by the name of Karen."

After several more minutes, Sheldon felt less uptight when she and George parted company in the parking lot. She drove home listening to her favorite FM radio, playing show tunes from "My Fair Lady." As she hummed along, she was unaware that a black truck had started following her nor could she have guessed who was uppermost in that driver's mind.

Sheldon Merrill. You little dish. Real soon now, you're in for a big surprise. You're so fresh and pretty. You can say goodbye to your buddies. It'll be just you and me. All alone. Nothing will stop me now. It's right. No one can say different. You're mine. You'll always be mine. You won't go off and work somewhere and leave me alone. You'll stay with me. That's the way it should be.

CHAPTER 7

❀

George had no idea what he was watching on TV. The memory of seeing Sheldon get into her car and drive away from him left him with a feeling of loneliness he hadn't known for a long time. She had no idea how much he cared for her, probably wouldn't be impressed if she knew, although she always seemed interested when they talked. Hell, she was always interested when anyone talked. But, still, sometimes there was a special light in her eye, like maybe she cared. Maybe she did. Some.

Now he was indulging in wishful thinking. No, she had made it clear that she could easily fall for someone like David Bradford. Well, why not? Rich, handsome, powerful. All the things that George wasn't. He knew from experience that women could like him, even make out with him, but they never fell in love with him.

He recalled the goodbye in the parking lot when she'd said, "Thanks George. Next to Dee, you're my best friend." Next to Dee. Well that was better than not being a friend at all, he guessed.

When he had walked back across the street then toward the office to pick up his camera, he thought about his former wife and why he had married her. It was for all the wrong reasons, a fact he had regretted soon enough. Odd that he hadn't seen her shallowness before they married, just doted on her pretty face and figure, attributes that did intrigue him for a few weeks. But then she began whining and crying and screaming over trivial things, all of which could have been discussed and resolved with a reasonable person like Shellie.

Shellie. The first day he met her, she intrigued him. She had such open sincerity and a huge curiosity about everything. She was a good reporter. She was a good friend, and a good person. Oddly enough, she didn't even know how pretty she was. He'd heard her say to Dee she hated to have her picture taken because her "buck teeth", as she called that cute overbite, were ugly.

For two years, he had watched her, talked with her, worked with her, laughed with her, yes even cried with her. And in all that time he had made every effort to keep their relationship strictly business. It was getting to be impossible. He wanted her too much. He wanted to be with her all the time. She'd make a wonderful wife, and he'd like to make her *his* wife. Would that be so unreasonable? Probably.

Maybe he should do something about his appearance, he had thought, as he entered the office and went to his desk. He smoothed the corners of his mustache. He could shave it off, but it had become so much a part of him, he'd feel naked without it. He could get some decent clothes. He hadn't bought any for a couple of years or more. Hadn't really cared how he looked. Not until now. Now that he would like to woo Shellie seriously. Yet, she didn't seem to be impressed greatly with clothing. She herself wasn't stylish; always neat and clean, but not stylish. Just his kind of woman.

His mind distracted by these thoughts, he didn't notice the nearly full cup of coffee he had left on the corner of his desk until he knocked it over as he reached for the camera and heard the splat of liquid on the floor. Coffee with cream and sugar.

"Damn. That will be sticky. Guess I'd better find something to clean it up with."

He went out through the composing room expecting to see Hugh, but upon hearing loud music coming from Hugh's portable radio in the press room, he decided he wouldn't bother him, simply go do it himself. He knew where the mops were kept, in Hugh's workroom. He climbed the stairs and turned right. Next to the bathrooms was a door that was seldom open, Hugh's "office." Tonight the door was ajar, and he pushed it open.

"What a mess," he said to himself as he surveyed the tiny room, so full of brooms, shovels, rakes, tin waste cans, rags, tools and an old reel type lawn mower, that he wondered how Hugh found anything. Giving it a long hard look, George finally spotted a mop and pail by a tiny desk in the far corner.

He eased himself around the obstacles to the desk, where he hesitated long enough to note the large bulletin board, covered with newspaper clippings, mostly agricultural pages.

"Looks like Hugh has an interest in farming. I didn't even know he could read," he thought. He got his equipment and left to clean up the coffee spill.

Now, staring at TV news, he felt some misgiving that he hadn't even kissed Sheldon before she left him in the parking lot. What stopped him? That open, innocent look of hers, that's what. She seemed almost untouchable to him when she put on that face. Could he get past it and suggest an overnight in Ottawa? God only knew. Whew! He had it bad, and he knew it.

"This won't do. I've got to think about something else."

Then he remembered that Sheldon had said she was going to call her mother tonight. How long had it been since he'd talked with his Aunt Betty? Too long.

He went to the kitchen and sat down, telephone in hand, trying to think of pleasant things to say to Aunt Betty. He smiled when he thought how caring she was of him, and had been all of his life. She was a brick, a solid influence on his life after his mother died when he was only five. She didn't have to take responsibility for bringing him up, but she did, and she showered him with affection, just as if he were her own son.

Although she was his father's sister, Aunt Betty had none of that restlessness or the gambling disease that he had, a sickness that won out over family and lured him to big-time stakes at cassinos out west when George was only a toddler. He'd often wondered what had become of the old man, even though he had long ago written him off as callous, without natural love in his heart. His father didn't care about his family or friends, only money. The bastard wouldn't even work for it. He expected it to come to him in one heavenly load at a gambling table. Inwardly, George had always felt that his mother had pined away for the useless man, who never even sent a Christmas card, until she finally died of pneumonia, her body weakened from lack of proper nourishment.

George long ago vowed he would not be like his father. Even though he had enlisted to fight in Vietnam, he would have returned to his wife, had she not filed for divorce herself. But it would have been a life of misery, he knew that. Like his aunt used to say, "You made your bed, now lie in it," and he would have done just that.

How different life would be if he married Shellie. What a life they could have. They didn't have to stay here forever. They might want to try for a larger newspaper and better positions. Have a couple of kids. Or maybe…

He shook his head and dialed the number. "It's no good, Georgie boy," he said. "She won't give you a nod, and you know it."

When his aunt answered he said, "Hi, Aunt Betty. I'm not lost, sick, or hurt."

She laughed. "Well, I should hope not. I had begun to wonder, though. I'm glad you called, dear. I have a bit of news for you."

"Do I need a pen and paper?"

"No, you old news hound. But you do need to be sitting down. George, I'm going to be married."

"Married!" He hadn't meant for it to sound so incredulous. Yet, that's what he really felt. He couldn't believe that, after all these years of being single, she would even think of marriage. Running her own accounting business, she had been extremely independent. How old was she? He began to figure. Well, not that old. Only in her early forties. God, she was young when she took him in and when she set up that business in the front room. Now she had a downtown office with a staff of five.

"Oh, I hope you aren't going to take it badly," she said, her voice going weak.

"No, no. Good lord, not at all. I just thought you were…" How could he put this? He didn't want to sound as if he thought she wasn't marriageable.

"That I was what? Too old? Too ugly? Too hard to get along with?"

"No, no, no. You're none of those things. Hardly." He laughed. "It's funny. When you're a kid you think of older people as being forever set in their lifestyle. Believe me, I'm happy as can be to hear this. You deserve happiness. Tell me about him. Who is he? He'd better be good enough for you."

She spared no details in telling about her new-found love, how they met quite accidentally at a flea market, how their relationship had developed, that he had his own business as a home builder, and that he had been a widower for five years.

Her breathless excitement got to him. He knew just how she felt. He, too, would be in a euphoric state if he were going to marry Shellie. One part of him wanted to discuss Shellie with his aunt, but the other part of him…that barrier that always threw itself up when it came to divulging his feelings to anyone…clamped his mouth shut, tamped down his need for asking someone for advice. Who better than Aunt Betty? But, no. He couldn't do that. If he asked Shellie for her hand, and she refused, it would be too embarrassing in the end. Aunt Betty often complained that he told her so little about himself. But that was the way he was made. No confidences, no embarrassments.

When she stopped to take a deep breath, George said, "Sounds like he's a good man. I'm truly happy for you. Have you set the date?"

"Yes. In October. The tenth. Can you come, dear?"

"Just try to stop me. Of course I'll come. Where are you going to live?"

She had her own lovely home, inherited from her parents. Every time George thought about the printing business that those same parents had left to his father, he wished he could belt him in the nose. It was a thriving business, one George would like to have today. But his father couldn't bear to be tied down to it, and sold it so that he could finance his big gambling tour, the one he never returned from.

"Well, that's something I wanted to talk with you about. Is there any chance you might want this house, George? If you do, I'll keep it. You won't have to pay me a dime for it. Better to give it to you now than to wait until I die. I expect I'll live to be a ripe old age." George smiled at that. She probably would, too. "I'm going to move in with him, since his house is larger and he has three grown children who will come to visit from time to time with their children. I don't need the money from this house, so if you think you will ever want to return here, I'll just maintain it and pay the taxes until such time as you do come back and move in."

George was dumbstruck. That beautiful house…all hardwood floors and woodwork, ornate windows, a big front porch. And the town was small, just great for children to grow up in. He could take Shellie there and they could…

What was he thinking?

"George? If you don't know right at the moment, it's okay. Think about it. You can tell me what to do with it when you come to the wedding."

"Yes. That's a good idea. It's a big decision. I must say I'm surprised at your offer. Why would you do that?"

"Because you're my boy, dear. You've always been like a son to me and I love you."

He swiped at the sudden dampness in his eyes. He wished he didn't have this sentimental streak in him. But his aunt could do that to him, make him go all wishy washy with her talk of loving him. It was time he told her the same.

"Aw, Aunt Betty. You know I love you, too."

That must have shaken her up. He never said words like that, and for a long moment she said nothing.

Finally, "Thank you, sweetie. That means so much to me."

When they finished talking, George hung up and sat staring at the phone. His grandparents' home. The one in which he was so happy growing up under Aunt Betty's loving care. Shellie would love it. If she would agree to marry him, he'd suggest they sell this house and go live there. Maybe he could set himself up in a carpentry business with the proceeds from this house. It wouldn't hurt having a new uncle in the building trade.

His heart was racing as he picked up the phone to call Shellie. Then he put it down. This wasn't the time to mention it to her. Perhaps Sunday night in Ottawa.

Life in the Berkshires had been idyllic, he reflected, once he became accustomed to not having either father or mother. And that took a while, as he recalled. Once again, his aunt had been steady, loving, explaining to him what had happened and that no one really wanted to leave their little boy behind, but that it was nothing that either of them had control over. And now he guessed she was probably right. Though he still found it hard to forgive his father for leaving them, he probably didn't have control over his addiction. Like most addicts, he wouldn't have looked favorably on finding help for the disease, either.

As for death, that was a whole new experience for him, and until he saw a pet turtle die, he didn't understand. Then he looked at Aunt Betty and asked if they could have a funeral and bury the turtle in the back yard. She had been just as serious as he was while they prepared a shoe box for the burial, said solemn words, then together pushed the dirt over the box. He even prepared a cross to mark the grave.

As the years went by, he came to regard her as his mother. She nursed him through the childhood diseases, babied him when he had bad colds, talked with his teachers about his school work, and helped him with homework. She encouraged him to take part in Little League baseball, cheered for him at basketball games, taught him to skate, and patched cuts after hockey games. If he cried in the night, no matter how softly, she was instantly there to hold him and soothe him back to sleep.

Then it struck George. His aunt should have married when she was young enough to have children of her own. Instead, she spent all her efforts on him. Did she refuse marriage proposals because of having him to care for? He wondered.

He wandered into the living room and sat on the sofa, still thinking about his years with Aunt Betty. He remembered the tree house he built all by himself and how proud he was of it. It was a darn good one, too, as he recalled with a smile. And the lemonade stand he and the next door neighbor girl used to set up in the summer to earn some extra pennies. What was her name? He thought for a long while. Ah yes, Caroline. Hadn't thought of her for years. She moved away when they were both nine and then an older couple moved into the house. He liked them, Florence and Mack. They were very good to him. Mack taught him a lot about woodworking and Florence loved to bake molasses cookies. Mmm. They were good. Wonder if they still live there. He should ask Aunt Betty when they talked again.

And there was his best friend, Kenny. They were pals all through school until high school graduation. What a live wire he was, always thinking up some deviltry. Poor Ken. Another victim of that lousy war in Nam.

Girls came into his life at age thirteen when he met Patsy Lovely at a church fair to raise money for the Missionary Fund. He was bored stiff and wanted to get over to the baseball field, but his aunt said they should spend just a little while at the fair, since it was for a good cause. She urged him to play some of the handmade games, all of which looked pretty stupid to him. So he finally sauntered over to the dart game and popped a couple of balloons, winning a small fuzzy dog.

"Oh isn't that cute," a girl's voice said, and he looked up into beautiful pale blue eyes. He was instantly smitten. All embarrassed and tongue-tied, he stood as tall as he could and said it was just something he'd won at the silly dart game. She asked him his name, and then said she was Patsy, and told him where she lived and what school she went to. Then she asked him if he'd had a hot dog yet, and he said no. Finally he found words and asked her to join him for one. Before the next hour was over, he had given her the furry dog and asked her to go to the movies with him next Saturday. Over the next year the two of them did some rather intimate explorations, and he always had a soft spot in his heart for that first romantic experience.

He sighed and smiled. He felt about Patsy a little like he did for Sheldon, only in a much less serious way, of course. At the end of that year, she began dating other boys and he squired other girls to dances and movies. Their paths seldom crossed after they entered high school, as they took totally different studies. Their separation was such a gradual thing that he had never suffered heartache over it.

He realized now that things were different. His feelings for Shellie ran deep, and his desire to have a lifetime commitment with her was so strong that he honestly felt he'd go out of his mind if she refused him.

Funny how content he had been with his life before she arrived in Westburgh. He enjoyed fishing by himself, and going to games with Jon Phelps, and making furniture in his own shop. He had put a lot of time into this house and he was satisfied with it. He occasionally dated Donna Brace, even though she was a couple of years older than he. She was a good soul, and a comfortable date. But she was just a companion when he needed one, he realized that. Perhaps it wasn't right that a man used a woman like that, and he certainly didn't mean to lead her on. In fact, they had discussed the issue and he'd told her flat out that there would be no long-term relationship, to which she agreed. He suspected that she saw other men, but it didn't bother him.

But now. He got to his feet and paced restlessly. Now life seemed almost turbulent. Shellie occupied his mind day and night of late. It finally occurred to him that he'd better get it off his chest, try to convince her how he felt. And even though he dreaded possible rejection, it would be better than living like this in limbo, being merely sociable and friendly at work. At least if she said no, he could always take his aunt up on the offer of that house and start over again, away from that very tempting woman.

He went to the refrigerator and took out a can of Coke, all the while wondering if he should call Shellie. He could at least tell her about his aunt and her offer, just drop the hint that he might like to move if he were married and his wife liked the idea.

No. That would sound childish. No need to beat around the bush with her. When the time was right, he should just tell her that he loved her and wanted to marry her. Still, he'd like to hear her voice tonight. Just a friendly call…

And while he thought about it, the phone rang. To his utter amazement, it was Sheldon.

CHAPTER 8

❀

Sheldon locked her car door out of habit and started up the stairs to her apartment. The sky was darkening and the wind, which had died down to a hot and heavy breeze, had shifted, carrying a strong stench from the direction of the Mollison farm. She looked around to see if Spence was home, but there was no light in the kitchen and the workshop out back appeared to be quiet, also. Maybe he had a wiring job today, she thought, and paused to unlock the apartment door. She heard a car engine on the other side of the house, sounding like it had driven into the other driveway that led to Spencer's workshop. Yes, there. A car door closed. Must be Spence just getting back. Well, she'd talk with him tomorrow. She was too tired tonight to be much company for anyone right now.

Entering the pretty apartment always lifted her spirits. Julia had decorated in warm country tones, antique red cabinets, beige counter tops and touches of green throughout the compact kitchen. Beige vinyl covered the kitchen floor, and extended to the light birch living room flooring, at left. A counter, topped by trellis work, separated the two rooms. The large braided rug at the center of the living area set the color scheme for the furniture, in shades of beige, rust, green, and brown. A sofa on one side faced two overstuffed chairs on the other wall, with a maple coffee table between, and a television set as the focal point. Mid way down the hall Sheldon had made a mini office in a dormer alcove under the skylight. Beyond were bathroom and bedroom. She loved the coziness of her garret apartment.

Going directly to the bedroom, she set her two bags on the floor, kicked off her shoes and slid her feet into shaggy red slippers. She wiggled her toes, enjoying the soft comfort. Now she would call her mother and then watch TV before gong to bed. She had missed the six o'clock news and would have to wait up until eleven to find out what was said about the fire.

She began to dial when a loud banging startled her. She set the receiver back and headed toward the door with foreboding. She seldom had visitors unannounced, so it couldn't be good news. Maybe more trouble from her story. Then she shrugged it off as her own paranoia, deciding it was probably Spencer.

"I'm coming," she yelled as the pounding got louder. Then muttered, "Don't take my door down."

Dread tugged at her gut when she saw Deputy Eugene Luce, dressed in jeans and sweat-stained navy T-shirt, obviously having just come from a dirty job. His green eyes fairly shone with excitement, and she could only guess that the emotion was anger at her.

"What…?" She didn't finish asking what he wanted. Likely he was about to chew her out for quoting him. "How did you know where I live?"

"Can I come in, Shellie?" She stepped aside and gestured to him to do so. "I'm with the Sheriff's Department. We know where everyone lives," he said, brushing past her.

"Oh, of course, Well…uh…what…what's the problem?" She could feel the flush in her face as her heart tripped. She would not back down, no matter what.

"I have some news for you."

"If it's about Sheriff Beaulieu's reaction to my story, I already know. And I'm sorry if you were offended, too." She couldn't help the pique in her voice.

"No, no. It didn't bother me. The sheriff has a short fuse, everyone knows that. Don't worry about him. He'll cool off. But I just came from the Mollisons'. After I went off duty, I returned to help them out if I could."

"That was a nice thing to do," she said flatly.

He took her hand and led her into the living room where he sat on the couch and pulled her down beside him. Instinctively, she recoiled, leaning away from him.

"You say you have news?"

"I guess I do, my sweet." Sheldon scowled at the endearment. "I went out there about mid-afternoon. There wasn't any more fire, but a lot of hot spots. So I thought I could help put out new flames or whatever Don might need for help. As it turned out, I was rounding up cows for a while. Imagine me, a cowpoke."

A dimple dented his left cheek when he laughed.

"When suppertime came, a lot of the volunteers left. Some of the women had brought things like beans and sandwiches for those who stayed."

Sheldon wanted to move away from the sofa, but waited to hear what else he had to say. His aggressive posture, leaning toward her with his arm over the sofa back, bothered her.

"I was still looking for stray animals…they'd gone everywhere…along an old logging road behind the barn when I saw something ahead of me at the edge of the road. When I got to it I found that it was a body, Shellie. A human body."

"Oh, my lord! A body!" Her hands flew to her mouth. "What was it doing there? How did it get there?"

"That's the sixty-four-thousand dollar question. I called Beaulieu. When there's a death, we give a certain code so anyone monitoring the police ban won't know. He said he would be right there and not to say anything to anyone. He and the coroner came up the woods road, so no one would see them."

Sheldon's mind was racing. The other end of that woods road came out past Spencer's workshop, but there were a couple of branches that went elsewhere. She had followed one of them one day when she was out for a walk, and it started just above the Mollison farm. Anyone coming from Westburgh could turn in there without being seen from the farm buildings.

"Everything was going fine while I waited for them, I was alone with the body, until I heard someone coming and there were two more volunteers walking toward me. One was a fireman and the other was another off-duty deputy. I told them both what the sheriff said about secrecy, and they said they would not breathe a word of it. They stayed with me until the sheriff came."

"The body. Was it a man or a woman?"

"A woman."

Sheldon got to her feet and began pacing, barely able to breathe.

"What happened to her? How did she die?"

"She was shot, but here's the odd thing. It wasn't a fatal shot. It hit the shoulder, nothing all that serious."

"So…?"

His mouth twisted as he thought for a moment, then he said, "There's more. But first I have to ask you not to tell anyone where you got this story. I'll lose my job if the sheriff finds out. He told the three of us that he'd call a news conference for the media on Monday, but that we weren't to say anything to anyone before that. So I'm telling you at risk of losing my job."

She dropped to a chair and stared at him, wondering why he would put his job on the line by giving her this scoop. She had mixed emotions about this Eugene Luce. He was obviously a good person, one who would work off-duty to help out a family in need. He had good looks and a generous helping of charm. But she had a feeling that he was ready to pounce on her any minute, that she needed to keep her distance. This whole revelation of a possible murder showed a reckless side, one that could only be for a selfish motive. She shouldn't have to feel that she was indebted to him, for anything.

"I don't have to reveal my sources," she said. "But why are you doing this? Why tell me? You know we'll publish on Sunday. And when we do, the story will be out."

Now it was his turn to stand and pace. He stopped at the divider and leaned back against the counter. His sly smile did nothing to reassure her that he was totally open with her.

"I'm doing it just for you, of course. Why else? When you like someone, you find ways to show them. I know what it means for you to scoop the competition. And for you, it will be a feather in your cap. Who knows? Maybe you'll get a raise."

Why didn't she feel that she could trust this man?

"I don't know, Gene. This is a very big story, but I don't like the idea of feeling in some way obligated to pay a debt for news information."

"There's no obligation. This is for free, totally. Merely an expression of my admiration for you. And I do admire you, Shellie. You're a hard-working, terrific young woman."

"We only just met this morning, and that was only briefly. How can you suddenly feel this admiration without even knowing me?"

"Well that's gratitude. You're questioning my motives? You think I'm not being up front with you?"

His raised voice, and the hurt it carried further worried her. It was apparent that the sheriff was not the only one with a short fuse. She wished he hadn't come to her door. On the other hand, she wanted to know about the body and would like nothing better than to have the *Press* scoop Channel Nine. The story would go out over the AP and UPI wire services. Like she said, this was a very big story.

"I just don't want to have you come to me sometime and say that I owe you, that's all."

She knew well enough that she would owe him no matter what, once she accepted the story. But she didn't have to owe him sexually, and he knew what she meant.

"Now why would I do that? You don't owe me a thing, Shellie. I repeat, I'll give you this for free. My motives are clean on this. I promise."

He held up his hands, palms out, as a show of surrender to her terms.

"All right then. You have my word that I won't reveal my source on this story. Now, what else is there?"

He walked to her chair and stood in front of her. His eyes, always full of secret messages, told her that he had won some kind of strategic move here, and she wished she knew what it was all about. She didn't trust his denial of expecting a reward later on.

"The coroner thinks the woman was beaten and then shot. Possibly whoever did this wanted to have her blown to pieces in the barn explosion, because there were signs that she had dragged herself from that direction. Her hands and arms were burned badly and some of her clothing was burned off her body. Her face…"

He turned away and cleared his throat. "We see some pretty bad things on this job," he said with a slight break in his voice. "This was about the worst I've seen. She had been beaten so bad…" He hung his head, shaking it in disbelief. "I don't know how she ever lived long enough to drag herself that far."

Sheldon shivered, thankful that she hadn't seen the body.

"The will to live is a powerful drive." Sheldon considered her own statement and wondered if she could ever have such a will to endure the pain that woman must have suffered. She must have been a very strong woman. "Was there any identification on her?

"No. But there was an odd thing, which may identify her. There wasn't just one wedding band on her ring finger, but two. Looked as if her husband put his ring on her thinking the rings would never be found once the explosion blew everything apart. And they wouldn't have been, either. Bulldozing has already started. All the evidence would have been buried. Maybe the rings have inscriptions or something to go on. Or maybe her dental work will provide ID."

"I can't believe that something like this could happen in Westburgh." This type of thing happened in large cities or places she'd never heard of. But here in this rural city, it felt like a horrid violation of privacy, hers and all the good people of the area.

"You know," she said almost in a whisper. "I've never covered a murder before. I never thought I would have to. Murder. I can't believe this."

She folded her arms around her middle and rocked, trying to hold back the threatening tears.

"Goddam." Luce balanced himself on the chair arm and pulled her to him, encircling her shoulders with both arms. "Can I get you something? A drink of water, maybe?"

"No," she said, once again pulling away from his touch. "I'm okay. Horrified, but okay."

Even though he was being gentle enough and his concern for her welfare showed through quite clearly, Sheldon wished he would leave. He wasn't the one she wanted to comfort her. She needed to talk with George.

"Is there anything else?" she asked. When he said she had all that he knew, she went to her desk and brought back a notepad.

"Then let's go over it again, so that I can write it down and be sure I have the facts correct."

When she finished, Sheldon again assured him she would not betray his confidence. At the open door, he reached into his back pocket for his wallet.

"I had some cards made up last week. Here. You're the first to get one. It has my home phone, as well as the office number. If you need me, day or night, just call and I'll come running."

His eyes wandered over her face with interest. "You were so cute in that hard hat."

"Hard hat. Oh-my-goodness. It's still in my car. I'll get it for you. Wait a minute."

She ran back to the bedroom, kicked off slippers and slid her feet into loafers, took the car keys from her bag, and returned, then followed him down the stairs. Unlocking the car door, she reached in back and brought out the hard hat.

"Thanks for the use of it. I meant to give it back to you this morning, but I didn't see you when I was finished and I had to leave."

"No problem. I keep a couple with me in case of emergencies, like this one. Now remember, if you need me, just call. And I mean that."

He twirled the hat in his hands. "By-the-way, about the pig. I found Don later and shot it with his permission. A neighbor was there with a front-end loader and simply scooped it up and took it to the rubble where the other carcasses were."

"Oh." Sheldon lowered her eyes. She could have spared herself and everyone else a lot of trouble if she hadn't made an issue of that policy against killing an animal without the owner's permission. But, as always, she jumped in with both feet whenever she was moved by what she saw as injustice or silly rule. As much as she opposed killing, she couldn't stand to see the animal suffer.

"It's nothing to worry about. Forget it."

He leaned toward her as if to kiss her. She stepped away, suspicion blazing. He threw back his head and laughed.

"You really are shy, aren't you? Like I said, no strings attached. Maybe later, though, you might enjoy a free kiss. I'd be happy to give it to you."

She locked both the car door and the one to her apartment after he drove away leaving her with a certainty that his motive in giving her this story was more selfish than generous. She hoped she had been right in believing him, but her conscience kept waging battle with her trust.

He was a little too smooth, that one, too cocksure of himself, and too friendly. However, she didn't have time to think about it right now. She had decided to believe him, and she needed to call Harry. Laying her notes and Gene's card on the desk, she reached for the phone and closed her eyes.

What a day it had been. Who could have predicted the finding of a body at the fire scene? Who would do such a grisly act? And suddenly Spence popped into her mind...his anger at Don Mollison for not giving him the wiring job on the milk house, his depressed appearance today when he said Julia had left. Was Julia really at her sister's? Or was she...good heavens...was she dead? Her eyes flew wide open. No, it couldn't be Spence. He was just simply too good a man. He wouldn't murder Julia. They loved each other, for heaven's sake. No. Not possible.

She dialed and when Harry answered, she told him all that she had learned, and that the sheriff had said he would call a news conference on Monday.

"Where did you get this, Shellie?"

"I promised that I wouldn't tell. Please trust me. It's a reliable source. The person was there, saw the body, talked with the sheriff, and the sheriff swore everyone to secrecy, so my informant is breaking a trust. There's no question about validity."

When she said the words, she lifted her eyes heavenward and said a secret prayer that she wasn't lying. But what if Gene Luce were just getting even with her for her story?

"I'll take your word on it. Now. Can you write up a story and bring it in? In the meantime, I'll talk with the coroner. It's time I called in a couple of markers from him. And don't worry about Beaulieu. He'll never know how I found out about it. Mmm. Come to think of it, maybe it's better if you just type up the facts, and I'll write the story. That way, if the sheriff gets nasty about it, I can take the flak instead of you. I'm sure he won't want to see more about his fits of temper in my column right now. I know what he had in mind. Call a news conference on Monday, just after our deadline. Then TV breaks it first and we come out with stale news, a day late. I expect he wanted to wait until there was a positive ID on the body before going before the cameras. You did a good job, Shellie. Real good."

Hoping he was right, and that the story was not a hoax, she said, "I'll bring the notes by tomorrow, after I go to the hairdresser in the morning. About nine-thirty. Okay?"

"I'll still be home, since it's Saturday. So bring them by the house."

After hanging up, she turned to her typewriter and quickly typed the notes from what Gene had told her. If this information was false, she'd be in real hot water. Harry might even fire her over it. Was that what Gene was up to? Did he want to get her fired? Perhaps the sheriff called him down over the pig episode, and this was his way of getting even with her. Lord, she wished she felt he was really trustworthy, but this dark cloud kept getting darker.

She didn't know when she had felt more tired than she did right now. She had to get on with things, but her stomach felt like it was full of hot pokers. She would call George and then her mother. George should know what was going on, and her mother would be expecting her call. It was eight-fifteen, so she could wait a few minutes before calling Mum.

"Shellie? I was just thinking about you. What's up?" George asked as soon as he heard her voice.

"No good, that's for sure. George, a woman's body was found near the fire scene late this afternoon. And my source says it looks like murder, with arson to cover it up. A gruesome murder, at that."

"Good God. Who told you that?"

"Please don't ask me. I promised I wouldn't reveal the person's name, and I don't want to break my word, even to you, though I know you wouldn't repeat it. Harry asked me, too, and I told him the same thing. But it's someone we can trust." Her fingers were crossed.

"I'll read you the notes I've made for Harry. He's going to write the story, because Sheriff Beaulieu has warned those who were near the body that they weren't to say anything about it until after he held a press conference on Monday."

"Ah ha. Fix it so TV would run it first, complete with his mug all serious in front of the camera, telling how he found the body, no doubt. That's our modest sheriff for you."

"You're right on that score," Sheldon said. "He'll really blow his rigging when he reads it in the *Press* Sunday."

"And he'll go after Harry. I know it's your story, but I'm glad he offered to write it. I'd hate to see Beaulieu attacking you. I'd blow *my* rigging if that happened."

She got the mental picture of George squaring off to Beaulieu, who was at least two inches taller and twenty-five pounds heavier. She smiled at the thought that George might do that for her.

She read the notes to him.

"Whew. This is hot stuff. She had to have been murdered, so badly beaten and then burned. Our arsonist must have put her there to try to blow her to bits. God. We have a real sicko around here, Shellie. That farm's not far from you, and you don't have any idea who the murderer might be, so you be sure to lock up tight, day and night."

"I do. Always. I'm just a bit worried about..." She had started to say that she was worried about the validity of the story, then checked herself. She believed that Eugene Luce might be a woman chaser, but she sincerely hoped he wouldn't deliberately pull such a big hoax on her. It was too serious a matter. Surely he would not. He seemed to be genuinely upset over the condition of the body when he talked with her. No, he couldn't be faking that.

"What? You're worried about something?"

"Oh nothing. Actually I have to go now. This is the night that I call my mother and I usually do it around seven. I'm late."

"You're sure nothing's wrong? If there is, please tell me."

"No. Nothing's wrong. I'm just very tired."

"So I'll see you Sunday, if not before?"

"You know it. Did you think I'd renege?"

"Possibly. I did apply some unfair pressure."

"That's okay. I was about to say yes anyway."

"Really? You were going to say yes?"

"Yeah. I was."

She listened and was about to say he sounded like an obscene caller, breathing so heavy.

"Thanks Shel. I…uh…" Another long pause. Then he let out a deep sigh. "You get a good night's rest now."

He's such a nice guy, Sheldon thought as she hung up and then dialed her mother's number. She hoped with all her heart that Gene Luce was a nice guy, too, and not just using her.

After hellos, her mother said, "I didn't think you were going to call tonight."

"I always call on Friday night. Unless there's something that I'm covering for the newspaper. You know that. Have I failed yet?"

"I hoped you were on your way over here to see me. This is your long weekend isn't it?"

"Yes, it is, but I had extra work to do for the newspaper today, so I couldn't really come over. Also, I need to shop for a dress to wear to Ottawa Sunday evening and get my hair done tomorrow. So I just didn't have time this weekend. I'll try to make it the next time around."

There was silence. Sheldon squirmed in her chair. Her mother wouldn't ask about why she needed to be all dressed up for a trip to Ottawa, and Sheldon would love to tell her about her date. But why do it when she just wasn't interested? Mum never understood why Sheldon took a job out of town, and in another state, at that. She thought her daughter should live with her and stay on the same job for the rest of her life just like she had done. Sheldon didn't want to get into that argument again.

"So. Did you buy a raincoat?" Sheldon tried to sound light and cheerful.

"No." The little whine now. "I really don't need a new one."

"Mum. You *do* need a new one. That old thing you've been wearing for the past twenty years is so thin the rain soaks right through it the minute you step outdoors. I sent you the money. It was supposed to be a birthday gift. Why don't you use it?"

"I can't find anything I like. There isn't much to choose from in this town, you know. I need to go to a shopping mall to find one. And I can't get there."

Sheldon sighed. Of course. The only one who can drive you there is me.

"You know that Theresa Andrews will take you, gladly. She loves to shop and loves to take you places. If you'd only ask her."

"I don't like to bother her. I'm fine. We haven't had much rain this summer, anyway."

"But it will get rainy and cold this fall, and you should have a coat with a zip-out lining."

"Hmm. Maybe."

Sheldon wanted to go to bed. She yawned, trying to be silent. Why did her mother lay these guilt trips on her?

"When will your next long weekend come?"

"In five weeks. It's every five weeks." She turned and looked at her wall calendar. August featured a picture of a covered bridge in Vermont, with a white farmhouse and red barn in the background. So charming.

"Maybe we can go then, when you come over to see me."

"Okay. We'll plan on it. And we'll find you a coat."

"Hmm. I saw Mary today and she asked how you were. She said Joe is doing real well at the insurance company. He hasn't missed a day of work in over six months and he's making good money, she said."

Sheldon nodded. Her mother would make a pitch to get her back to Middleton, go to work at her old job, and marry Joe Johnson. Of course, Mum never knew what broke them up and always believed it was Sheldon's fault for running off to Westburgh.

"Do you ever hear from Joe?"

"No, Mum, I don't. And I don't want to. I hope you haven't given him my address or phone number."

"Oh no. Of course not. It just seems too bad that you two split up. He's such a nice young man. If you had married him, you would be here in town."

"Yeah. Well, some things just aren't meant to be."

"I'll never understand you. You're so much like your father was. He wouldn't stay with one thing, either. Always dreaming, and always had to be trying something new, something that was going to make us rich. And look where it got him. Nowhere."

"I know. I'm doing just fine. In less than two years I've become editor of my own page, and I get to interview really fascinating people, Mum. I'm doing a story right now on a multi-millionaire who has built an intensive care unit on the hospital here, a huge new wing. He…"

"That's nice. You should have been here for the Fourth of July parade." She had said the same thing in their previous conversation, but as she so often did, she repeated the details. "It was the best they've ever put on. Some of the Shriners were dressed like clowns, driving those little cars. And then we had the pot luck dinner at the Shrine Club. I took my chicken noodle casserole and a pumpkin pie. The Country Squires played. It was real nice. I saw your high school friend, Jane Larrabee. She's married and has two children, you know. Such lovely little children, a boy and a girl."

Sheldon stifled a groan.

"Too bad you're missing out on children. You're at just the right age to enjoy them. Don't you want to have children, Sheldon?"

"Yes, Mum, some day, but not right now. Look, I'm really exhausted tonight. I need to go to bed. I'll call you next Friday. Okay?"

When she hung up, Sheldon dropped her head onto folded arms. She loved her mother, but why couldn't she understand things? Even when Sheldon lived at home, there was always that whining accusation that she was just like her father, or that she hadn't learned to cook like Linda's daughter did, or she kept too busy at the office and was never at home.

"Oh dear. I know you mean well, Mum, but why don't you find a man yourself and stop trying to get me married off to Joe Johnson?"

If her mother only knew. Hard to believe that someone hadn't gossiped about him at the store. He was indiscreet enough. Maybe she had heard about him, but she would never say anything bad about Joe. He had her so buffaloed. Even if he hadn't been running around on her, Sheldon wouldn't have married him.

"I don't want a possessive husband like you had, Mum. And I sure don't want a cheap woman-chaser for a husband."

Every week she went through the same thing, the guilt trip for not being close to her mother and not marrying and not having children. Every week Sheldon tried to explain how she felt and what a good life she was making for herself, how much she enjoyed her newspaper work here. But her mother never listened.

Well, things were what they were. It was late now, and there wasn't a thing to be done about their differing views on men and life in general.

"Besides, I have bigger things to think about right now."

Sheldon got up and went to the kitchen to make a cup of hot chocolate. She'd try to stay awake until news time, but wasn't too sure she could make it. As she looked in the refrigerator for something to eat with the drink, a crash jumped her. She straightened and listened closely to see if she could tell where it came from.

She quickly turned out the light and went to the window to look outside, but despite a bright moon, she could see nothing. Could it be a prowler? Or maybe Spence? It sounded like…oh, of course. The trash can was knocked over. Must be a neighbor's dog or maybe a raccoon trying to get into the can. He'd find poor pickings today. This was the day that Spence always took the trash to the dump. She snapped the light back on and fixed herself a bologna sandwich, then carried drink and sandwich to the living room where she turned on the TV.

※ ※ ※

Damned garbage can. At least no one came out to check. Lucky for me. Sheldon looks tired. She works too hard. She needs to stop working. It won't be much longer. You'll get rest very soon, my dear one. I'll take care of you and it'll be just you and me. Forever.

CHAPTER 9

❀

The beauty shop, with its white lace curtains and pale yellow front, was quiet. Its downtown location, between Jack's Hardware and Bernstein's Furniture Store, made parking sometimes difficult. But at this hour of the day, only a few cars were moving on Main Street.

Receiving Adrian's usual warm greeting, Sheldon took the first chair of the three, swivelled around and studied the photographic array of hairdos on flawless faces that would glamorize any cut, and decided to go for a real change. Long ago she had learned not to be overly vain, more from her mother's nagging in high school than personal preference. "The vain woman is everybody's fool," Mum would paraphrase William Penn. Hairstyle was straight and parted in the middle, clothes revealed minimum leg and bosom, shoes were serviceable. Sheldon became accustomed to the conservative look, though she caught herself secretly envying women like Dee, whose styles were current and often provocative.

Now, she decided, was the time to make her final statement of independence and update her appearance. "Do you think you can give me that second hairstyle, Adrian? The short one with curls around the face."

"You bet I can, dearie." Everyone was dearie to Adrian, who was probably the best hair stylist in the county. Even when she cut Sheldon's hair in the shoulder-length style, Adrian managed to give it a bit of pizzaz, with varying lengths creating a feathery appearance.

"That's a good choice, too," Adrian said. "It'll look great on you, Shellie. Just go over to the shampoo chair."

After the shampoo, Sheldon sat for the long process of rolling her hair onto little rollers with tissue papers; but Adrian didn't give a woman a chance to become bored with the process. She liked to talk.

"So you have a big date. Who you going out with?"

"I'm just going for dinner and theater in Ottawa with George Durant. He's a fellow I work with. It's no big deal."

"I love Ottawa. Have you been up there when the tulips are in bloom?"

Sheldon said she had not. It was difficult concentrating on the chit chat, with the murder, or possible hoax, still uppermost in her mind. As tired as she was last night, sleep was intermittent, and horrible dreams kept waking her up. Then she would think of the dreadful murder, followed by anxiety over whether Deputy Luce had told her the truth.

"You must go next spring. They're so beautiful. All over the city, thousands and thousands of them, just like in Holland. Not that I've ever been to Holland." Her hearty laugh was infectious, just as one would expect from a hearty woman. Sheldon wondered how she could stand on her feet all day with that extra weight she carried. With such a pretty face, she'd be a knock-out if she were fifty pounds lighter.

"I've heard so much about them. Guess I'd better plan to go."

"I've never been much of a gardener myself, but I'll tell you someone who has a huge garden of tulips as well as everything else you can imagine each spring, and that's Bev Stoner. You know her, don't you?"

"No, I don't think so."

"She's Pat Mollison's mother. Lives in Ashton."

"Oh? I didn't know she lived in Ashton. I never met Pat's mother. Seems like everyone lives in Ashton."

"Well, a lot do live there and work here in the city, especially since the town was bypassed by the highway. I live there. Two houses down the road from Bev, in fact. We're good friends. It's just a shame about the fire. Poor Pat. My God, that family seems to be plagued by fires. You knew that her parents lost their place in almost the same way some years back?"

Not waiting for an answer, she continued. "Of course, barns are notorious for catching fire for one reason or another. My folks had a barn fire years ago, but we didn't lose the house, nor the main barn, for that matter. Just the old carriage shed attached to the barn and some moldy hay. I think my brothers were smoking out there is how it started, but they both deny it to this day."

She laughed again. Sheldon looked into the mirror at Adrian's friendly face with the deep laugh lines cutting up to her eyes and could picture her as a young girl with rowdy brothers who smoked behind the barn.

"Did the Stoners know how their fire started?"

"No, never did find out. But they felt quite sure it was set. They had fired a farm hand the week before, and he was pretty bitter, I guess. But they could never prove that he set it."

"Anyone hurt in it?"

"No. That was a blessing, but it sure broke Pat up. She was in 4-H and raised prize sheep for show. She lost them all. And the family dog was killed. Now look at what Pat's lost. Everything. After all the years of hard work she and Don put into making a success of that operation. God. It seems like some people get all the hard breaks in this life. And they're such good folks, too. Just a crying shame."

Adrian paused to answer the phone and take an appointment. Sheldon studied the cans and bottles of products on the shelves at the sides of the mirror. She reminded herself to buy some decent shampoo and hair spray before leaving.

Returning, Adrian said, "Almost finished with this. My regular customer is due in about five minutes."

"If you live in Ashton, then you must know David Bradford," Sheldon said.

"Oh yes. Everyone knows David Bradford. At least they all know what he gives to the town. And the county. Now he's built that hospital wing. A real philanthropist, that one. Odd duck, but generous."

"Do you know about the painting he has in his living room? The one of a beautiful blond woman?"

Adrian laughed. "Really? No, I don't know about it. I've never been in his spooky house. But if there's a painting of a woman there, it could be just for the sake of appearance."

"Why do you say that?"

"You don't know the scuttlebutt? I shouldn't talk about him. People in town know that Dave has a way of getting back at anyone who talks against him or anything connected to him. But, between us, rumor has it that he's gay."

"I did hear something to that effect. I find it hard to believe, though."

"Well, I certainly don't know. All I know is that he does some very weird things, and he is never seen with a woman. He keeps company with drinking buddies, like Bill Ferguson, where he kennels his hunting dogs. Has a farm the other side of Ashton, near the Bethany line."

"You mean to say he's never had a girl friend?"

"When he was in high school he used to go with Faustina Roselawn. He was a year ahead of me in school, but Faustina was in my class. Everyone thought they would get married, but then he went off to college, and she married a local guy. He was gone for several years, building up that empire of his, I guess. He'd come back for brief vacations in the summer, but never for long, and most of what we saw of him was when he donated something to the town."

Adrian began drizzling a cold liquid over the rollers, and Sheldon's eyes watered.

"That's strong stuff," she said.

Adrian nodded. "Sets the perm. If David has a woman friend, she's in New York and he never brings her here. But that could well be, since he's so damned secretive. He delights in doing some crazy things that people are bound to talk about, but doesn't let anyone know what his private life is like."

"What kinds of things does he do? Everyone says he's eccentric, and in some ways I can see it, but it also seems as though that's exaggerated."

"No, not really. For instance, when hunting season comes, he'll put on his sister's big straw hat with lots of flowers on it and a red feather boa around his neck, and walk from his house to his cabin by the lake, and he only walks over there during hunting season. Now that's strange. But he laughs and says no hunter will shoot him wearing that get-up."

Sheldon chuckled. "Well, he's right, isn't he."

"The funny part is that he's a hunter himself. So go figure. Is he putting on a show? I think maybe so, mainly because I knew him in school. He was smart, but he was the class clown, always pulling oddball tricks. But a lot of people are saying it's because he's gay. I don't give it too much thought. As long as he keeps up our fire house and gives us new fire engines and new books for the library and money for the school and on and on, I'm satisfied to let him go his way, whatever way that is. Besides, he's not really the problem in the family, you know."

"What do you mean by that?" Sheldon's interest suddenly surged as she detected her beautician's eagerness to tell her some juicy gossip.

Adrian looked at her in the mirror while she tied a plastic bonnet over the curlers.

"His sister. Lucille. She's the problem. I think that's why he doesn't come to Ashton all that much…or at least he didn't until the last couple of years. Now that she's sick, he tends out on her. But she was a real lush. Heavy drinker. Everyone in town knew it. She's just the opposite of Dave. Won't socialize, doesn't shop at the general store. Doesn't have anything to do with anyone. But she kept the liquor store open. Literally. She not only bought enough liquor to give old Milt Coombs a good living, but when he wanted to fix up his house and add onto it, she gave him a loan to do it. I doubt that he ever paid her a cent, between us. But he kept her liquor cabinet well stocked. Used to deliver it to her personally."

Adrian said the last as if maybe the delivery was for more than taking liquor to Miss Bradford. But before Sheldon could ask, the doorbell tinkled and a middle-aged woman walked in, greeting Adrian warmly.

"Sit right here, dearie," Adrian called. "I'm always alone on Saturday. I'll have to watch this perm, but it should work in okay without holding you up too much."

She turned the chair and pointed to the dryer chair where Sheldon was to wait for the perm to set. "Here's a towel in case of drips."

Sheldon took it and picked up an old magazine to read. But her eyes remained on only one page as she waited, her mind racing through all the questions she had about the Bradfords and then back to the fire.

How demoralizing for Pat Mollison to go through a devastating fire for the second time, to lose everything, to face starting over from scratch. She wondered if the Mollisons had been told about the body, and whether the woman would turn out to be someone Pat and Don knew. Just knowing that someone had come onto their property, put a battered woman in their barn, and then started a fire would be terrifying. If there *was* a body. Oh dear, she thought. I hope I was right in believing Gene Luce.

The most frightening of all was to know that someone in the area might be a sadistic murderer and arsonist, that maybe others would be targeted. She fidgeted as thoughts of the possible danger began to escalate, and she could even imagine herself being in jeopardy.

Death itself was horrible enough. But to be at the mercy of someone intent on killing you was a horror that she didn't want to contemplate. As a ten-year-old, she had looked into her dying father's haggard face and felt total helplessness, a deep inner sense of futility, even at that young age. And when he died, despite the fear she had of his strict ways, she begged for him to come back. She needed him. She loved him. And he was gone from her forever. The man whose ability to make her laugh and enjoy life remained a far greater memory than the man who dealt her strict discipline. But his death was from an unseen hand, a power so great that no one could alter it, "natural" causes, they said. Cancer didn't seem natural to Sheldon, but it was a fact of life that the body would die one way or another since it was finite.

How unthinkable that an individual, a finite person himself, would assume the role of ending another's life. Anyone with an ego so inflated that he could believe his life was more important than another's, that he had the right to snuff out that life, must be full of hate, thoroughly lacking in compassion.

What if the identity of this man were never discovered and he wasn't brought to trial for this terrible crime? Sheldon thought how she would react if she had murdered someone. Her life would fall apart. She could never hide the fact that she was guilty. She would go insane.

Most likely the murderer was insane already. Anyone capable of deliberate, brutal murder had no conscience, had to believe anything he did was all right. As she thought about it, she knew her ex-lover was that way, to some extent. Joe believed he shouldn't be questioned about his actions and that he owed no one anything, certainly no apologies. But Joe's problem was all about his manhood, and Sheldon couldn't believe that he would ever go so far as to murder, like the arsonist did. If there really was a murder. Once again, that nagging doubt. She had to believe Deputy Luce. After all, he couldn't afford to have his reputation besmirched with a false report like that.

Sheldon shook her head in bewilderment. It was all too much to contemplate. She had never studied psychology, but it seemed to her that a person had to be born with a genetic flaw to commit murder. It was the worst of all crimes in her book. She had written about capital punishment, in a special series, and cited statistics that it did not deter crime, and she felt at the time that all states should do away with it. Now as the full impact of violent murder so close to home flooded over her, the ground of that belief began to move. She was beginning to understand what David Bradford meant when he said he could kill under certain circumstances. But killing a human being, snuffing out a life! How could you do that? She finally shrugged off the thoughts. No sense dwelling on a subject that would likely never apply to her.

*   *   *

An hour later at Harry's house, she rang the doorbell and heard the scrambling of kids' feet beyond the door.

"I'll get it."

"I got it."

"Get out of the way, you."

Sheldon smiled, reflecting on the family Harry had. The young O'Brien boys were typically active and noisy, and their mother was a saint in Sheldon's eyes.

When the door opened, it was Kate, the saint herself, who stood there, the boys apparently having been shooed off to another part of the house. She was dressed in uniform, so she must be getting ready to go to work.

"Ah Sheldon. I'm glad to see you. Harry said you'd be in. And you left a note for me to call you. I'm sorry I didn't get back to you. We've been so busy."

"I understand, believe me. Probably nothing important anyway."

"You look terrific. Had your hair done?"

Sheldon nodded, "Just now." She felt like a new person with short hair all curled and framing her face, somewhat like a twenties flapper. Adrian had said she looked like Gene Tierney, with the pouty overbite and now the short hair. But she knew she wasn't glamorous, just well-coiffed. It felt so good that she wished she had done this years ago.

She stepped into the hallway, where the rough plaster walls were evidence of the constant renovations being undertaken by the O'Briens.

"We're having the hall papered next week," Kate said, sweeping her hand toward the bare walls. "Harry was going to do it six months ago, but never could get to it. I'm tired of having it like this, especially since it's the first thing a visitor sees. I'm having a professional do it. At least the dining room is all finished. Come and see it."

They walked the length of the hallway and entered the dining room, papered in red with tiny white dots. The woodwork, molding and fireplace were painted white and the antique oak table, chairs, and sideboard had all been stripped and refinished.

"Wow!" Sheldon said. "You've been busy. It's really striking. Just right for this old house. Did you refinish the furniture?"

"Harry and I did it all, and we're not doing any more. I'm through with this house renovation. I told Harry that from now on everything is being done by professionals. We're both too busy to be using our precious spare time for this kind of work. The children need our attention. Besides that, I hate the constant mess."

They both turned as Harry entered the room. His presence always demanded attention, both because of his size and his no-nonsense, bigger-than-life aura.

"Here you are," he said, his eyebrows knit for serious business. "The boys said you had come. You got the notes?"

"Right here." Sheldon set her bag on the table and opened it.

"Before you leave, Shellie, stop in the kitchen." She nodded at Kate, who quickly left them alone.

Harry read down through the notes, shaking his head from time to time, then he indicated he wanted Sheldon to sit, and he took the chair next to hers.

"I've had a development here that may be linked to this." His voice was lowered.

"Oh?"

"I got a note." He pulled it from his pocket. "Here. Read this."

She took it in hands that were beginning to feel weak and shaky. The barely legible note, scribbled on a torn scrap of white paper, said, "Watch your step or you'll end up in a furniss to."

"Obviously not a Rhodes scholar. Furniss to? What do you think it means? You think it's the murderer?" If so, she thought, then my story is correct.

"Maybe. Telling me to back off from printing the story. I'd think it was from Beaulieu, but I don't see him as a murderer. And he can spell better than that. Of course, the spelling could be a ploy to make me think the murderer is illiterate."

"But why you? I mean, this is all going to hit the media on Monday anyway. And how would he know that you have the information already? It doesn't make sense."

"No. It doesn't make sense. The fire, the murder, now this note…none of it makes sense. And we don't even know if this is related to the murder. Well, we'll see just what kind of game someone is playing tomorrow when the story breaks on page one. If he comes after me, we'll know it's our killer. All the more reason for it to have my byline, though it robs you of a big story."

Dismissing the apology with a wave of her hand, Sheldon said, "This really scares me, Harry. Don't you think you should take this to the police chief?"

"He already knows. I called him this morning just after I got it. It was shoved under the front door sometime during the night."

"How will you be protected? If someone is out to even a score…I mean, well, maybe…"

"Maybe they want to kill me? I know. I'm thinking about it. But I can't hide in a cocoon. And if there's news to print, I won't be scared off. The chief thinks maybe I should wear a bullet-proof vest. We'll see."

Of course Harry wouldn't want to wear such a thing, but Sheldon wished he would. Never had she been involved in anything so serious. And now it looked like a threat on Harry's life. Police Chief Ken Ott was a far better choice of protection than the sheriff, especially under the circumstances. They both knew that Chief Ott was a more discreet investigator than Beaulieu, and if it appeared that the sheriff was involved in the threat, the chief could call in the state police. Besides, Beaulieu would likely give only lip service to the investigation.

"The fact that he said you'd end up in a furnace, too, does sound as if it could be the murderer, implying the fire was a furnace."

"Well, until he makes his move, we have no way of knowing who he is or what he's up to, assuming that it's a man. Ken is coming to the office in half an hour and I'll give him the note. They'll see if they can do anything with it, but it's doubtful. Fingerprints are out, since I had no way of knowing that I should be careful about them when I picked it up, but they'll do what they can."

When Sheldon stood up quickly to leave, she suddenly felt light-headed. She leaned against the table and fiddled with her purse so that Harry wouldn't notice. When the dizziness passed, she turned to leave.

"By-the-way Shellie, that new hair style looks good on you."

She felt her face redden. A compliment from Harry was a rare treat.

🍁   🍁   🍁

Just as she entered Dee's apartment, she remembered that she didn't go see Kate before she left the O'Brien house. She had been so befogged by the threatening note that she'd forgotten about the

Bradfords and Lucille's nurse, Karen. And then her lightheadedness had temporarily shaken her. The tension was just too much.

From the bedroom she heard a groan.

"Dee? Is that you, Dee? Are you all right?"

She was walking toward the door through the plush living area of the contemporary apartment when she heard, "Come in here, Shel. I'm dying."

Sheldon ran the rest of the way, only to find Dee still in her shorty nightdress, half in and half out of bed, her head over a floor pail. Her dark hair was matted and stuck to her face.

"What in the world has happened to you?"

"I believe they call it a hangover." Dee said in a raspy voice.

"Hangover! But you don't…"

"Put that in the past tense. I didn't drink. Until last night. And that bum Conrad Drew is past tense, too."

"Connie? He got you drunk? But…"

"Ohhhh." Dee jerked her head back over the pail and gagged with dry heaves.

"I'm so-o-o sick, Shel. I can't go with you today. Please don't be mad."

"Mad. Of course not. But what can I do for you? You really are sick."

"Just get me some cold water, will you? After that leave me alone. I'd like to die by myself."

"You're not going to die. But I'll get the water. Hold on."

Sheldon went back through the living room where Dee's decorating eye was fully evident in soft blue, rose and white, complementing a royal blue carpet that swallowed each footstep. On the wall of windows, a French door led to a covered terrace that, from the sixth floor, gave a panoramic view of the Border River. Oh, to be rich, Sheldon said to herself every time she came into this lovely haven. The white kitchenette was miniature compared to the spacious living area, yet it boasted a large bay window nook for the round dining set.

Sheldon poured the glass of water and fished ice cubes from a tray in the freezer.

"Thank you," Dee whispered when she returned and handed the glass to her. "Now go."

"Well gee. I feel terrible leaving you here like this," Sheldon said. Dee looked so tiny in the queen-size bed with its pink and white covers. This room had no view, but the double closet doors were fronted by mirrors that gave the impression of a much larger space. "You sure you don't want me to stay?"

"For what? I can be sick by myself with a lot less embarrassment."

"How come you drank last night? You never do. You always order Coke at the pub."

"Oh, I don't know. Connie gave me a glass of orange juice. I thought. After about three of them, he confessed that there was vodka in them. By that time, I was having a pretty good time, felt wonderful, so just went on with it. We danced and laughed and ended up here in my bed. You can guess the rest."

Dee moaned again and reached for the water.

"I'm so sorry. I know you've been so careful on both counts." Sheldon was sure she felt as downhearted as Dee did. After all, Dee had always boasted that she would wait to have sex with the man she'd marry. As for drinking, she had said little, but had given the impression that someone in her family had been an alcoholic and that she detested it.

"Yeah. Well, it's the last time mister good-time Charley gets the chance to make a fool of me. His name is mud. And I told him so when he left this morning. Believe me, he didn't think it was all so funny any more. He said he thought it would be easier for me to be a bit tipsy…*tipsy* he called it…for my first sex. I told him maybe it was, for all I knew, because I couldn't even remember it, and who said I wanted my first sex with him last night? Oh my head. Oh my stomach. Why do people drink? I'm so miserable."

"That must have burst his ego a bit, that you couldn't even remember it."

"You bet it did. Worse than that, though, was when I told him to get out and not ever to call me again."

"I truly am sorry." Sheldon patted Dee's arm and gave her a light kiss on the forehead. Alcohol smelled bad, but a hangover smelled really bad. "I'll leave. Try to get some sleep. Do you have something that you could take? Aspirin, maybe?"

"No. I don't take pills. You know that. I'll talk with you later, if I feel better. Have a good time shopping. You look terrific. Short hair becomes you."

🍁 🍁 🍁

After two hours of shopping in Winterville, Sheldon was ready to go home. She was hungry, but she'd wait. She had bought two pants suits and a dress that she hoped looked at least a bit sexy. The strapless underdress, red with large white polka dots, rustled when she walked, and it had a sheer white overdress with stand-up collar, gauzy material that clearly showed her bare shoulders, something she had never done except in a swim suit. She had finally found red shoes and handbag that matched the dress.

On the way back to her car, she passed a florist shop and stopped in her tracks. The picture of Dee, hurting so badly both physically and emotionally, came to mind. She decided to do something nice to make her friend feel better.

Fifteen minutes later, she breathed deeply of the perfume from the floral arrangement of carnations and roses on the seat beside her as she drove up the highway toward Westburgh, passing the river, along which both old and new homes reflected the wealthy status of those who could afford river front property. An occasional glimpse of water revealed that pleasure boats were everywhere, speeding in all directions. Just like drivers on the highway, she thought. The sun glaring on the pink rock formations at her right, fueled the visual sense of heat. Fluffy clouds floated aimlessly about the blue sky, but it appeared to her that in the distance the sky was darkening. She wondered if they might get some badly needed rain. Lawns had long ago turned brown and yielded to prickly weeds, trees were losing their leaves, and cicadas held their monotonous notes without pity. Beyond the rock formations were sheep farms in this area, though they were greatly outnumbered by Holstein dairy herds to the north. She had interviewed one of the sheep ranchers for this week's agricultural page, Drew Backus and his wife, with the darling little boy Sean. She must send them the picture she took with the boy's arms around the lamb. So sweet.

She began to relax, feeling a wave of happiness over the new apparel and her new hair style and her upcoming date with George. Her thoughts turned to Dee and the seemingly irreparable damage which Conrad had done to their relationship. It was a sad development, since everyone had been certain that Dee would marry Connie. He was a good guy, maybe a bit eager, with that glad-hand type of personality that is so great for an admissions officer in a college. Hale fellow, well met, as the saying goes, Sheldon thought. But he shouldn't have treated Dee like that, getting her drunk. That was way beneath him.

She couldn't believe that Conrad was a heavy drinker, but then you never can tell. Look at Lucille Bradford. Sheldon had little experience with drinking and though she would have a couple of beers with friends, she never desired to drink more, and had never been drunk. Neither of her parents drank, and Mum would be appalled to know that her daughter even went into a pub. She wondered if Lucille got sick, like Dee did, every time she woke up with a hangover. If she got that sick, why would she continue to drink? And why had she started in the first place? The woman's father was a minister. And there they lived right in the same town together, all those years.

The poor woman was sick enough now, and Sheldon felt great sympathy for her. To be the brunt of town gossip must be demoralizing, especially now that she had so little time to live. The woman was so frail and helpless. Never mind what she was in the past, she was dying now. She needed some cheering up, if at all possible.

"Maybe Lucille Bradford needs these flowers more than Dee does," she muttered. And at the sign to turn right for Ashton, she turned right.

CHAPTER 10

❀

The nurse was reluctant to take Sheldon to Miss Bradford.

"I don't know. She's not been feeling at all well today. You'll have to see her in her bedroom, and she never likes company there," Rose said.

"I won't stay long. I just want to give her these flowers." She knew she could let Rose take them to Lucille, but Sheldon wanted to talk with her again. Somehow she was drawn to this sad and sick woman, this sister to a very handsome and very rich young man. Mystery surrounded their family, mystery that had stirred Sheldon's imagination and drawn her back here.

"You wait and I'll go ask if she wants a visitor."

Rose quickly disappeared and Sheldon waited in the foyer. An ornate grandfather's clock in the corner struck once and she saw that it was one-thirty. She had made good time shopping by skipping lunch. She sidled to the mirror and looked at herself. The change from the last time she looked into this mirror was dramatic. She couldn't help but smile, still not used to seeing herself with curls, especially short curls, and they did seem to emphasize the square chin and high cheekbones. Funny how cutting her hair had brought out shiny dark red highlights. Anyone would think it had been tinted.

Rose reappeared as quickly as she had left, and Sheldon whirled about feeling guilty to be caught studying her own face.

"Miss Bradford said she'll see you, but if she gets tired you'll have to go."

"Certainly. Thank you."

Sheldon followed Rose to a large, dark bedroom, where Lucille was propped up by several pillows, tubes still sprouting from her nose. Her skin was chalky white, her eyes were sunken into gray holes, her lips had no color. Though the room felt hot to Sheldon, Lucille was mostly all covered by sheet and crazywork quilt.

"Miss Merrill. So good of you to call. And what have we here?" Her weak voice barely carried across the room.

"Just some flowers to brighten your day a little."

Sheldon looked for a place to put the arrangement, but the night stand was filled with medications and water glass.

"Here. I'll put them on the bureau. She can see them there." Rose said, and she took them from Sheldon's hands, crossed the room and picked up an empty vase. She stepped into the adjoining bathroom and ran the water, returning with the flowers in the vase. She set them in the center of the dresser then left the room with the admonition, "If you need me, ding the bell."

"Throw my robe over the bed there and sit down," Lucille said.

Sheldon took her white satin robe from the chair and laid it across the foot of the bed, then sat down, tugging the chair closer. She hated sick rooms, hated seeing people so helpless. For years she wouldn't visit the sick following her father's death.

"How are you feeling today?" she asked.

"Not good. Can't do a thing. Sick most of the night. Woke up weak as a dishrag. David and Rose wanted me to go to the hospital, but I'm okay here. They can't do anything for me now, anyway."

Sheldon felt awkward, not knowing what to say that wouldn't further depress her. Finally, she broke the muffled silence of the room, which was darkened by heavy drapes at the windows, stifling with heat, and filled with stagnant odors.

"I got the flowers in Winterville. I was shopping for some new clothes. Got a date tomorrow evening."

"And you had your hair cut. You look lovely."

"Thank you. It feels strange, so short. I've worn it long for years." Absently, she touched the back of her head, feeling the short length and the softness of new curl.

"We're going to Ottawa for dinner and then a performance at the Arts Theatre."

"Oh, that's nice. I like Ottawa. Used to go there a lot." Lucille turned her head toward her table of pills and said in a whisper, "Too much."

"I don't know what's playing at the theater, but it doesn't really matter. I don't get there often, and it will be a treat."

"And with your beau. That's nice."

"He's not really my beau. Just someone I work with. But it is our first date, and he's a good friend, a good guy."

"Well, if he is good, hang onto him. The good ones are hard to find."

Sheldon smiled and, on sudden impulse, patted Lucille's hand where it rested on top of the quilt. As if the action were just the last straw, Lucille began to cry softly.

"Oh, I'm sorry," Sheldon said, withdrawing her hand. "I said something to upset you. Shall I call Rose? You want me to leave?"

"No. Not at all. Don't be concerned. I cry easily these days. You didn't say anything out of the way. You're very thoughtful to bring flowers."

"It's my pleasure, really."

Sheldon meant that. The picture of Lucille as an alcoholic just wouldn't form in her mind. This woman had a meek soul, a caring heart. She was suffering, but not just from a physical condition. Her eyes had the look of constant fear, a look that seemed to have intensified since their meeting yesterday.

"Is there anything that I can do for you?" Sheldon asked.

"Possibly. We'll see."

"Just name it. If I can do it, I will."

"I need to think about it. I may need you to do something for me." Lucille struggled to raise herself higher on the pillows.

"Let me," Sheldon said, placing her hand under Lucille's armpit to boost her upward, the body barely more than a skeleton. It was hard to believe that this emaciated woman was just fifty-five.

Settled back, Lucille said, "Thank you, dear. You know I don't have any friends now. Used to have lots of them, but one by one they all deserted me."

She could say only a few words before resting. When she had breathed deeply a few times, she said, "Not too surprising, but very distressing. Now there's no one to talk with. I need to talk with someone."

"Does your pastor call on you?"

"I don't want to talk with a minister. I don't trust ministers."

"But your father was a minister."

"Yes. He was a minister." Her weak laugh ended in a snort. "Imagine it. Giving advice to people when you don't even know anything about your own family. When you don't care about people in the least."

She sighed and looked away, reflective. As Sheldon waited, she wondered about this family, the brother who was rich and generous to the community but miserly with himself, a sister who obviously wasn't penny-pinching but so very unhappy with her life. Of course, as ill as she was, she would be sad, but there was something beyond the illness, something deeper about her unease.

"Damnation. That's what my father preached. Never heard him preach anything but damnation. He loved the topic. Relished the idea of people going to hell, I think. Townspeople held him in awe, someone with authority from God, who could quote chapter and verse for every sin he saw and when he preached, he'd pronounce the ultimate punishment on them for those sins, eternity in hell fire."

Lucille closed her eyes and sighed. "Christian or not, they got the same sermon. Repent or face hell fire. I saw one woman go down front to repent three times in one year…and she had been baptized. Of course, in his eyes, just the fact that other people lived was a sin in itself. The only one who was supposed to live without feelings of guilt was himself. Uncle Saul was the same, only worse. Much worse."

Lucille's rasping gulps for air made Sheldon nervous. She stood and walked to the window, where she pulled aside the heavy green velvet drape to look outdoors while Lucille rested. The room overlooked a small lily pond surrounded by a well-kept rock garden filled with a variety of greenery and colorful floral ground cover. An oblong bird feeder with a roof was alive with chickadees, wrens, and a pair of cardinals, all flitting and eating and squabbling, some flying down to the ground to peck at the seed that was flung out of the tray above.

"Don't worry. I'm not going to die just yet," the voice said behind her. Sheldon let go of the drape and returned to her chair.

"You probably shouldn't tire yourself so. I should leave."

"No. Please don't. I want to tell you a few things. Will you listen?"

"Of course."

Lucille swallowed and adjusted the tube in her nose. "I'm okay. Just hard to breathe. I need to talk. There is so much…I have to tell someone. I can't talk with the pastor, you see. I can't abide self-righteous preachers. They think they know the route to heaven. Every last one of them, no matter what the religion. They know the way." Her voice became stronger, "Every damned religious sect there is. No other faiths are right, of course. Ministers and monarchs. Kill, plunder, brow beat, and as long as it's in the name of religion, they're justified. 'Oh, someone believes different than we do. Annihilate them. Get rid of the non-believers.'"

With a violent shudder, she inhaled quickly. "Oh God. They don't know anything about truth. The awful **Truth**."

She waved her hand to dismiss Sheldon's concern when she began to cough.

"I had a towel once. It had been hemmed wrong, one side hemmed on the front and the other, on the back. Only I never knew which was the front and which was the back. And every time I'd fold it, I'd say to myself, 'Just like life. No right and no wrong side.'"

Sheldon giggled at that. "Well, maybe not always," she said. "But you have to admit that some things are totally right and some are totally wrong. Like murder, for instance."

Lucille shot her a quick look.

"Perhaps."

"You think there's justification for murder? That it isn't totally wrong?" Sheldon felt like she was continuing her discussion with David Bradford.

Lucille turned her head away and stared, as if in a trance state. Then she sighed and looked back at her guest, her eyes swimming in tears.

"Perhaps it is totally wrong. Or perhaps there are extenuating circumstances sometimes. What I believe is that we can't know the absolute truth because we see it from only one side. When we die and face that truth, it will be without the compromises that we make in this life based on what we feel or want or have been led to believe."

She wagged her finger at Sheldon. "We'll face what we are. What we are, like old Marley's ghost dragging that chain of lifetime wrongs, is the total being, not just what we show to the world. We won't need to be judged by a higher court. We'll judge ourselves. We'll look into a mirror that tells only the truth, a reflection of the real self, and there can be no changing it then."

Sheldon almost smiled as she conjured up the picture of Snow White's wicked step-mother asking the mirror on the wall who was fairest of all. Then Lucille began to cough and struggle for breath. Sheldon wrestled her own conscience, whether to let her go on and get it off her chest or to call Rose and make her calm down.

"Please. Don't you think you should just relax? You're upsetting yourself."

"I'm upset. But I have to be." Her words came in gusts of thin breath. "I have to tell you how it is. I have to tell someone that it's cold, hard Truth which we can't escape, no matter who or what God is, or what we believe for the convenient sake of hoping that we'll be saved from facing that Truth."

After a few seconds she went on, "Can you imagine your every word, your every thought, your every action, your attitude toward others, being judged in the light of absolute honesty? Is there anyone in the world who isn't hypocritical in some way?"

Again she struggled and gasped. Sheldon was listening closely and sensed an odd revelation in what Lucille said, slightly uncomfortable with the prospect of mirror judgment. She lived an honest life, but could everything be held up to the light, especially her attitudes? So often she had unkind thoughts about some of her fellow workers, even her mother.

"You see what I mean, don't you?" Lucille held out her hand and Sheldon took it in hers, appalled at its coldness.

"Yes, I understand. But still, since no one is perfect, isn't that why we have baptism? Isn't that why we believe that Christ interceded for our sins? It's what I've believed ever since I was baptized at the age of twelve."

"And you still believe that? You believe your sins were washed away?"

Sheldon replied that she didn't question that concept.

"Baptism. What a meaningful ritual that is." Lucille's attempted laugh bespoke her contempt for the rite. "Symbolic of what? Of having our sins washed away by the blood of Christ. Imagine! To even think of being bathed in some innocent person's blood is ghastly. Why are children baptized? Because they're 'born in sin.' Such absolute idiocy. And does baptism immunize us against guilt for sins from that day forward?"

"Well…" What could she say? Sheldon was no religious scholar.

More wheezing. "How fiendish is God that He'd create a man and a woman with sexual organs, and the…the…" her mouth twitched, "the resulting desire for each other, and just for the fun of it tell them to abstain from sex? Which is supposedly what the enlightenment was when Eve tempted Adam with the metaphorical apple. And then, when they experiment with the good feeling, to pronounce their action sin? Sin which He wouldn't forgive? Was He just playing games like teasing a cat with a catnip mouse? I find that too preposterous. And what about the resulting races? If He created them, as we're to believe from Biblical accounts, He made them with reproductive organs, set everything up for reproduction. Did He do all that and plan to have just that one couple inhabit the earth without generations of offspring to follow?"

After she gathered her thoughts and regained her breath, Lucille said, "We're born because it's the biological nature of this life, and that's no sin."

Sheldon felt compelled to respond in some way.

"I guess not. Although I have never really questioned that God created us or that Adam and Eve were sent from the Garden of Eden as sinners."

"No. Of course not. People with blind faith don't question. The fact is that everything religious leaders teach about God is self-serving, from the early days forward. Granted, church leaders may believe what they teach, but they carry on a long-established custom of teaching the uninformed and unthinking masses the dogma that served the church so well with power and riches, both at the expense of willing believers."

Breathing hard, her chest heaving in spasms, Lucille looked at Sheldon with wide eyes.

"Today's preachers do the same. They repeat the threat of damnation long and loud so that people will be lulled into thinking they're chosen when they're baptized and will congregate and give money to the religious cause."

Sheldon wanted to argue, but knew too little about the Bible's origins. This must be very important to Lucille the way she fought to continue talking, even though her pain was obvious.

"Sins washed away by blood requiring slaughter of a sacrificial lamb. Gruesome thought…pagan by nature. Just as pagan as the origin of Christmas. But we must believe it because *it's written*. Generations have taught their children what they call the word of God. Sometime compare pagan teachings, the myths, to our Christian heritage. You'll be surprised at the parallels. So few people seem capable, or daring enough, to question that so-called word. The *godly* delight in interpreting symbolisms, and reading all kinds of things into vague and meaningless statements in the Bible."

When Lucille appeared ready to resume, after a rest, Sheldon asked, "You don't believe in the word of God?"

"Word of God? If I heard a word from God, I would believe it. Who said it was the word of God? More the word of kings and despots than the word of God. But that's what leaders think of themselves, isn't it, as God? Interpretations of mythical writings had to suit the king, what he wanted commoners to believe. Pious men played on mass ignorance. Why do you think early writings about reincarnation don't appear in the King James version of the Bible? The masses shouldn't be allowed to hope they'd come back to this life happier or richer or maybe even as rulers themselves. They shouldn't know that they had the power themselves to enter a better life instead of bowing to the king or the priest as their attorney before God."

Sheldon had never questioned Christian teachings. In fact she had felt quite inspired many times listening to one of Reverend West's sermons. She had been baptized because she wanted to become a missionary, to help save the world, a twelve-year-old's ideal that soon vanished in light of reality. She couldn't afford to go on to college and she didn't feel that she should leave her mother alone at that time. But to hear Lucille talk about the fallacies of Christian teachings…no, of all religious teachings…took her by surprise and alarmed her. It seemed frightening to take on the very creator himself.

Lucille was not finished though every word shook as if torn from her.

"I can't accept the Christian Bible as the word of God, no. To know the nature of God is impossible. All we know is that there is one and only one Truth, and its quality is the absence of human guile. When a Christian argues that we were created in the image of God, I laugh. We worship a God with human traits?"

A long struggle for breath. "That's what pagans taught, that gods speak and hear, feel and love, laugh and cry, and on and on. All human attributes. No one knows about the supreme power of the universe, or of other universes. I certainly don't. But I believe it's a force, an energy, a knowledge that no intelligence in all this world can comprehend. It's absolute and doesn't cry or laugh."

More gasping and wheezing. Then, "I don't question life after death. And that's blind faith, too, you see, when I recognize the possibility that when we die there is no more life, that life's gone. Period. But I believe in eternity, in eternal life, without beginning, without ending. So when this life ends, and self-interest is ripped away, I will face my role and who I am by the rigid standard of almighty Truth. The question is where in the never-ending cycle will I be? I believe it. I cannot avoid my true self. How can it be otherwise?"

Lucille rubbed her throat. "You think some blood bath or the symbolism of it, washes away the dishonest part of the self? And you think because you believe that your every move is watched over by God that it really is? If prayer is so powerful, why have millions of people died in wars? And in floods, earthquakes, tornadoes. Why do mothers die in childbirth? Why is death taking lives daily, young and old, and why is the world so full of cruelty? Why do people still starve when they beg God for help? Believe me, we deceive ourselves. In this life, we don't know or understand Truth. And because we can't comprehend the tragedies we call them 'God's will.'"

She could barely be heard now, her voice had gone so weak. Tears rolled down her cheeks again and her hand fluttered as she tried to breathe.

Overwhelmed by the woman's passion, Sheldon said, "I've kept you talking too long."

"No. No. I just want you to…You see we have a selfish nature and what generations of worshipers have tried to do is avoid facing the Truth. And then the big question remains: what happens when we face the Truth? In the eternal life, where will the true being, or soul if you like, go next? I believe we should correct our attitudes here, while we live in this flesh. It's too late when we die. Just too late. The return, or whatever the future fate is, may be too grim."

Though she wanted to comfort her, Sheldon waited, and thought how strange that the daughter of a minister rebelled against religion and Christian beliefs. She wondered if David agreed with her. Had both of them been maverick in the eyes of their parents? David had mentioned not having been "called", and yet he had also said his sister was the reverent one of the two. That didn't sound like this woman who railed against church teachings.

When Lucille opened her eyes again, she said, "I'm tired, Sheldon, very tired. I need to tell you so much more. Promise me that you will listen to the rest that I have to say, when I can get it all out. I've decided. I do want you to do something for me."

As strange as Lucille's talk was, it also fascinated Sheldon. She recognized questions that had been arising in her own mind, and though she couldn't feel the hopelessness of Christianity that Lucille did, she was coming to believe there might be more than one path to heaven.

"Of course I will. I'll be only too glad to listen any time that I can. You just call me if you want me to come. I'll leave my telephone number." She picked up her bag, got out pen and paper, wrote down the information, then put the paper under a pill bottle.

"Just one more thing." Lucille's hand was moving nervously over the covers.

Sheldon waited.

"Where there is real love, there is Truth." She moaned. Her eyelids fluttered and she whispered, "You're just what I need. I have no one else to tell this to."

"Wouldn't your brother…"

"No! Never tell my brother what I reveal to you. Never. He must not know. Please promise me that, too. When we talk again, it will be more serious. And David cannot hear it. Will you promise?"

Sheldon couldn't bear to see Lucille suffering so. She had to leave. But deep down she wanted to stay and have Lucille tell her all. What could it be? That she had been drinking secretly? Surely David knew all about her drinking problem. And what did she want done for her?

Sheldon looked into Lucille's pleading eyes and promised that she would keep all that transpired between them secret.

※   ※   ※

She left the house feeling like she had just gotten off a speeded-up merry-go-round. Her head spun with the wild talk. Deep in her reflections as she went to her car, Sheldon didn't notice David Bradford walking along the driveway until he spoke to her. She had no reason to feel guilty, and yet that was just what she felt. He would think that she was visiting his sister to get information about him.

"Miss Merrill. You seem to be spending a lot of time with my sister."

He was, indeed, wary. His blue eyes squinted in distrust and he stopped in front of her, his body in an aggressive, tackling stance, only inches away from her.

Sheldon smiled, telling herself to stay calm. "Yes, I saw your sister yesterday to get her perspective on your growing up years here in Ashton. She was very polite, but didn't have much more to say than you had already told me. That was okay," she said with a shrug. "Today, I was shopping in Winterville and bought some flowers. I thought they might help cheer your sister. I was sorry to see that she's feeling worse."

He slowly unwound to a more relaxed position and studied her carefully.

"You've had your hair changed," he said simply.

"Yes. It was time to make a change, I thought." If she expected a compliment from him, she was mistaken.

"When did you say the story would be printed?"

"Next weekend."

"I see." He turned half way around and looked down the hillside toward his home, the roof of which could barely be seen over the thick growth of trees on his property. He looked so handsome to Sheldon that she blushed, ashamed that she would even think of an attraction to him. But in faded work jeans, a khaki shirt and ragged tennis shoes, he looked more like a handyman than a Wall Street tycoon. It was as flattering to him as the suit and tie had been.

"How was my sister?"

"She was tired and didn't want to talk long." It was only a slight lie.

"She was sick all night. She's stubborn, like me. Won't go to the hospital. If she gets worse, she won't have a say in the matter, but for now I'm letting her remain at home. The doctor was here earlier. He thought she might as well be here as not for now."

The thinness of his voice told her that he was very worried over his sister.

"She asked that I come see her again. Would that be all right, do you think?" Might as well stem any future blame for doing so right now.

"Why not? Company should do her some good, as long as she doesn't get overly tired."

He put his hands in his back pockets and stood gazing at her until she had to look away and try to focus on the colorful petunias lining the paved driveway. He really did have a strange way of doing that, she thought.

"Did you see it all?" he asked out of the blue.

"See it all?"

"You said you wanted to see the village and the lake. Did you do it?"

"Oh. No, I didn't. But it would be nice to do sometime."

"Why not now? I'll show you around, just as soon as I look in on my sister. And before we start, you can drive me down to my house. There's something I need to take to the lake."

※　　　　　※　　　　　※

Lucille knew he was there, though she hadn't opened her eyes yet. She had heard his voice as he spoke to Rose and then a deep sigh as he seated himself beside her bed.

"Hi Sister," he said softly. "Are you awake?"

She opened her eyes and nodded. She felt so tired, all she wanted was to go to sleep, but she never would refuse to talk with her little brother.

"I won't stay," he said, smoothing the quilt beneath her chin. "Just checking in."

Again, she nodded. As she looked into his sad eyes, she wanted to tell him it would be all right. She had never told him how she feared dying. More than anything, she wanted him to feel that she could brave this out. She wanted for once in her life to be the kind of sister that he deserved, not a whining loser who quivered in her boots because this was one more thing she couldn't escape.

"I'm okay, David," she said. "Don't worry about me."

She saw him now as she had seen him when he was eight years old, a beautiful boy, with a good and caring soul, and suddenly there was a scene crashing through her mind, one of those times that she had wished over and over again had never happened.

He had come over to this house and had sticky, dirty hands. She had always told him not to touch the grand piano with dirty hands, but that day he didn't think. Just sat down and started poking at the keys, leaving smudges on them.

"I told you never to do that," she screamed at him. She had been drinking hard. It was a Sunday afternoon and she was drunk. He poked a key again, and she lost her temper, grabbed him and turned him over her knee to spank him. But he was getting big enough to resist, and he did. He pulled at her blouse, ripping the sleeve. She tipped him over again, but he managed to swing around enough to pull at the front of her blouse, ripping it some more until it was hanging from only one shoulder.

"You won't get out of this," she yelled at him, and with all her might she got him over and spanked him hard.

How many times she had remembered that dreadful deed, as well as similar outbursts of drunken fury on her part, times when she had hurt him, if not physically, then emotionally, she was sure. She loved the boy so much, and yet knew no other way to discipline him except to physically hurt him, as she had been hurt growing up. Now her throat ached as she fought to keep the tears from moving up to her eyes. Here he was, the best person she knew, and she felt so much guilt over hurting him all those years ago.

"David," she said, holding out her hand for him to take. "I just want you to know that I love you."

"Yes, I know. And I love you. You rest now. I'll check in on you later."

When he left, Lucille felt the familiar shroud of loneliness wrap around her heart. Escape had seemed possible before, when a bottle of gin warmed her and dulled her pangs of guilt, eased the emptiness. Then she could be reckless and laugh in the face of propriety and forget all the evils that had invaded her life, including her own stupidity and cruelty. It had given her pleasure to fool the townspeople, with their know-it-all whispers about her. They knew nothing, nothing. What they gossiped about was so far from the truth. Wouldn't they be surprised if they knew?

Now, without the numbing comfort of alcohol, every memory was alive and sharp and pulling at her like a magnet toward that awful moment. The awful moment of facing her own judgment, the Truth.

CHAPTER 11

❈

Sheldon got into her car to wait, all the while considering Bradford's request...no, his order.

She didn't mind transporting something for the man, but each time she felt a bit flattered by him, she ended up being disillusioned. First she thought he was interested in her hairdo and how she looked, only to have him ask when his story would come out. Now, just when she thought how generous of him to offer to show her around Ashton and the lake area, it wasn't because of any particular interest in pleasing her. He wanted her to do an errand for him.

She smiled, realizing that she was learning some lessons here on never presuming anything about this man. He had a knack for keeping a person just a bit off balance, whether intentionally or not.

The Bradfords were independent individuals, without question. Lucille had certainly shocked her with all that talk about truth. Her departure from Christian doctrine might deserve consideration, Sheldon thought. Some of Lucille's observations, especially concerning the nature of God, coincided with her own recent doubts. But it might be that Lucille was merely substituting the word Truth for God. Semantics. The only problem with the woman's word games was that she had given up the one hope which Christians clung to. Salvation. Sheldon had the usual Bible school education concerning faith, and could probably name most of the New Testament books and maybe a quarter of the Old Testament books, and she knew the basics of St. Paul's letters and admonitions to the churches. And she could find the Beatitudes and Psalms. She remembered St. John 3:16, "For God so loved the world..." Well, probably a whole lot more if she strained.

It had always been her belief that the Bible was indisputable. She had even engaged in argument on occasion concerning the creation, the trinity, the usual controversial topics. Perhaps Lucille was right. Blind faith was just that...blind. She thought that for a faithful Christian to question, to challenge, and to depart from the basic doctrinal premise that the Bible was the word of God must have taken a great upheaval of some sort. Lucille's rebellion had to have been triggered by...

What? Sheldon searched for a plausible explanation, but knew that until she heard the rest of Lucille's story, she couldn't understand this magnitude of her rejection. She did understand, however, that the woman was truly disturbed and horribly afraid to die. So strange that one could disavow belief in salvation and damnation, yet fear death.

Death was frightening for everyone. She thought of the woman's body Deputy Luce told her about. Natural death held its own emotional terror, but what must it be for one to be tortured to death? She shuddered to think of it. So horrible.

Then she reminded herself, *if* there really was a body. Oh, dear, she shouldn't have thought of that. Now she began to worry again. What would happen if it was all a set-up that the sheriff and Deputy Luce had perpetrated to make the *Press* look stupid? Even though the note Harry received appeared to be related to the fire, and thus the murder, it might be totally unrelated. For the life of her, she couldn't think what it would be if not the fire, however.

"She's going to sleep now." David Bradford's deep voice through the open window startled her. She had been so absorbed in her thoughts that she hadn't heard him approach the car. He opened the door and slid onto the seat.

"She was tired when I left her," Sheldon said as she started the engine and drove around the drive to the road. "Talking was very difficult for her today."

"Damned emphysema. The doctor says it won't be long now."

No, Sheldon thought. It won't be long before Lucille will face what she fears so much. Truth. Perhaps merely her own demons.

Driving into his yard, Sheldon noted that the barrier was still there. Then it wasn't for the rain. It was a constant fixture.

"I'll only be a minute. It's in the hallway." Bradford slammed the door. He returned quickly, carrying a gasoline can.

"I'll set this in the back here," he said, not waiting for Sheldon to suggest putting it in the trunk where the odor wouldn't be quite so strong. Great, she thought. Stink up my whole car. She backed out of the driveway as soon as he was settled.

"Had to have gas for the outboard motor. Do you like fishing, Miss Merrill?"

"I went fishing just once in my life, when I was eight, with my father. We had a good time and he caught a couple of fish. They were lake trout. I recall that I couldn't bait my own hook with a worm." She laughed. "I'm not sure I could now, either."

She glanced at him and saw that he was smiling.

"Little girls never can bait a hook. Only one I ever saw that could was Faustina, a schoolgirl friend. She liked fishing, and hunting," he said, with emphasis on hunting.

Sheldon raised an eyebrow and looked sideways at him. Since he didn't offer further explanation about Faustina, Sheldon decided to let it alone. If he didn't want to talk about his high school girlfriend then she wouldn't pry. She had learned that much about him. He'd tell what he wanted to and nothing more. Perhaps that painting was of Faustina, she thought. Never thought to ask Adrian what she looked like.

They were coming into the town proper now, where she had talked with a few locals, prior to interviewing Bradford. She had driven into town from the opposite direction before interviewing Bradford and had not taken a very good look at things. Ashton, typical of early settlements, had grown and prospered for a long while, before automation propelled the world into high speed motion and left small towns bereft of self-sufficiency. Where once families could live together, work together, shop and play together, townspeople quickly took to the road that led to better paying jobs and versatile shopping opportunities and grander entertainment. They no longer needed to farm for food nor barter for goods and services. And the town's main street reflected the poverty of that wholesale abandonment, except for the three major buildings that Bradford had commissioned. Bradford pointed to the pretty library, constructed of pink Potsdam sandstone, with four white pillars at the front of a curved entryway. Although a small and declining town, Ashton could boast of a library offering one of the largest book collections in the county, the librarian had told her. And that was because of this man, this handsome David P. Bradford. Previously, what they called a library was housed in one room at the town hall.

"They wanted to put a plain front on the library," he said, "but I wouldn't have it. We have white columns, or we have no library, I told the committee. As you see, we have the library and we have white columns. Any building that I build has pillars."

Sheldon recalled that the ICU unit at the hospital had its own entrance, and it, too, had the columns.

"Why is that, Mr. Bradford?"

"I like them."

Well, ask a stupid question.

After only a brief silence, he added, "They're elegant. If you're going to have a public building, it should look stately."

Now somewhere there was logic to Bradford's philosophy, but Sheldon found it difficult to understand. His home was hardly a showplace, badly in need of renovations, sidewalk ugly. Yet he demanded that a public building look stately when he sponsored its construction. A Jekyll and Hyde, Bradford showed no one his true self, Sheldon guessed.

When they came to the red brick fire station, she noted it was one place where even he must have realized that white columns wouldn't work, not with the oversized doors for the trucks. Both doors were open and she could see several men polishing two fire engines.

"Did your engines go to the Mollison farm fire yesterday?" she asked.

"Yes. We were there."

He had said we.

"You mean you were there? You're a fireman?"

"When I'm here, I am. Yes, I was there."

"I didn't see you."

"No. But I saw you. You were all over the place. Wrote a good story, too."

"Well, it could have been better." She turned her head slightly toward the left so he wouldn't see her red cheeks.

Although homes in Ashton had a cared-for appearance, the mostly wood-constructed stores did not. The color of the town's one restaurant could barely be determined, its white paint so badly chipped and dirty. The hardware store was black with age.

"This town looks deadly now. I'd like to do something to bring it back to life, but I haven't decided what yet. Just look at that. Three stores in a row boarded up. Used to be a clothing store, an insurance company, and a candy shop. I remember especially buying maple candies that they made at that shop. I like maple flavor. They made all their chocolates, too. It's a wonder I have any teeth left, the way I ate that stuff." He laughed. "My sister used to tan my hide when I'd get my fingers sticky and then try to play a tune on her grand piano. I can't blame her. I could be a frustration."

He turned and looked at Sheldon. "That's progress for you. They built a highway so that Canadians could sail right down the pike and not be bothered to come through Ashton, where they might stop and buy a few things, like the candy. One woman sold handmade quilts and did a booming business until that bypass went through. Now she has to get welfare to survive since her husband died. Political scam, that road was. Even a high-paid lawyer couldn't stop that bit of so-called progress. Too many powerful politicians and greedy contractors involved."

Sheldon guessed that the high-paid lawyer would have been Bradford's. If he couldn't stop something from happening then it really was wheeling and dealing, big time. Too bad the media hadn't opposed it. Or had they? She'd have to ask Harry.

They had passed the general store with its Salada Tea sign in one window and Budweiser Beer neon sign in the other. Now they were on the central bridge that crossed over a barely trickling stream. Smooth rocks of all sizes nested in the stream bed, dry and white.

"That's the lumber mill on the left, across the river."

When she had passed it previously, her mind was totally consumed with thoughts of Bradford and the evasive answers she had received from those she interviewed about him.

There might have been a circus playing along the street, she wouldn't have noticed. The whole town was hazy in her mind after passing through earlier, but now she began to appreciate the damage the highway and automation in general had done to its business section. It obviously was once a busy and attractive village. Today, there was only a handful of cars on the street.

The mill's concrete structure stood straight and sturdy, two floors above a full story of sound rock foundation, planted solidly at the edge of the stream, the high water mark a dark contrast to the lighter concrete above. Logs littered its big wrap-around yard. Three teenage youths lolled about a stack of logs, two standing and one sitting on a low stack, leaning over his spread legs. Sheldon could see that they were passing a cigarette around, each taking a drag and then handing it on to another.

"Used to be a lot neater outside when Lucille ran it. Of course in the old days the water furnished power for the grist mill, and later for the lumber mill. Now, of course, commercial electricity is used. The dam and flume are gone."

They were past the mill now, but he continued, "In the early days of the mill, farmers grew their own grain, and hauled it to the grist mill where it was ground to flour or meal consistency. You can still see a couple millstones there. It must have been quite an operation. I wish I could have seen it."

Passing a half dozen cars parked in front of a large building still bearing the sign A&P, Bradford said, "There's one good business. We have a lot of poor people in this area, Miss Merrill. The owner of this place goes to large city stores and buys up loads of close-out stock, end-of-season clothing, shoes, and such. He opens this abandoned supermarket on weekends and, as you can see, gets plenty of business. His prices are reasonable, the goods are new, and customers can wear decent clothing, their children can have warm boots. I get all of my work clothes there."

She smiled at that, though she would have guessed that he bought his work clothes at the Salvation Army store.

They approached the school where she had talked with the principal, Celia McIntyre. It was a tall one-floor building with white trim and, of course, a white column on each side of the front entrance, over which the name Bradford Elementary School stood out in gold-bordered black letters. Set back from the road, the school did look stately, almost like an estate home with its curved driveway, and a large round flower bed with flagpole in the center.

"You have an attractive school," she said.

"Yes. And we have good teachers. Our students rank among the highest scholastically on entering high school. I plan one day soon to build a gymnasium across the road, a large gym that will put others in the county to shame."

"For elementary grades?"

"Not necessarily. I envision this town's hosting regional high school basketball tournaments. It could even serve as Westburgh High's home court. It's not that far from the city, only ten miles."

Sheldon changed her direction by driving around the driveway and heading back to the mill site, where she turned right.

"I see you know where you're going. You say you haven't been out here before?"

"Not on this road. But I was told how to get to the lake," she said.

Arriving at the head of the lake, Bradford pointed out that most of the cottages were at the far end, while this western end had only a few scattered camps.

"Most of this property has been in my family for several generations. I own a hundred acres on the lake side and most of the land on the other side of the road. It goes all the way back to the highway."

He was in a particularly talkative mood today, and Sheldon had been enjoying all of the family histories of residents whose homes they passed as they drove along.

When the camp-like house that George had described to her as being Hugh Webster's came into view, Bradford said, "That was one of my few mistakes."

"What's that?"

"Selling property to that no-good Webster. When he came to me and said he was out of a job and needed some place to live, I thought I'd give him a chance. He looked like an honest man, and I knew his family. They were all good workers. Now they're all gone, only him left."

Sheldon had slowed the car to a mere crawl as they passed the house, a nondescript structure fronted by a plain door and one window, its panes lined with brown paper. Tall dead grass showed no separation from the fields, indicating that a lawn never existed, and the driveway side looked like a junk yard. Automobile wheels, bicycle frames, rubber tires, a wringer washing machine, chunks of wood were all scattered about the straw-grass.

"Does he run a repair business on the side?" Sheldon asked.

"No. He doesn't repair, he destroys. That junk represents would-be projects that never materialized."

Sheldon thought about Bradford's house and its run-down appearance. But it didn't have a lot of junk in the yard.

"I practically gave him this place, which used to be a fairly decent cottage, charged him just enough to maintain his dignity. We staked out an acre from my property to go with it. Then I got him a job, and told him he could do odd jobs for me, too, like shoveling snow in the winter."

Bradford hesitated long enough to point to his own driveway. "Pull in there. We'll stop for a few minutes."

Sheldon did as directed, turning into a long drive that led to his camp. The handmade keep out sign, which George had mentioned, hardly prepared her for the sight of the large brown-stained chalet that came into view ahead of her through the wooded lane.

"Each time I was to come back to my Ashton village house in winter time," Bradford continued, "I'd call him and tell him to have the driveway shoveled, if it had snowed. We agreed on a price of ten dollars for the job. We had a big storm one day three winters ago just before I was to arrive, and he shoveled the drive. When he came for his pay, he wanted me to give him twenty dollars. Said it was more snow than usual, and should be worth twenty dollars to me.

"Well, I pulled out a twenty dollar bill and handed it to him and told him, 'I'll pay you this once, but this will be the last time. You're fired.' Like I said before, I don't get taken, at least not more than once."

As if he couldn't afford the twenty dollars. But she understood. It was a matter of principle. Bradford might give away money, but he did it on his own terms, like everything else. However, it appeared that the reverse could be said of what he would take, making demands on others without hesitation.

She had stopped the car next to the chalet and was waiting for further instructions. Perhaps they were just pausing to see the lake from here, a beautiful sight indeed, with an island in the middle. It was a long lake, and judging from the expanse of sand and gravel she could see, it was very low, like all the area water levels. Extending from a boathouse near the lodge was a long pier, sitting high and dry.

Bradford sat for a moment, as if deep in thought, his arm resting on the back of the car seat.

"Webster can't be trusted, Miss Merrill. I believe he works at your office. He has never been charged with any crime, but the general store owner here watches him closely when he comes in. He has a bad habit of tucking small things into his coat pocket without paying for them. Like I said, he's never been brought him up on shoplifting charges, but I pass on to you that he is a thief and will steal anything that takes his fancy if he gets a chance."

"I'm surprised to hear that. He seems very easy going, though maybe not too smart. He looks to be honest enough. But I'll pass the word on to Harry O'Brien. I doubt that he knows about it."

"You do that. Now, have you had lunch yet?"

"No, as a matter of fact, I haven't."

She brightened. Maybe he'd take her to lunch at the Ashton restaurant they had passed. Sheldon thought it would be a real kick to have lunch with her esteemed companion of the afternoon. It might be a first at the restaurant, even, having him come in with a woman.

"Good. I haven't either. Let's go inside. I keep a good supply of food on hand here. I'm sure you can whip us up something for lunch."

Blindsided again. Well, why not. Anything to save this poor man a buck. Sheldon climbed out of the car and slammed the door just a bit harder than she had intended.

After she made grilled cheese sandwiches and iced tea, they sat on the covered porch overlooking the lake to eat. If she had felt put-upon to get lunch, it was all forgotten now. This mesmerizing, peaceful setting would linger in her mind for a long time, she thought as she listened to the soulful cry of a loon, the gentle lap of water rippling on the shore, the shrill hum of locusts. A jet flew soundlessly overhead, so high that she could see only its white contrail. Against the pale blue sky, a hawk floated gracefully on wind currents, then dove straight down, rising again with some small prey in its beak. She breathed in deeply of the cedar-perfumed air and let out a deep sigh.

"This is so great. Why do you live in the village when you have a beautiful place like this?" she asked.

"You like it here, then?"

"Very much. I thought you said this was a camp. It's a gorgeous lodge." She had admired the interior with its spacious open living area, enormous rock fireplace, braided rugs and leather-upholstered furniture. Upper level bedrooms opened off a balcony. The generous size of the lodge was complemented by a kitchen ell, and an attached three-car garage.

"Uncle Saul visited a Swiss chalet once in his travels and liked it so much that he had it replicated here. Of course, the house where Lucille lives was his, too. He knew she had no interest in this property, so he willed her the house and mill, and he left this for me."

Bradford washed down a bite of sandwich with tea.

"I like the old house that my parents owned. I had happy times there in my youth. If townspeople think I live a contradictory life, let them. We each should live the way it pleases us. Don't you think so, Miss Merrill?"

"Yes, in theory. I guess, though, most of us don't do that. Convention seems to dictate much of how we live, I'm afraid. But ideally we should, indeed, live our own lives."

"Exactly. I like the old house just the way it is. I have happy memories of life in that house. The moldy smells, the old farm equipment in the barn, even the rustle of old hay in the mow when I go up there to check for possible hot spots. It's all home to me. My roots. You see?"

They sat on folding camp chairs, across from each other at a rough-hewn wood table with pitch oozing from tiny spots along the bark-covered legs. Though it was a hot day, a gently cooling breeze played around the porch, carrying the musky odor of lake water. Sheldon dropped a piece of sandwich in her lap, picked it up and threw it over the rail for the birds. When she had dressed in a blue cotton dress and white sandals this morning, it was for shopping in the hot city. She had no idea she was also dressing for lunch with David Bradford by the lake.

She observed that he seemed intent on letting her know why his life was that of an eccentric. Maybe he was trying to be sure she wouldn't write him up as a crazy coot living in a run-down old house. Of course she wouldn't do that. Despite his oddities, she really liked the man. Maybe she liked him too much.

"Yes, I see. It must be a pleasant contrast to life in the city. I hate cities myself. I feel so isolated when I'm in a big city among total strangers who seem always to want to get ahead of you, whether you're driving a car or walking on the sidewalk or shopping."

"Ah. The city. It's a necessary evil for me. But you've identified exactly what it is, a highly competitive and rude place, confining for those who like the freedom of the country, the woods, the waters. Freedom and solitude. They go hand in hand."

Sheldon knew she could easily fall in love with this man. She could hold him right now, feeling his aloneness, wanting to say, 'I'm here for you.' He had a strange power over her. His words thrilled her, more from warm emotion in the utterance, than what he said. When she was with him, looking into his magnetic eyes, she forgot about the office, her work, her co-workers. George. Oh, dear. She shouldn't be thinking of any man this way, especially not a man of Bradford's power and wealth. To even imagine a connection with him beyond the professional relationship they now had was foolhardy.

She needed to get on solid ground again, not to think of the man's loneliness or why he was lonely, or whether he had a woman friend in the city. That was none of her business.

"I didn't notice the Baptist Church when I went through town, Mr. Bradford. Where is it located?"

"It's on Crescent Street, the second right-hand street off Main. It curves around and comes out on Main Street farther down. You don't see the church from the main drag."

"Your father was its pastor for many years."

"All of his preaching career was right there in that one place, except for a few substitute ministries when called on. Some ministers get moved every few years, but the people here wanted him to stay. Of course, it being our town, so to speak, it was only natural."

"Is the church still operating?"

"Oh, yes. The preachers come and go with regularity. There's a young pastor there now. I don't think he'll last long, not in this town. I hear that he's a poor speaker and doesn't pay calls on the elderly, like my father did."

Sheldon had the distinct impression that she was getting two different views of the Reverend Bradford. Lucille's opinion was far less flattering than David's.

"You haven't heard him speak?"

"No. I don't attend church."

"How about your sister? Does she get to church?"

She detected a slight frown as Bradford's head tipped back in that arrogant manner he had of raising his chin and flexing his jaw muscles.

"My sister hasn't been well enough for about three years. But even before that she had left the church, which you may have heard already. She had a drinking problem. My father took a dim view of drinking, even as a social nicety. She decided she liked her way better than his and resigned from church membership."

"I see." She felt heat rising to her face. "I didn't mean to pry. Please excuse me."

"Not at all. Gossips have always had a field day with that one. There's no need to be devious about it. We can't change what is past."

"I haven't heard a lot of gossip, believe me."

"Maybe not. But you would, sooner or later."

She wanted to ask about Lucille and her current fears, but decided that she should keep her word and not repeat to Bradford what his sister had said.

"When we talked at your home, you didn't mention that you had another uncle who served in the second world war."

"Thomas. I never think of him, mainly because he went off to war the year I was born. So I never met him and I heard very little about him. Lucille knew him and he sent her gifts from overseas. She tell you about him, did she?"

"Uh huh. She said he was the one who started her collecting Hummel figurines."

"Yes, indeed. Her Hummels."

"I didn't think to ask you if you were a veteran."

"No." Hastily he added, "I wasn't a draft dodger, though. They just didn't like the way my feet hugged the floor. I'm flat-footed, you see. I'd have gone, if I'd passed the physical. It isn't right that Carter pardoned the draft dodgers. No one wants to kill, but that doesn't mean that we can evade our duty."

Sheldon didn't respond. She had a differing view of killing, especially in a war where the U.S. wasn't threatened. She could see the need for protecting the country when it was threatened, but not to be an aggressor for an unclear reason. With all of that, she did respect the Nam veterans and what they suffered. She just didn't think that it had been necessary.

He looked out over the lake as the sound of a motorboat reached them.

"Kids out joy riding," he said. "Parents don't control their kids any more. They don't need to race around making it hard for others to fish or even to enjoy a leisurely outing on the lake."

To her surprise, Bradford sniffed the air, then said, "It's going to rain tonight."

"It is? How do you know that?"

"I can smell it." With barely a breath between sentences, he said, "You enjoy your work, Miss Merrill?"

"Oh yes. I don't think I'd want to do anything else."

"I expect there will be more to write about the fire. I suppose they're looking for a cause. Will you write it up when they find out what happened?"

"It may be me, or it could be another reporter. It wouldn't really matter who."

"Even though it was your story?"

"Yes, well, we often follow up on another reporter's original story. It all depends on who is least busy to do it. Besides that, George Durant shared the assignment with me. I simply got to write the main story."

"It was a big fire and took everything the Mollisons had. I should think there would be a great deal to write about. And I should think you are the one to do it."

A follow-up story of this sort usually was routine, nothing more. Unless there was foul play involved. And of course there was that, as far as she knew.

"We'll follow up on it. There will be a lot of volunteer labor in helping Don rebuild, and no doubt there will be great involvement from the farming community. They always help each other in disasters. I'm the likely candidate for writing the follow-ups on my agriculture page. We'll see what happens."

He arced over the table, his eyes gleaming.

"Don't let them take anything from you, Miss Merrill. Whatever is rightfully yours, you fight for it. Women get passed over. I don't mean just this story. I mean when it comes to promotions and pay increases. Do you get bonuses?"

"No. Well, yes, we do get a bit extra at Christmas. It's not much, though. But every little bit helps, especially at that time of year."

"Hmm. Harry should do better by you."

"It's not Harry. It's the publisher, Jason Moon. He's generous about letting us have free newspaper space, like my ag page. There's no advertising on it. But he is known to be a bit tightfisted when it comes to salaries. I do all right, however, and he pays all of us reporters the same scale, men and women alike. And I really do love the work. I meet so many interesting people." She paused and looked into his eyes. "Like you."

He held her stare and slowly smiled. "You're a charmer, I think."

Why had she said that? It was too bold. But, she really wanted to tell him that he was a heart-stealer, and that she was in danger of losing hers to him. Every nerve in her body screamed to be caressed. She was sure she must be red all over, she felt so hot. His blue eyes studied her until she couldn't breathe. Could he possibly feel the same attraction for her that she felt for him? She was spared further embarrassment when he got up and walked to the rail.

"Would you mind dropping me off at a friend's farm? It's time I took my dogs out for a run. Before the rain."

"I'd be happy to," she said with a pang of disappointment.

CHAPTER 12

❦

The magic soon passed, and Sheldon delivered the enigmatic David Bradford to the farm where his friend Bill Ferguson, carrying a can of beer and wearing nothing but a pair of khaki shorts and sandals, emerged from a side porch. He greeted them with gusto.

"Hey, Davey boy. Wondered where you'd gone to. Who have we here? A new girl friend, huh?" His wink was exaggerated.

With the engine idling, Sheldon waited while Bradford exited the car.

"This is Sheldon Merrill. You know, the reporter who writes that agricultural page for the *Westburgh Press*. She's writing up a piece about the hospital unit. I've just been showing her around Ashton."

"Welcome to Shantytown, Sheldon." Ferguson wiped his hand on his shorts and shoved it through the open window. She guessed that this was not his first beer of the day. He was obviously joking, for his farm spread would not be mistaken for a Shantytown. The house was a charming blend of stone and wood construction. The long, single story main barn was abutted by a horse paddock. That and other outbuildings were neat and gleaming, as if it had all just been painted white.

"Nice to meet you," she said, putting her hand in his and fighting a grimace at his too-firm grip. "You raise horses, do you?"

"That's right." Tall, slender, and sun-browned as the fields behind him, Ferguson seemed to think everything was a joke. He laughed lustily. "I raise trotters for light-harness racing."

"This is the first horse farm I've seen here in the county. I'm running a series on diversified farming right now, to show that more than dairy farming goes on here. Yours would be an excellent example. Would you be willing to have it featured some week soon?"

"Great. Come over any time and do a story about Shantytown. I'm usually here. I'll give you a guided tour and we can have a beer. Well, hell, how about stopping now and tipping a cold one with ol' Davey and me?"

The man's genial personality made up for his lack of good looks. The bent nose and deep scar at the side of his left eye indicated he could have been a boxer in his younger years. Or maybe he had simply been in one too many bar brawls.

"No, thanks. I have things to do. But thanks anyway. And I will take you up on an interview about the horses."

She put the car in reverse and backed out. At the end of the drive, she looked back and saw Ferguson throw his arm around Bradford's shoulders as they walked toward the side porch, their heads close together.

She swallowed hard. Could it be that the gossips were right, that David Bradford was gay? And why should it matter to her? Why should she have this sick feeling in the pit of her stomach? She had no designs on the man. And she certainly had no reason to judge him. Didn't Bradford himself say that he believed in living his life his own way?

She drove on toward Westburgh trying to sort out her own feelings, asking herself hard questions. Maybe she had taken a liking to him, but did she really think she had a chance for a life with someone like Bradford? Why was she doing this to herself? Where did this fantasy come from? In all the years she had been interviewing people, she had never felt attracted to a man like this. She had always kept a cool head and maintained a professional attitude.

Besides, Bradford was an arrogant man, the type who believed that he was totally right and that he could control others with his money. Despite his bedroom eyes, he dismissed as easily as he invited. How much would he have talked with her had she not been writing a profile on him?

"Not at all, you dope," Sheldon said aloud. "Come back to earth and stop with the fantasies. Right now."

They were of different worlds. She was a working woman and always would be. She wanted it that way. To even indulge in a dream of marrying a rich man was folly.

If she were to compare Bradford to George, she would have to be honest and admit that George had a far better, sweeter disposition. He showed real concern. He treated people fairly and he allowed others to make mistakes. Even though Bradford seemed to care about humanity, he did it in a vainglorious manner, investing money where he would be honored. Even his apparent eccentricities served his purpose. He liked being able to shock and to displease, certain no one would dare suggest that he do something differently. He pushed people around, like putting a stinking gas can in her car and having her prepare his lunch. And firing poor Hugh Webster because he asked to be paid more for shoveling out that long drive.

No. There was no way that she would ever be able to live with a man like that, no matter how much sexual magnetism he generated. Hadn't she already experienced that kind of love? Joe was just that sort, too, demanding and taking, but giving nothing. Never again. She'd settle for the Georges of the world, without the surprises and heartaches.

Sighing in relief, telling herself that she had been sensible to analyze the situation and recognize her own temporary weakness, Sheldon once again drove off the main route onto the road leading to the Mollison farm, feeling only slightly uplifted. Now that she had brought herself out of the clouds, she told herself, there was work to do. She wanted to see what was going on at the farm and find out if she could help in some way. She also wanted to know if they had learned about the body yet. The Bradford mysteries were interesting, but not nearly so critical as this horrible scene, nor were her personal feelings at all important. She would survive her own stupidity.

It didn't surprise her to see Harry's station wagon among the many vehicles parked in the field when she drove up the driveway. When she got out of her car she was struck by the noises of bulldozers working out back and hammers pounding. Only a blackened shell remained of the house, and nothing of the barn, just the silos, standing tall and straight and colorful behind all the destruction. The smell of dying embers pressed in on her. Her footsteps crunched across dry grass to where a group of women had set up a long table under a big old maple tree. It looked like a church supper with casseroles, a ham, salads, breads, cakes, pies, and various soft drinks. The colorful group and the bountiful table contrasted sharply against the background of the gaping ruin of the house and the flattened and buried remains of the barn.

"Come on over, Shellie," she heard Pat call. Picking her way around the little groups where conversations centered on who was going to do what the next day, Sheldon reached Pat, still wearing the clothes she had on yesterday at the fire. However, the light had been turned on in her eyes again, as if making the adjustment from having a fine home and business to having nothing were an every day occurrence. What a brick she is, Sheldon thought.

"We're beginning to get organized," she said. "Don and I will go to my parents' tonight when we get through here. They're already starting to rebuild the barn. Isn't this something? An old-fashioned barn raising, complete with food from the ladies." She swept her hand in a semi circle at all the activity. "How fortunate we are to have so many good friends."

Sheldon agreed, and they continued to talk about the contributions of various retailers in Westburgh, lumber and hardware, windows, roofing.

"Even the John Deere dealer said we could have a new tractor at a forty percent discount. I couldn't believe it. Everyone has been so kind and generous. At first I cried over our loss. Now I have to cry over the outpouring of help. It's just too much, really."

Sheldon felt herself misting up, too, and took a second to collect herself.

"Well," she said, "this will certainly make a good story. I saw Harry O'Brien's car down the lane. Has he been interviewing?"

"Yes, as a matter of fact, he has. I was surprised to see him and not you."

"Believe it or not, yesterday, today and tomorrow are my days off this week."

"Then you had to come here yesterday and work."

"Yes. So inconsiderate of you to have a fire on my day off." Sheldon gave Pat a friendly shove and they laughed. Sheldon was glad to hear Pat so revived and ready to face the challenges that lay ahead.

"I'll try to do better next time," Pat said. A gray-haired woman extricated herself from a group of women and came toward the pair. As she approached, Pat asked, "Have you met my mother, Shellie?"

"No, I haven't."

"Mom, I'd like you to meet Shellie Merrill of the *Westburgh Press*. Shellie, this is my mother, Bev Stoner."

An older version of Pat held out her hand and warmly held Sheldon's while she said,

"I'm so happy to meet you finally. I did hear you speak at our Grange meeting one night, but you had gone before I could come out of the kitchen to say hello."

"I'm always in too much of a hurry. It's good to meet you. Pat looks just like you."

"Everyone says the same, but I don't see it."

After they finished chatting about the family, Sheldon said, "This must be a nightmare for you, too, a horrible re-enactment of your own fire."

"Oh yes, it is. It's so devastating to lose everything you own. But the one good thing about both fires is that no lives were lost. All the rest can be replaced. It certainly is *deja vu*, however, right down to the start of it in the barn, where we had explosives stored, also. And we couldn't get our livestock out, either. But we came back. Just the same as Pat and Don will. Takes a lot of hard work, but that's the nature of farming. Hard work. It either kills you young or toughens you to live to a ripe old age."

"Did you ever find out what caused your fire back then?"

"No, not really. We suspected arson. We'd fired a hand after we caught him stealing petty cash that I kept in the office. We just felt that he had set the fire out of revenge, but nothing could ever be proved. The young man we suspected had a sound alibi." She shrugged her square shoulders. "And it may not have been set. We'll never know."

Sheldon scowled. So apparently the Mollisons didn't know about the body.

"I hate to go, but I see Harry O'Brien over there by the workmen. I should speak to him before he gets away. It was nice meeting you Mrs. Stoner. Pat, I thought I'd make a plea for donations on my ag. page. You wouldn't mind, would you?"

"Of course we can use all the help we can get, but I'm not sure. It's like begging."

"Not if it comes from me. And it's something I'd really like to do for you."

Pat nodded reluctantly. "Do what you wish then."

Declining Beverly Stoner's invitation to stay for supper with everyone, Sheldon sought out Harry.

"I knew you were here," she said on approaching her boss. "I saw your wagon. Have you learned anything new?"

Harry took her by the elbow and steered her toward the driveway, out of earshot of the other men who were building a large frame.

"No, nothing new," he said. "As a matter of fact, the coroner wouldn't confirm that a body was found. I reminded him of a couple of favors I had done for him, but he still said he couldn't say yes or no to my questions. I guess the sheriff holds more over him than I do. That's politics for you."

"So what are you going to do?" Sheldon couldn't disguise the worry she felt. If he printed the story, they could be in real trouble should it turn out that there was no body, and the newspaper's credibility rating would be in the sewer. And she might be out of a job. Maybe it would be better to tell Harry right now who had tipped her off. At least, that way he would be able to judge better for himself whether he should run with it.

She didn't like to betray Gene Luce that way, hated to break her word, but she also didn't like bearing sole responsibility for the possible backlash. At least if Harry knew who the source was and still ran the story, he would be better prepared for a negative outcome.

Apparently sensing her reticence, he said, "I'll run the story if you're quite sure you can trust your source. You really believe that there was a murder? No one I talked with mentioned a body being found."

She could trust Harry to keep quiet if she told him about Luce, even though she had misgivings about doing so. But right now was the time to do it. He should be the one to judge the advisability of going ahead with the story.

"Harry, I'm not..." She didn't get a chance to finish. Bellowing from his car as he slammed the door was Sheriff Beaulieu, now running full-tilt toward them.

"Harry, you son-of-a-bitch. I want a word with you." The man's voice carried across the field.

Harry's mouth twitched in a suppressed smile. "Looks like we've got our answer."

Panting and sweating, Beaulieu waved his fist as he approached Harry.

"What the hell do you think you're doing? What do you mean by calling the coroner on a Saturday morning and asking questions about classified information?"

So there was a body. Sheldon wanted to laugh out loud as she listened to the exchange.

"When *should* I ask him about classified information?"

"Don't play dumb with me. I don't need that smart mouth of yours. Classified information is just that, not public, and you damned well know it."

"Classified information? What are you talking about, Beaulieu?" Harry stood square-footed in front of the much taller man, in a relaxed but defiant manner, almost inviting the sheriff to come at him. He was a scrappy Irishman who was proud of his wrestling record in high school. He feared no one.

"Wipe that goddamned smile off your fat face. You know what classified information. Where'd you get it? Huh? Who told you?"

"Told me what? Is there something that you haven't said here? You want to tell me something now, Beaulieu?"

Lines deepened around the sheriff's mouth. He swiped at a bead of sweat that slowly trickled into the corner of his eye. So dilated with anger were his eyes that they appeared to be black. Had she cared, Sheldon would have feared he might have a heart attack.

"Goddam your hide. I want to know who leaked it. How did you get it?"

The man could barely keep his fists at his sides. His face was red all the way into the bald spot at the part of his graying hair. It was easy to see how a man with a temper like this might beat up a prisoner who had no recourse for help.

"You'll have to spell it out for me, Sheriff. Tell me what it is that I'm supposed to know about."

Harry's eyes narrowed, but they held a challenge and a sparkle that revealed the pleasure he was getting out of the sheriff's dilemma.

"Damn you. I don't know how you got it, but you won't get away with this. I'll get you for this. No one steps on my toes and gets away with it. You may think you got ahead of me on this one, but you haven't. I'll take care of it."

"Seems to me that now would be a good time for you to give me a statement that I can use in my story tomorrow. That is, if there is a story, as you seem to suggest. Is that it? *Is* there a story, sheriff? Is there something that I'd be writing about, something to do with this fire?"

"You...you bastard. I don't know who leaked this, but I intend to find out. Someone is going to pay for this, and pay good. You don't quote me, either. You hear me on that? Don't you put any of this in your damned paper. And you hear me good." He jabbed a finger into Harry's shoulder. "I'm coming after you. I'll sue you. I'll see that you and your gossip rag both go bankrupt before we're through. I'll put a stop to this yellow journalism. That's a promise."

"Aren't you being a bit melodramatic? There may be a story here. I won't say there isn't. If there is, then it's mine as well as television's. I'm sure there wouldn't be a cover-up, now would there, Beaulieu? You wouldn't try to squeeze the *Press* out of the picture by calling a news conference just after we'd published, would you?"

"So I'm calling a news conference."

"Without letting me know?"

"I'd have gotten around to calling you."

"Monday afternoon, no doubt, after our paper was printed."

Beaulieu's mouth worked, but he said nothing. His eyes began to take in the scope of the scene, moving from Harry to the builders who had stopped hammering and were staring at the two men, to the table and the women there who had also stopped to observe, and back to Harry. Though they had never mentioned the body, it was there between them, along with the knowledge that these people would later recall this angry exchange and realize that the sheriff had held back initial reports of the discovery once the story appeared in the *Press* on Sunday.

"Actually," he said, his jaw set, and his eyes now studying the ground where they stood, "I was gong to call a conference for tomorrow morning at ten. This is your notice of it."

"I'll be there. At city hall?"

"Of course at city hall."

Watching him stride off, his hands fisted at his sides, Harry said, "Now there's an unhappy man. We may not be able to break the story first now, but at least we have the satisfaction of keeping the sheriff honest, if that's really possible. As a matter of fact, this little confrontation gives me an idea for my Sunday column. I'll give our readers another little insight into the way their elected official handles business."

"Do you think he'll sue you?"

"Don't know, don't care. The newspaper has a first-rate attorney for all that business."

"What about the Mollisons? I don't think they know about the body. It's going to be quite a shock when they hear about it tomorrow."

"Yeah. You're right. I'll take care of that. I'll go tell them now."

"Good. And I'm going home and do some laundry. See you Monday."

※　　　　※　　　　※

Finding the apartment stuffy, Sheldon began opening windows. She was humming no particular tune, just happy notes. The uncertainty was gone. She could breathe easier. They really had found a body and Gene Luce hadn't lied to her. Of course Harry couldn't be first with the story now, but at least the *Press* wouldn't be a day late with it, either, thanks to the sheriff's legendary temper. What a jerk he was.

She wanted to call George with the good news, but first she'd get supper. She would have stayed to eat at the farm, but not only was she not hungry then, but she badly needed to do some of her chores, which so far this weekend had been neglected. Spaghetti would do.

Before the water was boiling, she heard someone coming up the stairs, and she looked out the open window to see who was there. Seeing her landlord, she hurried to the door and opened it for him.

"Spence. Hi. What's up?" she called.

"Hate to bother you, Shellie. Just wondered if you really meant your offer for supper?"

"Sure. Of course I did. Come on in. As a matter of fact, I'm making spaghetti. I hope you like it."

"One of my favorites."

When he came in, Sheldon noted the dark sags under his eyes and a cover of speckled whiskers over the lower half of his face.

"You look tired, Spence. Are you all right?"

"I'm okay."

"Missing Julia, are you?"

"Funny how we get into habits that we never think about until change comes about. Hard to sleep alone now. Can I give you a hand there?"

"No. Just sit down and rest. This is a one-butt kitchen, as my southern friend used to say."

He nodded. "Small but serviceable. Julia and I worked hard to design it in a practical manner and then get it ready. You keep everything looking good. You're a good tenant." He paused, then said, "You're a good woman," with such tenderness that Sheldon quickly glanced at him. His heavy lidded look sent a chill through her. She turned to put spaghetti into the boiling water, wondering what had come over Spence. He was never anything but open, honest, full of energy and wit. This introspection of his made her uneasy.

"Well, I'm not home much more than to sleep most of the time so it's not too hard to keep the house in order. Have you heard from Julia today?"

"No. She's busy, I guess. Probably shopping for baby things. She keeps quiet now."

Such an odd thing for him to say. Something in his flat tone just didn't ring true. Like maybe Julia hadn't been in touch with him at all. Sheldon once again felt a gnawing suspicion about her landlord. It just couldn't be that he was a murderer and arsonist. She knew it couldn't. Yet his manner, his staring off into space, his lackluster speech, all pointed to something more than just Julia's being away from him for a few weeks. Lord, how she hoped she was wrong.

"When did you say you expect her back?"

"Not sure. Sometime after the baby comes. She'll want to stay longer, I guess."

"And when's the baby due?"

"Soon. I don't know. She didn't tell me the date."

He was being evasive. Why? He must know more than he was saying. He and Julia were close as pages in a book. Why was he acting this way?

She finished getting the spaghetti and salad ready while Spence looked out the window, not offering to initiate further conversation. That fact alone made Sheldon even more uneasy. It wasn't like him to be so withdrawn. And look at him. Not even shaved today.

When all was on the table, she said, "I have some red wine, if you'd like."

"Fine."

She got the wine from the refrigerator and poured, then sat opposite Spence.

"I guess I eat more of this than anything else. This and hamburgers," she said, stabbing at light conversation, unwilling to think further about the possible guilt of this man at her table. "It's the one thing I managed to learn to make. My mother, to this day, says she's a failure as a mother because she couldn't teach me to cook and bake."

She laughed. Spence managed a faint smile.

"Julia's a real good cook," Sheldon said. The words just spilled out even though she had meant to cheer Spence. She wanted to know what had happened. "But then, Julia does everything well. She's a very talented lady. You must be proud of her."

Spence set his fork on his plate and pushed his chair back. "This was a mistake. I shouldn't have bothered you for supper. Please excuse me."

"Don't leave. Please. Finish your supper. If I said something, I'm sorry."

"You didn't say anything. I'm not really hungry. I have to leave, that's all."

"You seem upset over Julia being gone. But she'll be back…what did you say? In a month at the most?"

"That's just it, Sheldon. Julia isn't coming back."

As the door closed and Spence pounded down over the steps, Sheldon sat perfectly still, stunned.

Julia isn't coming back. No! It can't be. You didn't kill her. Please God, don't let it be true. Don't let Spence be a murderer.

CHAPTER 13

❀

Beaten, shot, left to be blown apart. The mental picture of the victim's death sickened Sheldon. Anyone who could inflict that unspeakable pain and suffering had to be aberrant in the most horrible sense, full of rage, bestial, perhaps a sexual psychopath. The description just didn't fit Spence. He showed the greatest respect for Julia and others, never told an off-color joke, but was happy and full of lively anecdotes over almost anything that happened in his daily routine. He loved flowers, for goodness sake. How could anyone who loved flowers the way he did be a murderer?

Yet he had said Julia wouldn't be back.

Sheldon moaned. "Oh God. What will I do?"

She couldn't go to the authorities and express her fears about Spence. What if she were wrong? Another thought startled her as much as to think that Spence might be a killer. Was it possible that Julia had simply left Spence?

After all her suspicions about Spence, now it occurred to her that there could be more to the story, a completely different angle. She had jumped to conclusions. Circumstantial evidence certainly was against him, but that's all it was. Circumstantial.

She felt like a sleuth trying to put together pieces of a crime and come up with the real killer, only she was missing almost all the pieces. She must look at all sides of the picture, like writing a well-balanced newspaper story. Of course, she told herself, just because a couple has a fight and separates doesn't mean that the man kills the woman. Not always. She had never seen the two of them really argue. Julia sometimes shouted at Spence. Sheldon had heard her yell at him in the garden a few times, but it was never an argument. Spence always did whatever his wife wanted him to do and usually did it with a condescending smile.

Then again, in the hours when Sheldon wasn't around maybe they did argue. Who would know? She hadn't even been aware that Julia was gone until Spence told her yesterday.

So where was Julia? Alive at her sister's or dead in the morgue?

Never one to lose her appetite over worrisome matters, Sheldon continued eating. She would just have to wait until more information came in from the coroner. To sound the alarm about her landlord would be unfair if he was innocent.

It was after the last pot was washed and put away that Sheldon started toward the telephone. And then it hit her. Just suppose Spence was the murderer. Then she was living in the same house with a very dangerous man! Now her mind once more played over the possibilities, and she began again to question Julia's fate. Sitting at her desk, she stared at the phone. The more she thought about it, the more she felt that she should let someone know her suspicions in case something happened to herself. If for some crazy reason Spence had killed Julia, and he thought Sheldon knew it, he might...what? Kill her? Hurt her? But why? Why would Spence come after her? He didn't have anything against her. On the other hand, a man crazed enough to kill in a brutal, savage manner and then set a disastrous fire might not need much aggravation. Society's murderers didn't announce their intent to kill or the fact that they had killed. Obviously they weren't always recognizable, just ordinary-looking citizens mingling with other ordinary citizens. Only after a heinous crime was committed did others begin to think about possible signs, a retrospective look at the killer that generally produced some earlier indications, if only someone had been looking for them.

Maybe she was thinking with her emotions, but Sheldon remembered the strange look he gave her when he said she was a good woman. It was suggestive and so unlike Spence who doted on Julia. Or at least Sheldon thought he doted on Julia.

She knew she must talk it over with someone. She dialed.

George sounded surprised to hear her voice. "There have been some developments in the murder. I'd like to talk with you. Are you busy? Could I come over now?"

"Developments? How so?"

"Well, I'd like to tell you in person."

"You bet, okay. Sure, come on along. How about stopping and picking up some cookies, or something? I have the coffee to go with them."

When she arrived at his ranch style home on Outer Maple Street, just outside Westburgh's city limits, she handed him a bag of groceries.

"Didn't know for sure what you'd want to snack on, so I picked up some chips and dips as well as two kinds of cookies, chocolate and oatmeal."

"Guess I won't have to shop for a week," he quipped. Then he did a double-take, stepping back to get a good look at her. "Good God. Look at you. That's some sexy hairdo. You should always keep it short like that. You look terrific."

She smiled with genuine pride. She had secretly hoped he'd notice, and he did.

"I'm glad you like it." Especially since she'd had it done for his sake.

"I do, I do like your do." He started for the kitchen and she followed. "I've made real coffee," he said, "not that instant near-beer stuff."

"Good. That's what I like, too."

He poured coffee into two mugs and set them on the table.

"You want to sit here or in the living room?"

"This will do fine." She sat down and pulled a cup toward her, then reached for the oatmeal cookies, opened the cellophane wrap, and took out one for herself, shoving the package toward him.

"I like chocolate myself," he said. "So what's up? Something new you said in the murder?"

His intensity seemed more than just interest in what she had to say about the murder, as if something were on the tip of his tongue to tell her, something exciting and important.

"Yes. At least now we know there was a body and that the information I received was correct."

"Was there question about it?" His eyebrows shot up, and Sheldon felt a pang of guilt for not having confided in him that there could be a problem with the story she'd received.

"Well, yes, in a way. I was quite sure it was okay, but there was a slight question in my mind. You know how it is. If you don't actually see something yourself and take second-hand information, you're never positively sure it's the way it was told to you."

He nodded but studied his cup for a second before saying, "Sure. So now you know. How come?"

"This afternoon I stopped at the Mollisons' and found Harry there. While we were talking, Sheriff Beaulieu drove in and stormed toward us, raving mad. Harry had tried to get confirmation from the coroner before writing the story, but the coroner wouldn't say one way or the other whether there was a body, even. So, again, we weren't totally sure we were on firm ground. Anyway, as soon as the sheriff lit into Harry over questioning the coroner about classified information, as he called it, we knew. He actually threatened Harry with a lawsuit if Harry quoted him."

"Good old Beaulieu."

"You should see the place, George. In less than a day all these volunteers have gathered and started rebuilding already. They've got all the dead animals buried and the barn leveled and ready for the new one. It looks like a church bazaar. The women have brought food for all the workers. It's so great to see that kind of compassion and cooperation. Anyway, all these people stopped working and just stood around listening and watching. It almost looked like the sheriff might hit Harry for a while, then he noticed the people watching and he backed off and said he'd hold a news conference tomorrow morning."

"So your story was validated but we lost the scoop."

"Like Harry said, at least he kept the sheriff honest."

They both laughed at that one. Sipping her coffee, Sheldon took notice of the house.

It was a roomy, open design, predominantly beige and brown in decor with colorful touches, like the orange counter tops and the forties aluminum kitchen table with yellow vinyl-covered chairs. She knew that he had a workshop at the back of his garage and made furniture, and presumed that the pine tables in the living area were his craftsmanship. Most impressive to Sheldon were the neatness and the clean-smelling atmosphere, something she would not have attributed to George considering his generally careless personal appearance. She remembered Joe's apartment, with its ratty furnishings and wet-dog smell, and yet Joe himself was always immaculate when it came to his person.

She turned her attention to George as he reached for his second chocolate cookie.

"There is something that I think I need to tell someone. I hesitate doing it, but in case there should be a problem later, it's probably the thing to do."

"What is it? What kind of problem?" He pulled himself straighter and leaned across the table, his brown eyes intense as they studied her.

"I'm probably being stupid. I mean, I have no real reason to think something's wrong, only just some circumstantial coincidences that probably all have a reasonable explanation. I don't know. But ever since the fire, I haven't been able to shake this feeling. And now it's stronger than ever."

She drummed her fingers on the table, trying to imagine just how ridiculous this was going to sound.

"Hey, come on. You got my attention. So give. What's the problem?"

"Well…" she sighed. "There are certain indications that my landlord may be the murderer."

"Your landlord! Why?"

"Do you know him at all?"

"Warren Spencer, isn't he?" Sheldon nodded. "The electrician. Yeah, I know him. I had him wire my workshop. Seemed like a good enough guy. Charged me a fair price, I recall."

"When Ken Mollison built his milk house, Spence went to him to see if he could get the contract to wire it. Ken told him that he would wire it himself and then have it inspected. Pat told me that Spence was very upset over that. And that was not at all like him. I don't know. When I heard about it, I began to think about the fact that Spence lives just a half mile from the Mollison farm, if you go by way of the old woods road that runs behind the house. He certainly had opportunity for access to the place without being observed."

She could tell by his silence that George thought she had a very flimsy argument for thinking her landlord guilty of murder.

"Then last evening when I got home, Spence came out to meet me, and he said his wife Julia had gone to be with her sister who's expecting a baby very soon. He seemed down-in-the-mouth, and when I suggested that he could go and be with her, since it's only in Syracuse, he adamantly put that suggestion down."

She paused for another drink of coffee, observing George. He looked uncomfortable, shifting in his chair, tipping his spoon end-over-end. She almost wished she hadn't come to tell him this.

"I told him that if he became lonely, I'd be glad to fix him a meal. Well, he came upstairs after I got home today and took me up on the offer. He looked like he had slept in his clothes, if he slept at all. He was unshaven. He's usually neat as a pin and always happy. But tonight he was moody, didn't talk much. And when we started to eat, I asked if he missed Julia. He just got up out of his chair and said that he'd made a mistake coming for supper. He went to the door and I pleaded with him to sit down and finish his meal. I said something to the effect that Julia would be back home in a few weeks. Well, then he gave me a real strange look and he said, 'Julia isn't coming back.'"

George half smiled. "So you think he did her in?"

"I don't know." Sheldon lowered her face to her hands and rubbed her temples. She wished she knew for sure. She wished she didn't have this gut feeling that Spence was guilty as sin. She wished she hadn't told George.

"I just don't know," she said with a sigh. "All I know is that Spence isn't acting at all like his normal self, he had motive for setting a fire at the Mollisons', and his wife is gone. I don't want to believe anything like this of Spence. I really don't. But why would he have jumped up from the table like that at mention of Julia? Why isn't she coming back?"

"Did you ask him that question?"

"No. He was out the door before I could."

"Maybe you should before getting all upset and trying to pin a murder on him."

"I'm not trying to pin a murder on him," Sheldon said, unable to tamp down her annoyance at his suggestion. "I'm not. I came here to tell you this for one reason only. If anything should happen to me, I wanted someone to know all this and that I had a concern over it. I can't picture Spence as a murderer. He loved Julia, I'm certain of it. They're a wonderful couple. They do everything together, and they grow beautiful, prize-winning roses. They renovated that house I live in. I always considered them to be the perfect example of a happy marriage. And then all this came up. And Julia's gone…somewhere."

"Calm down, Shellie. I spoke out of turn. I understand now. I see what you're getting at. If you feel that you may be in danger, real or imagined, why don't you take my guest room for a while? I'd be glad to have you here, you know."

She looked into those warm brown eyes and felt like a fool. Of all people, why had she flared up at George? He was as gentle as a lamb and he was absolutely right. She was trying to pin a murder on a man who was most likely as innocent as a babe.

"He gave me a rather suggestive look, too," she said, still trying to justify her cause.

"How's that? Spence gave you a suggestive look?"

"While I was getting supper. He spoke of how they had designed the apartment and said that I was a good tenant. Then he said, 'You're a good woman, Sheldon,' in a throaty whisper, and his eyes definitely carried a message that wasn't fatherly. I was embarrassed. And again, it was so uncharacteristic of Spence."

George stared at her for a second, then burst out laughing. "Excuse me, Shel. I can't help it. You get a compliment and you fall to pieces over it. You *are* a good woman. I don't blame him for saying that. He might have added that you're a very attractive woman, too, and I still wouldn't fault him for that. Now if he'd said 'Let's play cozy in the bedroom,' I'd kill him. But to state one of your obvious qualities is not tantamount to a sexual advance."

"You'd kill him?"

"A figure of speech, Shel. I'm not your killer."

"Of course not. I just thought it odd that you'd get upset over something like that."

Of late, she'd noticed that George had been making remarks similar to that as if he might have feelings for her, but like he said, she was quick to become embarrassed, to read the wrong message in such words. If she were honest with herself, she'd know that his kindness, the offer of the room, were not unusual for him. He was good to everyone.

But his next words almost undid her.

"I care for you, Shellie. Don't you know that yet?" His soft tone was so sincere she suddenly froze, her thoughts muddled, her feelings scattering like pick-up sticks.

"I...I...don't...No. I didn't...I don't know that." Sheldon concentrated on pushing crumbs around one spot on the table, unable to meet George's gaze.

"Dee told me you had a lover before moving here. Is he the reason that you don't trust men?"

"I didn't know that I don't trust men. What makes you think that?"

"You're always so defensive when it comes to compliments from a man. Like with your landlord. He's a decent man. Probably just admires you, and that's okay. Men are allowed to admire women, you know."

"I might not have thought anything of it if he hadn't said afterward that Julia wouldn't be coming back."

"That could mean that she has left him. Women have been known to do that."

Sheldon felt a prick of guilt. Poor George. His wife had left him when he was in the service overseas. It must have been a traumatic experience to be so far away and unable to talk with her to see if they could iron out their problems.

"Yes. I know. Like yours. You never mention your former wife. Do you miss her still?"

"Hell no. She was only nineteen when I married her. I must admit that back then I thought a good-looking woman was all I wanted. We hadn't been together a month when I realized how wrong I was. She was the quintessential beautiful but dumb blond. I enlisted in the service to get away from her and her constant prattle and whining."

He got up and refilled his coffee cup. Sheldon shook her head when he held up the pot, questioning a refill for her. She should be ashamed of her feeling of relief that he wasn't still carrying a torch for his ex-wife. After the let-down from her childish fantasy over David Bradford, however, she would be mortified if George was simply being nice to her, or worse yet, wanted to have an affair, all the while still in love with his ex.

"I had a low-paying job then, as a carpenter's assistant." He laughed. "I should say, a lower paying job. I'd come home tired, anxious to sit down to a hot meal, and she'd be all dressed up in a new outfit, ready to go out to a restaurant and then dancing. I'm not against eating out, mind you. But we were poor. Finally, I told her that if she wanted clothes, going out to restaurants, cosmetics, and all that stuff, she would have to go to work. I didn't make enough to cover it all. She carried on and said she was too nervous to work, that I was just being mean to her. Actually she screamed that at me. She was a screamer. Didn't have enough vocabulary or mental power for a normal discussion. That was when I decided that a war with guns was better than a wife with the gimmies."

He returned to the table and sat down, momentarily far away. "I was wrong, of course. There's no hell worse than war."

Sheldon had seen that haunted look of his before, as if he had just seen a fatal accident. Only war was no accident. And he had been obliged to kill other men not so much different from himself. To kill for the grand cause, whatever that was. She could only imagine what a horror that must be, to do it daily and to see no end to the carnage from one day to the next. No one had the right to take another's life. War was no exception in her view. Why couldn't world leaders negotiate without killing the innocent to get what they wanted?

"It was a relief when I got the letter telling me she was getting a divorce. For once in my life I said a prayer of thanks to God. I've been careful ever since. Haven't carried on very meaningful relationships."

"At least you've had some. I haven't even had one relationship, meaningful or otherwise," she said with a nervous laugh.

"Did you get burned so badly?"

"You might say that. We were actually making wedding plans. Then one day I was covering the county fair, just out of town. The fairgrounds are across from a seedy motel. While I was snapping pictures I happened to look toward the motel, and I saw my fiancee coming out of one of the rooms. He didn't see me with all the activity going on. He got into his car and drove off, and a few minutes later a redhead came sashaying out of the same room and got into a car and drove off in the same direction. If they thought they were being discreet by not coming out of the room together, they were pretty stupid. I saw Joe that night and confronted him with what I'd seen. He just laughed, didn't even try to lie. Said he had a right to a fling or two before we were married. That's all it meant, he said. Just a fling."

She rubbed her forehead to hide her moist eyes. She still felt the bitter hurt she had felt then. "How could he be so callous? We were committed to each other, I thought. Then when I told a very close friend of mine about it, she said that she had heard other stories about his escapades. That's when I broke off our engagement and answered an ad for a reporting position here in Westburgh. Two years ago."

"Well, you see? Maybe he broke your heart, but there has been a whole lot of good come from it. Besides, you deserve better than that. He was a fool. Not all men treat women badly. Most men would know when they're well off with a good woman, like you. They don't go looking around for new thrills any more. I know I wouldn't."

He took her hand. Her heart jumped and started pounding so hard she was sure he must hear it. She wanted to believe that someone really did care for her. She would welcome a close relationship. At the same time, she was apprehensive. It had been a long time since breaking up with Joe, her first and only lover, and she wasn't sure she could feel total relaxation in a sexual encounter. She hadn't been able to with him, and she had thought then that he would be the only man in her life, ever. Even his crudities hadn't deterred her, but now she saw him for what he was, self-absorbed and callous.

"You're afraid, aren't you?" George pulled his chair closer and began to rub her back in a calming gesture. "It's a terrible thing to be betrayed by a loved one. Makes you think twice before plunging into another affair."

"You understand that, don't you? I mean, I really am unworldly in the sense of lovers' trysts, and whatever."

His closeness, his woodsy essence combined with Old Spice, and the warmth of his body next to her arm raised her own body heat to an unbearable high. She leaned back against his arm and let him pull her toward him. His lips brushed hers. When his bristly mustache tickled her nose, she giggled and pulled back, but not for long. Like magnets, their lips joined once more and as he pressed harder, she sighed. His tongue touched hers, gently, not intruding. She liked that. She had never liked Joe's wet, tongue-thrusting kisses.

The kiss ended and he stayed with his face against hers, rubbing slowly. His arms pulled her to the edge of her chair and wrapped about her. Lord, he was a sweet person. It felt so good to be held and to have her arms around his body, to feel the closeness of another human being. There were no sharp edges with George, whether he was talking, or laughing, or telling a joke. And especially not now as he held her and comforted her. His gentling melted her. She knew she could easily be led to the bedroom at this moment. In fact, she burned to go there. Should she say so? Wasn't it his place to say the word? She wished she knew more about these things. The etiquette of love-making had not been her best subject.

"Shellie," he said softly in her ear. This would be it. She sensed what was coming next. She waited, barely breathing. She felt his hand move around to her breast and an "Oh," escaped her, as the kneading burned one continuous sensation from high point to low point in her body.

And as she anticipated the moment that he would suggest going to his bed to follow through with what he'd started, the telephone rang.

"Shit," she said under her breath. George pulled back and looked at her, his eyes twinkling. "I can't believe you said that."

"Neither can I."

Laughing, he got up and went to the wall phone over the counter. After the hellos, he said, "She's here, if you want to talk with her." Then his face turned serious. He looked across at Sheldon with a worried frown. "When…Where are you?…Yeah. We'll be right there."

"What?" Sheldon asked.

"It was Dee. She said fire trucks are at the *Press*. Apparently someone tried to burn the place down this evening."

※　　　　※　　　　※

Like an outdoor disco, red, yellow, and blue lights flashed from fire trucks, police cruisers, and an ambulance. Over the static of radios and the roar of engines, voices of the milling crowd sounded distant. The firemen were going in and out the back door, a single long hose snaking through the hallway, but there was no sign of smoke.

"Hi, Shellie, George. Over here." Waiting by the front door, Dee waved her hand to get their attention. As they jostled their way through the gathering sightseers, Sheldon wondered what prompted people to flock to fires and accidents. A month ago, she had been at an automobile accident, trying to get photos without actually looking at the body, as people jostled and shoved to get a better look at the mangled mass of steel and flesh. It had sickened her, but others seemed to take pleasure in the gore.

"How bad is it?" George asked as they reached Dee.

"Not too bad. Just a lot of smoke and water damage, except in Harry's office. Someone set fire on top of his desk, among all his papers. Of course, the fire sprinklers came on in the editorial room as well as his office, so our desks are soaked."

"We can go in?" Sheldon asked.

"Sure. Through the front. Come on."

"Uh-oh. Here come the Wicked Sisters." George nodded toward the edge of the crowd at the sidewalk. Sheldon and Dee moaned in unison. Before they could disappear inside, Janet stepped lively to reach them, all the while smoothing the front of her dress with both hands.

"Well, looks like someone wants us out of business. I hear the fire was set."

"It looks that way," Sheldon said. Now Candy was at Janet's side, looking as if she had just come from a ball, dressed in a pink linen suit with matching pink pumps.

"I don't see any flames. Is it bad?" Candy asked.

"No. Mostly water and smoke damage," Dee said.

"Well, and how are you feeling, Dee?" Janet had the triumphant expression of a cat holding down a live mouse. "I hear you had a rousing good time at the Bay last night."

"Oh, I'm fine, thanks," Dee said with a grin, as if she never felt better. "I got high as a kite, you know. Had a ball. You should try it sometime. Helps improve the disposition."

The three walked into the office, leaving Janet and Candy scowling and whispering.

"Now you've done it," Sheldon said. "They won't speak to us for a week."

"I hope not. It pays to be wicked, you see."

"I wouldn't know."

"Ha! You're a good one to talk. What about 'grey ghost'? Who said that, huh?"

Sheldon giggled, though she had been embarrassed when Janet walked in just as she was saying that the grey ghost must have taken to the skies since it was four o'clock and she hadn't returned from a luncheon fashion show. It was a moment that she re-lived with feelings of guilt. She meant no harm, but Sheldon knew she had sunk to the same spiteful depths of insult that she despised from the others. It bothered her that she wasn't above pettiness. When would she learn?

"Whew! This is a mess, all right," George said as they stood in the composing room doorway and surveyed their workplace. Dripping water sounded like a gentle indoor rain shower, pooling along the cement floor. The individual piles of newspapers at each desk were all soaked through as were baskets of current work.

"It smells like a goat shed," Sheldon said. She had walked inside just as far as Jon's desk and stopped. Harry nodded to the three as he talked with the fire chief outside his office door. Sheldon gave no sign of noticing Gene Luce, who stood behind the two men. When they finished talking, Harry came toward them.

"Well, the arsonist struck," he said. "Whoever he is, he's not too bright. Set a fire on my desk, right under the fire sprinklers."

"Did you lose much?" George asked.

"Burned all my papers. We've got a lot of water damage. At least out here it's all metal desks. The top of mine is scorched badly, but it can be refinished."

"Oh, my notes." Dee had gone to her desk. She held up a dripping notepad. "This is ruined. I've lost my interview with the senator." Carefully she opened the pages, one by one. "No. No, I can read this. I just need to dry it out. I'll take it home with me."

"Thank goodness I took my tape on David Bradford home with me, but the photo of Sean Backus must be ruined. It's on top in my wire basket." Sheldon was aware of the catch in her voice. The drama of the two days flooded over her with full force. A crazy murderer was far too close for comfort. What if Harry had been here when the arsonist came in? Would he have killed again? She looked at Harry and saw the worry lines in his forehead, his tight mouth.

"What will we do?" she asked, thinking out loud.

"Well, I've called for a professional cleaning crew to work in here tonight. I'll come in tomorrow. George, you come in, too. I'll let the women know they don't need to. Sheldon, you take an extra day off. Come in Tuesday. I already told Kate to bring in a couple of our big fans to help get rid of the smoke. It's suffocating in here."

"But, what about the killer? What's being done about him?"

"The police chief and the state police are working on that. As soon as they can identify the body, they'll have more to go on."

"Killer?" Dee asked. "Did you say killer?"

"I'll tell you outside," Sheldon said.

George reached out and touched Sheldon's arm. "What say? Shall we go? There's nothing we can do here."

"Yeah," Harry said. "All of you go. And watch yourselves. We don't know where this maniac will strike next."

As she passed Harry, Sheldon said quietly, "You be careful, too, Harry."

Outside, each one took deep breaths of the heavy night air, and coughed.

"I've had enough of fires to last a lifetime," George said.

"Me too." Sheldon coughed again. "Hey, there's Kate just driving up. Let's help her with the fans."

The crowd had dwindled to only half a half dozen lingerers, as everyone saw that the alarm was nothing spectacular and that the fire truck was getting ready to leave.

"Kate," Sheldon called. "Wait. We'll help." Dee and George followed to Kate's car. Sheldon turned to them and said, "Do you two mind taking these in while I have a word with Kate?"

When they'd gone, each carrying a window-sized fan by the handle, Sheldon slid into the front seat with Kate.

"I'm sorry that I forgot to go out to the kitchen this morning and talk with you. I was so preoccupied by all of this…" she waved her hand toward the office.

"I know. It's okay. You wanted to know about a nurse by the name of Karen?"

"Yes. Do you know one?"

"I knew a Karen Lockhart. She used to work at the hospital, worked there for about a year. Then she took a private nursing job, one that paid a whole lot better, I'm sure, than what she was making at the hospital. A real nice young woman. Very pretty. Very smart. And very caring. That's why she was hired by Miss Bradford."

"That's her. She's the nurse I've been trying to find out about."

"May I ask why?"

"I guess it's more out of curiosity than anything else. When I was at Miss Bradford's yesterday, she spoke of a nurse she'd had and said the name Karen. But then she looked as if she'd said something she shouldn't have. When I was leaving I asked her present nurse who Karen was, and she said she was told never to say the woman's name in that house. So I got nothing from her. And it intrigued me. Why would they be so secretive about her?"

"That's interesting." Kate, a petite woman and complete contrast to her husband, shifted her weight where she sat under the steering wheel, turning to face Sheldon squarely. "It may have something to do with her brother, David Bradford. You've interviewed him?"

"Yes. Two days ago. Found him quite…er…unusual."

Kate smiled. "Yes, very unusual. When Miss Bradford was in the hospital, her brother would come and raise holy hell. Nurses were running here and there to tend to all the things he said needed to be done for his sister. Karen returned from her vacation and took over with Miss Bradford, and all that complaining stopped. He seemed to be quite charmed by her."

"Oh, I see." Sheldon let her mind wander for a moment, thinking of the painting.

"I have no idea what went on, but everyone around the hospital was convinced that David Bradford was gay. Probably all the single nurses figured that if he wouldn't give one of them a second look, there had to be something wrong with him."

She laughed. "Whatever, all I know is that when Karen's shift was over, he'd be with her in the coffee shop. That went on for the all the rest of the time that Miss Bradford was there. And then when she went back home, Karen was hired as her personal nurse. Strange thing, though."

She looked thoughtful. Sheldon said, "What's strange?"

"Karen just disappeared off the face of the earth, it seemed. Miss Bradford called the administrator one day and asked if he could recommend a new nurse for her. She said Karen had left her. However, no one ever heard from her after that. And that was not like Karen. She was always calling her friends. She was very sociable."

Sheldon's flesh crawled. Karen had just disappeared, and the Bradfords would not have her name spoken. Why? What did it all mean?

❦ ❦ ❦

On the way back to George's house, Sheldon wanted to tell him about Karen, but the fires and the murder were uppermost in their minds. They had to share their horror, their fear of what might happen next, and the possibility that the murderer might never be apprehended.

When she got out of the car and they walked to hers, George took her chin in his hands and kissed her. "Would you like to stay the night?"

Even though his question sounded earnest, Sheldon could see the weariness and worry in his eyes. Her own ardor had diminished and now she felt bone weary.

"I'm very tired, George. I think I'd rather just go home tonight. But thanks for asking."

"You're not afraid to go home and be alone tonight?"

"No. I really don't think Spence is guilty. He couldn't have set that fire at the office. I'll be fine."

She turned the events of the previous few days over and over in her mind on the way home, and she barely noticed the dense darkness of the night, clouds moving fast and furiously overhead. Nor did she notice the black pick-up truck following her at a distance.

CHAPTER 14

❀

Finally it rained. Sometime in the night Sheldon woke and heard the welcome sound of water pounding on the eaves, a drumming that soothed her back to sleep immediately, total weariness having taken over her body. But it became a restless sleep, in which dreaming and waking blurred into a pattern of confusion and surrealism. She sensed danger. Her sleeping mind told her to wake up, that she was in jeopardy. But she couldn't seem to stir. She felt like she had a lead blanket over her and her arms and legs were helpless. From a distance she heard noises...a door closing, floorboards creaking, heavy breathing. A thin beam of light flashed around her.

Someone was standing over her. Hands were on her bare arm and shoulder, cold, wet hands. The light shone in her eyes. A ghoulish figure bent over and kissed her forehead. She pushed the figure away. The light vanished. Her eyes flew wide open and she found herself in a sweat, her heart beating as loud a timpani as the rain overhead. She trembled uncontrollably.

"Who's there? Is someone there?" Her teeth chattered as she called out. She clutched the covers tightly to her chin and strained to hear the slightest noise. But all was quiet except for the rain battering the roof and the constant howl of the wind whipping shutters and tree limbs loose. Impressions from the dream persisted for several minutes before she finally convinced herself that it was just a dream.

Only a dream, nothing more. But it had seemed so real. So very real. Her heartbeat slowed, she relaxed against the pillow and finally slept again.

🍁   🍁   🍁

The rain muffled the sound of his footsteps up to the door, which he opened easily. He smiled. It was so easy when you had a key. He only wanted to see her sleeping, but this was not the time to take her. She would come voluntarily when he was ready. Maybe tomorrow. For now, he turned on his penlight and eased his way to her room where her steady breathing told him she was unaware of his presence. He stood looking at her, playing the light over her partially covered body, lingering at the cleavage above her lace-topped nightie. He couldn't resist running his hand along her arm to her shoulder. How he wanted to caress the soft mounds and kiss those slightly parted lips, but he knew if he went that far he'd have to crawl in beside her and go all the rest of the way. Not yet. Not tonight. But he couldn't resist altogether. He leaned down and kissed her forehead. She mumbled something and swung her arm out at him. He jumped back and snapped off the light, then swiftly tiptoed down the hallway. He heard her cry out, "Who's there?" But he was already in the kitchen, where he waited and listened. There was only the sound of the rain, beating furiously against the windows. With all the noise outside he was sure she didn't hear him leave.

🍁   🍁   🍁

She looked at the clock on her dresser. Six-thirty. Of course, a Sunday when she could sleep in and she was wide awake at the usual time. It was such a restless night. Bad dreams. A frightening nightmare. So realistic. Might as well get up and get dressed. She sat on the edge of the bed and thought briefly about her nightmare, listening to the constant rain on the roof. She shuddered at the thought of that ugly face that had kissed her. Funny how real some dreams are, she thought. She was sure when she woke up that she could still feel the impression of wet lips on her forehead. But it was only a bad dream. Just a horrible dream. Still, she couldn't remember ever having one that seemed quite so real.

As she dressed in jeans and cotton shirt, she kept looking at her new red and white dress and thinking about what a great evening she would have with George in Ottawa. To think about him was almost as relaxing as to be in his company. He made her feel comfortable, only now she had a strange knot in her stomach over him. She could picture him as loving husband, ideal father, true friend. She could see him taking his children fishing and skiing, patiently teaching them to ride a bike, helping them with their lessons. He would never forget her birthday. She didn't know how she knew that. She just knew. He was the kind who would say, "You've had a bad day, Honey. Let's eat out."

So unlike David Bradford. Sure, Bradford was handsome and rich and could make you feel all tingly just by smiling at you. But he was like a carnival, in a way, full of promise, glitz and glitter, all the while playing a big con game. Just when you thought you had him figured out, you realized you had been suckered and that there was no prize. He was definitely a man of many faces. And what about Karen Lockhart? Had she been his lover? Why had she disappeared so suddenly? What happened to her?

"Big mystery," she thought as she walked out to the kitchen for breakfast. "Surely they didn't do away with her." Then she stopped in her tracks, realizing what she was thinking. Of course the Bradfords weren't murderers, for heaven's sake. Granted, they were both odd. David was eccentric and self-centered, and at the same time philanthropic, a benefactor to many causes and to the poor. And his sister was full of wild talk about the fallacy of organized religion, but she was harmless. She was certainly no Charlie's Aunt. "Good lord, Sheldon Marie Merrill, you think everyone is a killer. Stop that. Just stop it."

She prepared a breakfast of orange juice, cereal, and coffee, and sat by the window to eat, thinking what she needed to do today. Laundry first, since she was down to one pair of clean underpants. She needed to shop for groceries. She had letters to write. She had vacuumed three days ago, so all she needed to do today was dust.

And she should make some appointments for interviews in the coming week. The horse farm intrigued her, as did Bill Ferguson. Again her mind returned to David Bradford, and she remembered the sight of Ferguson walking with his arm around David's shoulders. So close. Did it mean anything? Did it confirm the rumors? Probably not, considering what Kate had said about Bradford's interest in Karen.

She gazed out the window and saw that Spence's roses were taking a beating in the rain, petals wilting and falling into mushy dark piles along the trellised, muddy rows. Dark and dismal though the day was, she could just imagine how much rejoicing there was in the farming community, although the rain was coming too late to do the farmers much good for this season's crops. However, wells and farm ponds would start to refill. If it would just keep raining for several days.

After the table was cleared and dishes were washed and put away, she got her raincoat and basket of laundry. The utility room was downstairs in the shed, which meant she had to go outside to reach it.

Squinting against the steady rain, she balanced the clothes basket on one hip in order to unlock the door. But as she started to put her key in the lock, she heard Spence call, "It's unlocked. Come on in." At the same time, the door opened and Spence took the basket from her. "Get in out of the rain," he said.

"It looks like it's going to last a while," Sheldon said, "and that's encouraging."

"Sure is. Weather report says we're going to get high winds with it tonight." Spence set her basket on the table next to the washer. He had built the little room at the end of his woodshed, complete with heat piped in from the main furnace.

"If you're doing a wash right now, I'll come back later," Sheldon said, hesitating to take off her coat.

"No, no. I was just drying some things that got wet last night. When I heard the wind, I put on some clothes and went out to put the lawn chairs under cover."

Spence avoided eye contact with her. She noticed that he still looked haggard and tired. Facial lines seemed to have deepened in just two days. Sheldon thought it better not to bring up Julia's name.

"Could you sleep with all that noise in the night?" Spence asked while he opened the dryer door and took out a cotton jacket and trousers.

"It was noisy, but there's something peaceful about sleeping under eaves in the rain. I slept quite well the first part of the night, but then I had a terrible nightmare, and my sleep for the rest of the night was fitful. I kept waking up and thinking about that awful dream."

"Dreams can seem real sometimes. I've had them when I could have sworn someone was in the same room with me."

"Exactly. That's just what happened. I thought someone had come into my apartment during the night and was standing by my bed." She omitted the part about the physical contact.

"I woke up just shaking all over, so sure that there had been someone there. But, of course, it was just a bad dream."

"Not likely anyone would get in without a key," Spence said with a little laugh.

"No, of course not."

"You have the day off, do you?"

"Yes. Actually today and tomorrow. There was a fire at our office. Not bad enough to stop publication of the newspaper, but quite smelly and everything is soaked from the sprinklers. My boss said to take tomorrow off. I have a lot to do today. I've been letting some of my regular chores, like laundry, pile up. And then tonight, I'm going to Ottawa with George Durant. We're having dinner and taking in a show at the theater. I'm so excited about it."

"That sounds like a good time. I hope you'll enjoy it."

"Oh, I will. By-the-way, I need to shop for some groceries today. Can I get anything for you while I'm at it?"

"No. Julia left me well supplied. Thanks anyway."

With that, Spence went into his house through the inside kitchen door, and Sheldon continued loading the washer, thinking that she'd missed the opportunity once again to ask him if Julia had left him voluntarily.

❀   ❀   ❀

She had finished the laundry and ironed what needed ironing, and had just sat down at the desk to write letters when the telephone at her elbow rang. To her surprise it was Lucille Bradford's nurse.

"I'm terribly sorry to disturb you today, of all days, a Sunday. But Miss Bradford has had a turn for the worse. She had to be hospitalized during the night. She's asking for you. She says there is something very important that she must tell you. Would it be possible for you to come see her? The doctor doesn't give her long now. A few days at the most."

"I'm so sorry to hear that." Sheldon closed her eyes. Oh God. She didn't want to talk with a dying woman today. She had so many things to think about. And she wanted to be in a happy mood for the evening. What should she say?

"Miss Merrill? Do you think you can come? She was most emphatic that she needed to tell you something important. I'm sorry that I don't know what it is, but I do hope you will grant her this wish. It would be such a help to her. She's very distressed."

Of course. It was only right to help the woman that much. It was obvious that this was very difficult for her, and someone needed to give her a bit of comfort.

"I'll be glad to visit her. When is a good time to come?"

"Just after lunch, about one o'clock, I would say."

"I'll be there."

Sheldon looked at her watch. Ten-thirty. She had plenty of time to finish up her projects, except for shopping, and she could do that on the way back home.

Poor Lucille Bradford. Probably more talk about her past, but she had said that there was something which she didn't want her brother to know. The conversation they had yesterday had been emotionally draining. Sheldon wasn't sure she really wanted to listen to the dying woman rant on about her fears. But what could she do? After all, she had no one except David, and apparently she had some reason for not wanting to tell him.

Being with a dying person was so unpleasant. She recalled her own horror when she saw her father, wasted away to a bony apparition, thrashing about the bed. She had not visited anyone in a hospital since his death. This would be the first time. Why did it have to be someone who was dying again? At least death was no mystery to her now, as it was then. She was old enough to understand what it was all about. But all the same, she dreaded the encounter.

She finished her letter-writing and made quick work of the dusting, then returned to the desk and found a telephone number in the phone directory.

The male voice that answered said simply, "Shantytown."

Sheldon told Bill Ferguson her name and her purpose for calling, that she wished to set up an interview with him for her agricultural page.

"Sure, Sweetheart. Come on out. When do you want to make it?" He sounded as cheerful as he had yesterday, laughing at nothing.

"How about Wednesday? In the late afternoon."

"Good by me. See you then."

"Oh, one thing. Will you tell me why you call your place Shantytown?"

He laughed heartily. "Everyone asks that. Well, it's not an original name. I bought eight hundred acres here ten years ago. On the back side of the property is an old mining site where the former owner thought he would make a killing in the mining of zinc and lead, like they did at St. Jameson's. They built some shacks for the miners and their families, and it got dubbed Shantytown."

He laughed again. "I guess they got some zinc, but not much. Produced quite a lot of lead, though. Then someone got real sick and died, and they blamed it on the lead. Since he couldn't make a profit out of it and there was no one who wanted to work there any more, anyway, the owner shut the place down. Some of the shacks are still there.

"So when I bought the place, I decided to leave the shacks and to call my farm Shantytown. It suits my sense of the absurd, you see. Sounds like a seedy, run-down part of town, when in reality I've got one of the finest horse ranches north of Kentucky. Sometimes I take visitors out through the farm to see the old mine and the little houses. Gives you an insight to the conditions that laborers like that often have to work and live under, even today."

Sheldon thanked Ferguson and reaffirmed that she would be there Wednesday afternoon.

"Unless we have a catastrophe of some sort." It was the usual condition she set.

While she was changing her clothes for the hospital visit, the phone rang again. This time it was Deputy Luce.

"Just wanted you to know that everyone has the story about the fire fatality now," he said, "and yours will be out only slightly later than TV airs it this noon."

"And how did the press conference go?"

"Just as you'd expect. The sheriff all but took credit for finding the body. He didn't have a lot to tell yet. Only that it was a woman who had apparently crawled from the fire. Everyone wanted to know who she was, but he said they'd have to wait for the investigation to be completed. When the TV reporter asked if the woman died from burns, Beaulieu said they'd have to wait for the autopsy report before be could say for certain."

"What you told me is that she was shot and beaten. Did he say that?"

"No. So you have some details that the other media don't have."

"Thanks to you. And I mean that, Gene. Thank you very much."

"No thanks necessary. Like I said before, if there's anything you need, any time, just ask. I'm yours to command."

His voice was so low and sexy that Sheldon had to laugh.

"'Yours to command?' That sounds dramatic."

"Dramatic or not, it's what I want you to remember. Do you still have my card?"

She picked it up from the desk and studied it. His name, Eugene R. Luce, and his telephone number, 321–0021. Easy number to remember, she thought.

"Yes, I have it right here."

"Good. By the way, I drove past your place last night after leaving your office. You go to bed early, I guess. All the lights were out."

"I was tired out. Been running for two days steady after the fire Friday morning. I guess I did go to bed early, about ten-thirty. Did you go by that late?"

"It was about eleven. Did you get a good night's rest?"

"Pretty good. The rain woke me up once. And then I had a bad dream. That woke me a second time. Other than that, I slept well, thanks."

Funny, she thought, two people have asked me that today.

"Why did you drive by?"

"I thought I'd stop and say good night. I couldn't very well say anything to you at your office."

"No, of course not." Not wanting to encourage him by inviting him to her home another time, as he probably would like to have her do, she changed the subject.

"Have you uncovered anything that would indicate who set that fire in Harry's office?"

"Not a thing. Whoever did it wasn't too serious about burning the place down. They set the fire in papers right under the sprinklers. If they really wanted the place to go, they'd have set it in the main building where the construction is wood."

"I wonder if it's the same one who set the farm fire. Harry got a threatening note. Did you know that?"

"No. What was it?"

"A note that said for him to be careful or he'd end up in a furnace, too. Only the writer spelled it f-u-r-n-i-s-s. Either a person who is illiterate to some extent, or who wants Harry to think he is. Anyway the note came yesterday, and sounds like a reference to the farm fire. We thought maybe he knew that Harry was going to publish a story about the body. But we couldn't see how he'd know that, so it's a mystery. And a scary one, at that."

"Did Harry report it to officials?"

"Yes. He went to Police Chief Ott. Thought it was a wiser idea than to go to Beaulieu, under the circumstances."

"Yeah. I'd say so."

"You must be worn out yourself. You were at the early morning fire, then back out there Friday afternoon. And then at the fire last night. Don't you ever sleep?" Sheldon asked

"There's a lot of sickness among our officers right now, and I've had to pull double duty. I don't mind. I don't require a lot of sleep."

"Well, I hate to cut you off, but I have to go to the hospital to visit a dying woman."

"That sounds like an excuse to me," he said, his voice teasing. "Tell me, who's the guy you were with at the office? You came in with him and left with him."

"George? You saw him at the fire. George Durant."

"He seemed very interested in you. You two have something going, do you?"

"I'm not sure I know what you mean by that, but what we have going is strictly friendship. We've known each other for two years, ever since I came to Westburgh. We quite often work on the same assignment together, as we did for the fire."

"I see. He's a pretty good friend then."

"Yes, a pretty good friend. I really do have to go. I'll talk with you later."

Why was Gene Luce so darned interested in her life? She wished he would leave her alone. On the other hand, she was grateful to him for his information about the body, and she really could not say why he bothered her. It was just that sly manner of his. His voice was just like his facial expression, always bearing a hint of insincerity, a lot like the wolf at Red Riding Hood's door.

CHAPTER 15

The day's darkness could not compare to the torpor emanating from Lucille Bradford, enshrouding the room in a twilight pallor, as ashen as the woman's flesh. Sheldon had thought she could handle this. Now she wasn't so sure. The prospect of listening to more ranting over truth versus religion was daunting enough without the added despair of fatality. The terrible part of watching another person at the end of life and recognizing one's own mortality was the preview of the certain time to come when all options are closed and all forks in the road of life are merged into one path straight out of it, closing off all ambitions and dreams, all hopes. Even at her young age when her father died, she had been shocked by that realization as he fought to breathe one more time.

Maybe Miss Bradford hadn't seen her, she thought as she stood in the open doorway. Or maybe she could say she had something she must do at her office and excuse herself from staying. She didn't like this. It was like signing herself into a prison. Once she stepped inside, she would be locked in by her own promise to listen to the dying woman.

"Sheldon? Is that you? Come here, dear, and sit beside me."

The voice was weak, more so than the last time they spoke, yet there was no hesitation. Lucille sounded determined. Trying to smile with conviction, Sheldon walked in.

"I'm sorry you're feeling worse," she said with the guilt of helplessness resting heavy on her chest. There could be no words of consolation now.

"Yes. Much worse. But there is so much I must tell you, and you must not interrupt. There isn't time for that. Press that button and raise my head."

Sheldon did as she was told, raised up the head of her bed, then sat beside Lucille, looking into that tired face with the sunken eyes, the cracked lips, and the tubes. A heart monitor blipped as bumpy lines scrolled along the screen, while fluid dripped from a bottle down a tube, through the catheter in her arm. The blue and white hospital johnny sagged on her thin body and drooped from her shoulders.

"Here," Sheldon said. "I'll fix that lovely hospital gown for you."

She re-tied the back and then straightened the sheet.

Lucille closed her eyes. She had rehearsed the way she would tell this young woman about her life, realizing that here was a person who had likely lived according to the rules of society and her faith all of her twenty-odd years and would be totally shocked if she heard the sordid details of a life gone so wrong from the very start. Nevertheless, it had to be done. There was no changing her past now. It was all there, weighing her down, killing her inch by inch.

She sighed and opened her eyes. Lucille read deep sympathy in Sheldon's expression. Would she turn away in disgust and tell her to find someone else to do her errand? Would she threaten to print the story? Lucille had to take a chance.

"I told you that I disdain organized religion and why. But I didn't tell you all of the story. To do so, I must start with my childhood."

Mentally, Sheldon groaned. Her childhood. This could take all the rest of the day. She managed a polite smile and nodded.

"Of course, David wasn't born until I was twenty, and until then I was an only child. My uncles were very good to me. My Uncle Saul was particularly attentive, always giving me gifts and taking me for rides in his big car. He would take me to movies on Saturdays. We had a theater in town then. And he'd buy me an ice cream sundae or a soda afterward at the ice cream parlor. Both places closed long ago.

"My father and mother were fundamentalists…Baptists. He had a strong belief in spare the rod, spoil the child."

Lucille took a deep breath. She could see her father, tall and strong, with penetrating dark eyes. She could hear his deep voice, full of accusation, *Why were you late for dinner? Where were you?* She tried to explain, *I was at Elizabeth's, playing dolls. I didn't know what time it was. Please don't spank me. I won't be late again.* She looked to her mother, who sat tight-lipped and quiet, keeping her head down and studying her empty dinner plate, her hands folded in her lap. When her father began to unbuckle his leather belt and pull it through the pants loops, Lucille started to cry. Why would he spank her for being late when she had no way of knowing what time it was? *Please don't…*

"Miss Bradford? Are you all right?" Sheldon's voice broke into her memory.

"Yes. I'm okay. As I was saying, the rules were rigid for me, but when David was born, the rules were relaxed for him. He wasn't treated as harshly as I was. Partly, I think, because they were so much older then. And partly because he was a boy."

Lucille began to cough.

"Would you like a drink of water?" Sheldon asked.

"Yes. Please."

Sheldon held the glass to her lips. She could relate to being reared under the stern hand of a parent. Her own father had been strict, too, until he became ill.

Regaining her composure, Lucille continued, "When I was about ten, I started turning to Uncle Saul with my troubles, and he was always most sympathetic, sometimes even providing me with an escape from my father's wrath. Uncle Saul was like a father to me, the understanding father that I didn't have, always supportive and never critical. He was usually cheerful, but I didn't know then that his happy moods came from a bottle."

Lucille remembered the first time Saul saved her from a sure beating. She had been told to wash the dishes from breakfast and dinner when she came home from school, since it was her mother's day to serve as an aide at the Westburgh Hospital. But there was a play rehearsal that afternoon and she was playing the piano for it, so she didn't get home before her father did.

How come these dishes aren't washed, girl? Weren't you told to clean up this mess after school?

Uncle Saul walked into the kitchen just then. *I had to stay for play rehearsal. I'm playing the piano for it.* Her tears had already started. When Saul saw his brother-in-law's motion toward his belt, he stepped between them. *Now, Nick, the girl has a good, legitimate excuse. Don't punish her for doing what she had to do. Cleaning up these dishes won't take two shakes. Come on, Lucy, let's go at it while your father reads his paper.* He was laughing then, and they washed the dishes together. Her father never mentioned the incident afterward, and she was so very grateful to her dear uncle.

"Uncle Saul had a serious drinking problem. Even so, he never hesitated quoting the Bible, going to church, being a pillar of society. Father frowned on his drinking, but as long as his brother-in-law was a generous contributing member of his congregation, they had few actual words over it. My uncle had the knack of performing his sins in private. He was not an openly obnoxious drunk, so he wasn't a public embarrassment to the family. Also, being a wealthy businessman put him in a respected position, and for some reason that meant a little thing like being a tippler could be overlooked."

She covered her eyes with a an almost transparent hand, and took long breaths.

Sheldon shifted her weight. The vinyl chair was uncomfortable. She had so many things to do. She wished again that she hadn't come. But she would listen.

"We had an old upright piano in our home, and I took lessons on it from a very young age. Early on, it became apparent that I had natural talent, and Uncle Saul would come to our house each Sunday, like everyone in the village did, it seemed. Mama always served goodies and they just wandered about, eating and talking. My uncle would insist that I play for the group. This did much to build my ego, and I became quite fearless playing in front of an audience. In fact, it gave me the incentive for wishing to become a professional performer. But, of course, the old piano had seen better days.

"On my twelfth birthday, Uncle Saul asked me to come to his house, the one I now own.

"He took me into the front parlor, where there was a large object covered over with a white sheet. 'Take the sheet off,' he said. He was grinning. By then I knew what that unpleasant odor was about my uncle. And it was strong that day.

"I pulled the sheet off, and there was the most beautiful grand piano, all shiny and new.

"'Happy birthday,' he said and he gave me a kiss on the lips. I didn't like the kiss, but I was overwhelmed by the gift. 'For me?' I couldn't believe it was for me. He explained that it would be mine but it would stay in that room. I could come over every day, if I wanted to, to practice."

Lucille could feel her strength slipping away, but she must finish this now.

"For about a year, I would go over each day after school and practice. Usually Uncle Saul wasn't there, since he ran the mill. I had such high hopes for a career in music. I had the skill and the determination. I was certain I would become a concert pianist.

"Then one day, shortly after I turned thirteen, Uncle Saul came home early, and he sat down and listened and watched while I played."

She had known by the twist of his mouth and the oily sheen on his skin that he had been drinking. He did that sometimes in his office, but more usually at home. Her stomach twisted when he walked over to her and began rubbing the back of her neck. She wanted to run. *I guess I'd better go now, Uncle Saul. I've practiced a long time.* She could smell the rank odor of booze strong on his breath. *No, I don't want you to go, Lucy.* She began to sweat. He was being so deliberate in his motions, running his hand up and down her back, pressing his lips against her hair. What could she do? *I told Mama I'd be home to help with supper. It must be about time to go.* Why was he doing this? What was he up to? *It will be all right. I called and told her you would eat with me tonight. She said that would be fine.* No! She wanted to scream, leave me alone. I want to go home. But she was trapped, with no way out.

Lucille groaned involuntarily.

"He asked me to stop playing after a few minutes. I had an odd dread in the pit of my stomach. I could tell he was up to something, but I had no idea what. Over the past year he had been doing little things, like touching my bottom, or pulling me close in a hug and managing to rub his hand over my chest. But I wasn't really afraid of him. I just thought I should avoid him when he was drinking."

Sheldon felt the chill of understanding coursing through her. She really didn't want to hear this.

Lucille turned her head away so that she wasn't looking at Sheldon. "'I have something to show you,' he said. 'We need to go upstairs. Come with me.' I pulled away, but he was big and strong. I asked why we had to go upstairs, but he just pulled me up over that long staircase and into his room at the far end. I knew I was trapped. What could I do? I couldn't run. Somehow I felt that he had been so good to me, it would be wrong of me to run away from him. I didn't want to create enmity between us. I was only thirteen. I needed to practice the piano for my career ahead. I couldn't jeopardize that privilege. What did I know? Nothing."

It was all so clear to her, the vision of Saul's bloodshot eyes leering at her, his heavy breathing, his command for her to come closer to him as he sat on the edge of the bed.

"It was all so humiliating and frightening. He said we'd play a little game, and he unbuttoned my blouse. I cried, and tried to push him away. I said I didn't want to play. But he kept saying, 'Oh, it's all right, my dear. You'll like this game.' He slowly took all my clothes off me, checking out each part of my body as he did it. I'd try to cover myself with my hands, but he'd push them aside and I stood there exposed. I'd never been naked in front of anyone, not since I was a young child. I felt sick and so degraded. But he kept telling me everything was all right. This was just a little game between the two of us, and I didn't need to be afraid. And then he undressed, and I couldn't bear to look at him. I sobbed harder, but he ignored that. He took me into his bathroom and made me shower with him. He made me touch him...oh, God almighty, I can't tell you the details. It was all so terrifying. So dirty and distasteful to me."

The fear she had felt when he pulled her into the shower soon turned to panic. *Please. Let me go. I don't want to do this. Please.* His grip was like steel on her arms, as he pulled her hands downward to touch him. *Just relax. This is what everyone wants. You will, too. Now, just do as I tell you and don't carry on so.*

"When he was finished with me that afternoon, I was no longer a virgin. I was in a state of shock, unable to talk even when I got home. I went to the bathroom afterward and bathed. I nearly scrubbed the skin off me. But, of course, the dirt that was under the skin wouldn't come out."

She had gone to bed, buried her face in the pillow, and cried. *Dear God, why? Why did he do that? Please, God, don't let him do it again.* She called on God over and over as she cried, until she finally fell asleep from exhaustion.

Sheldon watched while Lucille wiped away tears with the sheet, her own throat tight.

"How dreadful for you. Couldn't you get help?"

"I…had…no…one…to…tell." Lucille emphasized each word individually as she had done that night. *There is no one I can go to. Mama would blame me. I can't tell her. Why God? Why? Why did this happen? What will I do?*

"There was nothing I could do. My mother would have declared that it was my fault, not her brother's. And she would have told my father, who would surely have beaten me within an inch of my life. To make matters worse, Uncle Saul, from that day forward, drummed into me that I was not a virgin any more and that no man would want me. I was his. That's the way God had meant it to be. God wanted me to be with him, he said."

She had stayed away for several days, not daring to practice the piano in his house for fear he would come in. Then he came to her house on Sunday. *Where have you been, Lucy? I miss hearing that wonderful piano music that you make. Terry, have you been keeping her away to do housework? She needs to practice, you know.* Oh, yes, by bringing the subject up in front of Mama, he had assured that she would be back in his house again. *I didn't know you weren't practicing, Lucille,* her mother said. *Why? You know you must work at it if you're going to become truly good at it.* And so she had to return.

Remembering clearly, Lucille continued, "He used the Bible, which he knew just as well as my father did, to brainwash me into believing it was my duty to serve him. I was brought up to believe in the Bible as the word of God. Whatever it said was the truth. Saul constantly quoted from it, read scripture over and over again, scripture that strengthened his case."

How many times he had insisted on Bible study, and how many times he had chosen verses that would condemn a woman who committed adultery, knowing full well that Lucille could not and would not question the Word of God. One of his favorite chapters was Proverbs seven, warning against the harlot. *Her house is the way to hell, going down to the chambers of death.* And how he would stare at her with warning in his eyes. *Do you understand that, Lucy? You see what God thinks of a woman who strays from her place? You must be faithful.*

"My faith, when I was a teenager, was strong," she said to Sheldon. "I believed with all my heart that I should do as the Lord wanted me to do, and it somehow was right for me to do what my uncle said I should do. He made it clear that he needed me, and I came to believe that if I went away and left him, I would be doing wrong. But I always wanted a life of my own. I wanted freedom from him, yet I didn't want to hurt him."

Trying not to cry again, Lucille sighed heavily, her whole body sagging with it. The pain was terrible to see, and Sheldon wiped a tear from her own cheek.

"I told him once, when I was older, that I didn't want to go on like that, but he turned it all around that I had to be loyal, that my place was beside him. He needed me more than ever at the mill."

They were having supper. They had just finished a sexual tryst and Lucille wanted him to understand how she felt. *This isn't right, Uncle Saul. I don't feel right going on like this. I want to make a clean break of it and go away.* His eyes turned angry, his nostrils flared. *Leave? You want to leave? Don't you know what you're saying, Lucille? You have a duty here. This isn't just a little fling that we've had. You're mine now. Don't you love me?* Funny thing. He never said he loved her, but always demanded to have her love him. What could she say? She didn't hate him, so she guessed she must love him. Only her love was so much different than what he expected.

Lucille's eyes closed, every breath so difficult, her thoughts so punishing.

"I've often wondered what kind of love it was that made him ruin his niece. What kind of love takes all hope away from a young girl?"

Lucille was getting weaker, thrashing around to breathe, and Sheldon feared that the woman might die at any minute, she was so colorless and breathless. Each word came out of her with great difficulty, but still she plodded on, sometimes with long gaps between her words, but determined to get it all out.

"As I told you before, I thought my salvation would be to go away to a music conservatory. Then I would be free of him. But that didn't happen. I was forced to work in Uncle Saul's mill and to learn the business. I was hopeless by then, and tired of smelling the nasty smell of alcohol when I did what my dear uncle demanded in the bedroom. Finally, I gave up, totally."

She blinked as if fighting sleep and fatigue.

"Brainwashing is a terrible thing, Miss Merrill. If you're told long enough that white is black, you will believe that when you see a white sheet, it's black. I believed I had no alternative. I believed that if I had no alternative, then I should do what my uncle did. Drink. And I joined him. He had been wanting me to take a drink for years, and finally I did. I didn't just have a glass of wine for dinner. No. I drank until I was mindless. I would wake up in the morning and wonder what I had done the previous night. Some mornings I would be in my own bed, and some mornings I would be in Uncle Saul's. He would make an excuse to my parents that I had fallen asleep at the piano, and he had put me to bed on the couch."

She lifted her head slightly, her words tight with bitterness.

"How could they not have known what was going on? My mother should have known when I was a teenager and became depressed and withdrawn that something was wrong. But she never seemed to tumble. I became very forgetful, and still she never asked me if I was all right, if Uncle Saul had touched me. Imagine it. Her own daughter, and she never saw the signs. No. She didn't **want** to see the signs."

Sheldon shook her head. "She probably thought you were just going through the usual mood swings of puberty."

"No, I'm sure that's not so. She wouldn't even have thought of that. After a while, Uncle Saul devised a plan. I would move into his house where I could have my own efficiency apartment. It would give me more freedom, he told my parents, without the cost of having to rent an apartment. The rental would be included as part of my wages for my work as his secretary.

"He laid it out to them in such a genuinely disinterested manner that they never questioned the appearance of it. He said my apartment would have its own stairway and entrance. And they thought that was nice. He kept his word, but I seldom used that stairway. The door from my apartment into the house, where I really lived, was much handier.

"For some years, I kept my drinking quite secret. But when I was in my early thirties, I didn't care any more. If I got drunk and decided to walk into town, I'd do it. When my drinking became an embarrassment to my parents, my father called me on the carpet about it. There wasn't anything they could do to me. Papa couldn't beat me any more."

He'd walked in when Lucille was laughing loudly over some joke she'd heard and had just told to Uncle Saul. She was so drunk that she spilled her drink as she laughed. *Lucille!* Her father's angry voice almost caused her to topple over. *Well, well, it's dear old Dad. Won't you come in and join the party, Papa?* He looked from one to the other, Lucille standing in the middle of the game room and Saul lazing back in his recliner. Both had drinks in their hands. *What's going on here? Is this how you two keep the Sabbath?* It was Sunday, and they both had attended church earlier in the day. She always arrived at church ten minutes before Saul came in for propriety's sake. Saul was unflustered. *Don't get your dander up, Nick. We're just having a few drinks before supper. Everything's okay. Nothing to get excited about.*

She went on, "But he gave me a good tongue lashing about it one evening when he visited Uncle Saul and found me drunk. I laughed in his face and said he could assign me to the devil in church next Sunday. It wouldn't matter to me, because I wouldn't be there ever again. And I didn't go to church again. But I did begin to think a lot about what had been drummed into me all those years as God's will."

Lucille had sunk back into the pillow. She sighed "Oh" in a painful rasp.

"Let me get the nurse for you," Sheldon said.

"No. No. Stay. Listen. I'll make it through this. I have to. After I moved to Uncle's house, I hated my life, but felt that I was doing my duty, just as he told me. I had seen my high school friends either go on to college or get married, and I would cry at night alone, wishing I could have been normal like they were. Wishing so much I could have gone to the conservatory. But I knew that I wasn't supposed to have a normal life. I had to be with Uncle Saul. He needed me. I really did understand him. I knew he was a sick man, in a way. I always had liked him. Everyone liked him. He was a personable man. Only I had to stay with him because I believed all his lies. I believed I really was his to command."

Her laugh was feeble, but the irony was there.

"How little I knew of men. He failed to tell me that it just didn't matter to men whether you were a virgin or not, as long as they got their pleasure from you."

She rested, her eyes trying to focus on objects in the room. Then they found Sheldon.

"I hated myself so badly and was so miserable that I wanted to take my own life. I remember once taking a razor blade and holding it against my wrist, trying to will myself to cut deep. But I couldn't do it."

"Why didn't you just leave? You had money. You could have started a new life somewhere else."

"That's what I dreamed of daily. I'd make elaborate plans for escape, and then I'd get to the point of asking myself where would I go? What would I do then? I had never been beyond Westburgh, you see. I felt that Uncle Saul would surely find me wherever I might go. And the world was a frightening place to me. I would have gone to music school, but there I would have been in a structured setting, with people around me to help me. The prospect of being alone and having to make my own way was overwhelming. And then, remember, I had the long-held belief that I was good for only one thing. To serve my uncle. I would pray to God to help me. But because no help came, I concluded that I was just not supposed to have the normal life that my friends had. Their lives were different from mine. I was not meant to be a free person. I carried on in the workplace, at the mill, with the appearance of normalcy. Everyone thought I was an excellent business woman. And I was. But the personal side of my life was not excellent. It was disgusting."

After another long pause and much gasping, Lucille went on.

"Finally I thought I'd try it. I'd run away. Just take what clothes were on my back and a pocketful of money and go somewhere. Since I didn't drive then, I struck out on foot and walked for at least ten miles, mostly through woods, before I sat down and thought it all out. I knew it was no good to try to get away. He'd find me. He'd bring me back, and I'd be hearing about it for months to come. He was that way…always reminding me of my duty and my faults and my weaknesses. When I did something he thought I shouldn't do, he hammered at me verbally for days, sometimes weeks, until I wanted to scream. Verbal abuse is sometimes worse than physical abuse, for it never ends. So I walked that ten miles back to Ashton, convinced it was better to stay with what I knew than to attempt to enter a world I didn't know. It seemed less ominous in the long run."

She had walked into the kitchen at noon, thankful that Saul wasn't there. He'd be at her parents', as he always was on a Sunday after church. She poured herself a glass of water at the sink, then walked up the long stairway to the upstairs hall and down to the end opposite Saul's room, where he had had the small efficiency apartment made for her. She replaced the few things that she had taken, and collapsed onto the bed, falling asleep almost immediately. An hour or so later, she awakened when she heard the door creak open. *Oh, there you are. I wondered where you had gone. Didn't see you this morning.* Saul was dressed in his black Sunday suit, with white shirt and cranberry tie. He was a very good-looking man, with light brown hair and brown eyes. The rimless glasses gave him a distinguished, gentlemanly demeanor. *I went for a walk very early. Couldn't seem to sleep so I just went out for a walk and enjoyed nature.* There was a flicker of question in his eyes, then he smiled. *Well, now that you've communed with nature, how about communing with me?* She said nothing, but sat up and dutifully disrobed.

"My uncle was always right. Not once did he say that his act against me was sinful, nor did he ever express sorrow that he had ruined my life. Although he had taken my life into his own hands and shaped it to his desires, and made a drunk of me, he saw no wrong in it."

Once again, Lucille closed her eyes, her face twisted in agony. Her hand moved back and forth over the bedclothes. The blip, blip of the heart monitor slowed.

Sheldon looked toward the window and stared as driving rain turned the day to nighttime. She thought how life was such a blur of rights and wrongs. The poor woman had obviously lived a confusing life of hell. Taken at the age of thirteen, she had no choice in her future life.

Lucille's voice startled her.

"The one thing Uncle Saul did do, however, was to make out a will, leaving me the mill and the house. I didn't even know that. Not until after I killed him."

CHAPTER 16

❀

The hallway lights flickered as rain lashed out at the window in a furious attack. Elevator doors opened and closed down the hallway. Voices rose and fell, followed by laughter at the nurses' station. A cart clattered along the hallway and was rolled into the next room.

In the dark silence of Lucille's room, Sheldon felt numb. "You...killed him?" she said, barely above a whisper, unable to grasp the fact that this little woman had just confessed to murder.

Lucille looked shocked at her own words. Her eyes, dulled by pain, were wide and fearful. Her head rolled back and forth and short breaths came from her mouth in a loud huff, huff.

"Yes. I killed him. Please. You're the only person who knows it. I beg of you not to tell. My dear brother must not know."

"This is what you wanted to tell me? That you killed your uncle?" Sheldon was aghast. Why? If no one knew, why not go to her grave with the secret?

"No. Not all of it. Let me go on." She motioned for Sheldon to get the water for her, took a sip and lay back. "One day, a very handsome man came into the mill. He was new to the area. I'd never seen him before. We talked about business, but there seemed to be a spark between us."

He had a roguish expression, a dimple in his left cheek when he smiled, and eyes that instantly imparted adoration. His words were all flattery right from the beginning. *Don't tell me you run this place. A lovely young girl like you?* She had to look away so that he wouldn't see her shy smile. *No, not really. I'm the office manager for my uncle. How may I help you?* He grinned and winked. *I can think of at least a dozen ways to answer that question, but I don't want to get my face slapped on our very first meeting.*

"I was starved for real love. I was an easy target for most any man, I suppose. He came back at least three times the following week, flirting with me shamelessly, and finally he asked if I would go out with him."

Each of his visits had been for minor purchases and each had lasted longer than the last. One day he said, *You know, Lucille, I really take to you. You have a special quality about you that is rare in women. I can't believe the men here aren't fighting each other for the chance to go out with you. Maybe the men around here are stupid, but I'm not. How about going out with me tomorrow. You don't work on Saturday, do you? We can do whatever you like—just have dinner together, or go for a boat ride. Or...we could just shack up for a few hours and enjoy each other's company.* She couldn't believe her ears. Someone who really liked her. A most handsome man who wanted to date her.

"Of course, I refused. I wanted to. But I had never gone out with anyone. From the age of thirteen, I was not allowed to date a boy. I was my uncle's prisoner, his personal slave. I couldn't think of dating a man.

"So I just said no, I guessed not. But he was persistent. The next week he kept coming back, and asking me each time. Finally, I couldn't stand it any longer. I said I would meet him, but it would have to be in Winterville. And when the day came, I told my uncle that I needed to shop for several things. It was a Saturday morning and I told Saul I'd be back before supper, which I was.

"We met at a motel on the other side of the city, had lunch at a fine restaurant, then went back to the room he had engaged. We spent three hours there, making love."

A slight smile crossed her face. "I knew I wasn't a real beauty, but not bad looking at that. I had always wondered if someone would be attracted to me. Finally I knew what love was, what I had been missing all those years."

She was ecstatic. She had fallen in love with this man and he said he loved her. *You're the best, Lucille. Just the best. I love you. I want you to remember that. I'll always love you.*

Her heart was breaking with love. *And I love you. I feel like we're soul mates, part of each other in every sense.* She knew this was true love and she would never want to love anyone else in her life.

"I had to leave in time to grab some odds and ends at a store to make it look like I had really been shopping. I even picked up a pipe for Saul, and he seemed not to realize anything was amiss."

A sigh was followed by a fit of coughing and strangling sounds. But she held up her hand for Sheldon to wait it out.

"We continued to meet at that motel each Saturday for three weeks. I began to notice that Saul was drinking more and more, but he had never said anything to me about my shopping trips. At the same time, I was drinking less. I was so deeply in love with this man, I contemplated taking the plunge and just leaving."

She wanted to leave Saul then. But she had to tell her lover about him. It would be unfair not to. *It doesn't matter,* he had said after she told him the whole story and confessed that she was still living with her uncle. *You should free yourself, though, Lucille. You shouldn't feel that you're trapped there.*

Sheldon noticed that Lucille didn't mention her lover's name, but as she told the story and relived the days at the motel in her mind, a far-away dreaminess settled over her, soon replaced by the dark shadows of uglier things as her chest heaved on each intake of breath.

"Well, one Saturday when I got home Uncle Saul was more inebriated than I had ever seen him. Out of his mind. He accused me of seeing someone else, which I denied, of course."

Saul called to her from the kitchen when she came in the front door. *Come out here, Lucy. I want to talk with you.* Her heart skipped a beat. He was very drunk. He also sounded angry. Could it be that he suspected something? She went to the kitchen and found him sitting at the table, both hands clutching a tall drink. Apparently he had dismissed the housekeeper, for all was quiet except for the steady tick, tick of the grandfather clock in the hall corner. *I bought you a necktie, Saul.* She tried to sound carefree and happy, but Saul was having no part of it. *Another gift, huh? You think that will cover up this hypocrisy? You think I don't know what's going on? Who is he, Lucy? Who've you been seeing?* She wouldn't let him see her fear. *What on earth are you talking about? I haven't been seeing anyone.* He struggled to his feet and swore. *Damn you. You take me for an idiot? Four Saturdays in a row to go shopping in Winterville? When did you ever do that much shopping? Never. You've got somebody and I want to know who.* He grabbed for her, but she jumped out of his way and quickly darted out of the room toward the stairs. She would go to her apartment and lock the door, something she had never done since moving in with Saul. She was surprised at Saul's alacrity. He was behind her before she could reach the landing.

"Uncle Saul ranted and raved and when I started to go upstairs, he was right behind me, staggering, grabbing me and holding me back. It's a very long, high staircase. Finally I reached the top landing and he was dragging at my clothes, yelling at me. He struck out at me but only grazed my cheekbone. He got up to the top and he said, 'You're not going anywhere. Do you hear me? Nowhere except to my room. Now!' I remember the words as if he had just spoken them."

He lunged for her again, and she turned sideways to avoid his hand. He punched her in the shoulder, a hard punch that hurt. He was unsteady on his feet, and she kicked against his shins, screaming *No! Not any more, Uncle.* At the same time she brought her arm around and hit the back of his head. The swift movement, along with his own off-balance momentum, sent him over the rail.

"I was strong in those days. Somehow I managed to hit him just right, and he went over the rail. He tried to grab it. But he missed and plunged over it head-first and dropped hard to the floor below. In the fall, his head hit the corner of a marble top table and it killed him."

Lucille whimpered pitifully. She battled for air before going on. Sheldon could see that she was very tired, very weak. It was hard to believe that she was a murderer. No Charlie's Aunt? The irony of that thought struck Sheldon, but the awfulness of the murder scene held her ramrod straight, blinking in disbelief.

Lucille saw her uncle's body, sprawled in a disjointed manner, blood running from the corner of his mouth, his eyes wide with amazement, his glasses hanging from one ear. Constable Smith had been understanding. *You just came home, you say, Miss Bradford?* She sipped a glass of water that he had brought to her. *Yes, I was shopping in Winterville and when I came in he was going upstairs. He leaned over to say hello and then he just…he just sort of lost his balance and toppled over it. Oh, it was terrible. Horrifying. There was nothing I could do.* She was thankful she hadn't had the first drink that day. *Well, he reeks of alcohol, Miss Bradford. Seems pretty obvious. He was drunk. That's quite a drop, but the killer was the table. There's blood and hair on the corner where he hit.*

She couldn't keep her voice steady as she told Sheldon, "I didn't really intend to kill him. I just wanted him to leave me alone. David wasn't in Ashton at the time, so I called the local constable. Everyone accepted the fact that he had accidentally fallen over the banister, as drunk as he was. Especially since I was stone sober. They all accepted that lie. Everyone."

Lucille wrung the edge of the sheet. "It was a horrible lie, and that lie became a never-ending lie for the rest of my life. My whole life. Just one big lie. I'm not ready to face myself, bared of the insulation I wrapped around myself to keep out the past. Drinking does that for you. When you get drunk you're sure you're having a good time, even if you do think of the past and get maudlin sometimes, and with the hangover you're sick and unable to think beyond how to get through the day. The past is forgotten. But now…Oh, now, I can't live with it. I can't die with it. I'm so…I don't who I am any more."

She moaned and puffed for air. "The lies just never stopped. When I started the mill up again the following week, I was surprised that my gentleman friend didn't show up all that week. Nor the next. Finally, I looked up his telephone number in our files and called it. A woman answered, taking me by surprise, but I faked it. I learned that she was his wife—*his wife*. I told her that he had a load of lumber waiting for him at the mill. She said she was surprised because they were moving the very next day. He had finished repairing the farm buildings and had sold the farm which he had inherited from his mother. They were going back to Connecticut.

"I couldn't believe it. He was married and never told me. He said he loved me. And now he was moving away the next day with his wife. And he hadn't told me. He didn't give a damn about me. I had all I could do not to cry right there in the office."

That night she cried. She got drunk and she sobbed. *Why has all this happened to me? Why? Why, God?* And right then she knew. It was the very faith that she had never really abandoned, despite having ceased attending church. Her own faith was the basis of all her troubles. From early childhood she had accepted all of her father's teachings about God. She knew she had to obey God, and therefor, her father and her uncle, because they spoke for God. No, they were God! She understood. They assumed the role of God in her life. Her father had literally beaten faith into her, faith and obedience. Her uncle had capitalized on that treatment. And she had feared both of them, as if they were deity with terrible power. She had stood up to her father and dropped out of church, but she had never been able to free herself of her uncle. Not until the fatal shove. In all of it, she had believed in God, even with all the drinking and the wrongdoing with her uncle.

Swallowing and rasping, she continued, "I blamed my father and my uncle and all their self-righteousness in exercising power over me, in controlling my life and my mind. The only reason it had worked so completely, I realized, was because I believed the words they quoted from the Bible. I was a blind believer in the word of God, a young Christian who wanted nothing more than to be a good person. My uncle persuaded me of my *duty* simply because I believed that I must please God and respect the wishes of these men, these authority figures, never mind my own despair."

She made herself some promises that night. She would never let a man break her heart again. She would not accept what men preached. She would seek the truth herself.

"As time went on I read a great deal about other religions and philosophies. And I came to the conclusion that Christianity was no less false than any of the other cults. I agreed with Nietzsche. 'Faith means not *wanting* to know what is true.' But I realized in the end that we cannot find the truth. Not here. Not until we're free of this self-deceptive flesh. I cling to my excuses. What happens when those excuses are stripped away? When all that's left is the naked being without argument. Ohhh," she moaned, "I don't know. I don't know. I just know that the Truth will not set you free, because it's impossible for any of us to know the Truth. Search your own soul, Miss Merrill. Can you sort out the truth in it? Can you distance yourself and honestly say that you are totally objective, totally loving?"

Sheldon felt that statement like a blow to her mid-section. She wondered, who knows what we face then? We all think we know and we all want to believe that we're going to a better place for our comfort despite what we truly are. She was catching the fever that drove Lucille. She, too, would be hard pressed to say that she really was what she appeared to be to the world around her.

"That night I also promised myself that I wouldn't be controlled by religion or man again. I would live as I wanted to. And each day that went by my lie grew larger and larger. My chain of sins grew ever longer and heavier. I started leaving the area on weekends and going to cities like Ottawa, where it was easy to find pleasure. I didn't have to be a prostitute, I didn't need the money. So men liked having me join them for a night or a weekend. I'd usually pick up the tab. Most weekends were a blur, with no recollection of how I met the man I'd find in my bed when I woke up, or what we had done."

Sheldon wondered why the woman took that route after her liberation. Surely she could have lived a quieter life, even have found a decent man to marry. Why would she degrade herself so? As if in answer to her question, Lucille explained.

"Make no mistake, my dear, that life did not please me. I just got stuck in it, I couldn't stop. By then I liked to drink and I liked the idea of so much freedom. I would land in a city and feel the exhilaration of choice, of an exciting adventure. And Monday morning, in Ashton, I would suffer with the guilt of hedonism. I'd promise myself to stop drinking. But I couldn't. Alcohol was my only friend, but a most traitorous one. Oh, I ran the saw mill like a dictator and made a lot of money from it. But the lies I made up to cover for my weekends became increasingly similar. So many funerals, so many weddings, so many visits with friends, and on and on. All lies. My life was one big lie."

Her sigh was ragged and deep. She wanted to sleep. Her eyelids kept drooping. But she forced herself to continue.

"I had nightmares. Always I was running away from my uncle, but he was catching me. Horrible nightmares. I'd find myself in a house, a dirty little house, and I would try to find a way out. But there was never an exit. And Uncle Saul was always there, reaching for me."

Tears rolled freely down her cheeks.

"Such a paradoxical freedom. Free from my uncle and his imprisonment, only to enter a pleasure prison, a false, drunken freedom. It was ongoing torture. Revelry brought on sickness in body and mind. I didn't get so sick that I couldn't work, but I had to fight hard to do so. You don't know what a trap it is, this addiction not just to the booze but to the lifestyle. I loved it. I hated it. I felt giddy with in-your-face independence. I felt guilty for my recklessness. More and more I detested myself. And now, I fear facing myself, my true being, for I don't really know what it is. I don't know if I'm that terrible drunken slut or if I'm actually a decent being."

Pain contorted her face.

"To add to all the humiliation that I brought onto myself, I was arrested…not once, but twice…for common drunkenness and held in an overnight drunk tank both times. I don't even know where I was one of those times. The poor matrons who were called in to sit outside my cell had to listen to my ranting and raving all night. That was the way I'd go, reliving my past, trying to make sense of it when I was drunk, then trying to forget it when I was sober. I always felt lucky that I wasn't near enough to Ashton for the reports of those escapades to get back there. All they knew in Ashton was that I drank in the evening, but I seldom got drunk enough to go wandering about like I did on my weekend toots. I mostly kept to my house week nights."

Sheldon tried to imagine this sick woman as a young, strong, energetic mill manager and a weekend thrill-seeker. What a waste of brains and talent. How callously she had been abused by those she trusted. She had been her uncle's mistress against her will. It was enough to shatter anyone's objectivity. What a shame it had also dragged her down to unrelenting self-loathing.

"Through all the years, the one bright light in my life has been David. He was a wonderfully sweet child, just a joy to be with. Then he grew into a very assertive young man with a good head on his shoulders. I was so proud of him the day he graduated from college. And then he went to New York to work with Uncle Charles and he made an astounding fortune in just a short period of time. Already, at his young age, he has become a respected philanthropist.

"And not once has David questioned my lifestyle, nor has he reprimanded me. He has been a very understanding, caring brother. I love him more than I've ever loved anyone, more than life itself. More than he will ever know."

She panted, "I'm so sick, my dear. But I'm not going to die for a day or two. I can't. There is something yet to be done."

Sheldon's emotions were so riled and mixed, she felt like she was swimming in a sea of confusion. This woman's life had been so terribly convoluted. Would she ask something impossible?

"There is one lie that I regret more than any other in my life, more than the murder I lied about and more than my own indiscretions ever since. It's the lie that broke up David and his loved one, Karen Lighthart."

Sheldon slid to the edge of her chair. Karen Lighthart *was* David Bradford's lover, then.

"You see, Miss Merrill, Karen worked as my nurse. She and David became friendly and fell in love. I could see that they would be a wonderful couple. They had so much in common. She overlooked his odd ways, and he was becoming more gentle. They kept their relationship a secret from townspeople. David hates gossip and he likes to spring things on people, especially those who want to know all about his life.

"But if the two of them were to get married and move away, who would take care of me? They were talking about getting an estate outside New York City. I was ill with cancer. I knew I was dying. I needed David. I had to have someone who understood me and who forgave me and would care about me. He was the only one in the world.

"It was bad enough that I had to face my self after death. I am terrified of that. But I needed to have someone to encourage me before that time. I needed my little brother. Don't you see? I needed him."

Lucille made a frantic gesture, reaching out her hand. Sheldon grasped it. The icy skeletal fingers felt like claws holding her own with a surprisingly firm grip.

"I lied to break them up. I told Karen that the rumors going around the hospital, which we both had heard, were true…that David was gay. I said all he wanted from her was to create an heir to his fortune, someone to take over from him when he retired. I said once he knew she was pregnant, he would go back to his male companions and she would be lonely. I told her it would be in her own best interest to leave without his knowing it and that if she did that, I'd set her up in another city and see that she had a good nursing position there. But she had to leave quickly, without telling anyone where she was going. I made out that David would be furious with her if he knew she intended to leave, since he had chosen her to be the bearer of his child.

"And she did leave. David thought she had just simply run out on him. That was a year ago, and he is still not over the loss. It was wrong of me to do that and I must make this right for them. I want to see both of them happy. Will you help me?"

"What could I possibly do?"

"I want you to get in touch with Karen, today. Call her. I'll give you her telephone number. Tell her to come here on the next flight out of Boston. I have someone ready to pick her up at the airport and she can call him. I'll give you that number, too. Then I want you to have Karen come here when David is here. He must not know that she is coming. David comes each day at ten in the morning and three in the afternoon. Either would be a good time to bring Karen. Can she stay at your house when she arrives? Will you take care of this? I'll do the rest. I'll confess to my lie in front of them."

"Why don't you just tell David and have him call her?"

"No. He is too stubborn. He thinks she left him high and dry and that was a blow to his ego. He won't suddenly accept what I tell him. He'll think I'm covering up for her and trying to get him to make up. I know him so well. It is necessary that they both hear me out, then they can decide what to do."

Sheldon was full of doubt that she could pull this off, or that she even wanted further involvement in the Bradfords' lives. If David had really loved Karen, why hadn't he pursued her and brought her back himself? Maybe she knew the answer to that. Lucille had just said it. His pride. She recalled his animation about loyalty being all-important and his words that he was never taken more than once.

"Give me a few minutes to think," she said.

There was no doubt in Sheldon's mind that Lucille's ghosts were there, settled around her like so many mourners come early, whispering in her ear, reminding her that she was still alive, that she mustn't forget how the skein of life had tangled and mangled until her soul clung to a mere thread of hope for vindication. Not even the death-bed confession could unravel all the wrongs, they were likely telling her. How they must taunt and sicken her with details, spinning them through and through her head, sapping what little strength she had left.

Sheldon walked away from the hospital bed now, replaying Lucille's revelations. This soft-spoken, shrunken woman, this pastor's daughter, sister to rich and influential David P. Bradford, had told her of a life so totally opposite appearances that it could have been fiction. Yet Sheldon could not question the awful facts.

What if Lucille died before Sheldon could reach Karen? What if Karen refused to come?

But the biggest question was one of ethics, a moral judgment. She could walk away and forget all that had transpired here this afternoon, the painful confession. She could even betray the confidence and write an expose on what had really happened to Saul Bradford. Lord, she could sell that story to a big-time magazine, and justice would be served, in a way, even when Lucille died.

Or she could assure Lucille that she would do her best to get Karen here and help the woman undo at least one wrong act. It would give Lucille a little bit of comfort in all this agony. Sheldon questioned whether a self-confessed murderer deserved to be given sympathy. She wondered if she would have liked this Uncle Saul had she known him socially. Probably. Did he deserve to be killed? To kill someone was so terribly wrong. There could be no trial or retribution now for that murder, but should it go by without public knowledge? What a shocking story it would make, to reveal the ugly, unknown facts about the Bradford family.

And David Bradford, her beloved brother, what would become of him? Was it fair to him to drag his name through the mud? He more than made up for what Lucille did. He was keeping people alive, assuring that future generations would have skills. Didn't he deserve to have the love of his life back?

Sheldon stood at the window and looked out over the river, straining to see the Canadian side through the heavy rain. Spectral images, distorted by rivulets along the glass, were as indefinable as her own emotions at the moment. Looming out of the dusky fog, like a silent monster of the deep, a rust bucket oil tanker glided slowly upriver. The river. This would be a bad day to try to cross the choppy water to the other side.

She glanced back at Lucille and returned to the grim reality of pain and suffering. Lucille's gray pallor, stark against the white pillow, and her gasps for breath brought tears to Sheldon's eyes. Such a short and sad life the woman had lived.

Sheldon had absorbed the emotion, but not the dreadful pain of Lucille's life story. Mentally they had connected, but Sheldon knew she was only looking on, not able to comprehend such deep and compelling anguish. And yet the moral issue couldn't be ignored. Murder was not just a crime. It was a sin.

Whatever Sheldon had expected to hear when she came to the hospital could not begin to compare with what Lucille had just told her. The dreadful lie. Her whole life was a lie. And now the torture from the lies was as painful as death itself.

She walked back to the bed and stood there, her decision made.

"I'll do this for you, Miss Bradford. I'll call Karen Lockhart and try to get her here for you. Do you think you can wait?"

The sigh this time was of relief.

"I can wait," she said, then added with a little smile, "as long as you don't take too many months."

CHAPTER 17

❀

If she had ever had a confusing few days, this weekend topped all. Sheldon turned on the light at her desk in the gloomy darkness and sat rubbing her temples. Rain beat against the skylight above her. Lucille's story had shaken her in so many ways. What a horrible existence the woman had endured. Sheldon couldn't quite sort it all out, the why of it all, but she had promised to try to get Karen Lockhart to come from Boston. And, after all, she would be most happy to see David Bradford reunited with the woman he loved. He was a unique man and he deserved happiness.

She would call Karen and then she'd have to hurry if she was going to be ready for her date with George. Presuming he wouldn't cancel the date because of the heavy rain, he would be here to pick her up in just over an hour. Maybe he had tried to call her. She should touch base with him. She felt as wilted as the yellow rose that Spence had given her. Perhaps when she got the new dress on she'd perk up

Guessing that he wouldn't be home yet, she dialed the office. When he answered his extension ring, she said, "Hi. Just thought I'd check and see if you still plan to drive to Ottawa tonight."

"Of course, if I can ever get away from here. Why not?"

"Well, the rain is really bad. And the wind is very strong. I just drove home, and had all I could do to see the road."

"I've waited too long for this." His cautious low voice, she knew, was so the other men in the office wouldn't tumble that he was talking with her. "A little wind and rain won't stop me now. We'll make it okay."

She laughed. "Fine. I'll be so glad to have a break from what I've been through this afternoon. I'll tell you all about it later."

Next, she turned her attention to Karen Lockhart. She hoped Karen wouldn't just hang up on her. Although it sounded as if there had been no animosity between Lucille Bradford and Karen, it could be that the wound hadn't healed. When your heart is broken over lost love, for whatever reason, you don't just walk away and forget it in a moment. At least, Sheldon couldn't, despite the fact that Joe had treated her with shabby disregard.

She dialed and waited. At first she thought she had struck out, but after five rings, a click was followed by a sleepy "Hello."

Sheldon suddenly felt terribly warm. This was going to be difficult, she just knew it.

"Is this Karen Lockhart?"

"Yes." It sounded like a yawn. She must have been resting. Not a good start.

"My name is Sheldon Merrill, and I'm calling from Westburgh, New York. I'm very sorry if I've disturbed you. Were you resting?"

"I was about to get up. I'm working a night shift at the hospital."

"Well, again, I'm sorry to wake you. I'm calling on behalf of Lucille Bradford. I have just come from her room at the hospital. She is very ill and she asked me to do this favor for her."

"Lucille? How ill is she?"

"Very. Her doctor thinks she has only a few days left, at most."

A long pause was followed by, "I'm so very sorry to hear that. She hasn't been well for a long while." The mellow voice was just the comforting tone to soothe a sick person.

"No, I know."

"And she wanted you to call me? Why?"

"She has a special request. She spent considerable time this afternoon telling me about her life and things that she felt she had done very wrong during her lifetime. I don't know how much you know of all this."

"I know some of it. I always suspected there was a whole lot more to it than I knew, however." Karen sounded genuinely concerned. "I think her life has been more tragic than most people know."

"It has." Sheldon didn't want to betray Lucille's trust in her, so she said no more on that matter. "She feels that there is something she needs to do in relation to you, however. Therefore, she asked me to call you and see if you can take the next flight from Boston to Syracuse. She has a driver who will pick you up, if you'll call him to say when you'll be in. Is that possible for you?"

"No, I don't think so. I'm a nurse. I'll be going on duty in a couple of hours."

"But couldn't someone be brought in to substitute for you for a few days?"

"Well, maybe."

"This was a most urgent plea. Miss Bradford has a great fondness for you."

Karen was silent.

"Please try. It's so very important."

"There are a couple of substitutes available. But why should I do this? I mean, we had an understanding when I left, and I told Lucille I wouldn't return to that part of the country again. Why does she want to see me now?"

Sheldon decided to try to convince her without revealing that Lucille had lied about David.

"I know why she wants to see you, and believe me it would be to your great advantage to do so. I don't feel it is my place to tell you, however, since Miss Bradford wishes to do that. She asked if you could come here to my apartment to stay, and I told her that would be fine with me."

"I see. You think this is worth losing a few days' work for?"

"Oh, believe me, yes. You will be very glad you did."

"Well, you certainly have me curious. I would like to see her before she goes. She's a very good person. I enjoyed her company. When she felt well enough, she used to play the piano for me. Such a wonderful musician."

"I can imagine, though I've never heard her play."

"If it's about money, she doesn't have to give me anything. She did so much for me already."

Sheldon knew just how much Lucille had done for Karen, and when the truth came out, she wondered if Karen would still feel the same.

"As I said, it is to your advantage. That's all I can tell you. Anyway, if you'll do this, I'll give you the number for the driver. Oh, I almost forgot. If there is no commercial flight coming in tonight, Miss Bradford said to engage a private plane. She'll pay all your expenses, no matter what arrangements you have to make. You could even drive by car, I should think."

"Oh my. I don't know. I'd have to make arrangements for someone to take care of my cat. I guess my neighbor would do that. I'll have to call the hospital and the airport. I don't know. If I come it would be to see only Lucille, you understand. Only her."

Sheldon knew what she meant, but she kept quiet. There would be another Bradford present, but that was the surprise for both of them.

"Well, I guess I can. I'll make the calls. I don't know when I can get out of here. The weather's not good."

"It isn't here, either. If you come, I don't need to know when you'll arrive. Just call the driver. I'm going to the theater in Ottawa in just a few minutes. My landlord is Warren Spencer. If I shouldn't be back before you arrive, go to his door and he can let you in."

When Sheldon finished relating all the necessary information, including directions to her home, she said, "Undoubtedly I'll be here when you come, but even if I'm not, you may come into my apartment and make yourself at home. Do you mind sleeping on a pull-out sofa bed?"

"Not at all. And thank you. I wouldn't do this except that Lucille did me a big favor. I owe her this."

"Good enough. Miss Bradford will be comforted that you're coming."

Looking at her watch and realizing that time was running short, she called the nurses' station first and left a message for Lucille. Then she called Spence.

"George Durant is picking me up to take me to the theater in Ottawa in just a few minutes," she told him. "I expect sometime there will be a young woman coming here, and if I shouldn't be home, will you let her into my apartment? I'm not really certain when she'll arrive, but it could be tonight."

Sheldon did not expect to be out later than midnight, but then she couldn't be sure. Who knows, she thought. Maybe George would want to make it an overnight date. She was ambivalent about that at the moment. If she could just pull herself together and turn it all off for the evening, she would be happy. If the evening stretched out longer, she'd go with it.

"Yes, sure. I'll be glad to."

"Oh, and pull out the sofa bed, will you? You can point out the linen closet to her. That's just in case I shouldn't be home when she comes in. Her name is Karen Lockhart. OK?"

"Sure, glad to. Karen Lockhart. There I wrote it down."

Sheldon noticed a lightness to his voice that hadn't been there for a couple of days, but she didn't have time to chat.

"Shellie?" he said just as she was about to hang up.

"Yes?"

"Oh, nothing. I know you're in a hurry. Talk with you later."

Telephone calls made and obligations met, she hurried through a shower, and got into her new dress. Although she looked at herself in the full-length mirror with approval, she felt less than ready to go on a date. It was a flattering style for her, she had to admit. Her hair had stayed very nicely. But she felt only half put together.

A loud knock at the door startled her. She looked at the clock. George was five minutes early. She had just made it. She slipped into her new shoes and straightened her shoulders. "Oh, my bag." She had not yet transferred from her daily purse to the new one. She would come back and do that before they left.

She hurried to the door and opened it expectantly, only to be disappointed.

"Hugh! What on earth are you doing here?" she said, not able to hide the annoyance in her voice at seeing Hugh Webster at her door. "Come in. It's wet out there."

"I know," he said with a broad grin. Funny, she had never before noticed the blue line along his gums. That was a sign of some physical ailment, but she couldn't quite remember what. "I'm in a bit of trouble down the road. My truck died, and I knew you lived nearby. Wonder if you can give me a lift to the gas station."

He walked into the room and stood dripping on her floor, then seeing that he was leaving puddles of water on the wood, stepped back to the little rug by the door where he wiped his feet.

"I'll call someone for you, Hugh, but I have a date tonight. I can't drive you anywhere. My date's due to arrive any minute now."

"Is it that George at the office?"

"Yes, as a matter of fact, it is."

"Oh." Hugh suddenly turned sullen. His eyes darted around in a confused manner. She waited for him to tell her who to call, but instead he said, "Well, I guess that changes things. We'll have to speed this up then."

Swifter than she had ever seen him move, Hugh reached in his coat pocket and pulled out a handgun. Sheldon drew in a startled breath, then let it out slowly.

"What are you doing with that gun, Hugh?"

"I'm taking you with me. Now. Come on. Out the door."

"I can't. I'm going on a date, I told you."

"You're going on a date with me. Get going."

He opened the door and when she didn't move, he grabbed her arm and pulled it behind her. As hard as it was raining, Sheldon knew she wouldn't be heard if she screamed.

"Wait, Hugh. I can't go like this. It's raining. Let me get my coat."

"Where is it?"

"In the closet. Over there." She pointed to the closet door off the hallway. If only she could do something to distract him, or get the attention of Spence. She wouldn't be able to get to the phone. Maybe if she stalled long enough George would get here. But Hugh wasn't about to let grass grow.

"Come on," he said and roughly pulled her to the closet. "Get it."

As soon as she took it from the closet and put it on, he caught her arm again and twisted it behind her, then pulled her backward toward the door. She lurched toward the trellis work and swept a glass candy dish to the floor, shattering it.

"Oh no. Let me clean up the glass, Hugh."

"No. We're gettin' outa here right now."

Hugh pulled so hard on her bent arm that she cried out, but he held tight and told her to open the door when they reached it.

"Now you walk down the steps very slow ahead of me. I have this gun pointed at your head all the way." His big raincoat would cover it up, in case Spence was looking out his window. "So no funny little tricks, now."

Terror slowly swept over her as Sheldon began to understand what Hugh was up to. How well did she know this man? They'd had very brief conversations, but she had no idea what was inside the man. He was a thief, she knew that. But was he capable of murder? She didn't know that, and she wasn't about to do something foolish just to find out right now. One thing she did know. Hugh was not too smart. He had let her walk out of her apartment without her handbag, and she never went anywhere without that. If George should see it, he would realize that she had gone unwillingly.

She hoped Spence was looking out his kitchen window, but a glance in that direction told her he wasn't. There was no light, and the day had turned so dark it was like night.

She sensed that she must not show him how scared she was. She must somehow stay calm. Easier said than done, she realized, with her heart trying to pound its way out of her chest. Rain was pelting at her head and she regretted that she hadn't put on her rain bonnet. She hoped the perm would hold up. Then she thought, how silly. Here a man has a gun at my back and I'm worried about my new hairdo.

When they got to her car, Hugh told her to slide in on the passenger side before him.

"You'll drive," he said.

"Where? Where do you want me to go?" Well that little squeak certainly sounded courageous, she thought.

"You'll turn left at the corner."

"Past Mollisons' farm?"

"Yup. That's the way."

"That road goes back to the highway."

"The old county road turns off of it. We'll take that."

"Is it safe in this rain? Is it paved?"

"It's got some pot holes but it's paved."

How she hoped she'd meet George coming to get her before they reached the intersection. Oh, please, get here George. Please. Even if it meant trouble from Hugh, she'd toot the horn to get George's attention. Where was he? He was never late. Please come along George.

But he didn't. They were at the intersection and there were no cars in sight. Her hope sank while her fear mounted. Why was Hugh abducting her? What kind of man was he? He had always seemed so harmless at the office.

"Get going," Hugh urged. "We've got a ways to drive."
"Where? Are we going to your truck?"
"No."
"Where is your truck?"
"It's at my house."
"How did you get to my place?"
"I had a man leave me off near there. Then I walked."

Sheldon knew she must be tactful. She always had a way of talking to Hugh that seemed to please him. She had to assume a sympathetic tone, like a mother or a teacher. She hoped it would work.

"I've never seen you be violent, Hugh. Is something bothering you? What seems to be the trouble? You know I'll be glad to talk with you about it, if there is something wrong."

"Nothing's wrong. Everything's just right. I got you. That's what I wanted. That's what I been planning. Just to get you."

"Why?"

"Ha! Can't you see? I want you, that's why. I want you with me, forever."

Oh God! What in the world is he going to do? A shudder ran the length of Sheldon's spine and she started shaking all over.

"And where are we going? Will you tell me?"

"Sure. I've got a great place for us. You'll like it. It's our own hideaway near the mine. A house, all fixed up. I worked hard to fix it all up so you'd be comf'table. You'll like it."

"Near the mine? What mine?"

"In Shantytown. The old lead mine."

❦ ❦ ❦

George was late. He shouldn't have taken that last phone call. If the woman wanted her storm drain cleaned, she should have called the Highway Department. Unfortunately, he couldn't get a word in edgewise to tell her that and she ranted on for a full ten minutes.

When he finally got home and showered and dressed, he was already late. Not much traffic, though, on a late Sunday afternoon in pouring rain, so he made good time out to Sheldon's. Now as he drove into her yard, he saw no car, but her apartment lights were on. Maybe she had to have the car towed for some reason, he thought. That old Dart had seen its best days. She should trade it.

Rain and all, he bounded up the steps two at a time and rapped smartly on the door. To his surprise it opened under the pressure of his knock. He stepped in and called, "Hi. Anyone here ready to go to Ottawa?"

All was silent. Too silent.

"Shellie? Are you here?"

No answer. That was odd. She knew he would be here at five, and he was only twelve minutes late. Surely she hadn't given up on him.

"Shellie?" he called again, and then he saw the broken glass on the floor. He started down the hallway. "Shellie! Are you here?"

He reached her bedroom and glanced around. She was gone. But there on her bed were two handbags. Her daily bag and a new red one.

"What the...?" He would never get into a woman's purse, but he sensed something was wrong. She carried a bag with her always. He had to check to see if her driver's license was there. When he found it, he began to worry. Had something happened to her? Maybe she got hurt, maybe cut on that broken dish, and left her bag behind in her rush to get to the emergency room. That must be it.

He could call the hospital to check, but maybe she hadn't reached there yet. He thought of the landlord. He should know.

He ran down the stairs and over to Spencer's door, then pounded loudly. A light came on inside and the door opened.

"Yes? Can I help you?"

"You remember me, Mr. Spencer? I'm George Durant. You wired my workshop a couple of years ago."

"Yes. Yes, I remember you. You're Sheldon's friend from the newspaper. She speaks of you now and again. Come in. How can I help you? Aren't you two supposed to be going to Ottawa tonight?"

"Yes. I was to pick her up at five, but she's not home. Her car is gone, but her apartment lights are on." Panic began to set in. He talked faster, "The door was ajar, and I went in. There was a broken dish on the floor, and I found her handbag in the bedroom with her driver's license in it. She wouldn't leave that behind. Do you know where she is?"

Suddenly Shellie's concerns about Spencer shot through George's mind. Could it be that he had done something to her? She had been nervous about him. Perhaps...

Spencer scowled. "That's strange. I knew she had a date. She called me just a short time ago. She said she was expecting some young woman in and asked me to let her in if she wasn't back. It sounded like the woman might be arriving tonight."

"A young woman? I wonder who that is. Did she say?"

"She gave me a name. I wrote it down. Let's see." He took a piece of paper from his shirt and held it at arm's length.

"Karen Lockhart," he read.

"Ah yes. Karen. I wonder what that's all about. It wouldn't seem as if that would have anything to do with Shellie's leaving in such a hurry that she'd forget her purse. Do you suppose she hurt herself somehow?"

"Maybe. But I really think she'd have come to me for help, if she had. I'd have taken her to the hospital if she needed to go."

"What about her car? She might have had car trouble. Then again, she'd have taken her bag. I'm sure of that. Women always take that bag, no matter what."

George was getting a crawly feeling along his neck. Something was wrong. He was sure of it. He knew Sheldon well enough to know that she wouldn't take off like that without leaving him a note. Spencer sounded genuinely concerned, also. George just didn't think Spencer was behind this disappearance. Something had happened.

"This is wrong. I can feel it. Something has happened to her." George said. "Maybe she got a call from someone else who needed her. Maybe Dee. I'll go back up and look by her telephone. She usually takes notes when someone calls. She might even have left me a note somewhere and I just didn't notice."

"I'll go with you," Spence said. "Let me get my jacket."

Together they mounted the stairs and walked into the fully lit kitchen.

Spence put his hand on George's arm.

"Those dress shoes of yours don't look to have a tread on them," he said, pointing to the footprint on the floor.

"That's not mine and it surely isn't Shellie's. Someone else was here. Did you see anyone?"

"No. I've been tidying the house a bit." A smile lit up Spencer's face. "My wife is coming back. We'd had a bit of a misunderstanding and she left me. But she called this afternoon, and we talked it through. I was changing the bed when Sheldon called. Then I was out in the laundry room. Just got back in the house."

Well that answered one question, George thought. Shellie's fears about Spencer were unfounded.

"I don't like this," he said. "I'll check her desk. You look around in here."

George found the tidy desk, with notes on same-size paper torn from the notepad beside the telephone, all stacked neatly in three piles. He quickly looked down through each. On top of one pile, in which were various telephone numbers and notes on agricultural projects, he found a telephone number for a Bill Ferguson and notes on Shantytown. He quickly read that note, which was dated today, and found a description of a lead mine and shacks around it.

That didn't seem significant to the search. There was nothing. He picked up the business card for Deputy Eugene Luce. As he looked at it he began to wonder. The informant about the body had to have been an official of some kind for her to be willing to accept it as true. The fact that she had a card here on her desk might mean he had been here. Otherwise she likely would have tucked it into her bag and forgotten about it, much like a man puts a card in his pocket.

Without further thought, George picked up the phone and dialed the number.

"Deputy Luce here."

"And this is George Durant here. I'm at Sheldon Merrill's apartment, trying to locate her. She has disappeared somewhere. Any chance you know anything about it?"

"Good God, man. How long has she been gone?"

"Not long, but she left under unusual circumstances. We were going to Ottawa this evening but she wasn't here when I arrived a few minutes ago. And her car is gone. She left her handbag with her driver's license, which leads me to think something is wrong. She always has that with her. I found your card on her desk."

"I gave it to her and told her to call if she ever needed help. Looks like maybe that's now. No other signs of what happened? Her landlord know anything?"

"No. He's here with me now. We found a dish broken on the floor and a footprint on her floor. It's from a boot-type shoe with cleats."

"Stay right there and I'll come over. She knew you were coming, so if she should call, it would be there, don't you think?"

"That makes sense. Yeah. I'll wait for you."

Hanging up, he waited a couple of seconds, then dialed again. Harry answered.

"This is George. You haven't seen anything of Shellie, have you?" He was trying to stay calm, but he knew he was talking too loudly for anyone to believe that.

"No. Should I have?"

"I was hoping so. She wasn't here when I got here to pick her up for our date tonight. It looks very suspicious and I'm getting concerned."

George related the findings again, and asked, "Can you think of where she might have gone in such a rush?"

"I haven't a clue. It's kind of soon to alert the police. She may have wanted to get something at the store in a hurry. She'll probably be back."

"She couldn't shop without her money. I just have a feeling that something's wrong. Things have been crazy ever since the fire. They find a body, and then your desk gets set on fire. I just hope Shellie won't be counted as the third disaster."

"Let's hope not. Speaking of the body, though, I got a call from the coroner. He said he felt that he should give me something on this case, since he didn't cooperate about affirming there was a body at the fire site. He found initials in the rings. The man's ring was initialed HTW and the woman's initials were GBW."

"Does it tell us anything?"

"I'm not sure. The first name that came to my mind was Hugh Webster. Maybe it was because I was thinking of him about the time of the call because he didn't show up for work tonight. I was about to go up to the archives room and look up the announcement of his wedding. I remember that he got married the week after he came to work for me last year. That was in March. I'll go upstairs now and find it."

"Hugh. Oh man. If it's Hugh…" George didn't finish the sentence. "Okay. Look, will you call me back and tell me? I'm at Shellie's."

"I'll do that."

Hugh. George remembered walking into the office and finding Hugh at Shellie's desk. He remembered how Shellie was always kind to Hugh and how Hugh followed her with his eyes everywhere she went. He felt helplessness coursing through him, but he'd wait it out. It wouldn't take Harry long to find the wedding notice.

Hugh. Something about him skittered through George's brain, then disappeared, something that had given him a flash of suspicion.

"Find anything?" he said, walking down the hall to where Spencer was in Sheldon's room.

"No. I took the liberty of looking through her handbag, too. Nothing. I feel like a voyeur, looking through her things. I hope she doesn't suddenly pop in and find us snooping."

"I wish she would. Somehow I have a terrible feeling that's not going to happen. Just keep looking. Deputy Gene Luce is coming out. Should be here any time now. I don't know what he thinks he can do any more than we can. Where in the world do you look for a missing person? We wouldn't even know what direction to go in."

Spencer saw George slowly falling apart and felt a fatherly concern. This young man obviously cared for Shellie. Well, they both did. She was a good girl.

"We can't let our imaginations run away with us," he said as calmly as he could. "There's probably a logical answer to all this. We'll just have to wait for a bit and see what develops. Just stay calm. Even though she's not here, it doesn't mean that she's in harm's way."

He wished he believed his own words. Obviously George didn't, either. They went through the motions of hunting through other parts of the apartment, even in the bathroom where the wet towel told them she had showered recently. But there were no clues, nothing to start them on their way to search for her.

As George walked by the divider, his foot crunched down on glass.

"I'd better clean up this broken dish," he said. "Don't want anyone to…" Then he remembered. It was when he went to clean up the coffee at the office.

"Oh God. The clippings." He ran to the phone and dialed the office, knowing that Harry would answer in the archives room.

When he did, George said, "Harry. I just remembered. Hugh has a bulletin board in his store room, at the back. All of the pages and articles that are on that board are stories that Shellie wrote."

"That sounds bad, because I do believe he's the killer and arsonist. If he isn't, then it's a very strange coincidence that Hugh's initials are HTW and his wife's are GBW.

CHAPTER 18

❁

Sheldon found it hard to breathe as her fear mounted. It flashed across her mind that this must be what it had been like for Lucille, being held captive against her wishes, loathing the man who robbed her of choices. No wonder she lost perspective on life. She had been a young and totally innocent girl, she trusted her uncle, and then he turned on her with a single-minded purpose. He trespassed into her soul and claimed it for his own, robbed her of individuality. He crushed her hopes and goals, molded her into a drunk and left her with nothing but cynicism and self-loathing. He made her his slave for life.

Just as Hugh would do with Sheldon. Full understanding hit her. No one had the right to do this. No one! Never had she felt so helpless. Never more alert. Never more angry. There must be a way to stop Hugh from carrying out whatever bizarre plan he had made.

Now on the Old County Road, it took Sheldon's full concentration to avoid the many holes. Her headlights could barely penetrate the heavy rain, nor could the wipers clear it from the windshield, the speeded-up clonk, clonk swishing water, like oil on the glass. She leaned over the steering wheel trying to see far enough ahead to avoid driving onto a soft shoulder. Her mind was on fire with disjointed thoughts and ineffective plans for escaping this madman holding a cannon of a gun over his arm, aimed directly at her mid-section. She prayed she wouldn't hit a pot hole hard enough to cause his finger to jerk against the trigger.

George must know by now that something had happened to her. She could cry, thinking of him waiting for her and worrying about her. But he just wouldn't know where she had gone. She pictured him pacing and looking at his watch every two seconds. Suppose he thought she had just skipped out on him? No. He wouldn't think that. He would have seen the broken candy dish and her pocketbook. He knew she wanted to go with him. He knew she had bought a lovely new dress and had her hair permed and had kissed him. Oh dear. Would she ever get to kiss him again? Would she ever joke and laugh with Dee again? Would she ever suffer through another of her mother's conversations? She wanted to hear her mother's voice again. She wanted to take her shopping for that raincoat. She wanted to exchange barbs with the Two Wicked Sisters at the office. She wanted to smell Spence's roses again. And she wanted so much to be with George again.

There must be something she could do to get away from Hugh. She could crash the car, but she might get killed doing it, so that wasn't an option. She couldn't wrestle the gun away from him, that was for sure. He was far too tall and strong for her, even if there weren't danger of the gun's discharging. If she could slow the car just enough so that she could open the door and jump…well, that was a movie stunt that she didn't feel too comfortable contemplating. She didn't have any poisons with her. Not that she ever did have any poisons. Oh, now she was getting silly. Think! she told herself. You have to think your way through this. Your mind is the only defense you have against this mad man.

"Hugh, where does this road come out?" she asked in as coy a voice as she could muster.

"Near the Lake Road. We'll take that to go to Shantytown. It goes past my house. I need to pick up clothes there, since we couldn't take yours."

He spoke with breathless anticipation. His expression when he came into her apartment had been wild, his eyes glazed with excitement behind his big glasses. Sheldon knew this was a real kick for him. He had mapped out a plan and he was certain it was going to work.

"Clothes?"

"Yeah. My wife's clothes. She don't need 'em any more."

"She doesn't? Why?"

"She just don't. She's gone."

"Where did she go?"

"Into the furniss."

Sheldon's hair positively stood on end. The "furniss". Hugh was the killer! That was his wife in the fire. Oh my God, she thought, he's a killer. Now she knew just how dangerous he was. Now she knew that she had to do whatever she could to get free of him.

"How would she get into a furnace?" she asked innocently.

"I put her there. She got in the way, and she cried. She cried all the time. I hate women to cry. I told her to stop it. If she would've stopped, I wouldn't've had to do it. But she wouldn't settle down. She never liked what I had for her. Never wanted to stay with me. She wanted to get out. After all I did for her."

Sheldon would have laughed if she weren't so frightened. She could imagine just how much Hugh Webster did for his wife. She had seen the outside of his house.

"Where was the furnace, Hugh?" Sheldon tried to sound only casually interested.

"At Mollisons' Farm, of course. You was there. You worked that day, and it was your day off. You shouldn't have worked that day. Harry shouldn't've made you do that."

"Harry? You were angry with Harry for making me work?"

"You bet I was. But he paid for it. I burned his papers. If the sprinklers hadn't gone off I'd'a burned the whole place down, and you wouldn't have to work there any more. I don't like to have you working so hard. You weren't supposed to be at the farm fire. I didn't do it to make you work. Honest. I wouldn't do that to you. I don't want you to work. I have to take care of you."

"Why should you do that?"

"'Cause a man should take care of his woman. He shouldn't make her go away and work."

Sheldon swerved the car around a large pothole and for a moment the gun waved wildly as Hugh made a grab for the dashboard. Her heart nearly stopped beating, then kicked in hard. The gun could have gone off accidentally. She slowed the car to a crawl.

"Is that what your father did? Made your mother go away to work?"

"Yeah. She worked hard and she wasn't home. She would'nt've died if she'd been home."

"What did she do?"

"Odd jobs on a farm. She mucked out stalls and pitched hay and worked in the fields."

"How did she die?"

"Poles under the hay mow broke one day and it all came down on top of her."

His mother was killed when a hay mow collapsed on a farm. Sheldon's mind, already in overdrive, thought of the farm fires, Hugh's wife, the man who was fired by the Stoners.

"What farm did she work at, Hugh? One that I know?"

"I don't know. It was Frank Stoner's place."

"Oh yes. I've heard of it." Pat's parents. His mother died on their farm. She drove on, cautiously, wishing she had the courage to slam the car into a tree. "You ever work on a farm, Hugh?"

"Yes," he said hesitantly. "After Pa died, I went to the Stoners and got work. Go faster. We need to get there."

Good lord. He must have set that fire for revenge. Was the Mollisons' fire for revenge, too? Sheldon was amazed at Hugh's candor, but she knew he thought she was going to stay with him and never be able to tell anyone what she had just learned. A shudder passed through her at the thought. How did he expect to keep her there? Didn't he think she could escape? If not, then he must have some kind of prison prepared.

"I can't drive too fast. It's dangerous. I don't want to break an axle on one of these pot holes," she said. Then, "Did you come to the *Press* after you stopped working at the farm?"

"No. That was years ago. I had a lot of jobs after I got fired by Stoner. I never went back to the mine, though. Pa died from the poison there."

"Poison? What poison?"

"Lead poison. I didn't get it, but Pa did. Anyway, they stopped mining after a while."

Lead poison. That was it. The blue line on Hugh's gums was a sign of lead poison. She had read that once in a murder mystery. Odd that she should remember that fact. She also remembered that the same ailment could cause brain damage.

"Had you been married long?"

"Anyone would know you're a reporter," Hugh said. "You ask a lot of questions."

She couldn't risk taking her eyes from the road, but she imagined his grin.

"Just interested. But reporting is my life, you know. I do love my work."

"I don't like your work. You won't work any more."

"You'd be taking away from me something I truly enjoy. Why would you do that, Hugh?"

"'Cause. It's not right. I told you. I have to take care of you. You can work at home and take care of our children."

Sheldon felt a wave of nausea. Children. With Hugh. It was the most repulsive thought she could imagine at the moment. It will never happen, she silently vowed, no matter what I have to do.

"Did you and your wife have any children?"

"No. She didn't give me none. She was no good. I didn't like her, not like you."

"You don't really know me."

"Yes I do. I watch you a lot. You didn't know that, did you? I've watched you at the office and I've watched you at home. I even saw you sleeping."

His laugh set her skin crawling. The nightmare had been real. Just as she had sensed, there had been someone in her bedroom and it was Hugh. She gripped the wheel so hard her hands ached.

"You was so lovely. Soft. Just like a baby. I felt your arm. I kissed you, too. I like kissing you."

If she held the wheel any tighter it would break in two. Dear God, this is a nightmare.

"How did you get into my apartment?" she asked through gritted teeth.

"I took your key one day while you was busy, and I had a copy made over at the hardware store. You didn't even know the key was gone. I put it back before you got back to your desk."

Fighting down her intense rage, Sheldon almost overshot the stop sign. She had to turn either right or left.

"Where are we? Where do I go now?"

"Turn right. The Lake Road is just a little bit up the road and you turn left there."

Sheldon drove on, unable to ask more questions. She knew all she needed to know about Hugh. He was crazy, and he was holding a gun on her. Remembering the condition of his wife's body when they found it, she knew she would have to do something, but if she didn't succeed in her first attempt at whatever she would try to do, it would probably be her last action. She had no doubt that Hugh would kill her as surely as he did his own wife if he thought she intended to get away from him.

❦　　　❦　　　❦

George couldn't sit still. Even as he related to Spencer what he and Harry had discovered, he was pacing. He had not felt so helpless in years, not since he watched his buddy die in Vietnam, unable to ease his pain or to save his life. That image flashed across his mind and he slammed his fist into the sofa back.

"Where is she?" He wanted to take off on a dead run. He ran his hand through his hair and pulled the tie from his neck, tossing it onto the coffee table.

"Try to calm down," Spencer said. "I know it's hard, but the one thing you need to do is keep a cool head. Becoming hysterical won't solve a thing."

"I know. I know. It's just that…I never even told her how much I love her. We've never even…"

"It's okay. She'll be okay. She's smart. You can bet she's thinking. If there's something she can do, assuming she's been kidnaped, she'll do it."

George sighed. "I expect you're right. God! If only I'd have gotten here sooner."

"Don't go blaming yourself. I've just gone down that path myself. When my wife called to say she was sorry for leaving the way she did, I nearly cried. I did manage to tell her it wasn't her fault. At first I blamed her when she walked out that door, but then I began to see things the way I thought she did, and my heart grew sick. I knew she was right and I was wrong. Every time she said she needed something or we should get something for the house, I acted as if we didn't have any more money left to do it. We're not rich, but we aren't hurting any more, and she should have some freedom to spend. Only I thought I needed to hold tight to the purse strings. The guilt trip I went on over it nearly did me in. It's best to let come what may, to see the problem, to figure out how to solve it. And to understand that, even if you didn't do something you should have, an action wasn't necessarily caused by you. My wife said she left because she thought she wanted a more meaningful life than she had here, not because I was too tightfisted. We'll work it out on both counts."

Despite the tension building in him, George had to smile over Spencer's words, and realized that here was a very good man. Sheldon would be happy that he wasn't the killer. That thought triggered another dread that started his pacing again. Why didn't Luce get here? He couldn't wait much longer.

"If the deputy doesn't get here within five minutes, I'm taking off for Ashton," George said. "I know where Hugh Webster lives. It's a place to start and it's better than waiting here for a phone call that doesn't seem to be coming."

"If you leave, I might as well go back to my place. If Sheldon should call here and not get an answer, chances are she'd call me."

George nodded. Within seconds, they heard footsteps on the stairs. George opened the door before Deputy Luce got to the top.

"Anything new?" he asked.

"Yeah. We've got a real development here. We think we know who the killer of that woman in the fire is."

"No kidding. Who is it?"

George explained about the initials in the rings and who they fit.

"And if it's Hugh Webster, it's very likely he has Shellie."

"How can you be so sure?"

"Hugh's the night janitor at the *Press*. He's had eyes for Shellie ever since he came there to work."

"That's understandable," Gene said under his breath, but not so low that George didn't hear it.

"The most damning thing is that I found Sheldon's stories on a bulletin board over Hugh's desk at the office, including the Mollison farm fire. I didn't think anything of it at the time, but in light of all this, I'm convinced that Hugh somehow came here and took Shellie. He must have had her drive her own car."

"That does seem to point the finger, doesn't it. Do away with his wife in an explosion and fire, thinking no one would discover the body, then go after Shellie."

"We all thought he was goofy," George said. "But not so far out that he'd kill someone, or set fires." He turned aside to hide his face. "Or kidnap someone. The question is where did he take her? I know where his house is, on the Lake Road in Ashton. I was just about to go there."

"We'll both go in the cruiser, and I'll call in on the way. Let's go." To Spencer, Luce said, "You stay here. Would she call her own number or yours?"

"Mine, likely. She'd know that no one should be here."

"Okay then. Give me your phone number. If we locate her, I'll give you a call."

※   ※   ※

The ride to the highway was painfully slow for George, but he set his jaw and forced himself to stay calm, listening to the crackle of radio calls, the ten-fours, and the splat, splat of the windshield wipers. But his mind registered none of what he heard. His mind saw a pretty young face with a charming new hairdo and laughing brown eyes, and a ready blush at a compliment. This night was supposed to turn into something memorable, but not this memorable. He had planned dinner and theater and then a very expensive hotel room, if she had been willing. Somewhere in that scenario he was going to propose to her.

Mentally he said her name over and over and prayed they wouldn't be too late.

CHAPTER 19

❈

When Sheldon walked into Hugh's house at gunpoint, she felt sick. It was dark, damp, and cold, with the fetid odor of rotting wood and mold. Hugh pulled a string for light and in the faint glow of the bare lightbulb, hanging from a wire strung along the ceiling, she saw a card table, a ladder-back chair with a broken back slat and a folding metal chair, an iron wood stove, a rusted iron sink with no faucets in a roughly constructed cabinet of warped plywood, and a grimy pantry cabinet. The bare wood floor, greasy underfoot, looked as if it had never been washed.

No wonder Hugh's wife cried all the time. Sheldon knew she would, too, if she had to live here. God, she thought, don't let that happen. Don't let me be trapped by this maniac. I have to find a way out of this nightmare.

She cast another frantic look around the room. On the back of the stove was an iron frying pan, on the table were a half-full glass sugar bowl, mismatched salt and pepper shakers, and some odds and ends flatware, by the sink were a chipped porcelain water pail, a dirty huck towel and a butcher knife. A butcher knife! She did not let her eyes linger there, for fear Hugh would notice and remove the knife. But she thought, if I can just get my hands on that knife. Then what? Will I stab him? Can I do it? What if I miss or he gets the knife away from me? He might slash me or maybe beat me up and I'd be helpless. I mustn't let that happen. I could hit him with the frying pan, but he's so tall. God, I don't know what to do.

Her thoughts took only seconds after they entered the kitchen. Now Hugh said, "Come on. This way. Her clothes is upstairs."

He picked up a flashlight from the windowsill and pointed the way with it, still aiming the gun at her. Sheldon was in good shape, but not particularly athletic. She knew her limitations. Even though she'd like to knock away the gun and attempt to run, it would be foolhardy. A gun would fire a fatal bullet much faster than she could move.

She did as he commanded, walking through a small, unlit living room where she could make out images of chairs and a couch, and into a short hallway with stairs. She hesitated at the foot of the stairs, but when he jammed the gun into her back she ascended, her heart speeding up with each step. She prayed he wouldn't get any ideas about the bed.

As they walked into the bedroom, he told her to pull the string for the light, another small-watt bulb hanging from the ceiling.

She took quick inventory of the bedroom: an iron bed with stained, sagging mattress and no sheets, a four-drawer bureau, a metal folding chair that matched the one in the kitchen, and a slop pail at the foot of the bed, which she avoided looking at. The malodorous air told her its probable condition. She covered her mouth and nose to keep from gagging.

"Clothes is in there," Hugh said, pointing to the closet without a door. "Grab some and let's get goin'. I wanna get to our place."

Sheldon went to the closet and peered into its darkness. Her own clothes were a bit out of fashion, but what she saw here made her cringe. These things must date back to World War Two, she thought, as she held out a couple of badly stained and yellowed cotton dresses, the cuffs on their long sleeves frayed. From the same era was a gathered cotton skirt of three tiers, part of the old eyelet at the gathers ripped and hanging. She saw one pair of double knit slacks, pilled and stretched out of shape. The four nylon tops were in equally shabby state, and obviously about two sizes too large for Sheldon. There was no sign of Hugh's clothes. He must have already transferred his to wherever it was that he intended for them to live. She shuddered.

She looked back at Hugh, whose determined expression left no doubt he was intent on carrying out his mission.

"Take everything. You'll need it. And hurry."

"I can't..." No, she thought, better not oppose him right now. Better get out of this place. She swept the stale-smelling collection onto one arm and they went back down the stairs.

In the kitchen, Sheldon stopped. This was far enough. No more. She couldn't go through with this, no matter what it meant. If they got out to Shantytown, no one would find her. She had to do something, and she made up her mind to make a stand right now. She laid the clothes over the table, took a deep breath, and turned around.

"Hugh, why don't you put down that gun and talk with me so that I can understand what you're trying to do?"

He looked from her to the gun in his hand and scowled, but he continued to point it at her. "I told you. I'm taking you to live with me. I want you to be my wife. There's nothing more to talk about." His voice seldom changed inflection, always a monotone. She noticed now that it was beginning to be ragged, as he took short breaths before every couple of words.

"But why this way? You wouldn't really harm me, would you?"

She hoped she sounded a whole lot more confident than she felt. It wasn't easy pretending to be calm when every nerve in her body was jumping, when she wanted to scream and run.

"Why don't you understand?" he said impatiently. "Why can't you see I don't want anyone else in the world, just you. I had Gwen, but she was no good. She yelled and she wanted too much. I hit her to shut her up. I hated her crying and screaming. You wouldn't do that. You'd be good to me. You're always good to me. You stop and talk with me, and you smile at me. And I want you. That's all. I want you. You'll be mine. I don't want you to be in that office. I don't want you to be near that George…"

Sheldon thought of how she wished she'd gone to Ottawa with George. She thought, Oh, George. Will I ever see you again?

"I don't want you to run around everywhere for stories and then at that desk for hours. No. No. I want you home. My home. Where you belong. You belong with me. You…you need to be with me."

Sheldon jumped when a door banged in the wind out back somewhere. The window panes rattled as rain beat against them in a sudden fury. Sheldon heard the increasing agitation in Hugh's voice and she fought down the frantic feeling that he might imprison her. He was a man who took what he wanted, stole from local stores, with apparently no thought that it was wrong to do that. He stole, he killed, and he destroyed. She needed to be careful now, or she'd lose it altogether. How could she appeal to him?

"But, Hugh, wouldn't it be better if you courted me if you want me? Don't you know that a woman isn't the same as a dog or a cat? You don't just pick up a woman and take her home. You have to be gentle and caring and show the woman that you care and then you ask her if she'll have you. A woman likes a man to do that."

Confusion flashed in his eyes, then distrust. Then anger.

"No! I don't do that. It don't work. I tried doing all that. It never worked. This is the only way." His voice grew louder, more insistent. "I do it my way. I…everything's ready. I'm ready. I'm not waiting any more. You have to come with me now."

He started toward her and she moved away in the direction of the sink, her stomach sick with fear. She felt water trickling down her sides. This man was so dangerous. How could she save herself?

"I'm not going anywhere with you, Hugh. We're going to stop this nonsense right now. You didn't really think I would live with you, did you?" Her bluster was so forced even she wouldn't believe it.

His pale eyes, owlish through the big glasses, looked dead, without feeling.

"Yes, you're goin' with me." He made a growling sound. "I fixed us up a nice place."

"In Shantytown?" She had inched toward the plywood counter but still had a few steps to go before she would be within reach of the knife.

He nodded. "It was my home once. No one can find us there. Just the two of us. You'll like it."

Was he trying to convince her or himself? Did he believe that this would work, this weird, crazy plan of his? Was he beginning to see the fallacy of it? She could only hope so.

"I got new sheets, and new linolyum for the floor and…and a sewing machine for you, that works. It's clean, not like this place. She didn't keep house good."

"Gwen?"

"Yeah, Gwen. She's not my wife any more. She's gone now. I blew her up."

"No, Hugh, you didn't. She managed to crawl out of the fire before she died. Her body was found on a woods road, away from the barn. The authorities know she was murdered. They'll be looking for you soon enough."

The air wooshed out of Hugh's lungs as if he'd been punched in the belly, and he stepped backward until he was resting his weight against the cold stove. Slowly he turned his head from side to side, an incredulous expression on his face.

"No. She was blown up. I blew her up. I watched the barn explode. She had to be there. I put her there. You're lying. She was dead, I know it. I killed her."

Sheldon felt a glimmer of hope. Maybe now he'd give up, let her go.

"She must have come to after you left her and had life enough to drag herself out of the barn and away from it before it exploded."

"But…but…but…I shot her. She was dead before."

"She died, all right, but after she got out of the fire. You killed her, Hugh. What do you feel about that? Aren't you sorry for that? Don't you know it was wrong?"

"Yes…no…it wasn't wrong. I wanted you. It's not wrong. I had to get rid of her."

"Why didn't you just divorce her, then?"

"Because. She was Cath'lic and she said we couldn't get divorced. She wanted me to move into town so she could see people. She hated this house. It's not so bad. But she cried. She said I should let her work to get more things."

"Did you tell her you wanted me?"

"No. I said I wanted to get divorced."

"And she said no?"

"Yeah. We got into a fight, and she wouldn't stop crying. And I told her to stop crying. And she said I wasn't good to her. I was. I always was good to her."

"If you were good to her, why did you kill her?"

"She made me. She wouldn't do what I said. She got me mad. I got mad. And I hit her and she wouldn't stop crying. I got my gun out and I shot her to shut her up. She…she was dead. So I took a can of kerosene and I put her in that barn. I saw the dynamite and I soaked the hay with kerosene and went out the back door. I tossed a match on the hay. I ran back to the woods and watched. It took a long time for the dynamite to blow. But it did blow. I knew she was gone then."

He pulled at his hair. "I know she was dead. You're lying. I wanted her to be gone."

"Why did you put her in the Mollisons' barn?"

"Because Pat was mean to me when she lived at her father's. She wouldn't like me. I tried to kiss her and she scratched my face."

"Did you set that fire at the Stoners'?"

"They weren't good to me. I needed some money one day. She found me taking some from their box and they fired me. I would'a paid it back. But they fired me. I got mad. I went back that night and started a fire. Where my Ma died, in the hay there. And the barn blew up."

"And you did the same thing to the Mollisons."

He grinned as if it was a big joke.

"Yeah. I did the same thing. Not hard to do. And Gwen was in it. She was dead."

"Only she got out, and the authorities will find out who she was and who killed her."

The gun nearly forgotten in his hand, Hugh slumped forward, his mouth open, as he thought about what Sheldon had said. For just a few seconds, she was relieved, sure that she had reached him, that he would give up this plan of his and let her go. Then suddenly he came alert, straightened, and pointed the gun toward her head.

"I don't care. They don't know I did it. We'll go to Shantytown now. They won't find us there."

"Yes they will, Hugh. They'll find you. You know they will. You have to work. You can't just hide out."

"I can go out at night. I can get food and clothes. No one will know where we are."

"You mean you'd steal food and clothes?"

"I know how to do it. It's easy. I've done it before. Come on. We're going now. No more talk."

He made a motion with his gun toward the door and started toward her. This was it. Sheldon's chest felt like it would explode, as she stepped backward, away from him, and felt the counter behind her.

"No. I'm not going with you. I'm going to get into my car and drive back to Westburgh. You can't keep me against my will."

It took her by surprise, the look of fear that so quickly turned to madness, and as he lurched toward her, she knew he intended to hurt her. She tried to stop him by speaking his name in a firm tone, but he apparently couldn't hear her through the storm of confusion rushing in his head. He looked as if he were in battle, rushing at an enemy soldier, his eyes wild.

"You'll come with me!"

The smack of his left-handed blow to her face sent her sprawling across the sink. Her face felt like it was burned with a branding iron. Pain shot through her forearm where it hit the plywood edge, and she prayed the bone wasn't broken.

She looked up and said his name again. "Hugh. Stop this. You don't want to hurt me."

But she might as well have spoken to a wild dog. She saw in his face no humanity, only wild rage. The vision of a beaten, shot, and burned woman flashed across her mind, as vivid as if she had actually seen the body. In that instant she knew he would kill her, just like he had killed Gwen, only for the reverse reason. To keep her, not to get rid of her.

"You won't go anywhere." He yelled hysterically. "I'll take you to our house. I fixed it up for you. You're mine."

She closed her eyes and ducked as he struck at her again, this time the blow hitting the back of her head. When she opened her eyes, she saw the knife, right in front of her. She bent lower over it, as if to regain her wind. He was so close to her she could hear his heavy breathing, smell his rancid breath. If he hit her as hard again, she would likely go down, maybe unconscious…maybe dead.

In one motion, she grabbed the knife with both hands, swung toward him, and with a strength she never guessed she had, plunged the knife through his coat and into his flesh. She had calculated how to grab the knife handle and swing it up all in one motion. What she had not calculated on was the gun's exploding at the same instant.

🍁   🍁   🍁

George glanced over at Deputy Luce, who had the patrol car's light flashing and siren whining as they sailed down the slick and almost obscured highway toward Ashton. The overhead road lamps looked to be moving, their beams of light whipping wildly in the rain like frantic ghostly dancers, only briefly lighting the road.

"This is about as bad a storm as I've seen in this part of the country," he said.

"It's bad all right. Acts like we're in a hurricane. I'll call in and see."

Luce made the call to the central station and learned that winds weren't quite hurricane force, but that warnings were going out over TV and radio for people to stay off the road.

Then he informed the dispatcher where he was headed, said he didn't need backup yet, but to be alert to the fact that he might need help and an ambulance.

"An ambulance," George said after the conversation was finished. "Damn, I hope not. At least not for Shellie. I don't think I've ever been more scared in my life."

"You got it bad for her?"

"Yeah. I guess you could say that."

"You two engaged?"

"Not yet."

"I see. But you're going to ask her, huh?"

"I certainly intend to. If…when we get through this night."

"Well, I can see I'd better not be knocking at her door, then."

"You did, didn't you? You're the one who gave her the tip about the body?"

Eugene chuckled. "Yeah, I guess I thought I could get on the good side of her. She's a pretty special person I would say from what little I know of her. She didn't tell you it was me?"

"No. She didn't tell Harry, either. I guessed when I saw your card on her desk."

"Well, at least we know she can be trusted. That's more than you can say for some women."

"You're right there." George blinked back a sudden dampness in his eyes. Trustworthy, sweet, smart, and a real pleasure to hold. He had never felt for any woman, especially not his former wife, what he felt for Shellie. She was the woman he wanted to share his future years with, to have a family with. God, please let us have a future together, he thought.

"If Hugh Webster so much as touches a hair on her head, I'll kill him," he said, his jaw tight.

"It might be better if I handled that end of it. I wouldn't mind eliminating the competition, but I really don't want to have to put you behind bars for murder."

They were now going through the village of Ashton.

"You know where the Lake Road is?" George asked.

"I know. And I know where David Bradford's place is. You say it's just this side of it?"

"Yes. On the right."

"We'll be there in just a few minutes now."

Despite the darkness of the country roads and at times nearly impenetrable rain, Deputy Luce didn't slow down. Under different circumstances George would be gripping anything he could get hold of, but he was oblivious to the speed and the danger of the road.

The tension in his gut built until George wanted to jump from the car and run the rest of the way. In war, he had steeled himself against emotion, had not let the dangers around him unsettle his reason, and had come through some of the worst fighting conditions. He'd seen fellow soldiers go to pieces, lose their sense of self-preservation and die because of fear and carelessness. But he had stayed alert, aware, and careful.

This was different. He couldn't protect Shellie. She was on her own. When they first got in the car, Gene had told him about Hugh's wife and what she looked like when he found the body. George fisted his hands and forced himself to concentrate on staying calm. He knew it wouldn't do any good to go off half-cocked when they got to Hugh's house. He didn't want to jeopardize Shellie's life.

Finally the house came into view. "That's it."

The deputy had turned off the siren and flashing lights when they entered the Lake Road. Now he slowly drove into the driveway, the patrol car's light illuminating a car and a black truck in front of it.

"That's Shelllie's car," George said. "She must be here."

"I'll go through the back door. You stay put. Don't go trying to be a hero."

He left the car, and George squinted through the rain to watch. He could see a very dim light through the hazy window. This was too much. He couldn't wait any longer. He quietly opened the door and left it ajar, then moved swiftly to the door through which Gene had just gone. The sight that greeted him inside gave wings to his feet.

Eugene knelt beside Hugh Webster, who was writhing in pain on the floor with a knife protruding from his coat.

"Shellie," George yelled. "Where is she?"

"I don't know. But this one's bleeding a lot. Looks like Shellie must have gotten the drop on him with that butcher knife. He's also got a gunshot wound in the foot."

It took George only seconds to bound through the house and discover that they were alone. When he returned, Webster was moaning loudly.

"I'm hurt bad. She tried to kill me. She cut me."

"Just stay put, Webster." The gun was on the kitchen table now. "There'll be an ambulance here soon."

"I'm dying."

"No. Sorry to say you're not dying. What did you find, George?"

"Nothing. She's not here." He fought an impulse to grab Hugh Webster by the throat and finish the job.

Just as Luce said, "Okay, Webster. Where's Sheldon Merrill?" David Bradford burst through the door, looking like a Maine lobsterman, his long yellow slicker and matching wide-brimmed hat dripping.

"Webster's alive?" Bradford sounded surprised.

"He's alive," Luce replied. "A little the worse for wear, though. How come you're here?"

"Sheldon Merrill pounded on my door a few minutes ago, babbling so I couldn't understand her at first. Finally when she calmed down, she said she had killed Hugh Webster, that she'd stabbed him with a knife and that a gun went off. She said he was on the floor, dead."

"Is she at your place now?" George asked.

"Yes. She's there." Bradford stood over Hugh Webster, whose moans continued. "For a woman who doesn't believe in killing…"

George didn't hear the rest. He was out the door, running through the rain, his head down, his breath coming harder with each stride. At the lodge, he opened the door and saw her slumped over her knees where she sat on a deacon's bench, her hair soaked and matted to her head, coat hanging open, new red shoes covered with mud.

"Shellie."

She didn't respond.

"Shellie, it's me, George."

He went to her and put his hands on her shoulders.

"Honey, look at me and listen. You didn't kill Hugh." He eased himself down beside her. "You only wounded him. Do you hear me? He's alive."

Slowly she raised her head and gripped his arm.

"He…he's not dead? Are you sure?"

"My God. What's he done to you?" She winced when he gently touched the side of her face and studied the bright red bruise that was swelling beneath her eye. "He beat you? That no-good bastard. How bad are you hurt?"

"Not bad. He hit me a couple of times. And then I got my hand on the knife and stabbed him. And the gun went off. I thought I was shot at first. When I looked at him he was so white…and…and dead. I didn't know what to do. I was so scared. And I thought of this place and hoped Mr. Bradford was here. I just ran. I thought I was a killer."

"It's okay now. It's all over."

"He killed his wife and put her in the barn. He thought he could blow her up and no one would know. He's crazy, George. Really crazy."

George held her closer.

"I know. The rings had initials in them and Harry looked up their wedding announcement. He discovered that the two sets of initials matched Hugh's and his wife's. So we were pretty certain that he was the killer. We put a few other things together and guessed it was you he was after."

Shaking all over, she began to sob again

"Someone like that…I don't know. He's cruel. He just thinks that whatever he wants it's okay to take. I know he's a sick man, but right now I just don't know what to think about him. When I went at him with the knife, I wanted him dead. I did, George. I wanted him dead. And now…I guess I still want him dead. He wanted me so bad, yet he would have killed me. I could see it in his eyes. He just lost control and began to hit me. I knew he'd beat me up, maybe kill me."

A great sob racked her body. "You're sure he's alive? He looked dead to me. His eyes were staring."

"No. He's not dead. He's awake and talking. He'll be okay, unfortunately."

"I…I would have killed him. And I thought I had, George. I can't believe I could do that. It's such a horrible thing. If I had killed him, I don't know how I could have lived with myself."

Neither one noticed the brief sound of the storm as David Bradford opened the door.

"No, no. Now listen to me." George held her at arm's length and cupped her chin in his hand to make her look into his eyes. "You acted in self-defense. You know what he's capable of doing. I don't know what he had in mind, but he had kidnaped you. He hit you and you knew he might even kill you. You had to save yourself. If you had killed him, you would have to realize that you had no choice. You did what you had to do to save your own life."

Words began to flow from Sheldon non-stop.

"He was going to make me his prisoner in some shack out in Shantytown at the lead mine. He wanted me to wear those awful dirty old clothes that his poor wife wore. Oh lord. He's a horrible man. He killed his wife and he set both farm fires, the one at Mollisons' and the one at her parents' years ago, all for revenge. He told me he beat his wife and shot her because she wouldn't give him a divorce and because she wouldn't stop crying. He did all that because of me. He wanted me. Then he put her in the barn. He was sure she had been blown to bits. He actually told me that just as if it was an every day thing and he had no remorse whatsoever. All he could think of was taking me out there and keeping me and not letting me work. Said he'd take care of me. He'd steal food and clothes. Oh-my-god, this is all such a terrible nightmare. I know he's probably brain damaged from lead poisoning, but to have no compassion…he just doesn't value life, except his own. George," her head came up and she stared him in the eyes, "he actually came into my apartment, into my bedroom last night. He'd had a key made from my house key and he came in and he stood over me while I was sleeping…"

She heard a light cough and looked across the room to find that Bradford was watching them from just inside the doorway. He removed his slicker and hat and hung them on a clothes tree by the door, then he walked toward the fireplace where he picked up a log and threw it onto the dying fire.

When he turned toward them, he said in a slightly amused voice, "Now you see, Miss Merrill." He had the good grace not to say I told you so, but she knew what he meant.

She felt small, like a child who has just experienced why not to put her hand on a hot stove. "Yes, I see."

"See what?" George asked.

"I'll tell you later. Mr. Bradford, I'd like to go home. Do you think I can, or should I stay for questioning?"

"The deputy told me to let you know you could go on home. He'll get a statement from you later, at your place. The ambulance is on its way to pick up Webster."

"My car's over there," she said to George. "I left my car at his house."

"I know. I'll get it," Looking down at her blood-stained raincoat and her muddied red shoes, he grinned. "I think a date in Ottawa would have been a lot more fun than this."

CHAPTER 20

❀

Monday dawned damp but sunny. For once Sheldon had slept in, after the late-night questions and discussion about Hugh Webster. Deputy Luce had come to the apartment for her statement, rather than take her into headquarters, and left at about eleven o'clock, half an hour before George left. They called Harry and told him what had happened, and George said he would write it up.

"Never thought anyone would steal me," she told Harry with a laugh. It seemed good to be laughing. In fact, she felt absolutely giddy now that it was all over and she knew that she was not a killer. It still bothered her to think that she might have been, though, and she knew she would never forget that sickening feeling when the knife in her hand sliced into Hugh's flesh.

She flung the covers back when she saw that it was eight o'clock. She had promised George she'd get to the office by nine in case there were still some points that they hadn't covered the night before. She was dressed and hastily eating breakfast when the phone rang.

"Miss Merrill?"

"Yes." She recognized the lyrical voice before hearing, "It's Karen Lockhart. I couldn't get out of Boston last night, but I got a private plane early this morning. I'm in Syracuse, and the driver is here. We should arrive there by eleven."

"Good. You have the directions I gave you?"

"Yes. I have them right here."

"Fine. I should be here by the time you arrive. Then we can go see Miss Bradford."

Sheldon drove into Westburgh humming her usual random musical notes. The roads were littered with leaves and small branches, but while the rain had been torrential, it still wouldn't do a lot of good. She was glad, all the same, to see sunshine this morning. It was like a sign that there was hope no matter how dire life might become. Of course, she knew that wasn't always true. It hadn't been true for Miss Bradford. Poor woman had been so misused. And when she killed her uncle, she couldn't live with her guilt. Actually she felt double guilt, not just for the murder, but for the incestuous relationship her uncle had forced her into when she was so young. She compounded the lie about his death being an accident by living two lives, degrading herself in the one way she knew went contrary to all the righteous pronouncements by both her father and her uncle. Her life of lies was now her deathbed torment, as if she hadn't had enough torment already. Sheldon wished Lucille could live longer. It just wasn't right.

The *Press* office smelled like wet charcoal, and only the men were working. Manfred and Jon each greeted her with joking remarks about the extremes some women went to in order to get out of a date with George. Their faces, however, showed their admiration and concern for her, and she touched her swollen face self-consciously. Fortunately, she could still see out of her eye, but it was colorful.

She exchanged a cheerful good-morning with George, blushing when he cocked an eyebrow and winked, their passionate good-night kiss still a pleasant, searing memory.

"Story's almost finished," he said. "Here, start reading." He handed her the first few takes. His tone softened, "Your face looks sore. Did you sleep okay last night?"

"Once I got to sleep, yes. But it wasn't easy to turn it all off. I put ice on this, but it's still ugly. How about you? Did you sleep okay?"

"Impossible. I was here at six. Seemed best to work under the circumstances."

She gave him a knowing look that said she was so very grateful for his concern and that he came to rescue her. What she didn't know was that George had a sleepless night, not because of the aftereffects of his fear for her life and then the rescue, but because of their second kiss that had set off fire bombs in his whole being. He had tossed and turned and then paced the floor until daylight, going over and over in his mind what he should say to her when he asked her to marry him.

As Sheldon read his story, she felt an uneasy tension build, reliving the ordeal with Hugh.

The newsprint was becoming smudged from her sweaty hands. Now she understood how Gwen Webster was able to crawl from the fire and get as far as she did, despite her many wounds. Sheldon had never before experienced that heightened sense of survival at all costs and the super strength that went with it. With a shudder, she remembered the cracking blow he gave her, and the moment she knew she would plunge the knife into Hugh. So effortless was the motion that she wasn't sure she had hurt him until she saw the blood. Raw panic sent her flying from the house afterward. Despite her high heels, she barely felt her feet hit the ground when she ran through the rain toward Bradford's lodge, praying he was there. When he opened the door, she collapsed against him, sobbing hysterically that she had just killed Hugh Webster. Her instinct to survive had taken over and she learned that she was capable of what she had always considered the unthinkable, unforgivable deed…killing to save herself. The aftermath left her horrified, both at Hugh's calculated actions and at what she could do.

She had an uneasy feeling that if she could sit on a jury to judge Hugh, she would recommend the death penalty. Perhaps that was why she had been able to drive the knife into him, her moral outrage at its zenith, much the same as Lucille Bradford's had been when she killed her uncle.

Perhaps she was no better than Hugh if she felt that he should die for his cruelty. When she could think rationally, she would have to weigh the life and death questions more thoroughly, but so much had been thrust into her thinking in these past few days that all her long-held beliefs had been shaken, just as her whole life was shaken.

"It's a good story," Sheldon said after she had read all of it. "Gave me the creeps to read about my own abduction. So I didn't deal Hugh such a terrible blow after all."

"No, the doctor said the foot wound from the gunshot did more damage than your knife wound, though it was painful. The knife hit flesh, nothing critical. The gunshot, however, shattered bone."

"Good. I'm glad he suffered pain, at least."

Harry had come to her desk as she said the last, and he laid his hand on her shoulder.

"You did all right, kid. You had us all pretty worried, though."

"I'm truly surprised that you guys figured out who it was in such short order."

Harry repeated what George had told her concerning the rings and also about the newspaper clippings that Hugh had posted over his desk, all written by Sheldon. "Since he hadn't come in to work, we just put it all together. It was a long shot, of course, but George and I agreed that it was better than waiting for more conclusive evidence."

George added, "I knew that he'd been ogling you for months, Shellie. I just sensed that he had somehow gotten you. Even though your car was gone and there wasn't any other vehicle there, I still thought he'd managed to get you away from your place. It was more instinct than anything else."

Telephones were ringing, and since Sheldon had no more work to do there, she left to go to the hospital. As she drove out of the parking lot, she saw a tan patrol car drive in. The driver was Deputy Luce.

Time was short now, so she merely gave him a hearty wave and drove on. She had thanked him last night and given him a peck on the cheek, aware that he held her hand a bit too long before leaving, and that George scowled as he watched.

At the hospital, she sighed, remembering the kiss she shared with George afterward. Yet, he didn't press her further. "You're tired. You need to rest after all you've been through," he said. "But we have some serious talking to do."

Serious talking. That could mean most anything, but likely meant he wanted a romantic relationship, and she didn't object to that. Of one thing she was certain. He was the best thing to come into her life ever. Part of her light feeling today was because of him. He had come to rescue her. He cared for her. Yes, and she cared for him. If she were honest with herself, she was in love with him. But he had said he kept his romances very casual, and she supposed he would want it that way with her.

She did hope he wouldn't ask her to move in with him. Somehow she never liked the idea of living with a man without being married. She thought of Sally James, her high school friend who had done that and had lived with a man for almost three years. Then they broke up. The problem was in what they owned, who would take what. They became so contentious over their possessions that they ended up in court when she sued him over a recliner and an expensive clock that he claimed were his, though she had the receipts showing she paid for them.

Just as she feared, David Bradford was still there when she arrived at Lucille's room.

When she saw him, bending over his sister and speaking in a hushed voice, she hesitated. What would she do now? She couldn't very well tell Lucille that Karen had arrived while David was there.

"Oh, excuse me," she said. They both looked in her direction. "I'll come back later."

"No, my dear," Lucille said. Her short breaths were labored, her voice weaker still. "David has had his visit. He was just saying good-bye. Come right in. He'll be back this afternoon."

"Yes, I'm leaving, Miss Merrill. You look like you're getting a good shiner there. Put ice on it."

Sheldon glanced at Lucille, and guessed that he hadn't told her about the excitement.

"I'm fine," she said, still standing by the doorway as he approached it. When he passed her, she whispered, "And thank you."

He smiled and patted her arm. "Life's full of surprising lessons, isn't it?"

Not expecting an answer, he strode down the hall like a king, head high, nodding to the nurses. As Sheldon watched him, she thought what a grand person he was and she hoped he would reconcile with Karen. Apparently he had truly loved her. She hoped the feeling was mutual. He deserved a good woman, but he needed one who could stand up to him.

Not like me, she thought. I really am more George's type.

She went to the bedside and said, "Karen is coming. She'll be here late this morning."

"Thank you. You don't know how relieved I am to hear that. Get her here this afternoon at three."

"Yes, I will. What do you think they'll do?"

"They love each other still, I'm sure of it. I wish I could see their wedding, but I'll be content to know that they are together again."

After struggling for breath and much wheezing, Lucille said, "I must see them today. I couldn't have waited longer."

"Oh." Sheldon couldn't say any more. She knew what Lucille meant, and it hurt. How she wished that they might have known each other long ago, that Lucille might have forgiven herself and have found happiness in a calmer state of life.

Little more could be said, and Sheldon bent down to kiss her cheek, then left. Her presence only tired Lucille more. There was still one more call she had to make before going back home.

"Come in. It's open," Dee called.

Sheldon opened the door and began, "I came over to tell you what…" then she stopped, her mouth open. "Dee. What in the world are you doing?"

Sitting in the middle of the floor, wearing jeans and T-shirt, her hair tied back with a red bandanna, and surrounded by packing boxes, books, and dishes, Dee looked up and said, "Come on over. Maybe you'd like some of these books. Have you ever read *The Tontine*? It's a really good story. Long, but good."

"Dee! What are you doing? Answer me?"

"Oh, I'm packing. Can't you tell?"

"I can see that you're packing. But why are you packing?"

Dee patted a spot next to her for Sheldon to sit. "What happened to your face? Did George hit you last night?"

"No, he didn't. I'll tell you as soon as you tell me why you're packing."

"You're the first to know this. I haven't given my notice yet, but I will tomorrow. I'm leaving, Shel. I'm going back home to Maine."

"No. Why? I hope it isn't because of Conrad's stupid stunt. He isn't worth giving up your job and life here for."

Dee pressed her hand on Sheldon's knee. "Never fear. I don't give up anything for a man. Not usually, anyway. You know that."

"Then why?" Sheldon knew Dee could hear the sob in her throat.

"I'm not going to the end of the world, dear friend. It's only to the coast of Maine. It's a ten-hour drive from here. That's all. We'll see each other from time to time."

"I know, but it won't be the same. Why are you leaving?"

"I need to make amends with my mother."

"Really? Was it that bad?"

"Yeah. It was that bad. I left Twin Ports in rather a huff. No. It was more than a huff. I was mad as hell at my mother."

"Why?"

"She's a very strong-willed woman, and our personalities have clashed ever since I was a child. I'm too much like her, I guess. We finally had just one too many battles on how I should conduct my life, and I packed up and headed west. Happened to pick up a copy of the *Press* at a lunch stand on the road and saw an ad for a reporter in Westburgh, New York. After asking myself, where the hell is Westburgh, New York, I decided wherever it was it might be just the thing for me right then."

Sheldon nodded. "That was after Joan Wight left."

"I came here, and walked in without even a telephone call to them. You know Harry. He looked at my college credentials and read some of my articles and gave me the job."

Harry had never attended college and he respected those who had. It always helped to hold a degree when applying for a job with him. Of course, the fact that Dee had been an associate editor in Twin Ports, Maine, didn't hurt, either. She had taken a demotion for the job he gave her.

"But why don't you just talk with her on the phone, or go visit for a while, if you want to make up? Why give up your life here?"

"My mother called me, actually. She said she has a problem. She asked me to come home and help her with it. I was stunned that she would ask me to help her. Anyway, I told her I'd let her know, and last night I called her. Said I'd be there in one week. It's not much notice for Harry, but it isn't as if I hold a top executive position. He'll find a reporter very soon."

"Did she tell you what the problem is?"

"No. But she sounded contrite enough and worried enough that I couldn't ignore her plea. I felt that if she could swallow her pride to call me, then I could swallow mine and go see if I can help, whatever is bothering. And to tell the truth, I miss the coast. That's why I decided to make it a permanent move."

"Oh dear. I can understand, but I just don't like losing my best friend."

※ ※ ※

That afternoon, trying to focus on a magazine article in the hospital waiting room, Sheldon lost her concentration and stared out the window. She had gone from a high this morning to a low this afternoon, from feeling liberated and free to now feeling empty over Dee's decision to leave Westburgh. Of course Dee should help her mother. Sheldon knew that deep in her heart, but it was hard to lose a close friend. She had been so upset that she nearly forgot to tell Dee about being kidnaped by Hugh.

Now as she waited for Karen, she tried to shake off the sadness over Dee's leaving and concentrate on what was happening here. She wished she could have listened at Miss Bradford's door, but had turned away as soon as she delivered Karen. She did see David stand up, and she heard him say, "Karen. What the hell are you doing here?"

She hoped Lucille could make it all right between them again. An hour later, it was obvious that she had.

"Miss Merrill," David said as he and Karen walked into the waiting room, "I understand that I have you to thank for bringing Karen back to me. I'm in your debt."

He held out his hand and they shook. Her own roller-coaster emotions were at the spilling over point and she could only force a smile to keep from crying. Karen's beautiful face reflected profound happiness.

"We were shocked, of course, to hear what Lucille had to say," Karen said. "I think at first neither one of us believed her. But she finally convinced us of her fear that I would take David away from her just when she needed him the most. In a way, I understand why she did what she did. When you're sick, you need someone there. She should have known that we would both have been there for her for as long as she lived, but her reasoning was understandably distorted. She had been through so much."

"I'm so glad she made it right," Sheldon said, thinking at the same time that she was glad she had helped Lucille do it. At least one lie was undone.

"We want to follow you home and pick up Karen's luggage," David said. He cleared his throat. "She'll be staying elsewhere from now on."

"Yes, of course." Sheldon managed a serious face.

❦   ❦   ❦

As Sheldon sat in front of her TV to watch the evening news, she felt lonelier than she had ever felt in her life. Perhaps it was the aftermath of so much spent emotion. She reflected on the unexpected turns each day had brought following the first encounter with David Bradford and then the Mollison farm fire. On the one hand, she was happy that David and Karen had been reunited, and that Spence had not killed Julia, and that Hugh had not gotten away with murder.

On the other hand, she wished that Lucille had been able to confide in someone who could have saved her from her uncle before serious damage was done to her all those years ago, and she wished the poor woman weren't dying with so much baggage. She wished Dee weren't moving away. She wished she hadn't lost so many pairs of shoes and that her new dress hadn't been ruined and that her face wasn't such a mess. Most of all, she wished George were beside her.

Five minutes later, as if in response to that last wish, she was shaken from her dark reverie by a knock at the door. She hurried to open it.

"George." Her heart suddenly seemed to be beating everywhere in her body. "I was just thinking about you," she said as she stepped aside for him to enter.

He swept her into his arms and kissed her warmly.

"And I've been thinking about you for too long," he said.

He walked past her to the TV and turned it off. Then, with a hand motion toward the sofa, he said, "Please sit down, Shellie. I have something to say."

He paced nervously, running his hand through his curly hair, looking down at the braided rug, wetting his lips, stroking his mustache. Sheldon sat with her hands folded in her lap, wishing he'd get on with it. Why was it taking him so long? If he wanted an affair, he could just come right out and say it.

Finally, he stopped in front of her. To her surprise he dropped to both knees and put his hands over hers. He looked deep into her eyes, his own dark eyes serious and full of passion.

"You have no idea how much I care for you," he said. "You are so tender-hearted, such a good person, beautiful in every sense of the word. The beauty in you is your honest soul. I've seen it since the first day I met you. But you stole my heart that day when you found me crying like a baby in the archives room. You didn't turn all embarrassed and run away, but waited to give me support while I collected myself."

"Oh George," she began. But he squeezed her hands as a signal not to say anything.

"Please. I need to tell you this, and I want it to be just right. I want you to know that I've never felt this way about any woman before. I've thought I was in love before, but it always ran very shallow. This love I feel for you is deep. I knew last night when I thought that you might be hurt or even killed that I couldn't bear to lose you. I'd have to kill him if he had seriously harmed you. As it was, I wanted to go back to his house and finish him off when I saw that he had hit you. Shellie, you're everything to me. I don't want to live without you."

He reached into his lightweight coat pocket and brought out a ring box. Sheldon's eyes widened. Good lord. He was proposing.

"I got this last week, expecting to give it to you in Ottawa. I didn't know your size, but the jeweler said he can adjust it to fit. That is, if you'll accept it, along with me. Shel, will you marry me?"

She had thought she loved Joe, but now she realized she hadn't begun to know what love was. Kneeling in front of her, not on just one knee but two, was a man so gentle, so wonderful, so everything that she ever could ask for in a partner for life. She felt a fire inside her so strong that she had to have it extinguished. She needed George. Needed him with such passion she could cry. In fact, tears started and she knew she couldn't turn them off.

"Now look what I've done. I've made you cry," George said, gently wiping a tear from her cheek with his thumb, careful not to press too hard on the sore part.

"I'm just so…so overwhelmed and so happy. Oh George. Of course I'll marry you. You're the best man I've ever known in my life. I do love you, with all my heart."

He rose up and slid onto the sofa beside her, opened the box and showed her a diamond-encrusted sapphire ring.

"George! It's beautiful. Oh, my goodness. It's much too elegant for me."

"Oh no. A beautiful woman deserves a beautiful engagement ring. Try it on."

It was too large, but after he slipped it onto her ring finger she held out the hand and admired it, recognizing that all the conservatism in her life had suddenly vanished. She would love wearing this ring, not just for its beauty, but because it represented George's love for her.

She flung her arms around his neck and hugged him. "Thank you. Thank you for asking me to marry you. Thank you for loving me. Thank you for being you. I love you."

The energy between them sparked stronger than ever. She felt like crawling inside his skin. How could she tell him this? How could she say she wanted his loving right now? She had never before expressed such emotions, even to Joe. She'd been so puritanical, in a way, brought up to guard her feelings. All she lacked in high school was a modesty belt. But she wanted to tear that belt away now. She wanted to explore with George and to let loose this passion she felt.

In a few moments, he rose and pulled her up to him, hugged her again, kissed her, gently at first, then deepened the kiss until desire took away their breaths as their two hearts beat faster.

"You know, I'd like to give you a chance to back out of the deal in case you're disappointed in me," he said in a whisper.

"Don't be silly. How could I be disappointed in you? I never have been."

"Well, there is a sure test. But this isn't the best place to perform it."

"Oh, I see. In that case, follow me down the hall. I don't think either of us will be disappointed."

※　　　　※　　　　※

Three weeks later, Sheldon and George walked into his house and set their luggage on the floor, having returned from a brief five-day honeymoon, first in New Hampshire where her mother finally warmed to George before they left for Massachusetts. There, she met George's aunt, who welcomed Sheldon with open arms. On the way there, George told Sheldon about the offer his aunt had made to give him her house, and when she saw it, she was so astounded by its beauty, as well as the friendliness of the town, that they were already making plans to move there within the next year.

"It's good to be home," George said, as he took Sheldon into his arms. "And welcome home, dear."

"I feel like an intruder moving into your home."

"No way. This is your home now, even if it is only for a short while." He kissed her again, then carried the luggage into the bedroom. As he went, he said over his shoulder, "See what's there for mail, will you?"

Since he hadn't stopped delivery while they were gone, the basket under the mail slot was filled and some had spilled onto the floor. Sheldon scooped it all into her arms and took it to the table, where she started to sort it.

"Anything besides bills?" he asked, coming into the kitchen.

"Yes, there is. Look, George. A letter from Dee. It was so good of her to wait before going back to Maine so that she could be my bridesmaid."

Sheldon instinctively looked at the two figurines sitting on the counter where she had left them before going on their honeymoon. What a surprise it had been when David Bradford, with Karen on his arm, came through the door at Harry's house where the intimate reception was held. "My sister wanted me to give you these," David had said.

The package was wrapped with artistic care, likely Karen's work, just as she had decorated David's living room, except for the bear. She would get to decorate the rest of the house following their wedding, but no one knew when or where that would be.

When Sheldon had opened the box, she found the Umbrella Girl and Boy, those two Hummel figurines that Lucille valued so much.

"Oh dear," Sheldon had said. "How wonderful. Thank you so much. I have to believe that deep down she was a good woman."

"I know my sister told you about her life," he said. "She thought she had kept it secret from me."

"Yes, I know."

"She lived a private hell. I was too young to be able to do anything about it, and my parents chose to ignore the obvious. The result was tragic all around. Whatever else she was, Lucille had a good and kind heart. She loved me unconditionally, even if she was rough on me sometimes when I was young. I can never blame her for whatever mistakes she made."

Now George brought her back to the moment. "I can see what your favorite wedding gift is. I'll make you a case to put those figurines in, if you'd like."

Sheldon realized she had been lost in her study of the Hummels. "That would be so nice. I'd really like that. I can't help thinking about Lucille. There was a quality of sincerity about her that just got to me. It's hard to explain. It makes me wonder about women on the streets now. We always think of someone like that as a cheap drunk or whore. It's a shame that society pastes labels onto people who don't conform. Lucille was a product, just as surely as a loaf of bread is a product, assembled and shaped and baked. Others did that to her and by the time she was free, it was too late. Her uncle's death plunged her even deeper into self-loathing. Such a shame."

George was the one person she had entrusted Lucille's confession to. "You can't live with guilt," he said.

"No, that's true enough. I wonder what she found after she left this life. Suppose she found peace, after all?"

"I'm not a religious man, you know that. But my belief is that death isn't something to be feared. It's release. There may be something more. I don't know. I find it hard to believe in hell, and I can't fathom heaven, either. Whatever awaits us after death, I don't think we need to dwell on it while we live. I think there's just one thing we need to do and that's to have compassion and true love for our fellow beings. We're all in the same finite boat together."

Sheldon turned loving eyes on her husband, so proud of him for his genuine goodness.

"I'm not certain about spiritual matters, but there's one thing I am certain of."

"What's that?" Sheldon read his meaning quite well.

He took the unopened envelope from her hand and laid it on the table, then pulled her to her feet.

"I think that letter of Dee's can wait a bit. There's a very comfortable bed, all empty and inviting in the other room. Would you care to join me there, Mrs. Durant?"

"Indeed, Mr. Durant. I do care to join you there."

It would be some time before Sheldon would get back to Dee's letter. But then she would read: "My arrival home was less than happy. I found that my mother was dead."

About The Author

Former journalist Camille Howland was an agricultural editor as well as columnist, and later editor of the Canton, NY, *St. Lawrence Plaindealer.* For twelve years she served as public relations director at New York State's Canton college.

In addition to a 70-year history of the Canton college, her published works include several articles for U.S. and Canadian magazines. Upon retirement, she and her husband Charles moved from Canton to Belfast, Maine, her hometown. There, among other writing projects, she published a 40-page tabloid on Solid Waste Management, commissioned by the publisher of *The Republican Journal.*

Currently, she resides in Sun City Center, Florida, where she not only continues to write, but also enjoys playing and recording organ music.

0-595-23216-7

Printed in the United States
80908LV00003B/157-162